Outstanding praise for the nov

THE SUMMER

"A satisfying and multifaceted ̲
guessing. For fans of similar w̲ ̲authors such as
Shelley Noble and Nancy Thayer." —*Library Journal*

THE SEASON OF US

"A warm and witty tale. This heartfelt and emotional story
will appeal to members of the Sandwich Generation or anyone
who has had to set aside long-buried childhood resentments
for the well-being of an aging parent. Fans of Elin Hilderbrand
and Wendy Wax will adore this genuine exploration of family
bonds, personal growth, and acceptance." —*Booklist*

THE BEACH QUILT

"Particularly compelling."
—*The Pilot*

SUMMER FRIENDS

"A thoughtful novel."
—*Shelf Awareness*

"A great summer read."
—*Fresh Fiction*

"A novel rich in drama and insights into what factors bring
people together and, just as fatefully, tear them apart."
—*The Portland Press Herald*

THE FAMILY BEACH HOUSE

"Explores questions about the meaning of home, family
dynamics and tolerance." —*The Bangor Daily News*

"An enjoyable summer read, but it's more. It is a novel for all
seasons that adds to the enduring excitement of Ogunquit."
—*The Maine Sunday Telegram*

"It does the trick as a beach book and provides a touristy taste
of Maine's seasonal attractions." —*Publishers Weekly*

Books by Holly Chamberlin

LIVING SINGLE
THE SUMMER OF US
BABYLAND
BACK IN THE GAME
THE FRIENDS WE KEEP
TUSCAN HOLIDAY
ONE WEEK IN DECEMBER
THE FAMILY BEACH HOUSE
SUMMER FRIENDS
LAST SUMMER
THE SUMMER EVERYTHING CHANGED
THE BEACH QUILT
SUMMER WITH MY SISTERS
SEASHELL SEASON
THE SEASON OF US
HOME FOR THE SUMMER
HOME FOR CHRISTMAS
THE SUMMER NANNY
A WEDDING ON THE BEACH
ALL OUR SUMMERS
BAREFOOT IN THE SAND
A SUMMER LOVE AFFAIR

Published by Kensington Publishing Corp.

A SUMMER LOVE AFFAIR

HOLLY CHAMBERLIN

KENSINGTON PUBLISHING CORP.

www.kensingtonbooks.com

As always, for Stephen
And this time, also for Madi

Acknowledgments

As always, thanks to John Scognamiglio, editor supreme.

Thanks also to Hank, Harry, and Sylvester for being so insanely cute and for keeping me busy and amused.

Children begin by loving their parents; as they grow older they judge them; sometimes they forgive them.

—Oscar Wilde, *The Picture of Dorian Gray*

Prologue

June 1982

Elizabeth saw him walking toward her across the green, and for a moment she had the strange impulse to flee, to get up from the bench on which she was seated and run, away from him and—

Just away.

But she remained where she was. She felt silly; the brief impulse had been ridiculous. Pre-wedding jitters or something like that. Christopher Ryan posed no threat.

None at all.

Chris was now close. He was tall and slim and fair-skinned. It wasn't lost on Chris—or on Elizabeth—that they looked alike, almost as if they might be brother and sister, or something even closer, two halves of a . . .

"May I join you?" Chris asked. His manner was always a bit formal, but it was natural to him. Elizabeth had known him long enough by then to understand that.

She nodded. "On one condition. Don't ask me if I'm ready for The Big Day. Honestly, if one more person asks me if I'm ready for The Big Day, I think I'll—"

"You'll what?" Chris asked, sitting at the other end of the bench.

She turned to him and smiled briefly, almost apologetically. "Nothing. People are just excited. Everybody loves a wedding."

"And you?" he asked quietly. "Are you excited?"

"I honestly don't know." Elizabeth looked away, off into the distance, and paused before going on. "That must mean that I'm *not* excited. If you're excited you're sure to know about it, aren't you? I mean, at the very least you'd have butterflies in your stomach or your nerves would be tingling or you'd be smiling all the time."

Chris nodded. "I suppose so," he said carefully. "But sometimes . . . Sometimes before a big event, before something you know is going to be life changing actually happens, you slip into a state of calm. Anticipation fades away. You're no longer looking forward or waiting impatiently. You just . . . are. At least, that's been my experience."

"Resigned?" Elizabeth asked. "You said 'you just are.' Do you mean that you're resigned to what's about to take place?" She was very aware of Chris sitting so close to her, close enough to touch if she . . .

"I . . . I suppose so," Chris replied. "Or, maybe I mean that you've achieved a state of acceptance."

"Isn't that the same thing as a state of resignation?" Elizabeth wondered aloud. She still had not turned back to look at Chris. "Just that 'acceptance' has a more positive connotation. Either way, you don't fight what's going to happen." Again, she paused before going on. "You decide, or you simply realize, that you're not going to do anything to stop that life-changing thing from happening. Unless . . ."

"Unless what?" Chris's voice was low.

Elizabeth swallowed hard. She felt suddenly terrified, tongue-tied. *Unless someone steps in and takes action for her. Unless someone she loves saves her.* How could she possibly speak those words aloud?

Her agony was suddenly both compounded and relieved by the appearance in the distance of Hugh Quirk. Tall, broad-shouldered, and heavily muscled, he came jogging toward them across the green.

"We've been found," Chris said softly.

Now, finally, Elizabeth looked directly at Chris again and felt that Time had suddenly stood still. But Time would start up again very soon.

And it would go on.

And then, Hugh was standing a few feet from the bench. "I've been looking all over for you, sweetie," he said; his breathing was slightly labored. "The minister needs us for one final rehearsal. And what are you doing out without a sweater? You don't want to catch a cold and be sick for our honeymoon."

Elizabeth stood. She didn't look back at Chris, but neither did she take a step to join Hugh.

"Well, come on," Hugh urged, reaching for her left hand, the one on which she wore the diamond ring he had worked so hard to afford.

"You two go ahead," Chris said. "I need to make a quick phone call first from the hotel."

Hugh shrugged. "Just don't be long about it. You know how you tend to lose track of time."

Hand-in-hand, Elizabeth and the man she was about to wed walked across the expanse of green, toward the small stone church. She did not turn back to wave to Chris, Hugh's best friend, Hugh's best man. She thought about resignation, and about acceptance. Were they really the same thing? Did it matter in the end?

By four o'clock the following day it would all be over.

Chapter 1

June 2022

Elizabeth Quirk was weeding. She enjoyed hunting for and pulling weeds; the task gave her a sense of satisfaction not to be found with many other gardening chores. Maybe it was because there wasn't much at stake pulling weeds, whereas with planting and tending, well, so much could be done improperly, at the wrong time. Gardening had always been Hugh's specialty. Her husband's joy. Now, it was becoming hers, as well.

Yes, weeding was okay, Elizabeth thought, as she stood to her full, not inconsiderable height and put a slim hand to her lower back. Except when bending and crouching were no longer so easy to achieve without aches and pains. She looked down at the pile of weeds she had collected. Enough, she decided. At least for today.

Elizabeth was in the backyard of her home on Lavender Lane in Eliot's Corner, Maine. A pretty expanse of green grass. Two large beds of flowers and three round pots of herbs. In one corner, close to the house, a marble-topped table surrounded by four wrought iron chairs with rain-resistant cushions. There was a garage, too, at the far side of the yard, a structure large enough for two cars—though Elizabeth had sold Hugh's car after his passing—two bicycles that hadn't been taken for a ride in years, and an upright lawnmower. Once, long ago, Hugh had announced his intention of buying a riding mower; a few of his buddies at work had riding mowers, and Hugh was a competitive man, always needing to equal or one-up his friends. But for some reason it had been important to Elizabeth to put her foot down about the purchase. A marital power play? Later, she felt embarrassed about having made such a fuss. What harm would it have done for Hugh to ride around their lawn on what amounted to a toy car, earphones delivering music by the eighties bands he had never grown out of? No harm at all. It would have brought her husband pleasure.

It was a warm day. Elizabeth realized she was thirsty and headed toward the house, a large colonial style common throughout New England. The house was painted white; the shutters were dark green; the front door was bright red. There were four bedrooms, two and a half bathrooms, a den, a living room, and a kitchen. There was also a large attic, used for storage, and a semi-finished basement where Hugh had enjoyed his pool table and big screen television.

Elizabeth stepped through the back door and into the kitchen. She was fond of the house, but it was far too big for one person, and she was growing tired of living there. For many years—all the years of her marriage and the ones after Hugh's passing—it had been her home. The house had witnessed familial happiness as well as domestic strife; it had listened to the wailing of babies, the babbling of toddlers, the whining of adolescents; it had seen tears of sorrow and of joy; it had enjoyed the laughter of a family who genuinely cared about one another. Still, it might be good to start afresh all around, now that she was being forced to give up her career.

To retire. Definition: to withdraw. To fall back. To take out of circulation. To go to bed.

But Elizabeth didn't want to fall back. She wasn't ready to

withdraw from an active role in the world, or, at least, her small part of the world. This forced retirement from her teaching career was almost as big a change in her life as Hugh's death had been. Suddenly, at the age of sixty-two, she found herself poised at the threshold of a new phase of her life, and she was scared, not so much of what challenges the future might bring as of her ability to successfully meet those challenges.

Elizabeth went to the sink and poured herself a glass of cold water. A simple pleasure, an absolute necessity. She was not so far sunk in fear and self-pity that she didn't realize just how lucky she was to have a home, fresh running water, heat in the winter, and, should she want it, that big screen television in the basement.

Still, a career . . . The trouble was that there just weren't many teaching jobs around, and the ones that did exist went to the younger people, as they probably should. The old needed to step aside at some point so that the young might have a chance at making their mark. That was the nature of things. The parent became the child. The teacher became the pupil. But you didn't have to like it.

Elizabeth knew she could probably get a pleasant part-time job at a shop in town, maybe even at Arden Forest now that Arden's second-in-command in the bookshop had moved to Boston. Such a job wouldn't fulfill her like teaching had, but it would pass the time. And time could weigh heavily upon a person.

Elizabeth poured another half glass of water and drank it before rinsing the glass and setting it in the rubber drainer. Now what? She had never been entirely comfortable with the idea of leisure. There must be a job that needed to be done. . . .

Of course. Elizabeth headed upstairs. There was a bright spot on the horizon, if only a temporary one. Petra, her youngest child, was coming to stay for the summer; her companionship would be very welcome. Not that Elizabeth would burden her child with her personal worries or concerns. There were things, important things, none of her children needed to know. Elizabeth wanted them to feel that they could rely on her. Even after Hugh's death she had made it a point not to depend too much on her daughters' support, though it had been offered generously enough.

Elizabeth walked into the smallest of the four bedrooms. She had already cleaned it in anticipation of Petra's arrival, but another check wouldn't be amiss. If Elizabeth needed a reminder, a quick glance around the room would serve to illustrate Petra's uniqueness in the Quirk family. A macramé wall hanging. A statue of the Buddha. Books on philosophy, art, world religions. Novels. Lots of novels. A crocheted blanket draped across a vintage beanbag seat. A print of William Blake's *The Ancient of Days*. A bowl overflowing with stones and crystals.

Elizabeth's other daughters had never had time for the esoteric or the artistic, let alone for philosophical tracts. They were practical, focused people, who by their mid-twenties had achieved their stated goals.

The oldest, Camilla, known as Cam, had always been a caretaker; it gave her real pleasure to be of help to people. She was also efficient, competent, and down-to-earth. Physically, she resembled her mother a little and her father a lot, and had never been terribly happy having Hugh Quirk's slightly stocky build.

Jessica, Elizabeth's middle child, better known as Jess, wasn't the most empathetic of people. In that way, as in many others, she was a lot like her father, abrupt, unsentimental (or invested in appearing so; sometimes Elizabeth couldn't tell), focused. Also like Hugh, Jess had a good heart. As far as her appearance went, she combined her mother's height and slimness with her father's coloring, his thick, dark hair, and his natural athletic ability.

At thirty, and unlike her sisters, Petra still seemed a person very much in flux, still developing, still a mystery. On the one hand, Petra was intelligent, creative, and warmhearted. On the other hand, she was famously reluctant to commit herself to friendships, romantic ventures, and meaningful work. Why? Sometimes, Elizabeth thought she knew the answer to that question, but maybe she didn't really know anything.

Elizabeth plumped a bed pillow that had already been plumped, wiped an invisible bit of dust from the top of the bookshelf with her forefinger, and headed back downstairs. When she reached the final step, she stopped, gripping the handrail. Suddenly, she had the strangest sense that Time had come to a halt, just for a moment, that it was waiting, poised, anticipating . . .

She remembered having felt this way before, many, many years ago, very briefly. But then, Time had rushed on again, and that moment of stillness had been lost.

Elizabeth took a deep breath. Less than twenty-four hours until Petra's arrival.

Chapter 2

Petra Quirk liked traveling by bus. She had never taken a long train ride, but suspected she would enjoy that experience, too. And given the fact that she didn't own a car—she didn't have the money to buy one, let alone to keep one in good working condition—buses and trains were a necessity. Petra, who lived in Portsmouth, New Hampshire, got along fine without her own vehicle, walking to and from a destination whenever possible; riding her bike when she was in a cycling mood; and, if necessary, borrowing a car from one of her roommates. Petra tried not to make a habit of that last; borrowing still required gas money.

For some reason unknown to Petra, the bus's route north to Maine was taking its passengers through small towns and on back roads, which made the journey much more interesting than if they had traveled on highways. This route provided the sights of green fields studded with grazing horses; acres of active farmland; stands of old trees thick with leaves; and buildings that mostly dated from the early twentieth and nineteenth centuries.

Historical buildings interested Petra far more than modern or contemporary structures. Even as a kid she had been deeply drawn to the past, and not only in the form of its artifacts. She liked everything old. She enjoyed reading histories of nations and peoples. She liked biographies. She liked talking with people older than herself. The past had always held a fascination for her, sometimes, maybe, at least according to her father, to the detriment of her ability to pay attention to the present, to the passing moment.

Anyway, setting up a vintage business, albeit a small one, had seemed a no-brainer for Petra; learning how to use the technology necessary to that setting-up had cost a lot of brain power, most of it belonging to people other than Petra. Past Perfect had been up and running for two years now, earning Petra a steady if modest income. The website sold vintage clothing and personal accessories, as well as the occasional bit of kooky home décor, like a pair of salt and pepper shakers in the shape of black-and-white cats wearing top hats, or paintings of Elvis or Jesus on black velvet.

Amazingly, luckily, she had made a big sale in the spring, the biggest one she had ever made, but perhaps unwisely, she had since become lax about working the website. As long as the money from the sale held out, she told herself, she would be okay, but the money was now almost gone. She figured she could survive the summer if she paid enough attention to Past Perfect to generate a few decent sales per week, while scouting around for more stock that was both affordable and eye-catching. Her mother never let her pay for anything when she visited her childhood home, so her expenses would be low. Her rent was being covered by having sublet her room in the apartment she shared with two other women who she had met a few years earlier while working at a crystal shop.

Sara and Ellen, already roommates, had been regular customers, and, when the third bedroom in their place opened up, they had asked Petra if she would like to join them. It was perfect timing. Petra was being tossed out of her tiny flat on the top floor of an old, red brick Victorian because the landlord wanted to sell the building but before doing so he needed to make some major repairs and upgrades to the property. Without a lease, Petra had no legal leg on which to stand, so she jumped at Sara and Ellen's offer. So far, so good, and Petra's summer replacement, Lena, had been deemed a suitable housemate.

The apartment the women shared was right in the heart of Portsmouth, a charming old city located on the Piscataqua River, packed with things to do and places to explore. There was, for example, the Strawberry Banke Museum, which covered ten acres and included thirty-nine historic buildings. In winter, a skating rink was opened on the property. Petra wasn't athletic and the idea of sliding around on a sheet of ice didn't appeal in the least, but lots of people, old and young, enjoyed the cold weather activity.

One of her favorite places to hang out was the Portsmouth Book and Bar, located in the Old Custom House and Post Office; you could get a coffee or a beer, browse the books, and select one or two to buy. Some nights there was live music. There were also lots of good restaurants (not that Petra could afford to eat out much), and cute boutiques for browsing, like the awesome Market Square Jewelers. In Prescott Park, you could enjoy a variety of riverside gardens. The Music Hall, which had started way back when as a vaudeville theater, was now a hub for musicals, concerts, and movies.

Still, as much as she enjoyed living in Portsmouth, Petra was looking forward to spending the summer in quiet Eliot's Corner with her mother. She had wonderful memories of growing up in the small town. Her childhood had come close to being idyllic; not once had she felt frightened or threatened or anything but loved, and that of course was mostly thanks to her parents, Elizabeth and Hugh. Sadly, Hugh had died a little over nine years before, leaving the proverbial gaping hole in the Quirk family. Petra had worried—as had her sisters—about how her mother would make out after Hugh's death, but they had worried for naught. Elizabeth had done well. She had confronted the grief and embraced the loneliness. Elizabeth Quirk was one of those women who might look fragile or delicate but who were really very strong. Besides, her teaching career had provided a distraction of sorts from personal pain and sadness.

Petra frowned. Just weeks earlier, her mother had been forced into retirement as a result of some bureaucratic nonsense. Petra could never understand why administrators and other people in charge of things like companies and shops and schools couldn't make an effort to work things out so that everyone who wanted a job and who was good at what they did could keep that job. Maybe she shouldn't have dropped the Introduction to Economics class her freshman year in college. Too late now.

Petra dug into her bag for the novel she was currently reading. It was *The Glass Bead Game* by Hermann Hesse. She hadn't read the book since college, though the mood of it had stayed with her throughout the years. Only days earlier she had encountered a man on a bench in Prescott Park reading a worn paperback copy of the book. Petra had taken it for a sign that now was the time to revisit the novel. The moment she got back to her apartment she had hunted out her own worn copy. The pages were slightly yellowed and the back cover of the paperback was torn, but none of that mattered. The text was there.

No sooner than Petra had opened the novel, however, did she become aware that the bus was pulling to a stop. A few new passengers joined those already aboard, including an older woman dragging a massive wheelie bag. Without hesitation, Petra leapt from her seat to help the woman stow the unwieldy bag.

"I keep telling myself to toss this giant and buy something smaller," the woman said, after she had thanked Petra. "But I keep forgetting!"

Petra smiled. "My father used to say that if my head wasn't screwed on I'd lose it. Not that losing things is the same as forgetting things, but I guess neither is ideal!"

Petra got back into her seat with a feeling of satisfaction. She enjoyed being with strangers, imagining their lives. She liked brief but sincere interactions; living in Portsmouth allowed her many opportunities to chat with storekeepers and tourists, with bartenders and even passersby. Sometimes she wondered if she truly preferred these brief encounters to longer, lasting, and committed relationships. Sometimes she was afraid that the answer was yes. But maybe that was okay. Keeping a distance had its benefits.

In fact, she was pretty content with her life. It wasn't complete or fully developed—yet?—but she was pretty much okay with where and who she was. Not entirely, but was anybody ever entirely pleased or satisfied with her life at any given point? Petra didn't think so. Something deep inside told her that self-satisfaction wasn't really the point of life. If only that something would tell her what that point really was, assuming a point even existed.

Petra smiled. She could almost hear her father, not one for introspection, telling her to get her head out of the clouds, to focus on the day to day. If Hugh Quirk hadn't been the deepest person, he was still one of the kindest and most loving people Petra had ever met.

Suddenly, Petra recalled the time she and her father and sisters had gone down to Portland to see a hockey game. Jess was the one into sports, Jess and her father. Petra and Cam were along for the adventure, a trip away from Eliot's Corner and into the city. Their father had bought them snacks at the game—popcorn and hot dogs and ice cream and soda. Petra had had no idea what was going on so far below in the ice rink, other than that there were a bunch of men in bulky clothing and helmets chasing something small with long sticks; she hadn't once been able to locate the puck. But it had been so fun sitting in the stands, watching other people's excited reactions, listening to the roar of the crowd or, at other moments, the boos and groans of disappointed fans. Petra remembered that her father and Jess had been two of those spectators fully engaged with whatever was happening on the ice, while Cam had looked bored and only perked up when a cute guy, older than Cam but not by much, had joined his friends in the row in front of the Quirks.

Petra remembered that she had felt a bit sick to her stomach on the bus ride back to Eliot's Corner after having eaten all that junk food. She had sat next to her father, Jess and Cam in the seats in front of them, and he had put his arm around her, assuring her she would be fine. She remembered being lulled into a sort of sleep, her cheek against the smoothness of her father's winter jacket, the spicy scent of his aftershave soothing. By the time the bus had pulled into the station and Petra had woken to see her mother waving to them from the parking lot, she no longer felt sick. Her father had been right. She was fine.

It was funny the things you remembered. Not always the big moments, the official turning points, demarcations like graduations from high school or college, but the small moments, the feel of your father's jacket against your cheek as you dozed against his chest, the smell of the pine-scented candles your mother brought out in the winter months. The meaningful stuff after all.

Finally, Petra opened her book again, eager to get back to the story of Joseph Knecht's journey from a small, seeking child to the wise, learned Master of the Glass Bead Game. Briefly, she wondered if either of her parents had read the book, maybe back when they were in college. Her mother would have liked it. Her father . . . Petra smiled. Her father would have thought it a lot of hooey.

Chapter 3

Elizabeth was kneeling at one of the flowerbeds. She had finally gotten around to buying a pair of kneepads. Why she had waited so long to make the purchase was anyone's guess. The larger question might be, why did any reasonably intelligent person put off doing what they knew was the right or smart thing to do?

The sound of a car slowing made Elizabeth turn. An old, dark blue Volvo she didn't recognize as belonging to anyone she knew pulled up to the curb, and, a moment later, Petra climbed out. She waved her thanks to the two people in the front seat and came loping across the lawn.

Elizabeth smiled, stood, and opened her arms for a welcoming hug.

"Why didn't you call me?" she said. "I told you I'd pick you up at the bus station. Who were those people?"

"A very nice older couple who live in Sterne Hollow," Petra told her. "The wife was on the bus with me, and I helped her with her bag. Her husband was happy to give me a lift. They had the most adorable dog with them, a roly-poly pug. He sat on my lap the whole way from the bus stop to Eliot's Corner!"

The two women went into the house. Petra looked well, her

mother thought. She had been a very healthy child and teen, barely suffering the common cold, and so far, she had been as lucky in her adult life. Also, her capacity for food consumption was famous and often envied.

"You travel light," Elizabeth said, noting Petra's one large bag, an amorphous tapestry thing with leather handles. "You are planning to stay for the entire summer, aren't you?"

Petra shrugged. "I figured I could always borrow something from you if I need it. We're the same height and build."

Elizabeth noted her daughter's peasant-style blouse and linen harem pants. "But my style isn't nearly as bohemian as yours."

Petra smiled. "I'll throw a gauzy scarf over one of your classic button-down blouses and create an entirely new outfit."

Arm in arm, mother and daughter went into the kitchen.

"Are you hungry?" Elizabeth asked.

"Starved. I haven't eaten since I had a corn muffin early this morning."

Petra went to the fridge and began to rummage. This habit had annoyed Hugh, who had forever been reminding Petra that it wasn't economically smart to keep the door to the fridge open too long. Petra had never learned the lesson.

Elizabeth heard the front door open and shut; it had to be Jess. She was the only one in Eliot's Corner who felt comfortable enough to visit without notice and without knocking for entry once she arrived. A moment later, Jess was with her mother and sister in the kitchen.

"Hey," she said in the direction of Petra's back. "When did you arrive?"

Petra turned around to greet her sister and then went back to examining the contents of the fridge.

Jess was in her work clothes—a pair of black dress slacks; a white button-down blouse, all but the top two buttons done up; and a pair of low-heeled black pumps. Her only adornment was a pair of small diamond studs her parents had given her upon graduation from college. Elizabeth had seen other people who worked in Jess's office, and none of them, not even the senior people, wore such a—okay, she would say it—boring and unimaginative outfit. But it suited Jess and that was all that mattered.

"Would you like something to eat?" Elizabeth asked.

"I'll have a cup of coffee. Don't worry," Jess added, heading for the coffee maker. "I'll take care of myself."

"How's Eddie?" Petra asked, now piling supplies for a sandwich onto the cutting board.

Jess frowned. "A pain in the butt."

"If you don't like him very much why are you still with him?" Petra asked. It was a question that often had occurred to Elizabeth.

"Oh, I like him. I probably even love him. That doesn't mean I don't also want to strangle him."

Elizabeth declined to comment. The women gathered at the table a few moments later, Petra with her sandwich, Jess with a cup of coffee, Elizabeth with a cup of tea. The flatware they were using had been a wedding gift; the dishes, cups, and bowls were more recent purchases. The fancy china Elizabeth had inherited from her mother long ago hadn't seen the light of day since the year before Hugh's death. If she downsized, Elizabeth thought, sold this house and moved to a smaller place, maybe a condo, would her daughters want the fancy china, the silver tea service she had inherited from a great-aunt, the hand-embroidered tablecloth that had been passed down in Hugh's family? Or would she be forced to sell it all on eBay?

Moot questions for the moment, as Elizabeth was going nowhere.

"So, what are you going to do with yourself in Eliot's Corner for the summer?" Jess asked in the vaguely aggressive tone she often used when talking to her younger sister. "Laze around?"

Petra shrugged and finished chewing before replying. "Probably, at least some of the time. But I'll also be working. You

know I've got this online resale shop called Past Perfect special-
izing in vintage clothes and accessories. All the stuff is stored
in my apartment. If anything sells while I'm away, Lena, the
woman who's renting my room this summer, will package it up
and send it to the buyer. In the meantime, I'll scour local yard
sales and flea markets for more finds. Maybe I'll check out an
auction if I can find one not too far away."

"I haven't been to an auction in years," Elizabeth said. "I
might just go with you."

Jess frowned. "That can't be a very reliable way to earn a living, selling baggy old dresses and worn-out shoes."

Petra laughed. "It's as reliable as any other, I guess. Anything
can happen at any time to shake up people's lives and liveli-
hoods. Anyway, I enjoy it."

"But it can't allow you to put away money for your future,"
Jess went on.

Petra looked momentarily puzzled, then almost confused.

"It's Petra's choice," Elizabeth said firmly. "We each have to
make our own decisions."

Jess sighed. "You're right about that. Well, I gotta go. Thanks
for the coffee."

She was gone as abruptly as she had arrived, leaving through
the kitchen door and closing it firmly behind her.

"I get the feeling she thinks I'm a lost cause." Petra laughed
unhappily.

"Not at all," Elizabeth protested. "It's just that the idea of
not having a 'regular' job—if such a thing exists these days—
puzzles her. Upsets her even. It's her issue, not yours."

Petra finished her sandwich, and, by the time she had, her
good mood had returned. "It'll be fun hunting for treasures,"
she said. "Who knows? Maybe there's even something buried
up in our very own attic I could recycle."

Elizabeth smiled. "I doubt you'll find anything of interest. I
was never good about saving my clothes, not even special occasion dresses."

"What about your wedding dress? Would you be willing to sell that?"

Elizabeth was startled by the question. She supposed she had thought that Jess or Petra might want to wear it one day. Cam had wanted her own dress; besides, she had admitted she didn't care for her mother's. "Too fussy," was her judgment.

"I'm not sure, to be honest," Elizabeth said. "I never thought about selling it."

"I know it's a sentimental piece," Petra said, "but better to sell it to someone who will wear it than let it rot away unseen."

"That's a point," Elizabeth admitted. "My mother chose the dress for me, you know. I suppose I had some input, but really, we both knew the final decision would be hers."

"I think it's a pretty dress, not like some of the really awful stuff brides wore in the eighties. And you looked really lovely in it."

"Thanks. You wouldn't want to wear it one day, would you?"

"Me?" Petra chuckled. "At the rate I'm going, I won't be a bride until I'm fifty, if ever! No, I think that, if I ever do fall in love deeply enough to want to spend my life with someone, I'll opt for a very low-key wedding, maybe at the beach or in a beautiful field full of flowers. And I'll most probably wear a caftan, definitely not something with a defined waist!"

Elizabeth smiled but only briefly.

"What's wrong?" Petra asked. "You suddenly look . . . pensive."

"I was just thinking about how my mother commandeered so many aspects of my wedding, not only the choice of dress. She was older by then; you know I was born when both of my parents were in their mid-forties. I was one of what people called 'surprise' babies. Anyway, I guess I always saw my mother and father as sort of double adult figures, parents and grandparents. To say no to them was impossible. At least, it felt that way."

"Well, what sort of dress would you have chosen if you'd had your way?" Petra asked.

Elizabeth shrugged. "I don't know. Something less . . . exuberant, I guess. Then again, the dress was perfectly appropriate for the event. You've seen the photos. My wedding was a by-the-book affair. That was down to my mother as well as to your father. He wanted something very traditional, nothing oddball, he said." Elizabeth rolled her eyes. "As if I would have gone for 'oddball.'"

"But you might have gone for a smaller celebration?" Petra asked. "Something unique to you and Dad?"

"Maybe. None of that matters now."

"Okay. Just think about selling the dress. No pressure, though."

Elizabeth promised that she would give the idea due consideration.

"So, how are you feeling about this enforced retirement?" Petra asked. "It makes me so angry to think about it. I mean, you were the most popular English teacher at Eliot's Corner Primary School forever! You're not happy about being pushed out, are you?"

"No," Elizabeth admitted. "I'm not ready to retire. I was angry at first, too, then sort of resigned. Now, I don't know quite what I feel. Leaving my colleagues—not to mention the students—was very difficult. The administration had a party at the end of the term for those of us not moving over to MidCoast Primary. It was a bit of a nightmare. Very uncomfortable. Those moving on were looking sheepish; some looked out-and-out guilty. And those of us who had been let go were working hard on keeping a strained smile on our faces. I slipped out early and came home to drown my sorrows in ice cream."

Petra reached across the table and took her mother's hand. "I'm sorry, Mom. But hey, look at it this way. Now you'll finally be free to travel, maybe to meet someone fabulous and fall in love again!"

Ah, Elizabeth thought, the sincerity and innocence of youth. It was touching, when it wasn't mildly annoying. "That's the last thing I want to do," she said with a laugh. "Fall in love, I mean."

"Never say never. I know, that's an obnoxious bit of advice but—"

A chirping from the region of her harem pants caused Petra to dig for a pocket and pull out her cell phone. "I should take this. Lena told me right after I left this morning that there's a leak in the bathroom and that she left a message for the landlord but he hasn't gotten back to her. Ugh! I don't know what I can do from here but . . ."

Petra dashed from the kitchen; Elizabeth could hear her daughter's voice from the hall but not what she was saying.

A moment later, Petra bounced back into the kitchen. "I know!" she cried. "You can get a dog! It'll be a companion for you and help keep you fit, and it's easy to meet new people when you're out and about walking a cute dog!"

Elizabeth laughed. "We'll see."

Chapter 4

While her mother was at the eye doctor for her biannual checkup, Petra had decided she would pay a visit to Re-Turned, Eliot's Corner's only resale and vintage shop. The journey into town from Lavender Lane was about two miles, but with the summer weather so pleasantly warm and bright, Petra thoroughly enjoyed the walk. She loathed and despised formal exercise, but walking, now that was fun.

It took about forty-minutes for her to reach Main Street, home of Eliot's Corner's independent bookstore, Arden Forest. It had been in existence for as far back as Petra could remember, and some time before that. It was currently owned by a woman named Arden Bell (total coincidence), who had been left the shop by the original owner.

Arden's daughter also lived in town, though she was a relative newcomer. The story was that Arden had been forced to give up her baby at birth and that somehow, after thirty-some-odd years, the daughter, Laura, had found her mother. Petra couldn't recall who had told her the story; it was probably Jess because Jess liked to gossip. Everyone who knew Jess was aware that she couldn't keep a secret or a good story for long, her own or anyone else's. Her intentions weren't necessarily bad, but spreading gossip—especially the kind that hadn't been verified—was, in Petra's mind, a pretty foul thing to do.

Petra walked on but vowed she would stop into the bookstore soon; maybe she could go along with her mother to a book club meeting or two this summer. That would be fun. Generally speaking, Petra thought that life was far too short to spend your time reading anything you didn't really want to read (after you got out of school, of course), but she could make an exception this summer. Besides, maybe she would find a new favorite author, someone she had never even heard of. Discovery was fun.

Not that she had done much actual discovering lately. Alarmingly, she had begun to realize that in many ways she was stuck, spinning her wheels, wasting time. But why was she feeling that way? What was it she was supposed to be doing, other than or in addition to what she already was doing with her life? What was there to feel discontented about?

If only her father could hear her now! Hugh Quirk would shake his head and tell his youngest child, for the umpteenth time, to stop thinking so much, to get her head out of the clouds, to have a little fun. Suddenly, she could see herself belted into one of those swings made for babies and small children, her father pushing her while she laughed and called "Higher, Daddy, higher!" Hugh Quirk had enjoyed playing with his children almost as if he were a child again himself, laughing, and tumbling, and exclaiming over found treasures like glittery rocks or perfect white shells.

Petra didn't always miss her father, not in any active, day-to-day way, if that made sense, but there were moments when his loss seemed brutally fresh and even startling. It was as if she were hearing the words of the hospice nurse for the first time, words she had been expecting but that had shocked and devastated her all the same. "I'm sorry. He's gone."

Dead. Deceased. Passed. No more. It was all the same.

Petra now came to Re-Turned, a place where at least inanimate items were able to live on. She hadn't visited the shop in ages and was eager to discover what treasures it might hold, either for sale on Past Perfect or for her own possession. She opened the heavy glass door and went inside. The man standing behind the counter was about forty, Petra thought (though she was pretty bad at determining people's ages), with the most gorgeous natural blond hair she had seen on anyone in a long time. His eyes were large and brown, the proverbial bedroom eyes, and if Petra had been a woman vastly susceptible to male beauty she might have blushed or fainted. In fact, she was more interested in the wild paisley shirt he was wearing.

"Vintage seventies?" she asked with a smile.

The man nodded. "I couldn't bear to sell it."

"The shop looks really different from the last time I was in," Petra noted. "And I don't think I've met you?"

"It does look different, and, unless you've visited in the past eighteen months, you haven't met me. I'm Michael Brooks. I bought the shop from the original owner."

Michael came out from behind the counter, and Petra stepped forth to shake his hand. "I'm Petra Quirk," she explained. "I grew up in Eliot's Corner. I'm spending the summer here with my mom, Elizabeth."

"And you're a fan of vintage clothes?"

"I am," she told him and went on to describe her vintage business, small as it was. "I don't think I'd like to have a brick and mortar shop though," she admitted. "That means rent, and I have enough trouble paying the rent on my apartment."

Michael laughed. "I hear you. Look, I'd be happy to give you some advice about where you might poke around while you're in town. There are definitely some honey spots out in the country you wouldn't know about without the inside scoop. In the meantime, feel free to look around. Take as much time as you'd like. It's the only way to uncover gold."

He left Petra alone to wander and explore the racks of shirts and pants, the shelves of hats and shoes, the baskets filled with funky costume jewelry. Who had worn this pair of bell-bottom cords? Was he—or she—still alive? If the cords had been longer, Petra would have snapped them up. And what had made someone want this sickly yellow blouse? Seriously, Petra thought, no one could possibly look good in that shade of yellow. But someone had worn the blouse and someone had kept it because here it was, being sold yet again in the year 2022.

Petra wandered on until her eye was caught by an amazing Art Deco-style Lucite box purse in a faux tortoiseshell color and pattern, complete with top handle and a lock that actually worked. Petra had seen hundreds of this sort of purse over the years but nothing quite as perfect as this example. In short, it spoke to her.

Petra immediately brought the vintage piece to the counter. "I have to have this," she told Michael. "Not to sell, just for me."

"A must-have item. There are so many of them! Must-haves, I mean. You know, you're lucky. I only put this bag out yesterday. There's a woman who comes in here two or three times a month who usually snaps up anything Lucite."

"May I ask you a question?" Petra said as Michael rang up the purchase. "My mother has her wedding dress from 1982 and is thinking about maybe selling it. Her mother picked it out for her, and she was never really in love with it. Anyway, I have no idea what condition it's in but if it's whole, can I bring it in for your opinion on its salability?"

"Sure," Michael said. "I'd love to take a look at it some time." After they had chatted for a few minutes about the current market for recycled and upcycled clothing, Michael asked: "Is your grandmother, the one who chose your mother's dress, still with us, by the way?"

"No," Petra told him. "She and my grandfather died before I was born. My sisters might have a vague memory or impression of them, but if they do I've never heard them mention it. Anyway, I guess I should get going."

Petra thanked Michael, and, with a final wave and a promise to pay another visit, she left the shop. Jess would probably scold her for spending almost two hundred dollars on something Jess would consider frivolous—"Where are you going to wear that thing? It's totally impractical. And you make hardly any money. Why are you spending it on an old bag?"—but Petra wasn't like Jess. She didn't see the world in the same way that Jess saw it, or maybe it was that she and her sister saw different worlds.

Either way, they would probably never agree on most things, and that was okay. Petra was used to feeling like the odd one out in her family. It was who she was.

Chapter 5

"How was the drive north?" Elizabeth asked, tucking a stray strand of hair behind her ear.

"Not bad. Not like driving to Maine from Boston on a Saturday or Sunday in summer." Cam shrugged. "Still, there were the usual stupid drivers to contend with."

Elizabeth's oldest daughter had called early that morning, before Elizabeth had gone off for her appointment with the eye doctor, to ask if she could pay a flying visit to Lavender Lane. It was an unusual but not an unwelcome request. Cam was and always had been easy to get along with; she made no fuss, and, unlike Jess, she was never combative, which made her a welcome addition to any day.

Thanks to Cam and Ralph, Elizabeth had three grandchildren: six-year-old Beth, her namesake, and the twins, eighteen months old, Jake and Joe. Elizabeth didn't see them as often as she would like—the family lived in South Portland—but now that it was summer and Elizabeth had no lessons to prepare in anticipation of the fall semester, maybe they could get together more often than had become the norm. It wasn't as easy to see your grandchildren as it had been in Elizabeth's own grandmother's time. Kids were so completely scheduled;

at any given time, they might be busy with dance class, playing on the school's soccer team, or learning film photography at a local community center. Elizabeth often thought about how Hugh would have felt about this situation, if he had lived long enough to meet his grandchildren. There was little doubt in her mind that Hugh would have made it a habit simply to show up at the Perrys' house in South Portland, announcing that it was Grandpa Time. Hugh had been like that. He wanted what he wanted when he wanted it. That wasn't always a bad thing, but it could be trying on those around him.

In contrast to Jess's severe, minimalist style, and to Petra's bohemian, eclectic choices, Cam's mode of self-presentation could be described as what Elizabeth had heard referred to (albeit a few years back) as normcore. Today she was wearing a white Oxford cloth shirt with the cuffs turned back, navy chinos, and black ballet flats. The bag she carried was a simple tan leather shopper; around one of the handles she had tied a silk scarf in a pattern of red, white, and blue. As always, Cam's jewelry was simple and classic—a yellow gold wedding band, small yellow gold hoop earrings, and a thin yellow gold chain on which hung a small single diamond pendant.

"So, how are things going here?" Cam asked.

Before Elizabeth could reply, Petra came bounding into the kitchen. "Hi," she said brightly to her sister. "Mom told me you were coming, but I'm on my way out again. I'm soaking up the atmosphere of Eliot's Corner. See you later!"

When she was gone, Elizabeth sighed. "She's hardly sat still since she got here."

"What's she going to do all summer?" Cam asked, taking a seat at the kitchen table. "Are you two planning a few day-trips or overnights? A jaunt to Acadia or a visit to the Farnsworth? Is she going to work? I'm not sure what sort of job she could find here in Eliot's Corner though. Summer jobs go to local kids, don't they? And Petra's no longer local or a kid."

"I'm not sure Petra has much of a plan," Elizabeth replied,

"other than to collect vintage pieces to sell on her website. I'll suggest a few activities of course—day-trips; some good local theater—but I'll be the one doing the organizing. She's—"

"A bit of a fly-by-night. But she's young. And smart. She'll settle down at some point."

"Will she?" Elizabeth said. "Maybe settling down isn't for Petra. I do wish though that she'd find her passion, something to which she can devote herself. Vintage clothing can't be enough for her, at least not forever. She's so intelligent and sensitive, so curious about the world. At least, she was. I don't know what she thinks about these days, not really. Well, time will tell, as it does for all of us. So, what made you want to visit today?" she asked. "Is everything all right at home? The children doing well? Ralph okay?"

Cam smiled. "Everything's fine, Mom. I just wanted a little break. I had the day off, and the sitter was happy for the extra hours so, here I am."

Elizabeth was convinced that Cam wasn't telling the full or the real truth, but decided not to question her further. "Not that I don't enjoy getting some alone time with my oldest child," she said, "but I am a grandmother. Maybe next time you could bring the kids?"

Cam nodded. "I promise next time I'll bring Beth. She loves spending time with her normal grandmother."

Elizabeth let that remark go, as well. Cam's mother-in-law, Abigail Perry, was notoriously nutty but, as far as Elizabeth could tell, harmless.

"Jess popped in yesterday," she told her eldest daughter. "I guess to say hi to Petra. She quizzed her on her financial plans—rather, her lack thereof—and complained about Eddie."

"I don't know what she sees in him, but then again, Jess and I were always so different. We could never even agree on the same sandwich cookie when we were kids. I was all for Oreos, and she was all for Hydrox. It stands to reason our taste in men would be almost directly opposite. Any word about her new venture? Did she finally land the partner she was hoping to bring on board to help get her scheme of her own marketing firm up and running?"

"Yes. She told me last week. She says she was very lucky to have hooked up with her. The woman's experience and contacts are supposedly a lot more extensive than Jess's own. I hope everything goes well. The idea of taking such a big risk . . ."

Cam smiled. "Jess will be all right. She always is. She's like Dad in that way. Nothing seems to really knock her down, or not for long, anyway. They have a sort of supreme self-confidence, or maybe, I don't know, a sense that the world loves them and will take care of them. That's how I see it, anyway."

"That sort of attitude—deeper than merely an attitude; a character trait?—can be dangerous though. It can become . . . lazy self-satisfaction. It can slide into . . ."

"Into what?" Cam pressed.

Elizabeth hesitated before going on. "Into a blindness to what's really going on around them."

"Well, that's Jess's problem, not ours," Cam said briskly. "Come on, let's go have lunch at Martindale's. My treat. And you can tell me about your plans for retirement."

Elizabeth sighed. "I've been out of a job for less than a month."

"No time like the present to start planning your future."

It was becoming very clear to Elizabeth that her daughters were not going to let her forget for one minute that she was facing an unknown future, a future that needed to be planned for, filled with adopted dogs and travel and even—God forbid!—romance.

"If you say so," Elizabeth murmured as she followed her daughter from the house.

Chapter 6

Only when Petra was halfway to town did she realize she probably should have hung around with Cam for a while. She feared she had been rude by running off the way she had. But it was too late to do anything about that now. She would be sure to apologize later.

Opening the door to and stepping inside Arden Forest was an immediate mood booster, like that first bite into a good piece of dark chocolate or the sight of the first green buds of spring on the tree just outside your bedroom window.

Both Arden and her daughter, Laura, were there that morning. Laura, Petra knew, was earning a PhD online; in her spare time, Laura helped her mother in the bookstore. How did a PhD candidate have any spare time, Petra wondered? Maybe one day she would ask Laura about her experience of graduate school, how she handled the pressure and the competition. Not that the information would be useful to Petra. She wasn't going on to graduate school. That dream had died long ago.

Unlike Elizabeth and Petra, who were often mistaken for sisters, Arden and Laura didn't look much alike. Arden was tall, thin, and blond; Laura was average height with dark brown hair. Still, if you looked past those superficial aspects of the two women you could tell they were parent and child. At least, Petra thought that she could, just as people had been able to see that Hugh and Petra were father and daughter in spite of the fact that they appeared so different on the outside.

Petra greeted both women, asked after their health, partners, and Laura's father's family in Port George, and answered their questions about her decision to spend the summer in Eliot's Corner.

Suddenly, the door to the shop opened, and Petra turned to see her mother's dear friend and former colleague, Mrs. Shandy, sail in. That's how Petra saw the woman, as a noble ship in full sail. She was a large woman, tall and broad, who carried herself with a becoming dignity. Her hair was a beautiful shade of silver, worn in a neat, old-fashioned style. Today she was wearing a floral-patterned cotton dress that came below her knees, with a cardigan over her shoulders, held together by a lozenge-shaped brooch. As always, she wore a strand of lustrous pearls around her neck and no other jewelry.

Mrs. Shandy came right over to the three women, ex-changed greetings, and announced that she had just seen the most appalling thing on her way through town. As she was coming along Center Street she spotted a woman not from Eliot's Corner—"You know I know everyone at least by sight"—making off with a large potted plant from Mrs. White's front porch.

"I reached the villain just as she was stuffing the stolen prop-erty into the back seat of her car. I assure you I gave her a piece of my mind! Can you believe the nerve of some people?" she demanded. Petra and the others admitted that they could imag-ine that sort of nerve but would rather not.

"How did you know the woman was doing something wrong?" Petra asked. "I mean, maybe Mrs. White had told her she could take the plant or . . ."

"I know a criminal when I see one," Mrs. Shandy replied with a significant look. "I demanded she return the plant to the porch and never show her sorry face in Eliot's Corner again."

"Did she?" Laura asked, eyes wide. "Return the plant, I mean."

"Of course. She didn't say a word, just scurried back up to the porch with the plant, and as soon as she'd closed her car door behind her she was gone. Of course, I warned poor Mrs. White to keep an eye out for other thieving types."

"I admire you doing the right thing," Arden said, "stepping in to stop a crime, but wasn't it risky? What if this woman had hit you or worse?"

Mrs. Shandy narrowed her eyes. "She wouldn't have dared."

Petra laughed; she couldn't help herself. "Well done, Mrs. Shandy. I don't think I would have had the nerve to confront someone robbing a neighbor. I'd call the police and take down the number on her license plate, but I'd make sure to stay far away!"

Arden and Laura returned to work while Petra followed Mrs. Shandy to the section of the shop where the book group held their meetings. Elizabeth had mentioned that Arden had recently replaced the ancient couch and seats with newer, albeit secondhand, models, but the one piece she hadn't replaced was Mrs. Shandy's favorite old armchair. That was sacrosanct. Petra sat at one end of the new-old couch and noted that unlike the cushions of its predecessor, these cushions actually offered a degree of support.

"Elizabeth must be happy to have you home for the summer," Mrs. Shandy said with a genuine smile.

"I hope she is!" Petra smiled. "I'm glad to be here."

Mrs. Shandy further settled herself in her chair. "It's a disgrace your mother was forced out, a teacher of her skill and dedication."

"I agree, but Mom says it's good to make room for the young."

Mrs. Shandy frowned. "Not at the expense of experience."

"But the woman who will be replacing Mom, as it were, already works at MidCoast Primary. She's moving up from teaching assistant to full-time teacher. That seems fair."

"Did you ever consider going into teaching?" Mrs. Shandy asked suddenly. To Petra, the older woman's eyes seemed to pin her in place.

"Gosh, no. The idea never occurred to me." That was kind of odd, Petra realized. She had enjoyed school, loved almost every aspect of it, at times missed its steady rhythms, even the discipline and deadlines, both of which provided the impetus to complete projects and finish homework assignments. She missed the sheer joy of learning. Of course, learning could take place anywhere and at any time, but . . .

"Then what goal are you pursuing?" Mrs. Shandy went on after a moment.

Petra looked steadily at one of the purple flowers on her print dress, rather than at Mrs. Shandy. "I'm not really pursuing anything, I guess," she said. "I'm—"

"You're what?" Mrs. Shandy's tone was kindly, even if her words called for an answer.

Petra laughed nervously and looked up. "I don't know what I was going to say. I don't know what I can say." That she was lost? That she felt she had missed something, some vital clue, some bit of information she needed in order to—to do what?

"No matter. The answer will come if you pay enough attention."

Pay attention to what? At that moment, Petra felt very uncertain of just about everything.

"Are you here for something in particular?" she asked the older woman, hoping her question was successful in changing the topic.

"Yes, as a matter of fact I am. My copy of *A Distant Mirror* has just about fallen to shreds. I'm not going to throw it in the garbage of course, just buy a fresh copy that won't lose its pages when I open it. And you?"

"Oh, I just wandered in," Petra told her. "You know. Just passing time . . ."

Mrs. Shandy rose gracefully from her chair, a queen rising from her throne. "I hope we see much more of each other this summer, Petra." Her words were accompanied by a smile that for some bizarre reason made Petra want to cry.

Petra remained seated in a corner of the new-old couch until Mrs. Shandy was long gone, purchase in tow. Suddenly, she recalled almost word for word her brief exchange with Jess the day before, how Jess had asked if her younger sister planned to "laze around" for the summer, pronouncing her job selling vintage clothing online as an unreliable way to earn enough money so that she could put some away for her future. Petra hated when people talked about "financial health" and savings accounts and mortgage rates. Weren't there more important things to talk about, such as art and ideals? The encounter with Jess had left her feeling sour, if only briefly.

The exchange with her mother's friend, too, had rattled Petra. Was that really just what she was doing with her life, she wondered. Wandering? Just passing time? But time—life—was precious. Everyone agreed on that. What if she kept drifting along as she had been doing since college, wandering, not trying very hard to do much of anything, accomplishing little other than eating, drinking, sleeping, just breathing day after day. . . . Was that really living? Technically speaking, she supposed it was. Was it as valuable as a life lived with purpose? Of that, Petra was doubtful.

Eventually, realizing her thoughts were getting her nowhere closer to an answer to a question she didn't even know how to ask, Petra made herself rise from the couch, and, after waving farewell to Arden and Laura, she left the bookshop and headed for home. Well, her childhood home. Her own home was—where? The room she rented in the apartment she shared in Portsmouth with two other young women she could barely call friends?

Petra shook her head as if to clear the murky feeling that had come over her. Home was where your heart was. Wasn't that the saying? And Petra's heart was with her family, her mother, her father, and her sisters. And that meant that home was everywhere they were, even in her heart and her mind.

Or something like that.

Chapter 7

Dinner that evening was a tarragon chicken salad served on a bed of mixed greens, with a loaf of fresh bread from Chez Claudine, the French style bakery and café on Main Street. For dessert, Elizabeth had whipped up an apricot tart. She was a talented cook; even years of making breakfast, lunch, and dinner for a husband and three children hadn't dimmed her enjoyment of creating delicious meals if only for herself.

Petra, on the other hand, had little if any interest in cooking. The kitchen in her Portsmouth apartment was small, but one of Petra's roommates, who loved to cook, had equipped it with the essentials such as an omelet pan, a cast iron skillet, and a set of good knives. Sara had once offered to teach Petra a few basic kitchen skills so that she could provide a decent meal for herself when on her own. Petra had thanked Sara but declined the offer. Elizabeth had asked why. Petra had only shrugged.

Elizabeth poured them each a generous glass of a sauvignon blanc and joined Petra at the table.

"How did your visit with Cam go?" Petra asked as she dug in.

"Fine. She took me to lunch at Martindale's. I don't think I'd ever had lunch there before. It felt so different in the daytime, far more casual than it feels in the evening. Anyway, Cam headed back south after she'd dropped me home." Elizabeth paused. "Don't you think it's a bit of a long trek from South Portland to Eliot's Corner and back to make in one day, unless you have a specific reason for the journey?"

Petra shrugged. "Not necessarily. Cam likes to drive. She was the first of her friends to get her license. Remember how Dad used to say what a skilled driver she was, even better than he was. He called her a natural."

"That's true," Elizabeth admitted. "And at least when you're alone in your car you can play whatever music you want to play, without having to consider your passengers."

"And Ralph's taste in music is . . . Well, it's not great." Petra wasn't alone in her opinion—her father had outright refused to allow Ralph anywhere near the music source at parties—but hey, taste was a personal thing.

"How was your afternoon in Eliot's Corner?" her mother asked.

"Good. I stopped in to Arden Forest at one point. Mrs. Shandy was there, and we got talking. She is seriously angry about what the administration at Eliot's Corner Primary School, or the people at MidCoast, whoever it was, did to you. She said someone with your teaching reputation should never have been let go. A place should have been found for you in the new school."

Elizabeth smiled. "That's kind of her. She's a good friend and was an excellent colleague. When I first started teaching she helped show me the ropes, gave me sound advice, and very expertly set me straight when I made mistakes."

"So, she was your mentor in a way. I wonder if her students liked her or if she scared them. She is pretty . . . imposing."

"She is that," Elizabeth agreed, "but kids seemed to appreciate her honesty and her bluntness. I mean, you know where you stand with her. When she finally retired, there was an enormous outpouring of thanks and appreciation from students she had taught twenty and even thirty years before."

"She's certainly unforgettable! Actually, she kind of hit a

nerve with me today. I don't know, maybe it was the way she asked but . . ." Petra shrugged.

"But what?" Elizabeth asked.

"Oh, nothing. Anyway, I wonder what it must feel like, to know you've made a positive impact on so many lives. It must be wonderful."

Elizabeth wondered about her own impact on the people of Eliot's Corner. How would she be remembered by the children she had taught over the course of twenty-five years? No doubt there were a few former students, those who found correct grammar unnecessary and literature a bore, who had been tempted to aim spitballs at the back of her head. But in all honesty, Elizabeth felt fairly confident that the majority of children she had taught did and would remember her fondly as an inspiring teacher.

"Oh, Mrs. Shandy also asked if I knew what you had in mind for the future," Petra said. "I guess she meant work or travel but I don't know for sure."

Elizabeth hated this question. That the question was a valid one made no difference. She was tired of having to give the same answer. "I'm really not sure," she said now. "I guess I'd hoped your father, Hugh—"

Petra smiled. "I know who my father is, Mom!"

Elizabeth absentmindedly rubbed the fourth finger on her left hand with her thumb, a habit she had developed ages ago when she had worn a wedding ring. It had been four years since she had put the gold band away—it had become too small to wear—but the old nervous habit persisted. "Of course," she said. "Sorry. I guess I'd hoped that he and I would have the opportunity to travel a bit, maybe even get to Europe finally. London, Paris. Or to explore more of the United States, maybe go to San Francisco or New Orleans."

"You could go to any of those places on your own, or find one of those groups for women traveling alone. Or maybe Mrs. Shandy would—" Petra smiled. "No, forget that. I can't see her being a very good travel companion. Too bossy. She'd never let you sleep in or miss a historical site. You'd be exhausted by the end of the first day."

Mom laughed. "Mrs. Shandy is a dear friend, but you're right, not my ideal traveling companion. Anyway, if the travel bug bites badly I'll pack my bags and be off, alone or with a group. Don't you worry."

"That's the spirit. Oh, I meant to tell you that I talked to the new owner of Re-Turned about the market for vintage wedding dresses, well, for all vintage items. More and more people are becoming aware of the importance of sustainability in fashion as in every other area of life. Reselling, recycling, repurposing has really caught on, which of course is great for the planet."

"Yes," Elizabeth agreed, taking another sip of her wine. "It is great."

Petra chattered on for a bit; Elizabeth picked up a word here and there. Plant thief. The family-owned hardware store was replacing its old wooden sign with a flashy new one. A squirrel had dashed across the sidewalk, almost running over Petra's sneakers. But Elizabeth's mind was elsewhere. She wondered what nerve Mrs. Shandy had touched in Petra and if their conversation had had anything to do with Petra's future. Elizabeth had expressed her concern—however mild—about Petra's seeming lack of focus or purpose to Mrs. Shandy on a few occasions. Her friend hadn't seemed to share Elizabeth's worry. She had advised patience. But now it seemed that Mrs. Shandy might be concerned about Elizabeth's future. Would she also advise that Elizabeth be patient with herself, or would she urge her younger friend not to waste time in setting a goal and a course of action?

"So, what do you think?" Petra asked. "Yes or no?"

Elizabeth jumped a little in her seat and smiled. "I'm sorry. I was woolgathering. I have no idea what you're talking about."

Petra leaned across the table and patted her mother's hand. "And they say I'm the spacey one in the family!"

Chapter 8

"I didn't expect to see you again so soon!" Petra exclaimed. "Two visits in one week."

Cam shrugged and stepped inside. "Yes, well, I was thinking about how little time we've spent together in the past year or so and—"

"I'm a bad aunt," Petra said quickly, closing the door behind her sister. "I'm sorry. I should come to see you and Ralph and the kids more often. And I should have hung around the other day. Eliot's Corner could have waited."

"Oh, I didn't mean to blame you, Petra, really," Cam said as she put her overnight bag on the floor and removed her sunglasses. "Life gets busy. It's just the way it is. Anyway, I decided I'm going to try to come north as often as I can this summer to spend time with Mom and my sisters."

Petra smiled. "And to get a break from the kids?"

"A bit of that, yes. Though I did promise Mom I'd bring Beth the next time I visited. But as you can see, I failed to keep that promise. Beth has the sniffles."

"What about Ralph?" Petra asked, leading them to the kitchen.

"What about him?" Cam went to the fridge and began to take out the makings of an early lunch.

"I mean, does he mind you staying here overnight? Doesn't that put more of a burden on him? I mean, I know you have day care and a sitter, but still." Petra was truly curious; she didn't mean her questions as a rebuke.

Cam didn't reply at once, continuing to gather bits from the fridge and take them to the counter. When she did finally speak, her tone was strangely flat. "Ralph probably doesn't even notice I'm not there."

Petra laughed. "Cam, come on," she said. "I'm sure that's not true. Look, what are you not telling me?"

Again, Cam took time in replying. Finally, she looked up from the sandwich she had just assembled and sighed. "It's just that lately, over the past three or four months, Ralph's been—different."

"What do you mean, different?" Petra pressed. She felt worried now. Her sister was not an alarmist. "Distracted? Worried? Depressed?"

"No, none of that." Cam sighed and, for a moment, put her hands over her eyes. "Look, the thing is, gosh this is embarrassing, Ralph seems to have developed a crush on his old girlfriend, Lily."

Petra frowned. "Lily? The Lily I've met a few times? The one with the collection of funky glasses? The one who works in fashion?"

"Yes. That's the one. She and Ralph dated for about a year before she ended things. A few months later Ralph met me. Just about the time we were getting married—that was almost two years later—we ran into Lily in the Old Port in Portland one afternoon. We got chatting, and I liked her immediately. I'm not really sure how it happened, but Lily became a friend to both of us. I never for one minute doubted her intentions, or Ralph's, in becoming friends."

"Until now? Wait a minute," Petra said. "Where does Lily stand in this? I mean, do you think she's fallen in love again with Ralph?"

"No. As far as I can tell, this is all going on in Ralph's head."

"But how do you really know what Ralph is thinking or feeling?" Petra asked. "You couldn't be imagining things, could you?"

"No. You know how transparent Ralph is. He can't hide his feelings, and he can't even tell a white lie. Besides, here's an example of what's been going on. About a month ago Lily was in Portland for a meeting with some client or other and after that she came by the house to deliver a book she'd promised to loan me. I guess Ralph didn't know she was coming, but whether he knew or not, he was visibly agitated. He hovered around the two of us in the kitchen, laughing too loudly at anything that struck him as amusing in our conversation, until finally I couldn't take it and asked him to please go outside and clean the grill like he'd promised to do." Cam shook her head. "He didn't look happy about being dismissed. When he got almost to the doors—you know the glass sliding doors leading out to the backyard—he turned around to look at us, or rather at Lily, and when he turned back he walked right into the glass. He wasn't hurt, I could see that right away, but honestly, it was like watching a love-struck fourteen-year-old boy in the same room as his crush."

"Oh," Petra said. "That's not cool. I mean, it would be laughable if it weren't so upsetting."

"Not to mention pathetic." Cam sighed. "Lily said nothing about what had happened; it was almost as if she wasn't even aware that Ralph had been there. We chatted for another few minutes and then she left. Look, even if Ralph never sleeps with Lily again, even if he never kisses her or takes her hand, his being in love with her while he's married to me is wrong."

"I'm sure you're the one Ralph is in love with," Petra said with the sincere intention of consoling her sister. But did she believe her words? Yes, Petra decided. She did. She knew Ralph. She liked him. At least, she had until now. Now, she just didn't know.

"How can you be sure?" Cam asked. "I believe that Ralph loves me, but that's not the same as his being in love with me."

"Let's sit down," Petra said. "Eat your lunch. I'll make us some tea." She busied herself with filling the teakettle and putting it on to boil, with fetching tea bags and cups, milk and sugar. The domestic activity helped, she hoped, to hide the fact from her sister that she felt totally out of her depth. What did she know about relationships? Her own experience was woefully thin and unremarkable. Her longest relationship had lasted only five months, and she had been the one to end it for reasons that were still murky to her. There had been nothing wrong with Scott. He was a nice guy, smart, funny, cute. But none of that had been enough. Was that it? She just hadn't been in love with Scott. That was reason enough to end a relationship, wasn't it? Maybe the best reason.

Petra joined her sister bearing two cups of steaming hot tea. "Why does tea make so many people feel better? Is it really soothing or have we just convinced ourselves that it is? And why?"

Cam smiled. "It's no surprise you studied philosophy in college."

"I think about all sorts of things all the time, but I never seem to make any discoveries or come to any conclusions." Petra shrugged. "Sometimes I think my studies actually might have gotten in the way of my—"

The landline rang then, and Cam got up to answer it. "It's Jess," she told Petra. "What's up? No, Mom's not here. Look, let me put you on speaker so that Petra can hear you. Everything okay?"

"Everything is more than okay." Jess laughed. "We got the funding! Raven, my partner, came through like the powerhouse she is, and we sign the papers in two weeks, maybe three."

"Congratulations," Cam said. "I know you've worked hard to get to this point."

"Tell me about it!"

"That's great news," Petra said. "But why do you have to wait so long to sign the contract?"

"It's frustrating," Jess admitted, "but Raven assured me that's how business works, slowly at best. She says there's nothing to worry about. Anyway, be sure to tell Mom the minute she gets in. I know she worries about this venture of mine, leaving the security of a job with a paycheck to run my own business."

"We will," Cam promised. "And congratulations again."

Cam ended the call. "Sometimes," she said, "I think Jess is a breed apart from you and me. Like she just showed up on the doorstep one day wrapped in swaddling clothes with a note that said: 'Take me in. Now.'"

"I know what you mean," Petra said.

"She's always so sure of things, always in control. I can't imagine her winding up in my situation, suspecting her husband of being in love with another woman and not having the courage to confront him about it."

Before Petra could reply to this—and she wasn't sure what exactly to say—Cam hurried on.

"Look, keep what I've told you about Ralph to yourself, okay?" she asked. "I swore I wasn't going to say anything to anyone, but I guess I just couldn't keep it all inside."

Petra nodded. "Of course, I won't say anything. Don't worry."

Cam took her overnight bag up to her room while Petra cleared away the dirty dishes. She felt bothered by what her sister had told her. She had always thought of Cam's marriage as unassailable, certainly strong enough to make the idea of an affair impossible, even laughable. But that was naïve thinking. Any relationship was potentially vulnerable to damage, from within or from without. Everyone knew that or should know it.

And no matter what Cam thought of Jess's superhuman qualities, Jess, too, was vulnerable to life's trials and tribulations. Petra knew there would come a day when Jess would need her family's support, whether she wanted it or not.

That day would come for everyone.

Chapter 9

Elizabeth had never been interested in formal exercise, by which she meant lifting weights and running on treadmills and doing hundreds of squat thrusts, whatever they were. So far, in her adult life, daily activity had kept her fit. She walked everywhere she could walk and took stairs instead of elevators when there was an option. She carried bags of groceries to and from the car. She had only given up playing tennis the year before, when the enjoyment had taken second place to sore muscles. And she routinely and rigorously cleaned every inch of her house.

Housework was exercise. That was Elizabeth's story and she was sticking to it. And it could be dangerous. There had been the time many years before when she had been dusting the baseboards in the living room and had crashed her head into the sharp end of a shelf as she stood back up. Luckily, there had been no concussion, but the pain had been awful. And bending wasn't great for a middle-aged—or old—back. And reaching could be hazardous, too. Still, Elizabeth insisted on doing her own housework, even now when she could afford to hire professional help for the big chores. Hiring a housekeeping service seemed to Elizabeth like the first step in admitting to being defeated by old age.

One day. But not now.

At the moment, alone after Cam had left early that morning to head back home and Petra had gone wherever she had gone, Elizabeth was vacuuming the rug in the den, the loud drone of the machine blocking out the world and allowing her to think about the past few days. For one thing, why had Cam returned to Eliot's Corner so quickly after her visit earlier in the week? And without Beth. Well, if Beth really did have the sniffles, and Cam had no reason to lie about that, then Elizabeth supposed the best place for the little girl was at home.

For another thing, Petra's questions about her mother's wedding dress had gotten her wondering. In all honesty, Elizabeth wasn't entirely sure the dress was still in the attic. She was sure she hadn't thrown it out or given it away, but as for any firm idea of what exactly she had done with it when she and Hugh had moved into this house back when Cam was an infant, well, she had none. Things could go missing over time, even things that had once been important, such as wedding dresses and diplomas and cards celebrating milestone birthdays. Even pieces of jewelry inherited from a great-aunt or a grandmother could be inexplicably lost, like the tiny Victorian-era gold and amethyst ring Elizabeth had been given on her twelfth birthday by an elderly relative she now could barely recall. The ring had been in the Primer family for generations, and Elizabeth had kept it safely in her little jewelry box for years and years, through high school and college, only to realize about the time of her wedding to Hugh that it was no longer in the box. What had happened to the heirloom? Could it have been stolen? Had she worn it to a party and lost it there, failing to notice its absence when she snuck back into the house in the small hours of the morning? Elizabeth had racked her brain for an answer but had never found one.

Elizabeth turned off the vacuum, picked up the dust cloth, and went over to the built-in bookcases covering one wall of the den. She liked the spines of the books to be even with one another, just about at the edge of the shelves. Immediately she noted that one of the coffee table books was out of step with its neighbors; Petra, not much concerned with order and symmetry, must have been browsing. *Italian Vistas* was the book's title; for the life of her, Elizabeth couldn't remember where or when she had gotten the volume.

That got her wondering, too. How was it that she had never traveled out of the country? Well, other than to Canada a few times with Hugh who had loved to ski and ice skate and had even tried snowboarding once or twice before reluctantly admitting he didn't have what it took. She had wanted to visit France and Spain and Italy, England, Ireland, Scotland, and Wales—the four little puppy dogs without their tails—maybe even Russia. But Hugh hadn't shared her desire, and even though she might have taken a week or two-week vacation with one of her female colleagues, she had never seriously considered the idea. Hugh wouldn't have protested, much anyway, but . . .

Without the dulling roar of the vacuum, Elizabeth was now able to hear the music streaming from her laptop. Suddenly, she caught her breath. The opening bars of R.E.M.'s "Losing My Religion" sounded through the den. Her eyes began to water, and she reached for the edge of the bookshelf for support.

The song had always made her cry, and clearly, though she hadn't heard it in years, it still had a hold on her. She had never tried to discover what exactly it was about the song that moved her so deeply—the way Michael Stipe delivered the lyrics, the words themselves, the melody . . . For Elizabeth, all combined to form a perfect evocation of loss, regret, inevitable change. Whether or not that was the songwriter's intent, she didn't know. She guessed it didn't really matter.

What did matter was that the song was so strongly associated with everything that had happened to Elizabeth Quirk in the summer of 1991. That wonderful, terrible summer.

Just a dream. Just a dream.

When the song had faded into silence, Elizabeth crossed the

room and slumped onto the cushiony leather sofa Hugh had chosen for the room not long after their wedding. Every room in this house held something of Hugh's choosing, something Hugh had enjoyed, something he had held, used, broken, or repaired. Maybe she should have gotten rid of the old furnishings, streamlined the accumulation of knick-knacks, sold the house and moved into a far smaller place that might come to feel like hers alone. Maybe it would be easier to ignore the past that way, in an environment that didn't proclaim the existence of a relationship that while long-lasting had endured a moment of intense challenge and suffering.

The moment on the stairs the other day . . . She had had a sense of Time standing still for a moment, poised before going on. . . .

Elizabeth put her hands over her eyes and sighed heavily. It was too late now to try to ignore any of the past, good or bad, beautiful or dreadful.

Wonderful or terrible or both.

Chapter 10

Petra sighed. She felt momentarily overwhelmed. Why had her mother kept so much stuff? Elizabeth was an orderly person, a good housekeeper, someone who regularly cleaned out cupboards and closets. Well, that was the thing about attics and basements. Out of sight, out of mind. You could put off making a decision whether to keep or to toss something by stowing it away for consideration another day. Of course, for someone like Petra, this tendency people had of putting off today what they could do tomorrow could prove a goldmine. Okay, it hadn't yet; most of her profit came from reselling items she had bought from other established vintage sources. In fact, the most valuable item she had found in her rummages through the attics of friends and neighbors had been an iron doorstop in the shape of a cat with an arched back. But one day her searches might prove to be worth more than sixty dollars.

The air in the attic was warm and still. Petra wiped a bead of sweat from her forehead and realized—too late—that she should have asked her mother if there was a fan she could borrow for her treasure hunt. Next time—if there was a next time—she would try to remember.

The next box Petra opened, coughing at the dust that rose in the process, contained a jumble of books. At first glance, Petra saw nothing of particular interest. But as she rummaged past the first layer she discovered a book that had enchanted her as a child. It was a retelling of Hans Christian Andersen's *The Wild Swans* published by the Golden Press way back in 1968. She had often wondered where this book had gotten to; she remembered being convinced that if she just stared hard and long enough at the puppets on the 3-D cover, Elisa and one of her swan brothers would step out of their strange prison and speak to her. This was definitely a treasure to bring into the present. It might well be worth a fair amount of money, but this was an item Petra knew she would not put up for sale.

Maybe that was why she earned so little money. She was always falling in love with her finds!

She was just about to turn away from the box when a sliver of red caught her attention. She moved aside Volume 3 of a set of encyclopedias from the 1950s—where had that come from?—and a paperback thesaurus sans cover, to reveal a small, red leather notebook, possibly a diary or a journal. Carefully, she opened the front cover and saw on the first page, in her mother's handwriting, the dates 1991-92. Quickly, she closed the little book. Whatever the book contained, it belonged to her mother, not to her.

Petra placed both the copy of *The Wild Swans* and her mother's notebook in the canvas L. L. Bean bag she had brought to the attic in order to transport anything interesting she found down to the main part of the house.

She turned to another dusty cardboard box that proved full of old toys. A piano tiny enough for a toddler to bang away on. An old-fashioned set of grooved wooden building blocks that might have once been played with by one of her parents. A plastic yo-yo missing its string.

"Bunny!" she cried.

Unlike Cam, Petra had preferred stuffed toys to dolls; unlike Jess, she had had no interest in sports. Until she was in her teens, Cam's bed had been decorated with dolls of all description. Before she was five, Jess had been proficient at riding a bike, jumping rope, and roller-skating. Petra, of course, had no memory of the day her mother had discovered that her father had been teaching his four-year-old to roller-skate, but she had heard often enough the story of the massive showdown that had taken place. Elizabeth had thought roller-skating too dangerous for a four-year-old. Hugh disagreed. His opinion won out, though he did promise that from that point on, Jess would always wear a helmet, and knee and elbow pads.

Petra held her childhood companion carefully. Bunny had once been hugely fluffy and pink—Petra had seen the pictures to prove it—but had long ago lost her fur and most of her vibrant color, so that now she was a sorry version of her former self but no less remembered and loved.

But strolling down memory lane wasn't Petra's purpose. Finding vintage stuff that she could sell via Past Perfect was the goal of the moment. Petra gently laid Bunny aside and turned to the task at hand. She worked for over an hour, pulling old, no-longer-sticky tape off cardboard boxes and most often finding that the contents of these boxes were not in the greatest shape or of any resale importance. A cheap photo frame whose glass was cracked from top to bottom. Who would want that? One roller skate, the kind with leather ankle straps, the kind that required a key for tightening the toe clamps. That might have once belonged to her mother or her father and been kept for sentimental reasons, but without its mate it was worthless in terms of profit.

At some point her mother or father had started using plastic storage bins, the kind with the tops that snapped closed on either end. The stuff that had been stored in these bins was cleaner than what had been stored in the cardboard boxes, but, in most cases, at least for Petra's purposes, no more interesting. Why would anyone want to hang on to a pitcher missing its handle? And as far as Petra could tell it wasn't even an important pitcher, something made by Lenox or Mikasa, or even something obviously dating from the Arts and Crafts movement, or something wonderfully kitschy. Another item saved for its sentimental value? Maybe. Petra put the pitcher aside.

At that moment a long, flattish cardboard box caught her eye; she probably hadn't seen it earlier because it was at the bottom of a pile of open boxes labeled "tools" and "wires/cables" and "bike stuff."

With some difficulty, Petra was able to move aside the heavy boxes of uninteresting items and unearth the bottom box. Instinct had told her before lifting the flimsy, smashed lid what the box contained.

Her mother's wedding dress. In many ways, it was typical of the wedding gowns worn by the majority of brides in the 1980s. The sleeves boasted puffed shoulders; the neckline was in the sweetheart design, and the skirt was full, meant to be worn over a stiff petticoat. But the gown in no way mimicked the over-the-top gown worn by Lady Diana Spencer at her wedding to Prince Charles. To be fair, Petra had always thought that Diana's dress had suited who she was at that moment of her young life, and Petra had no doubt the workmanship had been superb. But you would be hard-pressed to find anyone eager to wear that puffy, overblown style for her wedding in the 2020s.

As Petra held her mother's dress out before her and examined it more closely, she was overcome by a wave of sadness. That an artifact of such a vitally important day could be so carelessly put aside without any evidence of ceremony. Why hadn't her mother ensured that it be properly stored to prevent the sort of damage Petra was seeing now? Moth damage, possibly also damage caused by mice. A stain, probably sustained at the reception, that had never been treated. A hemline that was ragged and torn in several places; who knew how that had happened. Petra had always thought her mother shared her passion for personal history. But maybe not. And then again, Petra herself had left Bunny to live out the years on her own with a toy cash register for company.

Enough was enough, Petra thought as she climbed to her feet and stretched. She was dirty and sweaty. Time to call the rummage to a halt for the day. Along with the canvas bag containing Bunny, the copy of *The Wild Swans*, and her mother's diary, Petra brought the dress to her room and laid it out on the bed to air. A few minutes later, she joined her mother in the kitchen.

"Boy, it's hot up there!" Petra exclaimed, pouring herself a glass of cold lemonade. "Attics aren't romantic at all. They're just . . . hot!"

Her mother smiled. "What were you doing up there? It sounded like a staged battle."

"Rummaging for Past Perfect."

"Find anything interesting?"

"Not much, to be honest. But I did rescue Bunny! Poor thing is pretty tired looking."

Her mother smiled. "I remember the day Bunny went missing. You were not quite two years old and absolutely inconsolable. It was a miracle your father managed to find her. He covered every inch of my usual route into and out of downtown Eliot's Corner, convinced Bunny had fallen out of your stroller that morning, and eventually, he brought her home. A little dirty, but that didn't bother you a bit."

"Dad was good at that sort of thing, wasn't he? Being the hero. Saving the day, coming to the rescue."

"Yes." Her mother smiled briefly. "He was."

"Speaking of Dad, I found your wedding dress. I'm sorry to say it's in bad shape. It wasn't properly stored, just folded into a cardboard box, and there's some significant damage. Moths, maybe. Or mice, I don't know. The box itself smelled a bit moldy."

Her mother cringed. "I'm sorry. Do you think it's at all salvageable?"

"Not sure," Petra admitted. "I laid it out on my bed hoping some fresh air will help bring some life back into it. I was thinking I could bring it to Michael at Re-Turned and see what he says. He might know a good fabric restorer around here. I'm sure there's someone in Boston who could, I don't know, maybe reconfigure the style? There are a few really lovely bits of lace that are still intact and a good deal of the satin is in okay condition."

A shadow seemed to pass over her mother's face; for a brief moment Petra thought her mother might cry. "I'm sorry the dress is proving a problem," Elizabeth said, a reply that didn't tell Petra anything at all to explain why the dress had been abandoned the way it had been.

"It's all right," Petra assured her. "I enjoy a good project, and I've seen dresses in worse shape come to life again."

"Anything else you might offer on the website? An amazing Betsey Johnson piece that might somehow have made it into my eighties wardrobe via Goodwill? I seem to remember having one or two antique beaded purses at some point in time, as well."

Petra frowned. "Nothing else interesting so far. But I'm an optimist! I'll keep digging."

She turned to leave the kitchen and then whirled back around. "Oh, I almost forgot!" she said, pulling the small leatherbound notebook from the pocket of her flowing skirt. "I found this. Don't worry; I didn't look inside. Diaries are private. If it is a diary and not just a datebook."

Elizabeth put out her hand and practically grabbed the book from Petra. "Thanks," she said shortly.

"It says 1991 on the inside cover. You were pregnant with me for part of that year. Gosh, I hope it's not all about what a nightmare I was in utero or what a bad-tempered infant I turned out to be!"

Elizabeth looked up from the cover of the small red leather book. "What?" she asked. She looked startled, Petra thought. Surprised.

"It was nothing," Petra replied. "So, what do you want to do for dinner? I haven't had fish and chips in a while. Any interest? We could go to the clam shack down by the water. The last time I was there they had an awesome dessert menu, too."

Her mother nodded. "Sure. Whatever you'd like. I'll just go and change into something presentable."

Petra headed back upstairs to take a shower; her exertions had left her feeling grimy. She hoped she hadn't upset her mother in some way by giving her the diary. Sometimes, maybe often, diaries—even datebooks—could contain embarrassing stuff about which a person would rather not be reminded. But it was more likely Elizabeth was upset by the fact that her wedding dress was in tatters. A wedding dress was a sentimental item, even, Petra guessed, for women whose marriages hadn't turned out so great. It was a tangible artifact or souvenir of a day of incredible hope. Maybe, too, of incredible naïveté. Maybe hope and naïveté went hand in hand. Maybe they had to.

Chapter 11

Elizabeth had changed into her nightgown, brushed her teeth, applied moisturizer to her hands, and turned off all of the lights but the one on her bedside table. The glow it gave off lent the room a comfortable and cozy feel.

But Elizabeth didn't feel comfortable or cozy.

She had tried hard not to let Petra see her agitation earlier, when Petra had handed her the diary, but she wasn't sure she had succeeded. Petra was a keen observer of people, but it could be difficult for a child to correctly read a parent's behavior, just as too often a mother could be so very wrong about her child's state of mind. The closeness could distort perspective.

After that, the two women had gone out to the clam shack. Though the weather had been near perfect, hot but not too hot, and the food its usual high-quality (if a bit on the expensive side), Elizabeth hadn't been able to enjoy the evening and had hardly been able to eat a bite. Petra hadn't commented on her mother's lack of appetite, so involved was she with scarfing her own meal and waving to people she had known since birth, some of whom she hadn't seen in ages.

Claiming exhaustion from having eaten so much food, Petra had gone to her room almost immediately after they got back to the house, leaving Elizabeth alone and free to examine her thoughts and feelings, as unsettling as that activity was proving.

Now, she looked out of the bedroom window at the lights glowing in neighbors' houses. She heard a dog bark, a distant laugh, and an owl hoot. Otherwise the night was quiet, soothingly so if only she had been receptive to soothing.

What had prompted Petra to suggest the idea of selling the wedding dress just at this moment in time? Did it mean anything that the dress was in bad shape? Was it a sign of coming disaster? Or evidence of past betrayal?

The dress was now in Petra's bedroom. Elizabeth could look at it in the morning, if she wanted to. But Elizabeth didn't think that she would.

And then, most important, there was the diary. Should she open the book, turn the pages, read the entries written during that long-ago summer? Maybe it wasn't necessary. She knew what she would find. She didn't need a visual reminder of a time in her life when it had seemed that everything wonderful was possible and, at the same time, that everything was coming to a crashing end.

Elizabeth turned away from the window, went to the tall dresser that had been hers for close to forty years, and tucked the diary in the bottom drawer, under a thick wool blanket where, she hoped, it would be safe for the time being.

It had all been just a dream.

A few minutes later, Elizabeth crawled into the bed she had shared with Hugh, her husband, for their entire marriage. The mattress had been replaced a few times, but the headboard and frame was the same one she had selected not long after their return from their honeymoon at Moosehead Lake. It had witnessed intimacies both physical and emotional; it had listened to arguments, laughter, serious conversations, and tears. It held the secrets of a relationship, the exalted and the mundane.

And as she lay there under the thin summer blanket, a distinct feeling of dread overcame her. Once a secret began to wriggle its way out of hiding, there was little one could do to halt its progress, to push it back into the dark earth where it had lain undetected for some time.

Secrets had a mind of their own.

Chapter 12

Summer 1991

It felt strange to be keeping such an enormous secret, Elizabeth thought as she watched Christopher dozing in the bed beside her. How was it possible that anyone, even a person not terribly skilled in reading other people, could take one look at her and not know that she was passionately in love with someone with whom she had no right to be in love? She was sure the truth was written all over her face. How could it not be when she felt it pulsing through every inch of her body with every breath she took, every step she made, every word, however ordinary, she spoke?

Chris stirred and lazily opened his eyes. With a drowsy smile, he turned toward her until their bodies, both long and lean, were pressed together.

"Was I asleep?" he asked.

Elizabeth nodded. "Did you feel me watching you? I couldn't help myself. I never thought we'd be here together, like this. It's like a dream come true."

Chris kissed her then, and it was some time before either spoke. When they did, it was of their love, kept so quietly over the years in the breast of each until just a few weeks earlier when they had left the theater after the ballet—*Swan Lake*—and found themselves clasped in an embrace.

The embrace and the kiss that had brought every tender feeling to the fore.

"I like this place," Elizabeth said. It was only the second time she had been to Chris's tiny, out of the way cottage about a half hour north of Eliot's Corner. He had bought the cottage several years before but had never, until now, invited anyone inside. It was almost, Elizabeth thought, as if the cottage had been waiting, patiently or perhaps impatiently, for her.

"I'm glad. It's simple and quiet and it makes a perfect retreat from the tensions of the outside world." Chris kissed the tip of her nose. "And a perfect retreat for us."

A retreat from the demands of husband and children, Elizabeth added silently. From the drain of a domestic life that had come to feel so empty of joy, so deadening of spirit. From the deep unhappiness of life with a man not Christopher Ryan.

"What are you thinking? You've a funny look on your face."

Elizabeth laughed. "Do I? I guess you're not used to seeing me happy. Oh, Chris, I love you so much I feel, I don't know, like I'm going to burst with joy."

"I feel the same way," he replied softly. "I don't know how I've lived so long keeping my love for you so hidden, even, to some extent, from myself. From the moment I met you in that awful pub way back when, I sensed we were meant to be together, even if I had no idea how it would come about."

"Ugh! It *was* awful, wasn't it? The floor was sticky with beer and the place smelled of old fried onions! But *you* stood out. You were different from everyone else there that night. I could tell immediately."

Chris smiled a bit sadly. "If only we had acted on that sense of being kindred spirits, grabbed each other's hand and rushed out into the night to live our own life together."

"You're a romantic man," Elizabeth murmured. So very different, she thought, from Hugh. Hugh was so very earthbound. "What's the song on the radio?" she asked then. She could hear enough of a melody coming from the radio in the living area to vaguely recognize the song but not enough to identify it.

Chris listened hard. "'Losing My Religion,' I think. I can't believe I know the song, but I do. I'm not exactly in sync with popular culture."

"It's one of the many things we share," Elizabeth said. "Being in some way out of step with the world around us. But tell me, do you like the song? I find it very moving."

"I do like it. Though it makes me feel sad."

"Me too. But feeling sad isn't necessarily a bad thing."

"I don't want you to feel sad ever again." Chris took her face in his hands and gazed deeply into her eyes. "I promise I'll never do anything to hurt you."

"I know you won't," Elizabeth breathed. "Kiss me, Christopher. Kiss me."

Chapter 13

Summer 2022

Petra was alone in the house on Lavender Lane. Her mother had left a note saying she had gone to the grocery store. While virtually all produce could be bought from local farmers, the grocery store was still the place to get items for the household cleaning, and dry goods such as pasta, canned soups, as well as the stuff of cravings like potato chips and ice cream.

The kitchen door swung open and Petra literally jumped. It was Jess. Jess never knocked. She never called ahead. Obviously, Jess felt it wasn't necessary to ask permission to visit her mother's home. Maybe it wasn't. Still, Petra thought a call would be a nice gesture.

"You startled me," she said. Her mood, which had been a wee bit on the melancholy side for no reason she could fathom, took a turn for the worse with Jess's abrupt appearance.

"Sorry." Jess removed her sunglasses and tucked them into a pocket of her soft briefcase. "Nice day out there. What are you doing inside?"

Petra ignored her sister's question. "What's brought you by?"

she asked. What she didn't say was: Shouldn't you be at the office? That might sound like a challenge.

"I've been doing some thinking about your business," Jess said, pulling out a chair and taking a seat at the table. "I took a long look at your website last night. I can't say I was impressed."

Petra leaned against the counter. "Gee, thanks."

"Hey, I'm not going to lie to you. But never fear; there's hope. I have a few suggestions, and I want you to take them seriously."

Petra could feel herself growing tenser by the moment. She so didn't want to have this conversation with her sister, now or ever, but couldn't bring herself to tell Jess to stop talking. To leave. Petra's fear of and distaste for confrontation was once again getting the better of her.

"Who designed your website?" Jess asked.

"A friend of one of my roommates," Petra said dully.

"Is she a professional web designer?"

"No, but—"

Jess sighed the sigh of the overly exasperated person. "Petra, you need to hire someone who really knows what she's doing. The site just isn't attractive enough. And the writing is a bit bland. Don't tell me—you wrote the text, didn't you?"

Petra nodded. She was a good writer. Her teachers had always praised her skills, as well as what they saw as her natural talent. But writing what amounted to marketing material was a skill she had never claimed to possess.

"Wrong. Don't stint on these things, Petra. You need a marketing specialist to work on your tactics, not a philosophy major. We have an excellent writer on the team at ATD Marketing, and I'd recommend him in a heartbeat, but I don't like to mix my job with my family."

"Tactics?" Petra repeated.

"Do you even take advantage of social media for promoting Past Perfect? By the way, the name isn't so hot. It's downright bland. Anyway, Twitter? TikTok? Facebook? Pinterest?

I couldn't find any online presence other than the website. I mean, why bother?"

Petra didn't need to reply. Obviously, Jess already knew the answer to her question.

Jess sighed and reached into her briefcase. "I put together a list of some people I know that you should talk with. They can help you. You'll have to pay for their expertise of course, but it will be well worth it, I promise. And I've added a few specific ideas for growing your business. I suggest you give them serious attention."

Jess held out the piece of paper. Petra went over to the table and took it. Then she returned to lean against the counter.

"With anyone else, I could have just texted that information, but with you," Jess went on, her tone smug (at least, Petra thought it was), "I thought I'd better use an old-fashioned method."

"Thanks," Petra mumbled. She was having a hard time now meeting her sister's intense and searching gaze.

"What's wrong?" Jess demanded. "Don't you want to do better? Don't you want to succeed?"

That word. *Succeed.* Petra hated that word. "What do you mean by 'better'?" she asked. "What do you mean by 'succeed'?" She could hear the anger in her voice. It upset her.

Jess rolled her eyes. "Come on, Petra. You can't be that naïve. Or are you just being stubborn, perverse? Everyone wants to have a nice, secure life, and to have that you need to have money, and, these days, as much of it as you can get. And it's not as if you're the type to marry into money, not going around looking like that! Not that I approve of marrying just for money. Anyway, rely on yourself! You're not stupid. You're probably more intelligent than Cam and me put together. Do something!"

The spark of anger that had come to life in Petra was extinguished as suddenly as it had flared, leaving her feeling slightly beat up, abused by her sister's assumption of superiority.

"I'm only saying these things for your own good," Jess told

her, in what just about passed as a kinder tone. "Someone's got to look out for you."

Petra stared down at the piece of paper in her hand. Her sister's handwriting was neat and bold. Jess always used black ink. An odd thought crossed Petra's mind. Who looked out for Jess? Who would dare?

"Well, I'm off," Jess announced, getting up from the table and loudly pushing her chair against it. "No hard feelings, right?"

Petra managed a smile. "Sure," she said. "No hard feelings."

When Jess had gone, Petra stuck the piece of paper with the names, contact information, and suggestions Jess had given her into her pocket. She didn't want Jess's help or her professional advice. Maybe she needed it—clearly, some people thought that she did—but that didn't mean she had to accept it. But she let the bit of paper stay in her pocket. For the moment.

Her mother returned not long after Jess's departure.

"Are you okay?" Elizabeth asked, setting several reusable bags of groceries on the table. "Did something happen?"

Petra managed a smile and joined her mother in unpacking the milk and other staples. "No. I mean, I'm okay. Jess came by."

"What did she want?" Elizabeth shook her head. "That sounds awful. As if she isn't welcome. I mean, did she have a particular reason for visiting?"

Yeah, Petra thought. To harass her younger sister. "No," she said, attempting another smile. "Just to say hello, I guess."

"Did she say anything else about the business? She must be concerned that someone at her office will find out that she's planning to leave and set up a rival company. Or, as she calls it, 'an alternative option to local marketing needs.' For all I know that might be cause for dismissal. Let's hope she's not planning on poaching clients from ATD."

"No. She didn't mention anything about the new company." For a brief moment, Petra felt remiss; she should have asked after her sister's new enterprise. But even if she had asked, Jess probably wouldn't have told her much. After all, Petra was too much of an airhead to understand business matters.

Elizabeth pulled a plastic tub of dishwasher pods from one of the bags and took it over to the cabinet under the sink. "Huh. Did she complain about Eddie?"

"Not this time."

"I've always felt sort of bad for him in that relationship," her mother said. "I'm not saying he doesn't have his own faults and flaws, but Jess can be a tough person to be around for long periods of time. And they seem so different. I never really understood what brought them together."

Petra shrugged and proceeded to fold the empty reusable bags. "Don't ask me. I'm not sure I've ever understood what brings two people together romantically. Other than sexual attraction, and that's not particularly special. What I mean is, in the course of a person's lifetime, it's likely she'll be sexually drawn to lots of people. That doesn't mean she wants to start a relationship with all of them. Why one person and not another?"

"The age-old question. The easiest answer is . . . love. But then you have to ask, what is love? Why does one person love another person? And from there . . ."

"You can drive yourself mad. Maybe it's better not to overthink relationships." Petra sighed. "Oh, I don't know."

Suddenly, her mother was at her side, smoothing a stray lock of hair from Petra's forehead. "I have an idea," she said. "It's a beautiful afternoon, and we're wasting it standing in the kitchen. Let's drive to the beach and watch the waves."

Petra was grateful for her mother's good care. Unlike most of the kids she had grown up with in Eliot's Corner, Petra had never felt she had a reason to complain about her mother. Elizabeth hadn't been too clingy or too strict or too much or too little of anything. She had been—she was—just fine. As close to perfect as a kid could ask for. And when a kid wanted the world, as they always did, that was saying something.

"I'll get the blanket and the sunscreen," Petra said with a smile.

Chapter 14

Elizabeth had to get away from the house that morning in order to think. Though exhausted from the strain of keeping up a pretense of normalcy with Petra all the previous afternoon and through dinner, she had been unable to sleep and was now dragging. Not surprising.

The turn onto Barnes Cove Road brought with it a sigh of relief. As she had hoped, there were very few other cars in the parking lot, and a quick glance around revealed only three people sitting on their own at various points across the massive gray rocks.

Elizabeth chose her own seat on a fairly flat, fairly smooth rock and looked out over the water. It appeared a gray-tinged blue through the lenses of her sunglasses, a slightly dull but soothing color, a perfect backdrop for introspection.

First, Petra's discovery of the damaged wedding gown.

Then, a song on the radio, a song that had sent Elizabeth tumbling through time back to that pivotal summer of 1991. Music, maybe the most powerful trigger of memories, in spite of what Proust had believed about the power of smell.

And then, the diary Petra had uncovered, a telling witness of secrets and lies that, were they to become public, would wreak havoc with Elizabeth's family.

Only a totally unimaginative person, someone innately opposed to any hint of the numinous in the mundane, could totally ignore these three events coming so soon upon one another as they had, could consider them random, meaningless, unrelated. Hugh, of course, had been one of those people. Maybe he had been better off for it. He had often teased his wife about her predilection for "reading into things"; he was an eminently practical and down-to-earth man who only believed what he could prove through the evidence of his senses.

Unlike Christopher Ryan, a man for whom a notion of God and a spiritual world coexisted comfortably alongside science and reason.

Elizabeth clasped her hands more tightly. At various times over the years she had toyed—only toyed—with the idea of telling her children about her long-ago relationship with Christopher Ryan, Hugh Quirk's oldest and dearest friend, best man at their wedding, good friend as well to Elizabeth, avuncular to Cam and Jess in the early years of their lives.

Christopher Ryan, a man highly respected in the important and contentious field of biomedical ethics. But for Elizabeth, the most important thing that Chris had ever done in his life was to be the biological father of her youngest daughter. And this was an achievement that no one but Elizabeth knew about.

No one.

Even after all these years she could so easily summon a memory of the day before the wedding when Chris had found her sitting alone on a bench at the edge of the village green in the quaint town where she and Hugh had gotten married. They had spoken of resignation and of acceptance. So much more had been left unspoken that morning.

Years later, when they had finally come together, they had talked about that brief moment at the edge of the village green. Elizabeth had lamented their lack of courage, their inability to say what it was they were feeling. Chris, his voice thin and his eyes sad, had counseled they not dwell on that missed opportunity. "We have to live in this moment," he had said.

Because that moment was all that they would ever have. Had they known from the start that their love was doomed? Even now, the answer to that question was unclear to Elizabeth.

What she was sure of was that, miraculously, there had never been rumors of the affair floating around Eliot's Corner. If anyone had hinted to Hugh that his wife might be cheating, he wouldn't have been able to keep silent, to let it go. He would have reacted with angry disbelief. He would have—

Elizabeth hadn't wanted to think about Hugh's potential reaction to the rumor of his wife's affair then, and she didn't want to think about it now.

One of the other people who were sharing the cove with Elizabeth that morning stood from her perch. She was an elderly woman, though not so frail that she must keep away from the rocky shore. Elizabeth watched as the woman made her way, slowly and deliberately, across the rocks and wondered if the woman was on her own in life, a widow, perhaps friendless, what remained of her family living far away. Elizabeth herself might be such a solitary person in twenty years' time, especially if she were to do something crazy such as alienate her children by telling them about her past.

How had it all begun? How had it all come about? For so long everything had been calm, pleasant, so very civilized. Since the very beginning of the Quirks' marriage, Chris had been a frequent visitor to the house; he and Elizabeth had often found themselves alone together. It was only in the two months leading up to that night at the ballet, only in the spring of 1991 that something had changed between them. For whatever reasons, it was as if a layer of protection had fallen away, their feelings finally breaking through the years of repression. Eyes quickly averted, pulses quickening, not so accidental touching of hands . . . It had been terribly, agonizingly exciting. But it had still been safe. Honest. Aboveboard.

Until one afternoon Hugh admitted to his wife that he really didn't want to join her at the ballet for which they had bought tickets ages ago. A colleague was retiring, and the party was bound to be outrageous, and Hugh really, really would prefer being at the pub to help send off Bob "Wildman" Collins rather than stuffed into a too-small seat in a stuffy theater watching a bunch of twinkle-toes do their thing.

"Chris will take you to the ballet," Hugh had said. "I'll ask him if you want. I mean, you don't want to go alone."

To Elizabeth, it had almost felt as if Hugh were offering her to Chris as a sort of gift. "Here, I know you guys get along, you spend time with her, I'm busy." Given Hugh's good-humored dismissal of Chris's manly appeal, he clearly saw no harm or threat in his wife and his best friend spending time together. In Hugh's estimation, Chris was no better than a eunuch.

Yes, that was how she had felt, as if she had been handed off, as one might pass on a trivial task to a junior colleague. "You'll have a good time with Chris," Hugh had said, as if she weren't capable of knowing her own feelings, as if she were a child being convinced by a parent that the babysitter he had hired was nice, really, and that all would be well. "He likes that sort of thing, culture and all. You know me. I'd be sure to fall asleep before the fat lady sings. Or is that opera?"

While the idea of spending an evening out with Chris was exciting, the idea also terrified her. Had she known what would happen when the two of them were alone in the dark at the end of the night? Had she wanted it to happen?

Elizabeth sighed. Whatever the answer to those questions, the fact was that after the ballet she and Chris had shared a passionate kiss and declared their love for each other. Over the next few weeks, they had talked endlessly about their feelings, about how nothing other than talk must be allowed to happen. No more kisses. No more embraces. Their intentions were good, but it was already too late to turn back.

Cam and Jess were young at the time—seven and five

respectively—and Elizabeth was their primary caretaker; there was no way she could just take off on her own for even a few minutes, let alone an hour or more, without a solid reason. So, she and Chris met when they could and, of course, as discreetly as they could, often just for coffee at some out of the way diner or for a stroll along a wooded path. Eventually, they started to meet at Chris's house, a small, out of the way cottage he kept for his visits to Maine from his primary residence in Boston.

There had been a few close calls in spite of every precaution.

One day Hugh had noticed that Elizabeth's car was low on gas. "I thought you told me you filled up just last Wednesday?" he had said to her.

Elizabeth had felt sick to her stomach. She had driven to and from Chris's house several times in the past few days. Of course, the gas tank was low. "Did I? Oh. I think I meant the Wednesday before that."

"No harm done. You know I just like to keep tabs on things. Did you put the credit card receipt on my desk?"

"Um, no. I think I must have paid with cash."

"I've told you it's better if you use the credit card for gas and most other expenditures. It makes my job easier when I pay the bills and review the monthly budget."

"Yes. I'm sorry. I must have forgotten."

"Try not to forget again, okay?"

Not that this sort of interrogation or, rather, paternalistic dynamic was unusual in the Quirk marriage. Hugh was a controlling man, no doubt well-meaning, but very sure that he knew what was best for the people in his world, especially his wife.

"Don't hold the knife that way, you'll cut yourself."

"I don't think you should watch that movie. You know how sensitive you are. It might upset you."

"You sound congested. I think you should stay in bed today and rest. You know how these things can get worse if you don't nip them in the bud."

For so many years Elizabeth had kept her temper, her replies restrained if slightly annoyed, but once the relationship with Chris had begun, this became almost impossible.

The exchanges now went like this:

"You look tired. Did you sleep badly? Maybe you should call Dr. Welsh, see if she has an opening this afternoon."

"Hugh, please. Just—leave me alone. I'm fine. You make me feel like an invalid. You make me feel like I'm stupid or incompetent."

"I never said you were stupid or incompetent."

"No, but you implied it."

"No I didn't. You're imagining things again."

Like a silly woman. Like a child with an overactive imagination. An adult could only take being talked down to for so long before she rebelled. Or before she backed down, exhausted, defeated.

Interestingly—perhaps tellingly—for all of his assumption of superiority, Hugh hadn't been the most intelligent guy around. And paying close attention had never been in his repertoire. Almost forty years after the moment, Elizabeth still retained a clear memory of one of their very first disagreements; it had been over choosing their wedding song. Hugh had suggested Willie Nelson's "Always on My Mind." "You can't beat Willie," he had said firmly. "He's the best."

Elizabeth had been a bit surprised, and a bit puzzled. "Willie Nelson is great, I agree," she said, "but Hugh, have you really listened to the lyrics?"

"Yeah. The guy's always thinking of his girlfriend. That's nice. That's the way it should be."

"There's a bit more to it than that," she had gone on to explain. "Basically, the singer is apologizing to his girlfriend for having ignored her. He asks her forgiveness and assures her that, even though he doesn't pay attention to her, she's still always on his mind. Don't you think that's a little, I don't know, grim, for a wedding song?"

Hugh had frowned. "That's really what it says? Huh. Okay then, how about "Every Little Thing She Does Is Magic"?"

Elizabeth remembered forcing a smile. It was dawning on her that Hugh might not be the most attentive of people. But that was okay. In fact, it was kind of cute. Endearing. "It's a good song, yes," she said carefully, "but . . . 'Must I always be alone?' Again, I'm not sure it really works for a wedding."

In the end, Hugh had agreed to let her choose a song she liked, and she had decided upon a classic, "The Twelfth of Never." Her mother had an old recording of the song as sung by Johnny Mathis. Elizabeth had always thought it super romantic.

"What does that even mean?" Hugh had asked after listening to the recording with her. "It doesn't make sense. I mean, it's a pretty song, I guess but, well, whatever you want. Weddings are really for the women, after all. I'm just there as a— Well, I don't know what my point is, really!"

Hugh had laughed at his own remark, and Elizabeth had joined him. Only later, months after the wedding, did she remember her new husband's words and find them bothersome. But only a little bit.

Now, in the summer of 2022, sitting on that smooth gray rock, looking out over the Atlantic, Elizabeth shivered and wondered why she had. The air wasn't particularly cool. It seemed a sign that she should leave the cove. As she carefully made her way back across the jagged rocks and to the parking lot, she wondered if her relationship with Christopher Ryan, Hugh's opposite in so many ways, had been preordained, fated to happen, written in the stars from the very beginning of Time.

In her head, she heard Hugh's mocking laughter.

Chapter 15

It was a sunny, cloudless afternoon. Downtown Eliot's Corner was busy with foot traffic, mostly, Petra guessed, other Mainers. The town did host the occasional group of tourists in summer, not enough to cause a significant rise in a shopkeeper's intake, but perhaps enough to briefly stimulate business in the restaurants and lobster shacks out along the coast.

Petra turned left onto the street that ran parallel to Main. It was almost as wide and had almost as many small stores, a perfect opportunity for window-shopping. She had always enjoyed a stroll, no destination necessary. There was always something exciting to see—a neighbor's new puppy; a tree suddenly in bloom; a house whose front door had been freshly painted red—even if your stroll took you along a route similar to the one you had taken the day before and the day before that. If you concentrated on seeing positive, even happy-making sights, you would invariably discover them. She knew that Jess would roll her eyes at the notion of wandering aimlessly, simply for the sake of what you might find; Jess would consider it a waste of time. But Jess was not Petra.

Suddenly, Petra spotted a former classmate not far ahead, and Petra's pleasant, carefree mood came to an abrupt halt.

Petra hadn't particularly liked Stephanie Taylor back when they were in school. Stephanie had hung out with a group of boys and girls who were Eliot's Corner's version of cool kids, mostly borderline bullies and poseurs. Honestly, Petra hoped that Stephanie would walk right by and ignore her. But that was probably hoping for too much.

"Petra, hey." Stephanie had come to stand within inches of Petra.

There was no way Petra could give her old classmate the cold shoulder; it just wasn't in her to be rude. Especially not when that someone was standing so close. "Hi," Petra said, taking a discreet step backwards.

Stephanie looked great in that way people not in financial straits often looked. Well cared for. Glossy. Trim. Effortlessly put together. Petra had heard Stephanie had married a guy who was involved with the sale of commercial property, or something like that. Supposedly, he was a big deal and made a ton of money. Stephanie, who had gone to law school, didn't practice as a lawyer. Word was that she was too busy shuttling among her various residences in New York's Hamptons, Connecticut's Greenwich, and just outside of Eliot's Corner, where her own family had a not-insubstantial home. Petra supposed staff needed directing, pools needed cleaning, and that major appliances such as a state-of-the-art barbeque station and a high-end Jacuzzi needed maintenance.

"So, what are you doing with yourself?" Stephanie asked, rapidly looking from Petra's face to her feet and back again.

Petra thought that an odd phrasing, but she knew what Stephanie meant. What are you doing to pay the rent? What is your job? Do you have a career worth mentioning?

"I have an online vintage clothing shop," Petra said, without the enthusiasm with which she had intended to reply.

Stephanie nodded. "Huh. Is that, uh, lucrative?"

At that moment, the sunlight struck Petra's former classmate's necklace, and the clear stones in the piece flashed brilliantly. They were probably diamonds, with sparkle like that; Petra knew the difference between real and faux. The necklace had probably cost more than Petra had earned in the past three years. But what did that matter?

"It depends on how much money you need to live," she said a bit boldly to Stephanie.

And then Petra wondered: Did a person really need money in order to live? Maybe not strictly speaking, but Petra didn't know many people—anyone really—who was equipped to survive in the wilderness (urban or rural) without food, clothing, and shelter, all of which were purchased with money unless you could produce the basics on your own. But was that even possible in this day and age? Where did a person get seeds with which to grow vegetables? Didn't she have to buy them? Buying meant you had to have money. And that meant—

Petra realized that Stephanie was laughing. "Good ole Petra Quirk," she said. "Head always in the clouds. Well, as long as you're having fun, that's what matters. Lord knows I would kill for more downtime, but I just have so many responsibilities, you know?"

Petra felt hurt. She was being mocked, if gently, and though she didn't want to admit to herself that she cared, she did. She wasn't laughable and didn't believe Stephanie or anyone else had a right to laugh at her. But maybe she was being oversensitive. She, herself, had often questioned her choice of . . . what? Lifestyle? But what about Stephanie's choice of lifestyle? Was it really any more valuable than Petra's? How could you spend all those years studying for a law degree and then decide not to use it? Wasn't that wasteful of time and money?

"Oh," Stephanie announced, looking pointedly at her heavy gold watch, "gotta dash. I'm meeting Rebecca Morris for lunch at Martindale's. You remember Rebecca, don't you? She's off to France the day after next for the rest of the summer, so this is a little bon voyage celebration."

With a wave of her well-manicured hand, Stephanie was

hurrying toward Main Street in the direction of the town's highest-end restaurant. The restaurant where Cam had taken their mother for lunch recently. Cam, a person with a successful career as a claims adjustor with a big insurance firm, even if, at the moment, it was part-time.

Petra hadn't been asked along to celebrate with her two former classmates—why would she have been?—and, strangely, the omission of an invitation rankled. But why should it rankle? Stephanie had insulted her, dismissed her choice of job as silly, more suited to a kid just out of college than to a thirty-year-old. . . . But Stephanie hadn't exactly said as much. Petra had sort of assumed her former classmate's negative judgment.

Anyway, what made Stephanie so much more adult than Petra? The fact that she was married? Big deal. Being married didn't prove anything other than . . .

Well, it proved nothing at all. Petra sighed. She felt deeply discontented and out of sorts, and it was all due to the questions and comments of other people. Jess confronting her the other day about the sorry state of Past Perfect had upset her. Then there had been Mrs. Shandy's questions about her goals. And now, Stephanie and her assumed superiority! Had Petra Quirk become a sort of universal joke in Eliot's Corner?

Whatever the answer to that disturbing question, Petra decided that it was time for a retreat to the grove of old pine trees. Growing up, it had been Petra's favorite spot to run off to when she wanted to be alone to think or read, to get far away from the busy house. If her father was at home, there was a good chance he was watching football with the sound turned way up or in the garage using a power tool while the radio blared his favorite rock standards. Cam was forever talking on the phone with her friends in an outdoor voice; and Jess, like Dad, loved to play her favorite bands at an insane volume, more than once leading to a justifiably angry phone call from the neighbors.

Only her mother seemed to share Petra's need and preference for silence in which to read and think things through.

But somehow, Elizabeth had managed to block out the chaos and noise of the lively Quirk household, doing her grading and other academic chores at the dining room table where she could expect her husband and her children to stomp through on their way to the kitchen or to suddenly, desperately need help with something only their mother could accomplish.

After a solitary walk that took Petra out of the town itself and within a mile of Lavender Lane, she arrived at the pine grove. It was located on land owned for centuries by the same family, and while, technically speaking, Petra's being there was considered trespassing, no one had ever chased her off.

The pines here were very old and very tall; the needles underfoot created a thick and somewhat slippery surface. Petra made directly for a particular tree, out of sight of the road, on which she had once carved her initials. She wouldn't do such a thing now—it was an unnecessary wounding—but at the age of twelve it had seemed important to mark her presence, to take possession in some way of this spot of nature that, in truth, in spite of land deeds, no one could ever really possess. She wouldn't have been the first child to leave her mark, and no doubt she wouldn't be the last.

Petra ran her forefinger over the wiggly and uneven marks that spelled out her name before settling on the ground with her back against the trunk of the large old tree.

She felt sad. She was bothered by the upsetting notion that she was wasting whatever talents she might indeed have. It didn't help that many of those around her, like Jess, weren't exactly sympathetic to the nature of Petra's business, what it was at its root, so of course Jess, and others, would see Past Perfect as only a vehicle—if a poor one—for making money. There was nothing wrong with making money. Petra knew that. It was how you went about making it and how you went about spending it that could be problematic.

And there was nothing wrong or time-wasting about selling vintage clothing; for one, it helped cut down on environmental stress by rejecting the throwaway culture that had reigned for so long. The problem, if there really was one, lay in the fact that deep down Petra knew—or at least suspected—there were other things she might be happier doing, or at least, that there were other things she felt she ought to attempt. She suspected there were ways in which she might make a better contribution to her fellow human beings and in the process, she, too, might benefit in a truly important way.

Maybe this summer would turn out to be a time of reckoning, a time of revelation. But reckonings and revelations didn't just happen; they didn't just land on you like an acorn falling out of a tree, did they? Well, maybe they did. Eureka moments. Sir Isaac Newton and the rumored apple. Epiphanies. Still, maybe urging something to happen, taking a conscious step in a particular direction might be helpful in—well, in getting the ball rolling.

Petra sighed. Every time she started to really think things through she got all muddled and agitated. It was probably a good thing she hadn't applied to graduate school all those years ago. She would never have been able to hack it. She would have had to drop out, which would have embarrassed her and disappointed her parents and, probably, made Jess laugh.

Anyway, right now, all Petra wanted was to enjoy the peace and quiet of this lovely spot, inhabit the moment, and forget about the past and the future.

This was not an easy thing to do.

Chapter 16

Elizabeth opened the driver's side window and welcomed the breeze that cooled her face. She enjoyed driving, though preferably not in cities; it allowed her to set her thoughts adrift. And in the past few days, her thoughts had been crowding upon her too thickly and heavily for comfort. Only that morning at breakfast Petra had observed her mother's low mood, asked if something was troubling her. Elizabeth had shrugged off her concern, said something to the effect of there being "a lot on her mind," assured her youngest child that all was perfectly well. All was not perfectly well; that part, at least, was a lie.

After breakfast, Petra had gone off for a walk to nowhere in particular, one of her favorite activities. Elizabeth had spent an hour cleaning and tidying up, and then she had taken to the road, not to Barnes Cove this time but to a stretch of land on the very edge of a marsh, that strange landscape of land and water exuding an air of ancient mysteries.

Elizabeth found herself entirely alone when she arrived at the pull-off used by those like her who found the marsh a place of beauty and fascination. She got out of her car and made her way to the old wooden fence almost buried at the moment in a profusion of dark pink beach roses. From this vantage point she had a full view of the various grasses, reeds, and sedges of the marsh in subtle shades of green and brown, rising, at the moment, above the pools of water. Elizabeth could think here without feeling entirely suffocated by her thoughts.

Think, for example, about the fact that at moments in her life she had been almost lulled into forgetting that her affair with Christopher Ryan had ever happened, too busy with or distracted by the challenge of work or the immediate demands of family matters. Daily life, alternately dull and full of the un-expected, could so easily obscure both what you wanted to re-member and what you wanted to forget.

And then, suddenly, a memory would force its way through the din of sudden demands and mundane responsibilities, and she would feel in every nerve ending the excitement as well as the fear that had gone along with being a deceiver, a per-son hating herself for what she was doing but knowing that she couldn't stop herself, at least not yet. The truth always came with the force of a blow. How could she have forgotten for even a moment that she had made love with a man not her husband? How could she have forgotten the fact that Petra was not Hugh Quirk's biological child?

It was at times such as those that she wondered most if she would ever truly be absolved of her moral crimes. At the time of the affair, her character hadn't yet been properly tried, and, when it was tried, when temptation beckoned that night at the ballet, she had so easily succumbed. Since then, she had made mistakes, but nothing to equal the transgression of having an affair with her husband's best friend—and withholding from that best friend the fact of his child's existence. Did that mean she had become a better person through the years? Did being a better person now somehow erase or negate the damage she had done before?

No. But at least she had never pitied her husband; that was one moral crime of which she was not guilty. To pity Hugh would have been the greatest insult of all. Still, it was too easy to feel pity for someone who didn't know they had been, or were being, betrayed. It was a terrible truth that the fact of a person's ignorance could lower the estimation of that person in the eyes of others. "How stupid is he that he didn't figure things out?" Or: "Poor woman. I wish someone could shake her out of her fantasy and show her what's really been going on right under her nose."

Of course, the situation had gotten insanely worse when Elizabeth learned that she was pregnant with Chris's child. It was then imperative that she and Hugh have sex right away. How could she otherwise explain a pregnancy to a husband with whom she hadn't been sleeping for several months? She hadn't been happy about committing a further act of deception, but she had done it. It hadn't been difficult to initiate a romantic encounter. Hugh hadn't been the one saying no since early spring.

Before her, two snowy egrets made their elegantly slow way through one of the bits of grassy land currently above the water. Elizabeth watched them intently for a few minutes. She wondered if egrets were one of those birds that mated for life, like swans and penguins. Was it easier for nonhuman animals to make that ultimate commitment to each other?

Elizabeth sighed as the birds dipped out of sight.

So, if she told her children about her affair with Hugh's dearest friend, what could she likely expect?

Oddly, she least feared Petra's reaction to the startling news. Petra was generally forgiving and understanding, empathetic as well as sympathetic. Even learning something as earth-shattering as the fact that Hugh Quirk was not her biological father wouldn't, Elizabeth believed, overwhelm Petra's good character.

Cam, though intelligent and open-minded, was also fairly conservative. Her shock might be very deep and might permanently damage her relationship with her mother. Still, Elizabeth felt sure that her oldest child would, over time, come to forgive and accept if not fully understand why her mother had done what she had done.

Jess was the problem. Like Hugh, the father she adored, she could be narrow-minded and unimaginative. And also like Hugh, she wasn't big on forgiveness; life for Jess was comprised of black and white, wrong and right, good people and bad people. Elizabeth's relationship with her middle child might never recover from the blow of revelation.

Elizabeth supposed that if she did decide to come clean she would simply have to trust in the love of her children, trust that they would ultimately forgive her for her transgression—and hope, also, that they would remain tight friends and allies. In spite of their unique natures, the three girls had always gotten along well. There had never been any big sibling rivalries, no fighting over boys or best friends, no fierce competition in school. When Cam married, she asked both Jess and Petra to be her maids of honor. That was Cam all over: fair, generous, concerned that everyone she cared about be content.

The same couldn't be said of her mother, though, could it? Elizabeth was afraid that she was fundamentally a selfish person. It would explain her decision to pursue the affair with Chris. It would explain her decision to keep Petra from her father. And it would explain her desire to tell her children about her past, knowing it would cause disruption in their lives.

But just how far was a mother compelled to sacrifice her own needs in favor of the needs of her offspring? There was no easy answer to that question, but Elizabeth knew, looking out over the ancient landscape of the marsh, that if she didn't make a decision soon, she would go mad.

Chapter 17

Petra had been looking forward all day to joining her mother at the meeting of the Arden Forest Book Club that evening.

The usual members were gathered, including Arden's elderly neighbor, Marla Swenson; thirteen-year-old Tami and her mother Tess Mogan; Lydia Austen (looking as chic as ever); the artist Jeanie Shardlake (Petra felt bad she had never checked out Jeanie's paintings, some of which were part of the public library's permanent collection); and a woman Petra hadn't met before that day. Her name was Edna Rogers. According to Elizabeth, Edna had once been a wealthy woman; her improvident husband had died and left her in debt up to the proverbial eyeballs. Petra observed Edna Rogers without seeming to do so and could tell that while her blouse and skirt were clean and obviously had been of excellent quality when purchased, they were now worse for the wear. There were a few other signs as well of a life deprived of the nicer things—Mrs. Rogers's hair clearly had been cut by her own hand—and Petra thought how difficult it must have been for the woman to deal with such a sudden and drastic change in circumstances.

The book chosen for this evening's meeting was *Cold Com-*

fort Farm by Stella Gibbons, published in 1932. Petra had sped through her mother's copy of the book the day before, thoroughly enjoying the rural adventures of the heroine, Flora Poste, with the exceptionally strange Starkadder family.

After a solid hour of discussion, Arden announced that it was time to linger and chat over Mrs. Shandy's shortbread cookies and tea, coffee, and wine provided by the bookshop's discretionary fund.

Petra heard a peal of laughter and turned to see her mother and another woman enjoying a conversation. She hadn't seen her mother smile so much in days, not since Petra had uncovered the tattered wedding dress, a discovery that seemed to have been the cause of Elizabeth's low or subdued mood.

Petra took a shortbread cookie from the pretty china plate on which they had been nicely arranged on a white paper doily. A few feet away, Laura Huntington, Arden's daughter, was in deep conversation with young Tami. What had happened to Laura's father all those years ago was almost too dreadful to contemplate, but at least mother and daughter were finally together, united.

Petra reached for another shortbread cookie—they were awfully good—and thought about her own childhood as the pampered youngest child in a stable family unit, with two parents who lived together under the same roof and who actually loved each other. How would she have fared not knowing her biological parents? How would she have fared learning only as an adult, as Laura had, that her father had been killed by her own grandmother and his body unceremoniously buried at the direction of her grandfather? At least Laura and her birth mother had found each other, and that was a gift.

Life could be so very difficult, full of the unknown, the unexpected, and the unwelcome. Petra felt very lucky that so far, her life had been pretty easy. Losing her father had been painful of course, but everyone kind of expected to lose their parents at some point, and she had known her father was sick and not expected to live for long. She hadn't wanted him to linger and suffer any more than he already had suffered.

"Penny for your thoughts?"

Petra smiled at Deborah Norrell, welcoming the distraction. Deborah, a real estate agent, was Arden's closest friend in Eliot's Corner—along with Gordon, Arden's romantic partner. In fact, Laura lived with Deborah in her spacious, beautifully decorated home. Both women had been married disastrously and had pretty much sworn off getting romantically involved with another man. But, of course, you never knew what might happen.

"I was just thinking about how amazing it is that Arden and Laura found each other. Their story makes me smile."

"Me too. It all could have gone so horribly wrong, but it didn't. I guess their guardian angels were being extra watchful."

Petra chatted with Deborah for a few minutes, then said her good-byes and joined her mother at the door of the shop.

"That was fun," Petra said as they stepped out into the warm night and headed in the direction of the car. "Eliot's Corner is so lucky to have Arden Forest."

Her mother nodded. "We are. It's a necessary hub for so many members of the community."

"You've seemed a bit distracted for the past few days. Well, you know that! But tonight, you seem like your old self. I mean, your usual self. What I mean is—"

Elizabeth laughed. "I get it. You know, it's nights like this, pleasantly warm, not a cloud in the sky, spending time with friends and neighbors, that I realize just how much I love this town. I wasn't sure when Hugh and I first came here that I would manage to fit in and be content but . . . Hugh had his heart set on raising our family in a small New England town. Eliot's Corner fit the bill to a tee."

"Would you have preferred to live in a city, Boston, or Portland maybe?" Petra asked.

"To be honest," her mother went on, "in those days I didn't really have a firm idea of what I wanted from my life. I let Hugh decide most of that." Her mother's tone was rueful but not angry. "Anyway, it all worked out in the end. Eliot's Corner has been good to me, and I hope I've been good to it. At least, to its children."

It was the first time that Petra had ever heard her mother talk about the earliest days of her marriage. She felt honored and, for some reason, a little bit sad.

"Do you think you let Dad make big decisions like where to live because he was ten years older than you?" she asked. "He could be pretty persuasive, and you were so young when you married."

"I suppose his being older and more experienced than I was did play a part," Elizabeth admitted. "And like you said, he did have a way of sweeping you up in his enthusiasm. My parents were totally awed by him. I think if I'd decided to break the engagement, they would have, well, they wouldn't have been happy."

"He was a force of nature," Petra agreed. "Sometimes I think that Jess feels she has to live up to his reputation, never show a moment of doubt or weakness, which is silly because of course Dad experienced moments of doubt and weakness; everyone does. He just didn't reveal them. Well, to his kids, anyway."

"And not often to his wife." Her mother sighed. "Yes, I do worry about Jess. Then again, I worry about all of my children. Worry is what mothers do."

"Doesn't it ever get any easier?" Petra asked. She was genuinely curious about this.

"Maybe a little. You have to learn to trust your children."

"To do the right thing?" Petra asked.

They had reached the car before her mother replied. "To do the smart thing," she said. "Now, let's get on home."

Chapter 18

"I'm at the office."

"Oh. Sorry. I guess I lost track of your schedule."

"That's okay. Is something up?"

Cam's tone was her professional one, polite but clipped.

"Nothing at all. I just called to say hello. But since this is a bad time—"

"You're sure everything is all right?"

Elizabeth had assured her that it was and ended the call.

A call to Jess had been even briefer.

"I'm driving. What is it?"

"You shouldn't have picked up if you're driving."

"I always pick up a call from you. What if you've had an accident? So, what is it?"

The aborted conversations had reminded Elizabeth yet again that both Cam and Jess had their own, busy lives. Maybe she was worrying too much about how her secret would impact their worlds. Maybe there was no such thing as too much worrying. Was she just trying to convince herself that telling her daughters about her long-ago affair was a perfectly fine, even a smart, thing to do?

A person could so easily trick herself, even a person who tried hard to live a conscious, examined life.

Today, Elizabeth had found solace in her own backyard, where she continued to ponder the wisdom or the folly of coming clean to her family and, possibly, one day, as the result of an ill-spoken word, to the town of Eliot's Corner.

For almost thirty years she had been respected and admired for her dedication to her students. The revelation of an affair that had produced a child—of an affair with her husband's best friend, a renowned voice in the field of biomedical ethics—might very possibly blacken the name of Elizabeth Quirk and erase all of the good she had done for the children of Eliot's Corner, so many now parents of their own children. To have her good reputation ruined by gossipy talk would be unbearable. As upstanding as the people of Eliot's Corner were, they were not immune to that all-too-human feeling of self-righteousness and self-satisfaction when a member of the community, always thought to be above moral reproach, was revealed to be an adulterer, or worse.

And should Elizabeth's secret be leaked outside the family, Petra's relation to the town in which she had grown up would change, as well. She might decide never to visit Eliot's Corner—or her mother—again, in order to spare herself the annoyance and embarrassment of being, even by association, notorious. It didn't take much to make a person notorious in a small town.

So many issues to consider! Still, this state of indecision was making her sick. Maybe, she thought, she needed to "force the moment to its crisis," to borrow a line from T. S. Eliot, one of her favorite poets, though she was pretty certain he wouldn't have appreciated her borrowing the phrase for this particular instance. Whatever Mr. Eliot might think, she couldn't keep running off to coves and marshes or sitting around her own backyard analyzing endlessly.

Prevaricating. Avoiding. Knowing that revealing the past to

her children was likely to bring her once more into contact with Christopher Ryan. And that he would have to be told that he was a father. He deserved that courtesy. To continue to keep the truth from him was almost criminal.

And so, like the proverbial lightbulb being switched on, that swiftly and definitely, Elizabeth made her decision. No matter the cost to her—and to others—the truth had to be told. She didn't want to be punished—she was not a masochist—but she craved an easing of the isolating burden of secrecy.

Now, with her husband dead, her daughters grown, and her career over or, at least, in need of a drastic reshaping, all the elements that had made it easier to avoid taking responsibility for her actions were gone.

Now, finally, she was ready do the right thing.

Chapter 19

Retro Groove was an okay name for a vintage shop, Petra supposed. She remembered feeling kind of proud when she had finally come up with Past Perfect as the name of her online shop. It was clever without being silly (no matter what Jess had said about it), and it was broad enough to attract people interested in finding gems from all periods of history, at least, from the Victorian era to the 1980s. This shop, as its name suggested, specialized in vintage items from the 1960s and 1970s.

Ever since she was a little girl Petra had enjoyed browsing—it was like hunting for treasure without the risks inherent in being a pirate!—but today, in this shop in Cousins Corner, it felt almost boring. It was making her all too aware of that deep but unnamed discontent, a restlessness that had made itself known pretty strongly in the last year. What had she really seen since she had walked into this shop? What had she really noticed? If she closed her eyes right then, what could she describe of the shop and its contents? She was afraid the answer to that question was that she had noticed nothing or, very little.

She remembered very clearly what her father would often say to her. He would tell her that when she grew up she would need to get serious about things, not walk around with her head in the clouds so much (even her former classmate Stephanie had used this expression), learn how to focus and concentrate on getting the job done.

"I'm telling you this for your own good," he would say, not unkindly. "The world is a tough place. You've got to keep your eyes open and your wits about you."

Clichés, but well meant, even if they did instill a certain layer of fear in the breast of his youngest, highly sensitive child, which might, Petra thought now, have something to do with her feeling that she didn't know her place in the world. For as far back as she could remember, she had been aware of a certain distance between herself and the people in her life, both people she knew personally and strangers, the wider community of Eliot's Corner, of Portsmouth, of the world.

Petra glanced across the shop to the only other customer, a skinny teenage boy searching very intently through a hanging rack of vintage pants. His head was partly shaved to reveal a tattoo of what looked like a roaring lion. She wondered if his parents were in the habit of telling him to get his head out of the clouds and buckle down, or if they let him be his authentic self, as alarming as that might appear to them.

Suddenly, Petra looked away from the teenage boy and left the shop, feeling the eyes of the sales person on her, as if the woman suspected her of—what? Stealing? Or of being a fake, a pretend person, someone who wasn't really who she said she was, whoever that was?

Instead of heading back to the car, Petra found herself wandering through the tiny town, noticing little, thinking a lot, like about Laura Huntington, Arden's daughter, whose academic career had been put on hold for several years thanks to a bad marriage and its ensuing debts. If Laura, who had been through so much, could grab hold of her life once again and move forward, well then . . .

But Petra Quirk wasn't Laura Huntington. Comparisons were most often useless and damaging.

Anyway, how could Petra even think about going back to school when her own business remained underdeveloped; when she couldn't even name a new special interest, something that she had discovered and dedicated herself to in the last few years; when she couldn't even always see physical, tangible items that were immediately in front of her, let alone grasp concepts and take hold of ideas?

Petra thought of the people in her own social sphere back in Portsmouth, such as those who had been at her thirtieth birthday party back in early May. About twenty people had gathered for pizza, beer, and wine, followed by a delicious cake made by one of the guests who worked at a local bakery. Among the guests were several artists; two or three people who worked in local retail or restaurants as servers or bartenders; a dog walker; a seasonal au pair; and a guy who was acknowledged as a brilliant gamer. As far as Petra knew, nobody gathered for the event worked in an office or had a career that might be considered "important" or, worse, "real." No doctors or lawyers. No nurses or financial advisors. No marketing experts or architects. In short, no one had much, if any money, and if they had specific ambitions or goals, Petra had never heard them spoken about.

But were these people content in their self-knowledge? Had each one of those party guests found their purpose in life? She couldn't be the only one floundering. Could she?

If only she could determine that purpose in life! Not her goal, that was different. At least, she thought that a purpose was different from a goal. But there was so much of which she was unsure. For example: Was a person's identity static? Was a core of it meant to remain stable over time? Or was every bit of a person's identity—whatever that was—always changing, for better or worse, evolving, devolving, revolving? In college, she had spent an awful lot of time reading works of philosophy, literature, social theory, even a smattering of theology, assuming, as youth does, that by the end of the four years she would be a mature adult in possession of Certain Knowledge, a Key to

Life, The Answers. Well, none of those things had been in her grasp when she was twenty-one, and they certainly weren't in her grasp now.

She couldn't recall the line exactly, but she thought that Hermann Hesse, in the persona of Joseph Knecht, had, in a student poem, talked about the fluidity of identity, of how a person took whatever form they found or . . . Maybe she was wrong about that. She knew that Bruce Springsteen had a line in one of his songs, something about being like a river not knowing where it was flowing. . . . Was he talking about what Hermann Hesse had been talking about? If only she could remember things precisely! If only she could learn how to pay closer attention!

Things look darkest before the dawn. Her father used to say that. But did they, really? Or was that an observation made in hindsight, or, maybe not an observation at all, but a useless fiction to make sense of, put order to, a time of chaos?

Maybe, Petra thought, what she was experiencing was a form of extended anxiety attack, or maybe it was a seriously bad bout of the blues. Whatever it was she was going through, she would have to ride it out, meet it head on, let it take its course. . . .

What did any of that even mean? More clichés. Convenient but empty.

It was time to head back to Lavender Lane. If only she could remember where she had parked the car . . .

Chapter 20

I feel elated to be carrying Chris's child, in spite of the terrible circumstances. How could our affair have been entirely wrong if it produced a new life? Or am I just deluding myself, making excuses for inexcusable behavior? I pray this baby will be born healthy and will never have to suffer as a result of my actions. . . .

Elizabeth closed the diary and went to her dresser, on top of which was a wooden box in which she kept less expensive items of jewelry. At the moment, she felt very strongly the need for a talisman of sorts, the small lavender agate pendant Chris had brought back from a working trip in Europe many years before, when Cam and Jess were small and the idea of an affair with her husband's best friend would have struck her as total insanity.

"Because this is your favorite color," Chris had said, handing her a small silk bag. She remembered uncovering the pendant and gasping when she saw the soft pastel of the stone, carved into the shape of a perfect circle.

"Her favorite color?" Hugh had boomed. "I thought that was blue."

"That's your favorite color," Elizabeth had reminded her

husband, who had then shaken his head and said: "I don't know how anyone keeps track of these things."

Maybe today, wearing the one gift she had ever received from Chris, hidden under her blouse, she would feel somehow protected—by the memory of his love?—and courageous.

Elizabeth joined her daughters in the living room. Jess was sitting in one of the high-backed armchairs. Petra sat at one end of the couch, Cam at the opposite end. Elizabeth took a seat in the other armchair facing all three girls.

"So, why are we all here like this?" Jess asked. "I feel like we're little kids again and about to be handed our punishment for not doing our chores."

"I was never punished for not doing my chores," Cam remarked.

Jess snorted. "That's because you were a goody-goody."

"Mom, what's wrong?" That was Petra; she looked truly worried. "What's going on?"

"Nothing's wrong," Elizabeth said, though that was debatable. "But I have something to tell you. I can't stay silent any longer. I wish that I could, truly."

Cam leaned forward, her hands clasped. "Mom, it's okay. Just tell us. It's got to be important for you to ask me to come north again so we could all be here together."

"It is important, even though what I have to tell you concerns Petra, mostly," Elizabeth began.

"Petra is in trouble?" Jess laughed. "What did she do? Forget to unplug the iron? Wait, she doesn't use an iron, does she? She prefers her clothes to be wrinkled and hanging off her like empty sacks."

"No one is in trouble," Elizabeth said quickly, hiding her annoyance at Jess's unpleasant attitude toward her younger sister. "I probably should have told you this years ago. I'm not entirely sure why I'm telling you now, at this particular moment, but there were signs. . . ." Elizabeth sighed. "When Petra found an old diary of mine—"

"I didn't know about that," Jess interrupted. "Cam?"

"Me, neither. But let Mom talk."

"The diary," Elizabeth went on, looking quickly from one daughter to the next, "was one I kept in 1991. It was a strange time in my life, strange and . . ."

"It's okay, Mom," Cam said. "Take your time."

After a moment, Elizabeth went on. "Well, the diary coming to light when it did—and honestly, I'd forgotten all about it—combining with a few other factors, things I'd begun to think seriously again about . . . You see, the diary contains the only written evidence, if it can be called that, of . . ."

Jess sighed. "Mom, you're killing me. Pretend like you've got a Band-Aid that needs to come off. Just yank it."

"Petra," Elizabeth blurted, "Hugh Quirk is not your father."

Petra laughed. "Sorry, Mom, but I think I misheard you. I thought you said that Dad isn't my father."

Elizabeth's hands were shaking. If only she hadn't opened her mouth! But it was too late now. The words couldn't be unspoken.

Jess frowned. "I heard it, too. What's going on, Mom?"

"Hugh, Dad, is not Petra's biological father," Elizabeth said, amazed at the steadiness of her voice. "In every other way, he was and still is the father of all you girls, equally. Nothing has changed."

"Nothing has changed?" Jess cried. "Are you insane?"

"Jess! Did Dad know?" Cam asked her mother softly.

"No one knew but me. Not even Petra's biological father."

Petra laughed again; this time it sounded ever so slightly hysterical. "Um, I feel like I'm being seriously dumb, but I don't get it. Mom, what exactly are you trying to say?"

Elizabeth felt her heart begin to pound in her chest. "I had an affair with Christopher Ryan, our family friend. Hugh's friend from childhood. Christopher is Petra's father."

Immediately, Cam scooted over to sit close to Petra and put her arm around her sister's shoulder. *I should have gone to her,*

Elizabeth thought. *I should have spoken to Petra alone, before telling the others. Oh, what have I done?*

"Well, at least you know who the guy is! Not just some pickup."

Elizabeth flinched. She probably deserved this attitude from Jess, as nasty as it was.

"How long did this—this relationship—go on?" Cam asked.

"All told, about two months. It was the summer of 1991. Chris and I attended a ballet together because your father didn't want to go. We had had tickets for some time but there was a retirement party for a colleague, and Hugh decided he wanted to go to the party instead, so he suggested that I ask Chris to accompany me to the ballet. I should probably have gone on my own, or asked a friend from town, even canceled my plans, given the tickets away. But I didn't. I was angry with Hugh for canceling on me. I called Chris, he said yes, and we went."

"You must have had feelings for a long time before that," Cam said quietly. "Affairs don't just happen."

"Yes, I'd had feelings for Chris for years," Elizabeth admitted. "And he'd felt the same about me. But neither of us had spoken a word or given the other a reason to hope in any way. Absolutely nothing improper had happened. Not until that night at the ballet. It was nothing either of us had planned, believe me."

"So, basically you had a summer fling?" Jess laughed harshly.

Elizabeth winced. "It wasn't a fling," she said evenly. She had expected Jess to take the news badly. Jess had worshipped her father. Still, her hostility was wounding.

"Oh, pardon me, it was a relationship. Well, that makes all the difference! Wait, a minute. Are you sure Dad is my father? What about Cam's? Did you have other flings? Oh, excuse me, relationships?"

Elizabeth willed herself not to burst into tears or to run from the room. It was difficult.

Cam cleared her throat. "So, what happened to end it?" she asked, again, quietly.

"The terrible guilt I felt. I broke things off with Chris, and he accepted my decision. He was as miserable as I was. And because I wouldn't leave Hugh, there was no choice but for us to part."

"Why wouldn't you leave Dad?" Cam asked.

Jess was clearly fuming, though silently now. Petra sat as if frozen.

Elizabeth knew she had to choose her words carefully. The last thing she wanted was to give the impression that she was blaming Hugh for her decisions. "I was afraid to leave Hugh," she said, "afraid of what might happen to us all, afraid of the damage a divorce might cause. And Chris and I were both so unhappy at that point that we knew we could have no future together. It would have been badly tainted by what we had done to Hugh. Parting ways seemed like the only solution."

"That was a brave decision," Cam said quietly.

Elizabeth gulped in an effort to hold back her tears. "Thank you. Anyway, a few weeks after I had ended our relationship, I learned that I was pregnant. It wasn't difficult to determine that Chris was the father. Hugh and I hadn't been intimate in a long time."

Jess snorted. "Nice. So, let me guess. To hide the fact that the baby wasn't Dad's, you had to have sex with him again. You had to add insult to injury, pretend you were interested in your husband. God, I can't believe this!"

"You must have been frightened," Cam said, ignoring her sister's outburst.

Elizabeth looked at her youngest child. Petra sat with folded hands, her eyes closed, silent.

"I panicked," she admitted. "The last thing I wanted was for your father to learn the truth about the affair. Sadly, Jess is right. I resumed intimacy with Hugh. Still, I was worried that the truth might come out at some point during the pregnancy, if something went wrong. But the pregnancy was remarkably smooth. A part of me had thought that a child conceived in a— in a dishonest way might . . . Well, I was in a strange, fearful state of mind, even superstitious. But I needn't have worried. Petra was born in perfect health and . . . and nobody was any the wiser."

Finally, Petra opened her eyes. "Why didn't you tell him, Mr. Ryan," she said, "that he was . . . He might have . . ."

Elizabeth tried to hold Petra's eyes as she spoke, willing her to understand. "There were several reasons I remained silent," she said. "Most important, I had to ask myself what it was I really wanted, and it was clear that what I most wanted was to protect my family, my children. I had no idea if Chris would agree to keep his being the baby's father a secret from Hugh. Every scenario I envisioned led to disaster. It seemed the wisest choice was to keep my secret, to bury it as deep as I could, and to atone for what I'd done to Hugh by falling in love with his dearest friend. If I could be a good wife, a partner to my husband, a good mother to his—to all of the children, that might go a long way toward paying a moral debt."

"You were afraid to tell Mr. Ryan," Petra said, her voice so low Elizabeth had to lean forward to hear it. "My father."

"Yes," Elizabeth admitted. So much had come about because of fear. If only she had been a braver person!

Cam rose from her seat next to Petra. "I need some water. Would anyone else—"

"Yes," Elizabeth said gratefully, wearily. "Thank you."

Chapter 21

While Cam was in the kitchen and Jess was angrily pacing the living room, muttering words Petra was happily unable to discern, Petra sat as still as the proverbial statue. She wasn't opposed to the idea of moving. In fact, if she could have moved she would have leapt from the couch and run from the house. After that?

Suddenly, Petra became aware of her mother getting up, slowly, from her seat. She tensed. Her mother was now crossing the short distance to where Petra was, on the couch. She sat, carefully, less than half a foot from Petra's side, and reached for her daughter's left hand where it sat limply on Petra's thigh. Petra didn't fight her mother's touch, but neither did she return her clasp.

Cam came back into the room then, carrying a tray on which were balanced four glasses of water with ice. She distributed the glasses—Petra, finally mobile again, pulled her hand from her mother's hand to take her glass—and took the seat their mother had vacated.

"I'm asking all of you to keep this a secret," Elizabeth went on after a long and uncomfortable silence. "I don't want anyone in Eliot's Corner to know the truth. This town has been my home for so long, I don't want my friends and neighbors to suddenly see me for . . . I mean, I have to live here for the rest of my life, I want to live here, and I can't bear the thought of becoming a topic of gossip and finger-pointing." She paused. "And I can't bear the thought of Hugh's memory being dragged through the mud."

Jess laughed bitterly. "Don't worry. The last thing I want is for anyone to know about this! Your secret is safe with me. And yeah, I know, I can be bad about keeping secrets, but there's no way this bit of family history is going anywhere. For *Dad's* sake."

Petra remained silent. She would keep her mother's secret to herself. Of course, she would. It touched her too deeply to be spread around like a bit of casual gossip. Besides, she had no one to tell.

"Of course, we'll keep this news to ourselves," Cam said then; she had gulped her glass of water as if she had never been thirstier. "But Ralph needs to know. I need to tell him."

"Yes, you do," Elizabeth agreed. "I don't believe there should be big secrets between husbands and wives. I know that sounds like hypocrisy," she added quickly. "To say or profess to believe one thing and to act another."

Jess snorted. "It is hypocrisy."

"Let she who is without sin cast the first stone," Cam murmured.

"I'm allowed to make a judgment in a case like this," Jess shot back.

Suddenly, Petra leaped to her feet, surprised by the rush of adrenaline coursing through her body. "Please, don't fight," she cried. "I can't bear it if we start fighting."

"I'm sorry, Petra," Cam said abruptly. "Really, I should have been more considerate of what you're going through right now."

"Me too," Jess mumbled. "Sorry."

"Petra . . ." That was her mother, speaking brokenly.

Petra worked to steady her breathing, to calm her racing

heart. Instead of sitting back down next to her mother she went across the room and stood looking blankly out of the window, her back to her family. At that moment, she didn't feel able to look her mother or her sisters in the eye, though she had no idea why. She wasn't the one who had done something wrong. She wasn't to blame. Why should she feel . . . ashamed? If ashamed was what she felt. And not—what? Repulsed? Oddly excited? Angry?

"I suppose you'll tell Eddie?" her mother asked Jess quietly.

"Why?" Jess sounded genuinely puzzled by their mother's question.

"For the same reason I'll tell Ralph," Cam said. "Because he's my partner."

"Maybe," Jess said dismissively. "I can't think about it now."

Petra placed both hands against the glass of the window. Again, she realized that she had no partner, no close friend, no boyfriend she wanted to tell, no one who *should* be told this explosive news in order to better support and understand her. At that moment, in the presence of her mother and sisters—no, her half-sisters; that made a difference, didn't it?—she felt more isolated than she had ever felt in her life, more at sea, more . . . unknown.

She remained at the window for what might have been a moment or an eternity until she heard each member of her family leave the room. Only then did she turn back around to face the empty living room. Though she recognized the couch, the rugs, the knickknacks on the coffee table, everything seemed changed, slightly altered, foreign, the painting over the couch sickeningly bright, the statuette of a classical nymph crassly erotic.

Yes, Petra thought. *I am in fact in the middle of a genuine identity crisis.*

Chapter 22

Elizabeth was alone in her bedroom, a sanctuary if only a temporary one, curled into the old armchair that had stood in one corner of the room for almost forty years.

The house was quiet. Jess had left once the conversation—if it could be called that—had wound down to a weary and confused silence, Petra staring out the window of the living room, her back to the others. Jess hadn't so much as glanced at her mother as she left the house and hadn't said farewell to any of them. Well, Elizabeth thought, that was no surprise.

Dinner later on had been a tense affair, over as quickly as it could be. Cam had been obviously nervous, attempting to make her mother and sister smile, trying to normalize a decidedly not-normal situation. For a caregiver like Cam, failing to make people feel comfortable was painful. She had escaped to her room as soon as they had cleared the table and gotten the dishwasher started.

Petra had been uncharacteristically but not unexpectedly quiet, eating swiftly but without any enjoyment as far as Elizabeth could tell. Before they parted for the evening, Petra had reached for her mother's hand. "It's all right, Mom," she had said so softly that Elizabeth wasn't entirely sure the words had been spoken. She hoped that they had.

Interestingly, as badly as Elizabeth felt for her children, she felt almost as badly for the two men in her life, both of whom had suffered as a result of her actions. For one, Hugh and Chris had effectively lost their friendship. Elizabeth knew for a fact that it had bothered Hugh more than he let on, Chris's unexplained disappearance from their lives. As for Chris, Elizabeth felt sure that he, too, had felt bereft.

It was an old story: a woman had come between two men, leaving destruction in her wake. Her affair with Chris had hardly mimicked a classic, tragic love triangle like that among Jules, Jim, and Catherine in François Truffaut's famous film *Jules et Jim*, but still, a woman had destroyed, however accidentally and without intention, a true friendship, and that was a shame.

It had been so important for Hugh to introduce Elizabeth to Chris before they married. Though he hadn't said as much, she knew that Hugh had needed his friend's approval in order to be absolutely sure that he was doing the right thing. Even back then Elizabeth was aware, if dimly, that, in spite of Hugh's air of bravado and bluster, he had moments of insecurity like everyone else; in fact, those moments, though not frequent, could be fairly severe.

So, one evening Hugh had taken her to a local pub popular with young professionals like Hugh and his officemates, and it was there that he introduced her to his best friend since childhood, second grade, to be precise. And at the very moment Elizabeth laid eyes on Christopher Ryan, she felt something inside her come to life. It should have been a warning sign, a signal that perhaps she was marrying the wrong man, but she had been so caught up in Hugh's dynamism and charisma, she could barely make a small decision on her own, let alone consider a major question involving her future. Besides, Hugh had presented Chris, who had just completed his PhD and was headed for "big things," as "one of those celibate academic sorts," a man whose ideal woman existed on a page in an old book if she existed at all. Not husband or family material. And Elizabeth had wanted a husband and a family.

It wasn't until several months later, on the eve of the wedding, when she and Chris had sat together on the bench across the village green from the little stone church, that Elizabeth had finally realized the depth of her attraction to her fiancé's best friend—and that she had finally known for sure that Chris had feelings for her as well.

Still, nothing had happened. Rather, nothing had been spoken, but something certainly had happened. Something subtle but sure.

Elizabeth looked across the room to the clock on her bedside table. It was past two in the morning. Sleep might not come this night. Better to accept the possibility than to argue against it. She considered fetching the diary from the bottom drawer of her dresser, maybe reading a few passages, and then, a terrifying thought struck her and she dashed across the room, retrieved the diary—thank God, it was still there!—and opened the door to her walk-in closet. At the back of the closet was the safe Hugh had insisted on installing. Elizabeth opened the safe and tucked the little red book at the back, behind a bundle of legal documents. She closed the safe, the closet door after it, and slumped back into the old armchair in the corner.

Only then, her hand around the lavender agate pendant at her throat, did she begin to cry.

Chapter 23

Petra stood at her bedroom window and looked out over the front yard. The street was quiet; only one house at the far end of Lavender Lane was lit up. It seemed an age since her mother had shared the truth of Petra's parentage with the family, but in fact it had been only a few hours since Petra had learned she was not, indeed, who she thought she was. She never had been.

Not surprisingly, Jess hadn't stayed on for dinner, and Cam had gone to her bedroom right after the meal. Petra assumed her sister had called Ralph and shared the shocking news their mother had revealed. She wondered what words of consolation he had offered. Ralph was a decent guy, in spite of what was looking like an inappropriate crush on his old girlfriend. Wasn't he? Now, Petra wasn't sure. If her mother, the one person—along with her father; Hugh Quirk that is—who Petra had always held above the rest of humankind as thoroughly good and honest, could prove to be merely human after all, then anyone . . . Petra sighed. How naïve she had been all her life. No one could transcend the frailties of humankind, not even parents. Too bad.

Suddenly, she remembered how just a few days before, while at a meeting of the Arden Forest Book Club, she had silently compared Laura Huntington's familial situation to her own and found them so very different. If only she had known that beneath the surface of her own happy, typical family lay a dark and dangerous secret! Maybe she and Laura shared more than Petra had assumed.

Petra turned from the window and began to pace the room. She was pretty sure she was in shock because she couldn't really ascertain or identify what she was feeling at the moment. She had told her mother that she was okay, but she had lied. She wasn't really okay. How could she be? Her identity, something that was already a mystery to her, had been called into question, if that was the right way to put it. Maybe this, the fact that she was the child of another man, not Hugh Quirk, explained why she had always felt somehow alien to herself as well as to others. Maybe this explained why she felt so lost, so unmoored, so uncomfortable with the person she was—with the person she had thought herself to be. The problem was that Petra hadn't known her origins. Rather, her origins had been hidden from her, no doubt for reasons that had seemed right to her mother at the time. And for the entire thirty years of Petra's life to date? Why, oh why, hadn't Elizabeth told her the truth before now?

The one thing Petra was certain she didn't feel at the moment was anger. She was not angry with her mother for having had an affair with Christopher Ryan. How could she be angry about that? The relationship had given her life. Still, she knew that she might feel angry at some point to come, once this shock had worn off. Anger was normal. She hated and feared anger, but it was a fact of life.

There was a muffled sound from the bedroom to the right of hers, her parents' room. Rather, the room her mother had shared with the man who had been Elizabeth's husband but not Petra's father. Did that make Hugh Quirk her stepfather? Had he really had any legal rights as one of her parents? A lawyer would know the answer to those questions, and maybe one day Petra would hire a lawyer to answer them. But for now . . .

Petra dropped onto the edge of the bed and clasped her hands in her lap.

"Dad," she whispered, "we're in a bit of a mess here. You were always good at fixing things. Flat tires on my bike. The food disposal in the kitchen sink. Remember how Jess was always dropping stuff down there she shouldn't have, chicken bones and spoons, even a hair tie once? You could fix everything that went wrong around the house. I know this isn't the same, and maybe you're upset about it—if you know about Mom's . . . The point is that we need you, Dad. I need you."

Petra couldn't go on. Tears slowly dripped down her cheeks; she felt them trickle along her neck. Would this Christopher Ryan have to be told that he was Petra's father? Why? Was he owed that information? Probably. Would he try to make up for lost time and act like a father was supposed to act? That would be awful. No. Hugh Quirk was her dad. Her daddy. And she was his daughter. They always would be father and daughter. No one could take that away from either of them. No one.

Besides, maybe Christopher Ryan wouldn't want to know his daughter. Maybe he would be horrified that she even existed, angry and annoyed that he had been bothered with the news after all the years of blissful ignorance, wary of any demands Petra might put on him, financial or emotional. Maybe he would never be a part of her future life, just like he had never been a part of her life to date. In that sense, maybe nothing would have really changed.

But Petra knew that it had. Everything had changed. Nothing at all was ever going to be the same.

Chapter 24

Jess hadn't been in touch with her mother since the revelation, but Elizabeth tried to convince herself that that was okay, to be expected. Jess had been the most obviously upset by her mother's news, and, given her volatile and prickly nature, she would need time to calm down, to reflect. How long? A week? A month? A year?

Cam, on the other hand, had gone back to South Portland early on the morning following the revelation, but not without taking a proper, loving leave of her mother and sister. Petra, in reality her half-sister. Not that it mattered. Since then, Cam had sent a text and an e-mail to Elizabeth, each with a message of genuine support. Elizabeth had replied with gratitude.

As for Elizabeth and Petra, they had been tiptoeing around each other for the past few days, avoiding entirely any mention of Christopher Ryan and the role he had played in their lives. The atmosphere had been less tense than determinedly calm. But it couldn't go on forever.

"We should talk," Elizabeth said. "We can't go on avoiding this."

She had come upon her daughter sitting at the kitchen table with a cup of milky coffee.

Petra glanced briefly at her mother and nodded. "I know. But I don't know where to begin."

"I guess I don't either," Elizabeth admitted. She joined Petra at the table, and, the moment had she taken her seat, Petra began to speak as if the words had been just waiting to come tumbling out.

"For the past few years," Petra said, staring down at her coffee, "it's become increasingly obvious to me that I don't have a strong sense of identity. That I have no idea where I am in the world or why. That there is so much more to life than I seem to be able to engage with. This is probably not really news to you, although maybe you haven't sensed the depth of my confusion or whatever it is. But this . . . this news about Dad and Christopher Ryan . . . It somehow makes it all worse. Now, I'm not at all who I thought I was, not even a little. And I'm not happy about it. How can I be?"

Elizabeth leaned forward and spoke earnestly. "Yes," she said, "you are who you've always been. This doesn't change the fact that you are Petra Quirk, daughter of Elizabeth and Hugh. Sister to—"

"Mom," Petra said impatiently, finally looking up with eyes that were sad. "You know what I mean. It's just that it's like suddenly finding out that I was adopted but . . . different. Worse. I don't know. I'm shocked. I feel betrayed. Why didn't you tell me before now? Didn't you trust me to keep my real parentage a secret from people who have no business knowing? I wouldn't have said a word. Why didn't you tell me when Dad died? And just so you know, I'm going to keep calling him Dad because he was my father and he still is my father and nothing can change that."

Elizabeth rubbed her forehead for a moment before speaking. "You were grieving when Hugh died. How could I have added to that grief by revealing that the man you loved and watched suffer was not in fact your biological father?"

"All right," Petra said after a moment. "That's a fair point.

But—I still wish you had spoken before now. Maybe. Oh, I don't know. I think I feel angry now. I hate feeling angry. I've always thought that most times when a person feels angry it's really something else she's feeling. Anger is so easy. It's right at hand, all the time. Our culture celebrates being pissed off, annoyed, slinging insults. When are those angry feelings covering for or masking other more complicated feelings, like maybe sadness or fear?"

Elizabeth attempted a consoling smile. "Your father always worried about you because he thought you spent too much time in your head. He could be suspicious of thinking."

Petra smiled fleetingly. "Maybe it's a tendency I got from Christopher Ryan, spending a lot of time in my head. Oh, it's all so terribly sad! When you found out that you were pregnant with me and knew Chris had to be the father, weren't you even tempted to involve him in your life again? Maybe get back together, tell Dad, get a divorce? Or even just tell Chris about the baby, ask for his silence or for his help?"

These were all reasonable questions, and Elizabeth owed her daughter answers.

"One of the reasons I never told Chris about your being his child," she began after a moment, "is that I was concerned for his reputation. What would people say if it was known that a specialist in ethical behavior had had an affair with the wife of his best friend and had fathered a child as a result? His career might have been seriously damaged, and Chris did such genuinely good work for people, especially for children. Add to that my feelings of guilt about what I had done to my husband, and the risk at which I had put my children, and it became impossible for me to tell Chris the truth about you."

"I wonder," Petra said after a moment, "if it was worth all the misery. I mean, all that pain for one short summer of love. Why?"

"I can't explain the whys," Elizabeth said with a small smile.

"But you being born into this world made every moment of anxiety and fear of exposure worthwhile."

"And if I hadn't been born? If you hadn't gotten pregnant? Would the relationship still have been worth the while, whether or not Dad ever learned about it?"

Elizabeth sat back in her seat. That was a question she had asked herself so many times through the years. And yet, she still had no firm answer. Maybe there was no answer to be had.

"Do you want to meet your father?" she asked, rather than replying to Petra's question.

"Yes," Petra said immediately. "Honestly, I wasn't sure about that until this very moment, but yes. I'm curious, if nothing else."

"Okay. I thought as much." Petra's contacting her father meant, of course, that before long Christopher Ryan would learn the truth, that the woman he had loved had betrayed him. And that would mean that at long last, Elizabeth would have to face Chris's anger and his judgment.

"Is Christopher Ryan dying or something?" Petra asked suddenly. "Is that why you told me now, this summer? Oh, my God, Mom, are you sick or—"

"No, I'm fine," Elizabeth assured her. "And honestly, I have no idea what's going on with Chris. I think I would have read about his death should he have died, so I'm assuming, I'm hoping, he's alive."

"So, why tell me now?" Petra pressed.

"Aside from the fact that the secrecy was weighing on me more heavily than ever, that I was beginning to feel like I couldn't breathe unless I spoke?" Elizabeth sighed. "Now that I think about it, maybe I did feel that now was a good time for you to learn the truth about Chris. Sometimes I— Sometimes I worry that you're floundering or lacking direction. Oh, that sounds like I'm criticizing you, and I'm not, really. Maybe my concerns have something to do with what you were telling me before, about your feeling lost, sort of without a purpose."

Petra nodded. "You sensed more than I thought you had."

"This might sound odd, but I've always believed that you, being Chris's child, are meant to be doing something really important, something more than—"

"Than selling vintage clothes?"

"Yes," Elizabeth said quietly.

Petra shook her head. "I've wondered the same thing, that I might be meant for something better. But if being in the vintage business is what makes me happy—"

"Then that's what you should be doing," Elizabeth said firmly. "I'm sorry. Maybe I've been wrongheaded, assuming you would share Chris's particular concerns and his drive. I've hoisted ambitions on you that might not be natural to you."

"The thing is, Mom," Petra said after a moment, "maybe I do have a desire for a different career, something that would allow me to make a positive difference in the world. I just don't know. I admit I haven't been as focused as I might have been, that maybe I've been just sort of shuffling through my life. But I'm not entirely a mess. I'm not something broken that needs to be fixed."

"I'm sorry," Elizabeth said earnestly. "I didn't mean to imply that you were. Anyway, my concerns about your path in life were only a part of why I spoke up now. Like I told you girls the other day, when you found my old diary from the summer of ninety-one, it seemed a sign. I just hope I made the right decision. I'm really not sure that I did. I suppose Jess hates me now."

"No," Petra declared. "She doesn't hate you. She's just having trouble wrapping her head around the news, and on top of that I have a feeling that things between her and Eddie aren't good. I mean, I know she's always complained about him, but something's different; maybe it's her tone when she talks about him—it's so unrelentingly harsh." Petra shrugged. "Maybe I'm wrong and everything's fine. I hope I'm wrong. Anyway, Jess will come around. With the new business and all she's under a lot of pressure."

"Thank you," Elizabeth said. She reached across the table, offering her hand for Petra to take. "Thank you for being who you are."

Petra smiled a wobbly smile and took her mother's hand. "It's okay, Mom," she said. "I love you."

"And I," Elizabeth promised, "love you."

Chapter 25

Summer 1991

"I love you."

"I know. And I love you."

"It's pretty amazing, isn't it?" Suddenly, Elizabeth laughed. "I can't seem to stop laughing these days! I'm just so happy."

The moment she had spoken the words, Elizabeth regretted them, not entirely, but she suspected that Chris would wonder if she was bursting into laughter at home, too, when she was with Hugh. And if she was behaving in a suddenly upbeat manner, to what was Hugh attributing her good mood? How, in fact, was Elizabeth keeping secret the fact that she was in love with her husband's best friend?

They had made it a point—more of an unspoken agreement—never to talk about Hugh when they were alone together. Neither had any desire to speak ill of him; each knew Hugh's flaws or limitations and had no need to rehearse them aloud. And neither wanted to waste one moment of their limited time together by allowing a third party into their intimate space. For an hour or two Elizabeth could pretend that Hugh didn't exist, that she wasn't married, that she didn't have a life back on Lavender Lane in Eliot's Corner.

"I'm glad that you're happy," Christopher said, drawing her into his arms. "You deserve a joyful life."

"Do I?" Elizabeth murmured as he leaned down to kiss her.

They went into the little bedroom, and, for a while, all that existed was that moment in time, the fact of their being together in body and in soul.

Later, as Chris slept for a bit, Elizabeth amused herself by reciting quietly several lines from poems written by John Donne, one of her favorite poets. He had spoken so beautifully, so convincingly of the importance of the personal and private sphere, the world created and inhabited by two lovers.

"'For love, all love of other sights controules, And makes one little roome, an every where.'"

Gently, so as not to wake him, Elizabeth ran a finger along Chris's arm.

"'Love, all alike, no season knowes, nor clyme, Nor houres, dayes, moneths, which are the rags of time.'"

Softly, she pressed her lips to Chris's shoulder.

"'Busie old foole, unruly Sunne . . . Shine here to us, and thou art every where; This bed thy center is, these walls, thy spheare.'"

Chris, Elizabeth knew, felt this, too, that together the two lovers constituted an everything and an everywhere, an entire universe. How Hugh would laugh at such an idea! How most people would mock.

Chris stirred, opened his eyes, and smiled. "Penny for your thoughts?"

"'I wonder, by my troth, what thou and I Did, till we lov'd?'"

"We waited for this very moment," Chris said, before he kissed her yet again.

Chapter 26

Summer 2022

Petra was driving her mother's car, her destination, the neighboring town of Cousins Corner. Cam was coming north specifically to meet her sisters and planned to return to South Portland that afternoon. Jess, who might have offered to drive Petra, hadn't offered. Not that Petra had expected her to.

The sisters had agreed to meet away from the house, as if a neutral setting might somehow help distance them from the strange and disturbing information they had so recently learned about their parents' marriage. At least, that was how Petra saw her sisters' insistence on gathering at a café in Cousins Corner.

Traffic was light on the back roads; in fact, it was virtually nonexistent, which was how Petra preferred it to be. Little traffic meant more room to think.

Petra loved her mother, and like all children had assumed she knew all there was to know about her. Mommy, whoever held that role in a relationship, was the greatest constant in a child's life. To discover something so unexpected, to realize that her mother was and always had been a stranger in some degree, was deeply disturbing. One day, would her mother make another monumental decision that might truly and irrevocably alienate her from her children? It seemed that anything was possible.

Suddenly, Petra realized that she felt like a little girl at a shopping center, who, becoming momentarily dazzled by a shiny object in a store window, turns around to discover that her parent is not in sight. Disoriented. Puzzled. Scared. She supposed this was what adult life, what maturity was all about. Accepting that no one was simply who she seemed to be or who you wanted her to be, that life was uncertain and chaotic and nobody—not even parents—could get away from that. Puppets in storybooks and pink plush toys could no longer comfort an adult the way they could a child. Nor could romantic clichés about living happily ever after without stress or strain.

The sisters arrived at the café within minutes of one another. Jess snagged a table with a large striped umbrella on the café's pleasant terrace while Petra ordered coffees and Cam selected a few treats.

"The blueish colored macaron is blueberry and cardamom," Cam explained as she set the plate in the center of the table. "The pink is strawberry and rose water, and the pale green one is pistachio."

"Why did Mom have to tell us?" Jess demanded as soon as each sister had chosen a macaron and taken a sip of her coffee. "Why not tell a therapist, get the secret off her chest that way?"

Cam sighed. "Maybe she did see a professional before she spoke to us. She must have been battling with the question of telling us for years."

"But why now?" Jess demanded.

"Why not now? She had to tell Petra one day. She owed it to her."

"Ok, but why did you and I have to know?"

Cam sighed. "Jess, come on."

Petra felt hurt by Jess's objection to being included in this family crisis. What was it, exactly, that she objected to? "Does it really make that much of a difference to you, Jess?" she asked.

"I mean, in terms of how you see me. I'm still your sister. Nothing about that has changed."

Jess didn't immediately reply.

Suddenly, Petra felt as if she might cry. "Don't you love me anymore?" she asked.

"Oh, for . . ." Jess reached for Petra's hand and gave it a painful squeeze. "Of course, I love you, you silly thing. Jeez. What I mean is, with all the other stuff going on in our lives, we don't need this on our plates."

"What other stuff do you mean?" Petra asked. "At the moment, my life is pretty boring. Well, it was."

Cam shook her head. "I wish I could say the same. Having three kids under the age of seven pretty much guarantees a life of—well, if not of excitement, then of borderline chaos."

"So, no additional pressing concern?" Jess asked. "No looming crisis at work or in the marital bedroom?"

Cam's cheeks flamed. She had always been a victim of extreme blushes. "Of course not," she declared. "Why would there be? Anyway, how's your big business venture coming along? Have you signed whatever it is you have to sign in order to get your funding?"

"Not yet," Jess replied shortly.

"Oh," Petra said. "Well, you did say that business happens slowly. I guess it's all right."

Jess shrugged.

"And things with Eddie?" Cam asked.

"Fine." Then, Jess turned again to Petra. "You didn't have to give the diary to Mom. You might have left it where you found it."

"Why would I have left it there in the attic?" Petra asked. "I had no idea the diary contained such incendiary information. Even if I had left it where I found it, I would have told Mom I'd come across it. Why not? Besides, she might have decided it was time to tell the truth about my parentage diary or no diary."

"Petra's not to blame for any of this," Cam insisted. Then, she shook her head. "What really puzzles me is why Mom kept that diary. I mean, leaving it around the house was a huge risk. Any of us might have found it at any time. Even Dad."

"People in love are careless," Jess said. "They don't think about the consequences of their words or actions on other people. They're selfish."

"That's a bit grim," Petra protested. "Some might say that people in love are courageous."

"You're free to have your opinion. I'll stick with selfish and maybe a bit insane."

Petra wondered but didn't ask her sister if she herself had acted selfishly and been a bit insane when she had fallen in love with Eddie. If she had fallen in love with him. Petra knew next to nothing about Jess's relationship, other than the fact that Jess complained about Eddie way more than she paid him compliments. Maybe Jess needed to be with someone she could complain about; maybe she needed to feel superior to her partner.

"Maybe on some level Mom wanted the diary to be found one day," Cam surmised. "After her death maybe? Oh, I don't know. I suspect she simply forgot the diary was still around. I often come across bits and pieces of the past tucked away in a book or a closet. Nine out of ten times I have to stop and really think about what it is and where it came from and what made me keep it. I can't always answer those questions."

"A trinket from a vacation or a movie ticket from a first date aren't the same as a diary," Petra pointed out. "A diary is hardly a souvenir. It's more like, I don't know, an artifact. Way more important."

"If I had kids," Jess said, folding her arms across her chest, "I wouldn't leave anything of mine around for them to find. That's what locks are for, to keep people out of your stuff."

Petra wondered if Jess kept her private things locked away from Eddie. She thought it was likely. Not that she could blame her sister for wanting personal space, but it would be nice if she trusted that Eddie would keep out of a certain drawer of her desk if she asked him to.

"I still don't understand," Jess went on. "Assuming Mom didn't want anyone to read the diary, why didn't she destroy it at some point after the affair?"

"To destroy something really personal like a diary or a love letter isn't an easy thing." Petra smiled grimly. "Not that I'd know about love letters, but I have kept diaries and journals through the years, and I've got them all. I don't have much of a desire to read them, but I just can't bring myself to throw them out. I don't know . . . It would feel like a betrayal of sorts, like turning my back on myself."

"Not my thing," Jess said brusquely. "Scribbling my thoughts. Waste of time."

"Just like Dad," Cam noted quietly. Then, she shot a worried look at Petra. "I'm sorry. I mean—"

"Hugh Quirk is still my father," Petra said. "One of them. Maybe the one who mattered most. I just don't know. This affects me way more than it affects you guys. I'm the one who found out her father isn't who she thought he was."

"I honestly can't imagine how you must be feeling," Cam said. "If I was suddenly faced with such news, if I suddenly had my entire life called into question—"

"It's hardly that drastic!" Petra protested. "My *life* hasn't been called into question. I am still breathing! It's just my identity that's been . . . disturbed."

"Is that all?!" Jess laughed. "What other secrets do you think Mom is hiding?"

"Why do there have to be other secrets?" Petra asked. "Mom isn't necessarily a dishonest person just because she kept one aspect of her life private for very good reasons."

Cam nodded. "Petra's right. I don't think there's ever been a person on this earth who has been totally honest at every single

moment of her life. It's not possible. Honesty is . . . complicated."

"And every family has secrets," Petra went on, all too aware
that she was holding Cam's biggest secret in her care. "I mean,
not every second cousin or great aunt needs to know what
grandparent said X when he was ten years old or what nephew
did Y when he got drunk at someone's anniversary party."

Necessary lies. Sins of omission. Choosing silence, when you
believed, rightly or wrongly, that telling a truth might hurt the
receiver. Cam was right. Honesty was complicated.

"I agree that every family has a bunch of skeletons in their
closet, and that the skeletons should stay there. How does it
help any of us knowing the dirty secrets of our parents' marriage?" Jess shook her head. "God knows what secrets Dad
might have been keeping, though I seriously don't like to think
of him as hiding stuff from us."

"But doesn't knowing that Mom and Dad kept their marriage alive for so long prove something wonderful about them?"
Cam asked.

"Maybe all it proves is that lethargy—i.e., maintaining the
status quo—wins in the end."

Petra shook her head. "I think you're wrong, Jess. I think
Mom and Dad were happy overall. I don't believe that happiness or genuine contentment can happen if lethargy is present."

Neither Cam nor Jess had anything to say in reply to that
statement, and for a moment Petra wondered if she herself
really believed what she claimed she believed.

"Still," Cam said finally, "do you think Mom was always miserable on some level after the affair with Chris ended? Do you
think she ever stopped loving Dad, even when she was seeing
Chris? Do you think she hated Dad, and that's why she had the
affair with Chris?"

"Why don't we just ask Mom for the answers to those questions?" Jess suggested.

"We can't!" Petra protested.

"Why not?" Jess asked. "She's the one who brought it all out into the open."

"Petra is right," Cam said firmly. "We can't badger Mom, like we're police detectives and she's a criminal. She is still our mother; she deserves our respect. I'm just voicing aloud some of the questions in my head. It doesn't mean I want to pose them to Mom."

Jess frowned but said nothing.

"Like I said before," Petra went on, "I think we have to focus on the fact that Mom and Dad seemed pretty content together. I can't believe they could have been faking things so well for so long. They had to have loved each other, even if it was in a way different from before Mom's affair. I mean, I remember them laughing together over television shows, taking long walks almost every afternoon, going on day-trips to Ogunquit and Portland, right up until Dad got sick. They had dinner at their favorite Italian place every other Saturday for years! You don't spend all that time together unless you like each other."

"Or," Jess said with an unpleasant smile, "unless you're so beyond bored it doesn't matter what you do or don't do with your spouse. I'm going to stick with the idea of lethargy for the moment."

Petra didn't bother to argue.

"Do you really believe that Dad didn't know about the affair?" Cam wondered. "He was a pretty savvy guy. I find it hard to believe he could have remained ignorant of his wife being in love with his best friend."

"Dad might have been savvy in business," Petra said, "but he wasn't the most emotionally astute man. That's not an insult; it's just the truth. We can all admit that."

"And," Jess said, "we're all blind to what we don't want to see. Even Mr. Ryan. You'd have thought a guy in his line of work would have been aware of the fact that sleeping with his best friend's wife was wrong."

"I'm sure he knew it was wrong," Petra argued. "Mom told us that the reason they ended things was because they both felt so guilty and unhappy."

"Still, I say he should have kept it in his pants for the sake of our father."

"Bashing him isn't helping, Jess," Cam said with a frown.

Petra sighed. "Can't we please talk about anything else besides the past? Just for a little while?"

"No," Jess said flatly. "No, we can't. There's nothing else to talk about now. No, I mean it. The cat's out of the bag. The elephant in the room has been painted with a big red X to mark the spot. Every single thing about this family, from now on, will be somehow in relation to Mom's affair with Christopher Ryan."

"That's not necessarily true," Petra said, if without spirit.

"Of course, it is! How can we talk about memories of our childhood without seeing them now as distorted, knowing that all the while Mom was unhappy in her marriage, in love with another man, that our little sister wasn't who we thought she was? Knowing this new stuff makes everything I thought was solid and true and simply there, suspicious, and tainted, crumpled around the edges. Wrong."

Cam stared down at the remains of the coffee in her cup.

Petra toyed with her napkin.

"But do you know what I really don't get?" Jess said, wiping invisible crumbs from her hands.

Petra held her breath. What rude or crass or insulting comment was coming next?

"What?" Cam asked wearily.

"Why doesn't this place just have regular stuff, like chocolate chip cookies or brownies? Why do we need fancy stuff like macarons?"

Petra's breath came out in a whoosh of laughter.

Chapter 27

Elizabeth knew the girls were meeting, and of course they would be talking about their mother and the bombshell she had dropped on them. It was good they had one another to talk to; Elizabeth believed that even Jess, the most independent of the three, knew she could turn to her sisters when she needed a new perspective on a problem.

But that didn't mean Elizabeth wasn't anxious about what might result from her children's discussions. She had been drinking cup after cup of ginger tea to help soothe her stomach, which felt as prickly as Jess's mood on an average day.

Maybe it would have been better, long ago, to tell someone outside the family about her relationship with Chris and his being Petra's father, a therapist, for example, or even a priest or a minister. Then maybe the burden of silence wouldn't have weighed so heavily on her all this time; then maybe she would have been able to keep the truth from her children forever. But would that have been the right thing to do? Would the continuation of secrecy truly have served Petra in the end?

Too late for what ifs.

Anyway, Elizabeth had been putting off an encounter with her wedding dress, and now seemed as good a time as any to confront the relic. Elizabeth went up to Petra's bedroom. The door was open; if it had been closed, Elizabeth might have hesitated to go inside.

Petra had never been the neatest person, but at least she had always been clean. Unlike Jess she had never been in the habit of leaving empty soda cans and chip bags lying around her bedroom. That Elizabeth strongly discouraged her children from drinking soda and eating too many chips never stopped Jess from doing exactly as she pleased.

The wedding dress wasn't draped across the bed or the armchair; unless Petra had hauled it back to the attic, it was likely in the closet, which was where Elizabeth found it.

Carefully, she laid it out on the bed. Petra was right. The dress was badly damaged. Elizabeth felt a wave of pity for it, almost as if it were a live thing that had been ignored and neglected, not simply a bit of fabric and beading. She sat on the edge of the bed, gazing down at the dress. A wedding came with so much baggage. There were so many rules, regulations, and expectations; it was surprising that anyone ever enjoyed their own wedding day. But no doubt the people who did enjoy their wedding day were in more control of their lives and were used to keeping a firm hand on the details, unlike Elizabeth who had been a person so easily swayed, even intimidated by other voices and opinions, so little confidence in her own wants and desires—forget about needs—that she had routinely bowed to the will and the vision of others.

Still, she felt a fondness for the garment and what it represented, even though if she had been able to speak up back then she would have said no to the big puffy shoulders, the elbow length sleeves, and the sweetheart neckline. But the dress was typical of its type for the early 1980s, and Elizabeth had been what she supposed might be called a typical young bride. Naïve. Innocent. Even a bit foolish.

She had loved her bouquet, if not the dress, though, composed as it had been of cream-colored and pale peach roses and

copious ferns, the stems wrapped in a cream-colored silk rib-
bon. At least she had taken charge of choosing the color scheme
for the wedding, though Elizabeth wondered, if her mother had
protested the choice of peach and pale green, would she have
stood her ground or caved as she had about so many other aspects of the wedding?

Gently, Elizabeth ran a finger along the neckline of the dress.
Had she carried a small bag, beaded or perhaps made of silk?
She couldn't recall. She had a vague memory of someone—
maybe a saleslady?—suggesting lace gloves, and her mother
firmly nixing the idea. Her mother had not been a bad person,
not even overly controlling. The fact was that Elizabeth had
been a compliant child and had grown into a compliant young
adult. How much of that compliant nature had been created
or nurtured by Marjorie Primer and how much was innate, her
daughter couldn't say. It hardly mattered now.

What meal had been served at the reception? Elizabeth
couldn't remember that, either, nor could she remember the
flavor of the wedding cake. Had there been a fruit filling, strawberry or apricot? A layer of chocolate? She did remember that
neither she nor Hugh had wanted anything to do with the garter
tradition; she found it humiliating and, though Hugh hadn't explained his resistance, Elizabeth suspected that he hadn't been
keen on his new wife revealing her leg to one and all. Hugh had
been pretty conservative about most things.

No one had had an objection to Elizabeth tossing her bouquet to the female guests. One of Elizabeth's young cousins
had caught it. Alice was only about ten at the time, and she had
been so thrilled to be the center of attention, though she had
probably been ignorant of the meaning behind the toss and her
catch. Next to be married. As if that was a sufficient goal for a
woman! Oh well.

Elizabeth got up from the bed and returned the dress to the
closet. Before she left the room, she took one last look around.
Resting against the pillows on the bed was Bunny, most defi-

nitely worse for the wear. On the bedside table was that old Golden Press edition of *The Wild Swans*. A wave of tenderness for her children washed over her. She so hoped they were able to help one another though this difficult time.

It was what she wanted more than anything.

Chapter 28

Petra was sitting in Chez Claudine drinking a cappuccino and eating a very buttery, very flaky croissant. She remembered Jess's remark about the café in Cousins Corner where the sisters had recently met, about it not offering the good stuff, like cookies and brownies.

It was typical of Jess to eschew—or to pretend to eschew—anything "fancy." Hugh Quirk had done the same, and whether that dismissive or critical attitude stemmed from a hidden sense of inferiority was anyone's guess. People like Hugh and Jess didn't admit to feelings of inferiority or self-doubt. She wondered how Jess felt about Chez Claudine, with its emphasis on French bread and pastries, and its décor that closely mimicked that of a classic Parisian café with its Beaux Arts posters of cancan girls at the Moulin Rouge and its Art Deco posters of sleek ocean-going cruise ships; the standing blackboard with the daily specials written on it in white chalk; the massive and gleaming espresso machine; the simple white crockery and a bud vase with a fresh bloom on every table. The owner of the café, a forty-ish-year-old man named Jim Hamill, had studied baking and pastry making at the Culinary Institute of America and had worked as head pastry chef at a well-regarded restaurant in Portland for ten years before deciding to open his own café in Eliot's Corner. His life here, Petra supposed, was probably a lot calmer than what he had known in the city. She wondered if Jim Hamill was sometimes bored. Boredom was a bad thing. Though, at the moment, being bored held a strange appeal. . . .

Petra took another sip of the good, strong coffee and silently thanked whomever it was who had discovered that a little brown bean could yield such pleasure. The coffee at the macaron café hadn't been half as good as the coffee here, though the meeting with her sisters had gone well enough. At least Cam and Jess hadn't come to blows, not that they ever had, not as far as Petra knew. And there was probably a lot she didn't know about the members of her family. One day, would Cam reveal that she loved women as well as men? Would Jess reveal that she had dabbled in the selling of marijuana? Had their father—Dad, Hugh Quirk—really been a secret agent and not a salesperson in the insurance industry?

Elizabeth hadn't pressed Petra for information about the sisters' meeting, but her interest was obviously and understandably keen. All Petra had told her mother was that the conversation had ended in laughter. That was the truth. Maybe Cam would share actual bits of the conversation over time. Most likely, Jess would tell their mother nothing. It was too bad there was so much tension between the two.

As for Petra and her mother, they had been getting along pretty well since Petra's brief experience of anger had subsided. Two nights ago, Elizabeth had shown her a lavender agate pendant Chris had given her upon his return from a working trip to Europe. Elizabeth hadn't worn the pendant often, and after the summer of 1991 she had tucked it away as too fraught a reminder of the affair. Still, she had chosen to wear the pendant as a sort of protective talisman the day she told her daughters about Christopher. It had made her feel marginally less alone, she said.

In spite of the détente in place on Lavender Lane, there had been one difficult moment between mother and daughter just the day before. Petra had returned to the attic with a sudden determination to find something that would verify that the man she had always believed to be her father was indeed her father in the ways that really counted.

She had rummaged through several boxes she hadn't bothered with the first time she had been in the attic searching for items she might sell via Past Perfect. Finally, after fifteen minutes or so of fruitless searching, she had found a folder that contained about twenty drawings—some in crayon, others in marker—made by Petra and her sisters when they were young. Originally, there must have been hundreds of such drawings; she remembered coloring and crafting as important pastimes. But her mother had probably chosen a selection from the entirety to keep. That made sense. A person couldn't hold on to everything.

Among the drawings, Petra found three of her own works. The first and the second depicted flowers of some sort, possibly imagined. They were of minor interest to Petra. It was the third drawing that commanded her attention. This drawing showed two stick figures holding hands. The tall one was a man; under his feet she had printed DAD. The short one was a girl. She was identified as PETRA. Both figures were smiling big, happy, wobbly smiles. There was a big yellow sun in the top right-hand corner of the paper. Behind the human figures, wildly out of proportion to them, was a house. A wiggle of smoke was straggling out of the chimney. Across the roof of the house was written: OUR HOME.

Leaving everything else behind, Petra had taken the drawing downstairs and confronted her mother with it. "This is real," she had said, her voice trembling with emotion. "This is my life and my father. You've assaulted my childhood, my memories. You should never have told me about Christopher Ryan. You should have kept your mouth shut."

Even at the moment she was shocked that she had used the term "assaulted." It described a brutal attack, a confrontation that was unwanted, unasked for. It presupposed intent to harm, and of course her mother had not meant to harm Petra or her sisters by revealing her long-held secret, though Elizabeth must have known that harm was a possible outcome.

For a moment, her mother had stood rigidly still, her face red with shock or perhaps with anger. Petra couldn't tell.

"I did no such thing," Elizabeth cried then, her voice shrill. "I did not assault you or anything about your life. You're my child, my daughter. I would never do anything to—"

Elizabeth had broken down then, sinking back against the counter, burying her face in her hands.

Petra, still in a state of high emotion, hadn't been able to make herself apologize, and certainly did not go over to her mother to offer comfort. Instead, Petra stood deadly still, hands clenched into fists.

How long the two women stood like that, together in the room but so very far apart, Petra was afterward unable to say. Finally, Elizabeth dropped her hands from her face. "I'm sorry," she said hoarsely. "I'm sorrier than I can ever say. Please, Petra, please forgive me."

Petra recalled feeling a surge of pure relief that the silence was broken, pure gratitude for her mother's sincere apology. She had rushed across the kitchen and into her mother's arms.

"I'm sorry, too, Mom," she had cried.

Mother and daughter had been tender with each other for the rest of the day, careful not to reawaken the hurt feelings of earlier. Petra honestly couldn't remember ever having had such a scene with her mother, not even during her sometimes emotionally turbulent teenage years. Thankfully, by morning all was back to the new normal on Lavender Lane.

Just as Petra was chewing the last bite of the excellent crois-sant, a woman passed by the table and smiled briefly at her. Petra nodded in return. She knew the woman but only vaguely;

she wasn't even sure of the woman's name, but she did know that before the woman had reached the age of thirty—she was about ten years Petra's senior—she had already completed a stint in the Peace Corps, had run for a local political office (and lost, but at least she had tried), and had begun what was now a steady career as a short story writer. Whether or not the woman was ever going to get rich writing short stories was beside the point. She was to be admired because she wanted to write, perhaps even needed to, and so was doing it.

What did Petra Quirk want or need to do? She supposed she was happy enough if the absence of pain was happiness, but she didn't want to go on this way. While it was true that life would present unlooked for and unasked for challenges all on its own volition, she had known for some time now that she needed to act. But how?

Sometimes, she wondered if she was fundamentally lazy. Being lazy was rarely if ever perceived as a good thing. Busy, productive, forward-facing people looked down on lazy people, condemned them, even, in certain religious traditions, viewed them as sinners. What was that adage? The Devil finds work for idle hands. Work kept a person out of trouble. She had heard her father—Hugh—say that often enough.

It was kinder to think that she was what some people called a late bloomer. Her mother could be considered a late bloomer, Petra supposed. She hadn't gone to graduate school until she was in her thirties. Then again, she had accomplished an awful lot before that—three children and marriage to a man who could be difficult, if loving. Motherhood and marriage were huge responsibilities, and, so far in her life, Petra hadn't felt drawn to undertake either one of them. Because she suspected she would fail? It was hard not to ask that question of herself.

A fear of failure wasn't new to Petra. Back in college she had seriously considered going on to graduate school but at the last minute had lost her nerve, like a horse who panics at the gate or who balks at the jump. Her friends had been curious as to why she wasn't making plans for the next stage of life, post-graduation. They wanted to know what she was going to do with herself. How she planned on making money. They asked about her goals and ambitions. Where did she want to be in five, ten, twenty years?

Her father hadn't been particularly helpful at that crucial moment in her life. Hugh had stressed that she had to earn a living and share in the household expenses if she was going to live at home until she could afford a place of her own. "Your sisters took charge of their lives after college," he had said. "Your mother and I expect you to do the same." He hadn't offered any specific advice about "taking charge of" her life. General encouragement or admonition was his habit and maybe all he was capable of offering. That was okay. It was more than a lot of people got from their parents.

Her mother had been more helpful, offering a few suggestions concerning particular schools and advising her daughter to pursue her dreams. But something had prevented Petra from acting on that advice; she had never before felt so stymied, stuck, unable to move and terribly unhappy about it. Petra had sometimes wondered if Hugh would be disappointed in her if he could see her now, at the age of thirty, fairly rootless, without an obvious goal or purpose in life. She wondered what Chris would make of her if they did indeed meet one day. Would he be disappointed that a child of his remained so unspectacular, so unformed, so useless to anyone but herself?

The bells over the door to the café tinkled, breaking Petra's train of thought. It was Jess. She spotted her sister, unceremoniously dumped her computer bag on the table, and went off to the counter.

"My afternoon fix," she said upon her return. "I probably drink way too much coffee."

Petra smiled. "You could try decaffeinated."

"Why bother?"

That was a point. "How's work?" Petra asked. What she

really wanted to ask was if Jess had spoken to their mother, but she figured she would learn the answer to that question by and by.

"Fine. So, what have you been up to since I saw you and Cam? Sitting around questioning your place in the universe?"

Petra laughed uncomfortably. "Not really. I mean, maybe I've been doing a little philosophical thinking. Mostly I've just been, you know, doing what I always do."

"Not that I've ever understood what that is, exactly, but whatever. You know," Jess went on, "I can't get over what a massive hypocrite that Chris Ryan is, claiming to be concerned with ethics and morality, having built this massive career around getting medical care to needy children or whatever it is he actually does, and yet in his personal life acting like a cad. I'm not a vindictive person—in spite of what you might think—but there's a part of me that wouldn't mind ratting him out to, I don't know, the people who idolize him." Jess sat back and shook her head.

"To what end?" Petra demanded, shaken by her sister's passion. "To punish him? Who are you to judge someone else's personal life? Besides, exposing Chris for a long-ago affair would put Mom in the spotlight and damage Dad's reputation."

Jess sighed. "I wouldn't actually do anything. I said it was only a part of me that wanted to cause trouble for him."

Petra was genuinely relieved. "Good," she said. "Because no one is perfect, and, as far as I know, Chris Ryan never claimed to be a saint. Besides, an affair, even one with your friend's wife, is hardly on the same scale as, I don't know, unfair distribution of organs for transplant or voter suppression."

"So, certain bad behaviors are less bad than others?" Jess asked with a bit of a smile.

Petra thought for a moment. "Yes," she said. "I think so. At least, certain bad behaviors don't have the same universal or large-scale impact as other bad behaviors."

Jess shrugged and finished her coffee in two large gulps. "Yeah, all right," she said. "I'd still like to know why Mom did what she did to Dad, and don't give me the line about mad, passionate love. I just don't buy it."

Petra sighed. "Okay, let's leave the simple answer—love—out of it. Think about this question: Do you understand everything you do? Why must a person's motives always be explored, brought to light? Maybe not every word or action can be understood. Maybe mystery or confusion is simply part of the human condition. Most of the world's favorite fictional characters act in ways that seem inexplicable to us and yet inevitable at the same time. That's why the characters are universally loved. They are us; we are them. Random. Flailing. Trying."

"A Freudian would say that a person who claims not to know why they did something is just avoiding or repressing the truth about their motives. Anyway, people don't just do stuff. There has to be a reason why they do what they do, say what they say. Otherwise it's all just chaos."

"Or human nature," Petra said quietly, "slippery, evading definition, and invariably messy."

Jess rolled her eyes. "Oh, goody! Like I don't have enough crap to deal with right now. All right, I give up. I'm done trying to understand why Mom did what she did."

"Good. There's no rule that says you have to understand. How's Eddie, by the way?"

"Eddie is always Eddie. At least that's something I can count on."

"Are you guys okay?"

"Yeah," Jess said with a dismissive wave of her hand. "We're fine. Why do people keep asking me that? Look, I have to run. Keep the faith."

Petra watched as her sister strode out of the café. Keep the faith? What did Jess mean by that? Maybe nothing. She seemed more tightly wound than ever lately, which was saying something. Then again, what would Petra know about the pressures and demands of starting one's own company? The most pressure she had ever experienced was the time she had been pitted against a far more experienced buyer at an auction. The bidding for the cloche hat, circa mid-1920s, had heated up unexpectedly, and Petra, knowing exactly how much she could afford to bid, nevertheless raised her hand to bid more than that amount. She doubted she would ever forget the panic she had felt in that moment—What had she done! She didn't have three-hundred dollars to spend!—until her adversary outbid her yet again and the moment of panic was over.

She had learned a lesson about herself that day, about seemingly inexplicable, self-destructive or self-sabotaging behavior that, she believed, no one was immune to experiencing. Could her mother's behavior in going ahead with an affair while married be described as self-destructive? Maybe.

Suddenly, Petra had had enough of sitting around wondering and supposing. As much as another croissant was tempting, a brisk walk would be the perfect thing to clear her head. She hoped.

Chapter 29

Elizabeth didn't like FaceTime or Skype or Zoom—and she didn't think her dislike could be solely put down to her age—but she had to admit the formats had their value. Petra, though a member of a generation that had grown up with a computer at hand, wasn't much of a fan of technology, either. Both mother and daughter acknowledged and were grateful for the conveniences certain technologies offered, but neither was under any illusion about technology's negative or damaging effects on the human animal.

"Here's our invitation," Elizabeth murmured, accepting admission to Cam's Zoom meeting. "And here's Cam."

Cam was sitting on a loveseat in the screened-in porch she and Ralph had added to the house not long before the arrival of the twins. On the wall behind her was a colorful, abstract painting dating from Cam's student days and her very brief foray into the arts. Elizabeth still wasn't sure why Cam had chosen to abandon all artistic endeavors after high school, but she had, and she didn't seem to miss them.

"Hi, you two," Cam said, tucking a strand of hair behind her ear. "How's everything on Lavender Lane?"

Before either Elizabeth or Petra could reply, there came the high-pitched shout of a little girl.

"Mommy!"

Cam put out her hand, and then Beth was in the picture. "Beth wants to say hello."

"Hi, Grandma!" Beth said loudly, as if aware of the actual, physical distance between them. "Hi, Aunt Petra!"

"Hi, Beth," Elizabeth said, noting the child's strong resemblance to her father. "What are you up to today?"

"My best friend is having a birthday party, she lives down the block, and I have to get into my new outfit now, so 'bye!"

Petra waved to an already empty space as Beth ran off.

"I guess Grandma and Aunt Petra come in second to birthday parties. Oh well. It was nice to see her for a moment."

"You know she loves you, Mom," Cam said. "And you, Petra."

Petra smiled. "We know."

"Well, I have something to tell you both," Elizabeth said. "There's been a wee bit of progress with Jess. This morning she finally answered a call from me. We had a brief, tense exchange, but at least we spoke. I feel cautiously hopeful that she'll come around to forgiving me for rocking the boat, as it were."

"You haven't actually done anything for which Jess and I have to forgive you," Cam said firmly.

"But Petra has a legitimate reason for needing an apology from me." Elizabeth looked to her youngest daughter and smiled ruefully. "For lying to her all these years, and perhaps for having an affair in the first place."

Petra looked embarrassed, and Elizabeth immediately regretted having spoken as she had.

"We'll be okay, Mom," Petra said, awkwardly patting her mother's arm.

"Changing the subject somewhat," Cam said brightly, "I guess I've always wondered about this but now, knowing what I know about your, well, your state of mind at the time, Mom, what made you decide to go back to school with three small kids at home? As a mother of three small children myself, I can't imagine having the energy! And how did you get Dad to agree? Did you give him an ultimatum? No, I can't see you doing that."

"You're right," Elizabeth replied, "I certainly didn't give your father an ultimatum, I simply spoke to him reasonably. When he said that we couldn't afford it, I told him that I'd already talked to a financial aid counselor at the university. I met his every objection with hard facts, and finally, he agreed. He did want me to be happy, after all. He just didn't understand that I was the only one who could determine what would make me happy. Hugh was repeating his parents' dynamic, which wasn't all that different from the dynamic between my parents, in fact. We were both acting out parts we'd learned as children. Not so uncommon."

"No," Cam said. "But unfortunate. I'm not sure anyone can really avoid repeating their parents' patterns."

"Just remember that some patterns or dynamics are positive," Petra said. "They just don't get the press the bad patterns get."

Elizabeth smiled. "True. Anyway, I remember Hugh saying, with that condescending way he had at the time, that having just had another baby, he thought I would be ecstatic, three beautiful children, every woman's dream. Why would I want to go back to school and then to work? He was astonishingly thick when it came to human relations, or at least, to relationships with women. To a relationship with me."

"But Dad was always proud of his children's school performance," Petra pointed out. "He supported the idea of our having careers, not just marrying and having a family."

"Yes," Elizabeth admitted. "He had no interest in keeping you girls in cotton wool the way he wanted to keep me. Of course, I came to understand that I was contributing to our dynamic, a realization I think I was afraid of admitting—until my relationship with Chris. Only then did I come to a turning point in my life. In a way, my life was made far better than it ever had been by my experience with Chris. I woke up to my potential and decided to become a teacher like I'd once dreamed of being. I don't know if I can say the same for him. I don't know if I helped him change in any productive way. Maybe all I did was hurt him."

"I'm sure that's not the case," Cam said quickly.

Petra nodded. "Cam's right."

Elizabeth appreciated her daughters' attempts, however unsuccessful, at soothing her guilty conscience. "What did Ralph have to say when you told him about my long-ago affair?" she asked Cam.

Suddenly, Cam cocked her head and frowned. "Wait," she said, "I hear the boys. Yup, they're waking up from their nap. I have to run. Love you both. Talk soon."

And she was gone.

"That was an abrupt exit," Petra said.

"Duty calls when you're a parent. You know," Elizabeth said musingly, "I like Ralph, and I think he's always liked me. I hope he still does. I hope he still has some respect for me now that he knows that I betrayed Hugh."

"Of course, Ralph still respects you," Petra said reassuringly. "Besides, what you did in the past has no direct bearing on his life now. Maybe if Cam was Chris's daughter . . . Anyway, I'm sure you don't have to worry about Ralph. And even if he did judge you harshly, he has no power over you or over Cam unless you allow him power."

Elizabeth smiled gratefully. "Thank you for the encouraging words. Can I convince you to come with me for ice cream?"

"Yes," Petra said. "You can. Easily."

Chapter 30

Petra loved black-and-white films from the thirties, forties, and fifties. Somehow, she had never seen *Scarlet Street*, starring Edward G. Robinson, Dan Duryea, and Joan Bennett, so when the funky little movie theater in Sterne Hollow announced it would be showing the film for one evening only, Petra jumped at the chance to see it.

She was now killing time—that was an interesting turn of phrase; the English language was full of them—before the start of the movie by poking around Sterne Hollow's Main Street, wondering, as she walked, if she would run into that nice older couple with the adorable pug who had given her a ride home from the bus station at the start of the summer.

Instead, she passed a couple, a man and a woman, about Cam and Ralph's age, and in an instant Petra saw her mother and father, Elizabeth and Hugh, in the couple, hand in hand, making their way through life. Was a dynamic similar to the one that had played out in the Quirks' marriage playing out now in the Perrys' marriage? And if it was, would things end as—as strangely—as they had for Elizabeth and Hugh?

People tended to repeat the patterns of their parents' relationship. They were doomed to repeat the patterns. Where did that phrase come from, Petra wondered? How closely was it re-lated to the notion of the sins of the father being revisited on the son? Or the sins of the mother being revisited on the daughter? Fate ruled lives, it seemed.

On a whim, Petra went into a high-end gift shop that sold the usual assortment of souvenirs for random tourists, from dish towels printed with images of blueberries and lobsters, to sachets of crushed pine needles, to books by Mainers and about Maine lives, to matted prints of ocean scenes and lobster boats, to items suited for a local or a tourist, like jewelry and pottery and beeswax candles handmade by local artisans. A large framed poster featuring the image of a rose in mid-bloom caught Petra's eye. Under the pretty image were the words:

And the day came when the risk to remain tight
in a bud was more painful than the risk it took to
blossom. –Anaïs Nin

Petra wondered. Maybe her mother's revelation would help her, Petra, in some way to blossom, to learn more about who she was deep down, as a person. Still, how did a person go about blossoming? What she meant was, how far was blossoming a natural thing, something that just happened, and how far was it a determined thing, something that required will and intent and a goal? Probably blossoming was a bit of both, maybe even an ever changing dynamic. Didn't gardeners or horticulturists "force" some flowers to bloom? But why?

Without answers to these questions, Petra left the store and continued to amble along—was ambling different from rambling? She would have to look up the definitions of the two words; there were bound to be distinctions and differences in usages.

She wondered if being curious about the origins of words or phrases, and pondering ideas and other abstract notions, was another trait or tendency she had inherited from her father, the biological one, not the one who had raised her. That old Nature versus nurture argument.

Certainly, Hugh wasn't the kind of guy who spent a lot of time—if any—pondering the abstracts of life. Petra imagined that he would have seen that sort of mental activity as a waste of time, unless, of course, it had a practical purpose and led to a useful end. Christopher Ryan had put his abstract thinking to good use, had used his intelligence for ends that helped people in concrete ways. He didn't dwell in an ivory tower. Petra knew this for certain. She had read about his career online. If he was like Joseph Knecht, searching for the truth, he seemed to have found it—or, at least, clues to it—in the real world, much as Joseph had finally decided to do.

Could Nature, Petra wondered, have supplied her tendency to investigate, to think? After all, it was not only Christopher Ryan who was an intellectual, but her mother as well.

And nurture, she supposed, could be responsible for her lack of drive or ambition. But Hugh had been an active man in his world. He had had a career in which he excelled. And what else? Aside from gardening and fixing things around the house and spending time with his kids, all of which was good stuff, what else had he accomplished? Could he be said to have achieved a successful marriage, when his wife had had a secret affair with his best friend? Could he be said to have been a boon to the community when he had never volunteered at the local food bank or run for town councillor?

Petra felt bothered by these traitorous thoughts about the man she had called Dad, the man who had taken his children to select a freshly cut tree each year for Christmas, the man who had attended every school performance in which his daughters had been involved, the man who had held his children's hair away from their faces when they were sick to their stomachs with some icky childhood crud. All of those acts were the stuff of the everyday heroic, the stuff that mattered as much as if not at times more than whatever Hugh Quirk might have done for the world at large.

Christopher Ryan, who had not had a family of his own, had nevertheless earned an undergraduate degree in philosophy and a PhD in biomedical ethics. He had built a strong career as a writer, lecturer, and advisor; for the past several years he had sat on the board of a philanthropic foundation concerned with providing health care for children in at-risk environments both in the United States and throughout the world. Petra couldn't help but wonder what sort of person she would be now if she had grown up with Chris as her father. Would she be more focused, have a career she was proud of, be in a loving relationship? It was silly to spend too much time wondering about unanswerable things, but it was hard to resist the urge.

But right now, it was time to get to the theater. She had bought her ticket earlier but wanted to get a good seat. Not that she anticipated a crowd. Just as she entered the lobby, her phone chirped. It was a notification from the Past Perfect website that a sale had just been registered. Three significant items had been purchased by one buyer, three items gone from her small but choice inventory, one potential repeat customer gained. She sent Lena a text detailing what needed to be done at this point in order for the customer to receive her purchases in a timely manner, and thanked her profusely.

Petra took her seat in the theater with a sense of satisfaction but not of pride.

Maybe satisfaction was enough for the moment.

Chapter 31

Petra had gone to a movie theater in Sterne Hollow to see a special showing of the 1945 black-and-white film *Scarlet Street*. Elizabeth had been tempted to join her; she had always been a fan of Edward G. Robinson as well as of Dan Duryea, and the movie was a long-time favorite—but something had held her back, some instinct, however vague. She had a sense that she was needed at home.

There was a sharp rap on the kitchen door, and then it opened and Jess came stomping inside. It was the first time that Elizabeth had seen her middle child since the afternoon she had revealed her past relationship with Christopher Ryan.

"I was just about to eat," Elizabeth said by way of greeting, wondering what was different about today that had caused Jess to announce her imminent arrival with a knock. Maybe she had just wanted to make noise. "Join me?"

"I can't eat a thing right now," her daughter growled. "I'm sick to my stomach."

Elizabeth looked more closely at Jess. She didn't look angry; she didn't seem to have come by to berate her mother. She did, however, look ill. Pained. Frightened almost, and that was what most worried Elizabeth. She was glad she had listened to her gut, stayed home, and not joined Petra in Sterne Hollow.

"What's happened?" she asked quietly.

Jess crossed her arms over her chest and gave a strange sort of laugh. "Oh, just the minor fact that my business partner has bailed. Family crisis of some sort. Can you believe it? And without Raven, everything falls apart. She was the one with the big connections. She was the one who convinced the investment people to back us. Without her, I'm sunk."

"Oh, Jess," Elizabeth said feelingly. "I'm so sorry."

Jess groaned and began to pace the kitchen. "This is the last thing I need on top of everything else that's exploding in my life!"

"What does Eddie—" Elizabeth began.

"Eddie!" Jess spat. "Don't talk to me about him. He's useless."

Elizabeth was wise enough to respect Jess's request, and also not to inquire as to the nature of Raven's family crisis, a crisis that hopefully wasn't too dire. "Surely there's something that can be done," she said calmly. "Can Raven hook you up with another potential business partner?"

"I don't know," Jess said; it was almost a shout. "I don't know anything. I literally just found out an hour ago that all my plans are destroyed. I haven't had time to . . ." Jess put a hand to her forehead.

"To process the news. But you will, and then you'll be able to figure out the next step."

"Will I?" Jess gave that strange laugh again. "Right now, I don't feel very optimistic about my ability to figure out anything. If you want to know the truth, right now, I feel pretty damn incompetent."

"Sit," Elizabeth said. "Let me get you a cup of tea or something."

In response, Jess took a step backwards and toward the door.

"No thanks. I need to go home. Eddie's hanging out with a friend tonight. At least he won't be there to annoy me."

Elizabeth wanted to say, "Please drive carefully. You're upset." Or, "Let me drive you home." But she said nothing. In Jess's current frame of mind, she would see both the plea and the offer as an insult.

Jess went off without a farewell, letting the door bang shut behind her.

When she had gone, Elizabeth sank into a chair. She felt absolutely drained by the encounter with her daughter. On the one hand, she was glad that Jess had been able to come to her mother with her bad news and to so easily reveal the depth of her distress. On the other, Elizabeth was alarmed by Jess's admission of a feeling of incompetence. Self-doubt had never been in Jess's repertoire. At least, as far as Elizabeth knew. But then again, how much did she really know about the private lives of her children? If she had been able to surprise them, they could very well be able to surprise her.

Elizabeth sighed. She could kick herself for having revealed her long-held secret at such an inopportune time. At that moment, she felt totally responsible for everything bad that had ever happened to her family, guilty for every skinned knee and adolescent heartache, for every minor frustration and every lost opportunity. She supposed that all mothers—and probably most fathers, too—felt this way at times, overwhelmed by the belief that they had failed to keep their children safe from the evils and annoyances of the world.

But how could she have foreseen that Jess's business partner would leave her high and dry at just this moment? No, Elizabeth knew she wasn't responsible for the success or failure of Jess's business. And she knew that Jess was tough and resourceful. Elizabeth had to believe that her daughter would find a way to go ahead with her plan, or to fashion a new plan for the new circumstances. And she also had to hope that Jess would offer her former business partner a degree of genuine sympathy, if she hadn't already. Sometimes, Jess could seem pretty self-centered.

Leaving her dinner untouched, Elizabeth went out to the backyard. The sun was still strong at six thirty, and Elizabeth shrugged off the light cotton sweater she had been wearing inside. The yard and garden looked lovely in the evening light. Elizabeth thought that Hugh would be proud of her, of how she had come to learn the joy of working with the soil. In some very real way, gardening had helped Elizabeth to keep Hugh close.

For that, Elizabeth was glad. She truly had loved her husband. She truly had enjoyed doing little services for him like ironing his dress shirts, and rubbing his temples when he had a headache, and baking him a birthday cake from scratch each year, devil's food cake with chocolate icing. She had truly enjoyed watching him eat his cake—with a dollop of vanilla ice cream on top—and would see him not as an adult man with a wife and children and career, but as his mother might see him, as any mother might see a son, as a child, innocent, deserving of love, needing protection. And she would wonder how she could ever have betrayed him, no matter how strong her feelings for Christopher Ryan had been and maybe, still were.

In moments like those, Elizabeth had known with absolute certainty that she genuinely loved her husband, in good times and in bad. At the time of Hugh's cancer scare, back in the summer of 1991, during her affair with Christopher Ryan, she had felt a surge of loyalty to Hugh so strong it had helped give her the courage to say farewell to Chris. And years later, when Hugh actually had been taken ill with cancer and had increasingly needed to rely on her, she had been a thoroughly dedicated nurse, uncomplaining and never resentful, grateful for every moment they had together, bright or grim.

Yet how much of her devotion to Hugh had derived from guilt and an almost talismanic hope that if she were very good to her husband, if she worked to make him happy, the terrible secret of her betrayal would never out? That question, Elizabeth believed, would continue to haunt her until the end of her life, as well it should.

Suddenly, Elizabeth heard a car pull into the driveway and turned. It was Petra, home from the movie. Elizabeth would tell her immediately about Jess's visit; there was no point in not sharing the news. And if Petra hadn't grabbed a bite in town, they could have dinner together. Elizabeth's emotions might be in turmoil, her mind caught in the grip of nostalgia for the quiet, stable days of her marriage, but her body was undeniably hungry.

Chapter 32

Summer 1991

"I'm so sorry I'm late," Elizabeth said even before Chris had completely opened the door to his cottage. "The woman who was supposed to pick up Jess at daycare and bring her to the sitter called at the very last minute to cancel, so I had to run and get Jess myself and drop her off. I didn't even have the time to stop and call you. I'm so sorry, Chris."

Chris smiled and ushered her inside. "It's all right, really. You don't have to explain or apologize. I know this situation is difficult, for you more than for me."

"I'm not so sure it's more difficult for me," Elizabeth said, moving easily into Chris's embrace. "I felt so bad when I had to cancel our getting together last Monday because Cam woke with a cold and I had to keep her home from school. If you had known ahead of time, you could have stayed on in Boston and not made a trip to Maine in vain. I wasted your time."

Chris kissed her before replying. "Elizabeth, really, it's okay. I don't harbor unreasonable expectations, or, really, any expectations at all from you."

But shouldn't lovers, Elizabeth thought, shouldn't two people who loved each other so deeply, like she and Chris did, shouldn't they be able to rely on each other to keep their word, most, if not all of the time? Chris was always so understanding. But how could he be? Was he lying to her? He had a life too, an important one. It could easily be argued that she and the children—because she did not come alone into his life, no matter what she wanted to believe—were drags on his time. Had there been a hint of annoyance in his tone when he'd spoken of having no expectations? He must want more of her attention than she could give, and it had to make him angry that he couldn't get it.

"Elizabeth? Say something."

She smiled up at the man she adored. "Sorry. Just woolgathering," she said, dismissing the troubling thoughts as best she could. Perhaps her guilt at not being entirely present for either man in her life was causing her to create problems where none existed.

They made love then in the little bedroom with its double bed and ancient, mottled mirror, and not much else. But nothing else was needed, Elizabeth felt, as long as she and Chris were there together, bodies entwined.

"What's wrong?" Chris asked, tracing the line of her jaw with his finger. "You look pensive again."

"Nothing is wrong," Elizabeth said, snuggling further into his embrace. "I'm happy. I'm where I want to be."

"Good. You know I'm leaving again for Europe on Saturday, which means I'll be heading down to Boston Friday afternoon or after dinner, at the latest. Do you think you can manage to see me before I go?"

"I don't know," Elizabeth admitted. "I'll try. You know I'll try my best."

"I know you will. But it's all right if you can't. I'll be back in Maine before long. I hate that you feel stressed by our relationship though I suppose there's no way you can feel anything other."

"I don't feel stressed!" she lied, looking into his beautiful blue eyes. "This relationship is the best thing about my life. Truly."

Was it? She wondered. What about the children? Weren't they—shouldn't they be—more precious to her than Christopher Ryan?

"You're the best thing about my life, too," Chris murmured. "I wasn't alive until I met you, and then not fully alive until we came together in this bed."

Elizabeth believed him. Chris was *not* a liar, even if she was.

"It will be okay, Elizabeth," Chris said suddenly. His tone was so reassuring; his eyes held such true promise.

But how could he know it would be okay? Again, Elizabeth wondered.

After another hour, Elizabeth left the cottage and headed home to Eliot's Corner. And as she drove she thought about how strongly she needed to believe that it *would* be okay with Chris. She loved Chris and needed him in her life to a degree she had never needed anyone else, not parent, husband, or, indeed, even her children. She knew that with every fiber of her being. It was her truth.

And yet, it was becoming more and more difficult to trust in the primacy and the power of the private world they had created, a world inhabited by just the two of them, their love alone enough to sustain each other and subdue every challenge they might encounter.

It was becoming so very difficult.

Chapter 33

When, Petra wondered, had the act of browsing first come about? Maybe when open-air markets and then indoor shops were established, when people finally had a little time and money for a leisure activity like choosing among various items, not all of which were necessary for the basic sustenance of life.

Petra even enjoyed browsing when in a place where it wasn't immediately obvious that she would discover something of interest to her. One time, she had accompanied a friend to a hardware store; Ben had needed a particular type of screw for a DIY project. While he searched for this particular screw, Petra had amused herself by strolling the aisles of hammers (who knew there were so many kinds of hammers?) and various power tools (ditto); gathering paint sample strips (so fun!); and finally, watching one of the store's employees working the key-cutting machine. Ben had had to drag her from the store.

Today found Petra browsing in Arden Forest and thinking about all the bastards, love children (what a creepy term!), or so-called natural children in literature. Bastards had always been a popular character, bastardy a popular theme. From the shelf just above her head, Petra pulled out an orange-spined Penguin paperback edition of Charles Dickens's *Bleak House*. How appropriate she thought, flipping through the many pages of small print. If there was such a thing as coming upon a sign—

It seemed there was. Petra looked down at the page and felt a shiver run through her. Here was Esther Summerson being spoken at by Miss Barbary, the nasty woman who raised her (Esther's aunt, if she had but known). "Your mother, Esther, is your disgrace, and you were hers."

Poor Lady Honoria Dedlock, Petra thought, remembering the storyline clearly, Esther's mother, dying at the grave of her child's father, full of shame and not knowing that her husband had forgiven her for her so-called sin and wanted her back with him in their home. It was terrible and unfair that Lady Dedlock had to be forgiven for having had an affair prior to her marriage, but that was the nineteenth-century for you. And how awful to have thought your child dead, though maybe it would have been better if Esther had been dead—no—or, rather, how awful that Lady Dedlock had never discovered her daughter. Petra closed the book and returned it to the shelf. What a mess all around.

Estella in *Great Expectations*. Oliver Twist. Anna Karenina's daughter, Annie. Adèle, Mr. Rochester's ward and possibly his child. So many fictional characters with uncertain parentage or dubious parentage, used as vehicles for stories centering on lies and deception, unjust actions and random fates. Rarely was one of these fictional characters granted a happy ending; if they were, the happy ending came only at great cost.

Henry VIII, Petra recalled suddenly, a real-life character larger and more frustrating than any writer of fiction could make him, was supposedly terribly fond of his bastard son, Henry Fitzroy, as were other powerful men fond of their by-blows. A testosterone thing? Children born on the wrong side of the blanket. There seemed to be an endless supply of terms in English alone for children who hadn't the social benefit of married parents. Petra, who sadly had no other language (though she could bungle her way through some Spanish, French, and Italian), thought it might be an interesting personal project to research the cultural or social history of bastardy and bastard children across the globe. A personal project she probably would never have the energy or focus to undertake.

Besides, there was another, more important project she did intend to undertake in the near future. Her desire to approach—not to confront—Christopher Ryan was stronger now than it had been when she and her mother had first talked about it.

And that, too, was a cliché of popular narrative, the unknown child turning up on the unsuspecting father's doorstep. "I think you're my father," she says. (It was usually a woman.) "Just before my mother died she told me about the relationship she'd had with you back in the summer of xxx." How the man reacted to such interesting news pretty much set the tone and direction of the subsequent action. Would he send her away? Embrace her wholeheartedly? Decide she must be kept at arm's length? Would he demand concrete proof of paternity? Offer her money to disappear, to keep her mouth shut?

"Looking for anything in particular, Petra?"

Petra hadn't been aware that Arden was standing close by. In truth, Petra hadn't stopped by the bookshop in search of a particular title, but after having spent almost half an hour meandering along the aisles, she felt duty-bound to make a purchase. "A new cozy mystery series to devour," she said brightly. "Any recommendations?"

Arden suggested several series, one well established, the others fairly new. Petra chose the first book in two series: Winnie Archer's A Bread Shop Mystery and Judi Lynn's A Jazzi Zanders Mystery. Neither of the books, as far as she could tell from Arden's descriptions or from the back-cover copy, centered on a bastard or love child.

Petra was glad about that.

* * *

Dinner at Lavender Lane that evening consisted of two small pizzas from the local Italian family-style restaurant. Elizabeth said she hadn't felt like cooking, though she had put together a green salad in a nod to the necessity of vegetables in one's diet. When Petra was on her own, she tended to forget to eat vegetables, or at least, to eat as many vegetables as she was supposed to be eating. She suspected she wasn't alone in that.

The atmosphere between the women was still not perfectly comfortable, but it wasn't half as uncomfortable as it might have been if Petra's relationship with her mother hadn't been as strong as it was.

Petra wolfed down a slice of mushroom pizza before announcing that she had decided to contact Christopher Ryan. "I mean, I was already pretty sure that I was going to reach out to him," she said. "I told you that before, but now I feel absolutely, a hundred percent certain."

Her mother's expression remained neutral. "It might," she said, "be easier on the both of you if I were the one to tell Chris he has a child. Sort of pave the way for you, let him know I've told all three of my children about our relationship. After all, I no longer know the man. Thirty years have passed. He might have a wife and other children. He might be ill. He might not want . . . He might not want to see you."

"I've thought about all that," Petra assured her mother. "I have no desire to shock him by just blurting the truth. I've decided to simply get in touch as Elizabeth Quirk's daughter. I'll say I've heard a lot about him and would like to hear back from him. I'll see how he responds and then decide where to go from there. If he doesn't respond at all . . ." Petra shrugged.

"What do you want from him?" Elizabeth asked. "I think it would be smart for you to know the answer to that question up front."

"Honestly," Petra admitted, "right now I'm not sure what I want from him. But I believe Chris has the right to know he's a father. Don't you agree?"

Elizabeth sighed. "Yes. I should have told him long ago. Look, assuming he does agree to talk with you, or even to meet, and if he asks to speak with me, tell him . . . Sorry. Forget I said anything. The last thing I want is for you to be acting as a go-between."

Frankly, that was the last thing Petra wanted, as well. She knew that going forward she would have to protect herself from becoming burdened by whatever emotional journey her parents found themselves taking. Her own emotional journey would be fraught enough. "Anyway," she said, "Chris might not want anything to do with either of us once he knows the whole truth."

Elizabeth took Petra's hand in hers. "I wouldn't blame him if he wanted nothing to do with *me*. But he won't turn you away, Petra. I truly believe that he won't."

"I'd like to think so," Petra said with a brave smile. "But there's only one way to find out."

Chapter 34

The Neale Gallery was to be found on a quiet street away from the heart of town in what had been the home of the Isaiah Neale family, residents of Eliot's Corner for four generations before they eventually died out. It was Elizabeth's favorite gallery space in Eliot's Corner—there was a more commonly popular gallery on Main Street—precisely because it provided so personal an experience, as if the homeowner had invited her neighbors in for a glass of wine, a chat, and a browse at her hand-picked works of art.

It was six o'clock on the evening of July third when Elizabeth and Petra arrived at the gallery. Elizabeth had harbored what was probably a silly hope in view of the current situation that all three of her daughters might be in town for the holiday. But Cam and her family were spending the holiday at home in South Portland. Their neighborhood organization (watch group, Cam sometimes critically called it) sponsored a block party to which everyone brought some sort of cold dish—potato salads; pasta salads; brownies; watermelon—while several of the men (why was it always men who manned the grills? Hugh had been so protective of his role as grill master!) supervised the charring of hamburgers and hotdogs. Some years there was a costume contest for the smaller children, and a professional clown making balloon animals, and games like ring toss. There was even a tombola; you could win what amounted to a neighbor's unwanted junk, but the money raised went directly to the local animal shelter, an undeniably good cause. Cam had admitted to her mother that she could live without the noisy, chatty, and sometimes catty affair, but Ralph and Beth looked forward to the event all year—the twins were too young to have much of an opinion on the matter—so at the event they all would be.

"Wow, it's pretty crowded already," Petra noted as she and Elizabeth stepped inside the gallery. "I guess folk art is more popular than I'd thought. Either that, or people are just in the mood to be out of the house on such a nice evening."

Elizabeth had always been drawn to American folk art, whether created by people long gone or by people working in the present. No matter the medium or the form, a metal weathervane, a portrait by an itinerant painter, a quilt stitched by an African American woman during her time as a slave or after she had been freed, the piece might reveal a strong individuality or express a sense of community, explore a religious theme, or speak of pride in a national identity.

This exhibit seemed to be wide-ranging. A glance showed that it contained everything from nineteenth-century landscapes of small New England towns, to handmade tune books or hymnals, to embroidered samplers, to a hooked rug displaying the image of a whaling vessel.

"Look, Mom," Petra whispered. "It's Jess and Eddie."

So it was. The pair were standing in front of a crudely charming wooden figure of a Revolutionary War soldier, regarding it closely; their backs were to Elizabeth and Petra. Elizabeth felt her stomach clench. She hadn't considered the fact that they might run into Jess and Eddie on this outing. And if she had? Would the possibility of an unplanned meeting with her middle child have stopped her from leaving the house? Should it have? Of course not.

"We should go over—" Petra began. But Eddie, who had turned away from the wooden figure, had already spotted them and now was walking across the gallery, Jess in reluctant tow.

"Hey, good to see you guys!" Eddie enthused. "Petra, it's been, like, forever. How've you been?"

Eddie was a good-looking man by just about anyone's standards. His features were strong but not gross. His smile was charming. His eyes were an unusual and compelling shade of green. His hair was thick and, even pulled back into what used to be called a man bun, it was evidently well cared for. He was tall but not too tall, well-built without being bulky. Elizabeth could easily see what Jess found attractive in him, though she had always wondered what other, more substantial things about Eddie had drawn Jess's attention. Even in the early days of their relationship, when most lovers couldn't stop going on about their partner's excellent attributes, Jess had never waxed poetic about her boyfriend's intelligence or sense of humor or kindness.

"Fine," Petra said. "Good. And you?"

Eddie shrugged. "Can't complain."

"But he does." That was Jess. Elizabeth noted that she was dressed as if for the office; indeed, maybe she had come directly from work.

If Eddie was offended by his girlfriend's remark he didn't let on. "Mrs. Q, what's been up with you?" he asked.

Elizabeth had never taken Eddie for a smooth liar; his open demeanor assured her that either Jess hadn't yet told him about the upheaval in the Quirk family, or that the knowledge of Jess's mother having had an affair didn't bother him. She chose to believe the former.

"Nothing much," she said with the best smile she could muster. "This is a wonderful exhibit, isn't it?"

"Can't say I know all that much about art," Eddie admitted, "but I know what I like, and a lot of this stuff is really cool. The portraits are whacky though! It's like some of those old itinerant painter guys had no idea what they were doing!"

"And that's what we find charming," Elizabeth said, ignoring Jess's eye roll. "This is art created by people who were—and are—self-taught, and often people on the outside of the social mainstream."

"We just got here so I don't have a favorite piece yet," Petra added, "but generally I love the wooden toys best."

Jess didn't offer an opinion on the works chosen for the show. Her eyes roamed restlessly around the room while managing to avoid her mother's eyes entirely. Elizabeth felt a tiny twinge of annoyance—Jess was acting like a child—but along with that feeling came an equally strong twinge of guilt. If Jess was misbehaving, it was because of something she, Elizabeth, had done.

Petra and Eddie were chatting away happily enough, so Elizabeth decided to take the risk. The worst that could happen was that Jess said no to her invitation.

"Do you want to join us tomorrow at the house, late afternoon?" Elizabeth said, as casually as she could manage. "Some of my friends from the book group will be coming over. I'll have the ingredients for ice cream sundaes. You know, strawberries for red, blueberries for blue, and vanilla ice cream for white. Oh, and chocolate sauce, of course, because, well, chocolate."

Eddie's face lit up; clearly, he hadn't been entirely focused on his conversation with Petra. "That sounds—"

"We're busy," Jess said firmly.

Eddie looked to her, his expression now puzzled. "We are?"

Jess frowned at him. "Besides, I'm not a fan of ice cream sundaes."

Before Eddie could contradict that—if he could—Jess had taken his arm and was guiding him toward the door of the gallery. "See you around," she called over her shoulder.

And then she and Eddie were gone.

Elizabeth smiled briefly. "I guess I'm not forgiven." In spite, she thought, of the fact that Jess had chosen to come to her mother directly after her erstwhile business partner had abandoned her.

"That was rude of Jess, to all of us," Petra said firmly. "There's no excuse for bad behavior like that. She's not a child."

"You sound like her mother. I think that's still my job."

Petra put her arm through Elizabeth's. "Sorry. I just don't like to see you hurt."

"I'm fine. Really." Elizabeth took a deep breath. "Now, I want to get a closer look at that quilt on the wall over there. Come on."

Chapter 35

Petra and her mother were part of the crowd who had come out to watch Eliot's Corner's annual Independence Day parade. It was, Petra thought, probably very similar to every other small town Fourth of July parade taking place that day across the country. The parade began with the town councillors and a few of the more important business people, looking summer-perfect in their navy blazers and chinos, their white jeans and espadrilles, walking along and waving. After that not very interesting group came a group of small children dressed like eighteenth-century American colonists—albeit very short ones. A wig falling over a pair of eyes, a skirt trailing along the pavement, and one little girl looking as if she were about to burst into tears, overwhelmed by the strangeness of her situation.

What members of the high school's marching band who could be wrangled to perform on a hot summer day came next. They looked a bit droopy in their heavy uniforms, but their efforts were earnest, and as Petra couldn't play any musical instrument, she was in no position to judge the actual performance. It probably didn't matter if one of the musician marchers hit a wrong note or two. Members of the fire department rode along at a snail's pace on the town's one ladder truck, followed by members of the choir belonging to the Baptist congregation in town. They were singing "God Bless America," not an easy song to sing standing still, let alone marching along in the full sun of a July morning.

Finally, a pale blue convertible, long and sleek with spectacular fins, a car that belonged to the most prosperous man in Eliot's Corner, rolled slowly along, signaling the end of the parade. In the backseat of the classic vehicle sat Gerald Keats, the town's last living survivor of World War II. He wore a baseball-style cap covered with various cloth badges, and a jacket—Petra thought it was his uniform coat!—pinned with medals.

"Gosh," Petra murmured, "Mr. Keats must be in his late nineties now, at least. That in itself is impressive, let alone the fact that he fought in the Second World War."

Elizabeth nodded and wiped her cheek. "I don't know why parades always make me cry. It's like I hear the first blast of a high schooler's trumpet or the first beat of the big drum and I'm overwhelmed by a sense of the fragility of human life, and yet, at the same time, I'm hyper aware of our seemingly endless ability to hope, to keep going, to believe in good things to come, to celebrate. It's all so touching. Oh, I'm not explaining it well."

"That's okay, Mom. I totally understand." Petra lowered her sunglasses and pointed to her watery eyes. "See?"

Elizabeth laughed. "Chris used to cry at parades, too. I wonder if he still does."

When the car ferrying Gerald Keats had passed out of view, the crowd began to trail off, heading for the next festivity of the day. The library, opened just for the morning, had mounted a special exhibit of the oldest books and papers in its possession, most of which had been bequeathed years earlier by the remnants of Eliot's Corner's founding families. The police force and their family members were hosting a bake sale on the front lawn of the courthouse. Several shop owners had elected to open from ten o'clock until noon with a pledge of donating one half of any proceeds earned during those two hours to the nearest food pantry.

"Let's not go home just yet," Elizabeth suggested. "How about we drive to the beach?"

Petra thought that sounded like a fine idea, even if the beach might already be crowded with merrymakers with their volleyball nets, Frisbees, and boogie boards.

"Dad, Hugh, liked parades," Petra said when they had gotten into the car and were headed out of town. "I remember he loved watching the Macy's Thanksgiving Day Parade on television, but I never saw him cry or get sentimental about it. Still, he'd get pretty excited when Santa Claus made an appearance at the end of the parade. It was like he was suddenly a child, full of joy and anticipation."

Elizabeth nodded. "Hugh was a man of simple pleasures, if that's the way to put it. Mostly, he saw things at face value. For him, a parade was just a parade, a gathering of people for the purpose of having a fun time. Nothing more poignant."

"Nothing is simple for me," Petra said quietly. "Everything seems poignant. That's not a complaint or a bid for pity! It's just that I think about every little thing, like I'm always asking questions of the universe or whatever, always wanting to know and understand and make connections. Honestly, it can be kind of exhausting."

"In that way, you're like Christopher. And me, to be honest, but more so Chris."

Petra thought about that for a while. The question was becoming one she couldn't avoid, not that she wanted to. How would she have been different if she had grown up with Chris's fatherly influence rather than with Hugh's?

"You know, I chose the name Petra as a quiet reference to Chris," Elizabeth said suddenly, into the silence of the car. "His confirmation name is Peter. Not many people would have known that, and even if Hugh had originally known—they were confirmed together—it was likely he would have forgotten it, being a proud ex-Catholic. None of that superstitious nonsense for me, he would say. And even if Hugh had remembered that Chris had taken the name Peter, my naming you Petra wouldn't have proved anything."

Petra smiled. "I like my name. I'm glad you chose it. Remember that time, I was in fourth or fifth grade, when that obnoxious girl in my art class—I can't remember her name!—started calling me Pet. When I asked her to call me by my full name, she was so rude about it, like it was her right and not mine to decide what people could call me."

"I know the feeling," Elizabeth said with a sigh. "People have always taken liberties with my name—including Hugh—assuming off the bat that I'm Betty or Betsy or Liz or Beth. I spent so much time correcting those people, telling them that my name is Elizabeth and that's what I prefer to be called, and still some refused to pay attention."

"By the way, did Dad have another name in mind for me?"

Her mother smiled. "He used to say that because the woman did all the hard work of pregnancy and delivery, the least the man could do was not to interfere with her choice of names for the baby. So, I got my way with Camilla, Jessica, and Petra."

"Dad could be pretty smart when he had to be!" Petra said with a laugh.

They made the final turn onto the road that ran along the beach for some way. Cars were parked bumper to bumper along both sides of the road, and a large, hand-painted sign announced that the parking lot was full.

"Um, I think this might have been a bad idea," Elizabeth noted. "I mean, I know it's a holiday, but I guess I hoped it was still too early for the hordes to descend."

Petra shrugged. "It's no big deal. Let's just turn around—if we can!—and head home."

With a skill that Petra wasn't sure she could manage, her mother extricated them from the mass of beachgoers in their cars and trucks loaded with boogie boards, coolers, umbrellas, and folding chairs, and before long they were on their way back to Lavender Lane.

As they drove along, Petra thought about Cam, who was spending the holiday with her family, possibly pretending that nothing was wrong in her marriage, certainly in front of her neighbors gathered for the block party. Petra hoped that her sister was able to enjoy at least some part of the day, let her guard down to enjoy a laugh with friends. And she seriously hoped that Lily didn't make an appearance at the block party. That, Petra felt sure, would be entirely uncalled for and would rightly result in disaster.

As for her other sister, well, Petra was sure Jess had been lying when she told them she and Eddie had previous plans for this afternoon. She wondered if Eddie had quizzed Jess about her rejection of Elizabeth's invitation, about her lie. Did he ever stand up to Jess? Petra knew so little about that relationship and realized now that she was okay with that.

"Home sweet home," Elizabeth murmured as she pulled the car into the driveway. "I guess we'd better get busy preparing for our little party."

The two women made their way inside the house and to the kitchen. Later, they would serve hot dogs, hamburgers, potato salad, fruit salad, and ice cream sundaes to Mrs. Shandy and a few others from the book group who preferred low-key celebrations to wild parties with the attendant risk of guests getting stupidly drunk and setting off illegal fireworks irresponsibly.

As Petra began to peel the potatoes, she found herself wondering what Christopher Ryan, her father, was doing at that very moment. Did he have a small but good group of friends with whom he routinely spent the holidays? Did he enjoy going to or giving parties, or did he prefer to socialize one-on-one? Was he an introvert—she thought he probably was—but also adept at getting along with strangers? There was so much she didn't know, so much to learn.

But that learning—that relationship—would wait. At the moment, Petra realized that she very much missed her dad, Hugh Quirk, life-of-the-party, chief reveler, master of the grill, cheerleader of the festivities, and all around perfect host. "Happy Independence Day, Dad," she whispered. "I really wish you were here."

Chapter 36

Elizabeth wasn't sure what exactly had made her contact two of her former colleagues and suggest they meet for lunch. She liked Emma and Tristan, and missed the conversations they had shared at lunch in the teachers' lounge, but they weren't close friends, and she had seen them fairly recently at the going-away party the staff of Eliot's Corner Primary had given for those teachers and administrative staff not moving on to MidCoast Primary. (Both Emma and Tristan were in fact moving on to MidCoast Primary.)

Maybe, Elizabeth thought, it was a desire to keep in her life those people who had witnessed her professional career first-hand; they could validate her as someone who had worked hard and made a positive difference in the lives of others not her immediate family. Whatever the source of the urge, a date and time had been set.

Elizabeth entered the small and casual lunch place to find her former colleagues already seated at a round, marble-topped table.

Emma Fry, mathematics teacher, had been divorced for about four years and had what she archly referred to as a gentleman friend. Her two teenage children lived with her while her former husband had moved to Chicago. Stuart didn't make much of an effort to visit his children though the child support arrived on time; Emma was fond of saying, with a shrug, "It could be worse." Her kids seemed well-adjusted. They didn't hate their father, nor did they clamor to talk with him on Face-Time, but they weren't averse to making a visit with benefits. "Tess wants to see the collection of Van Gogh's work at the Art Institute," Emma had told Elizabeth the last time they spoke, "so she's decided to ask Stuart if she can stay with him for a weekend before school starts in the fall. Frankly, I'm not sure how much time she wants to spend with her father. I think it's mostly about Vincent."

Seated to Emma's left was Tristan Meyer, teacher of social studies. He was in his late thirties, married, and, with his husband, planning to adopt a baby. Gary worked from home, and, as an educator, Tristan had summers off, but the couple wasn't silly enough to think they wouldn't need help with the child. Gary's parents had offered their babysitting services; they were both retired and eager to be hands-on grandparents. "Don't get me wrong," Tristan had told Elizabeth, "we're grateful to the Murphys. But my parents are making a fuss about wanting to help out as well, and Gary and I foresee Grandparent Wars."

"Before either of you asks," Elizabeth said, once they had settled with their drinks and sandwiches, "I have no idea what I'm going to do with my future. Suddenly, the future is something that needs doing to, and I just haven't given it much thought."

Tristan nodded. "Understandable. Losing your job did come out of the blue. No one can expect you to have firm plans only months after sustaining such a big blow."

It had indeed been a blow, one that Elizabeth was still absorbing. "My children seem eager for me to make decisions," she admitted.

"They just love you," Tristan assured her. "Adult kids worry. I drive my parents nuts on a regular basis asking if they've installed a safety bar in the shower yet and if they're sure their living wills are current."

Emma laughed. "I look forward to the day when my kids are old enough to be concerned about Mom. Don't get me wrong, they love me, but it's still mostly because of what I do for them."

"It's funny," Elizabeth went on, "but since Hugh died I never once thought about retiring. It never occurred to me that one day I would have to—or would want to—stop getting up early and heading off to spend eight or so hours hard at work."

"Did you and Hugh have retirement plans in place before he got sick?" Emma asked.

"Not plans so much as ideas. We talked about doing some traveling, maybe taking up golf, nothing outrageous. But when he died, those ideas died with him, I guess. Teaching took on even more importance in my life. It filled emotional spaces once filled by my marriage." Elizabeth shook her head. "I'm sorry. I didn't mean to—"

Tristan put his hand on her arm. "Don't apologize. These are situations that will come to most, if not all, of us."

Elizabeth smiled, grateful for these two good people in her life.

"I know I shouldn't suggest this," Tristan said when they had finished their sandwiches and talked for almost an hour, "but what about sharing a piece of that decadent chocolate hazelnut cake on today's menu. Freshly baked this morning. All organic ingredients."

Emma laughed. "You had me at decadent. I'm in."

Elizabeth shrugged. "Why not?"

Finally, cake eaten, the former colleagues made their fare-wells. Emma and Tristan promised to keep in touch with Elizabeth and to let her know the news from MidCoast Primary once they were settled into the fall semester.

As Elizabeth walked to her car at the far end of the parking lot, she wondered when she would next see Emma and Tristan. She was glad they had all gotten together—it had been a poignant meeting for her—and she was grateful that neither of them had, even jokingly, mentioned the possibility of her dating. Maybe they knew her well enough to know that the very idea of "going on a date" at this point in her life made her feel sick to her stomach. No doubt neither had mentioned dating because they were smart and sensitive, aware that a new romance was rarely a cure for anything other than momentary boredom. Life just wasn't that easy, not for most people.

Besides, how could she possibly consider a new relationship when there was unfinished business with Christopher Ryan to attend to? At the very least, she owed him an apology. At the most, she owed him a lifetime of gratitude for the gift he had given her.

Elizabeth got behind the wheel of her car, opened all of the windows, and began the journey back to Lavender Lane. She wondered how Emma and Tristan would react to her secret, should she ever be crazy enough to share it outside of the family. She suspected her former colleagues would be understanding, maybe surprised, but not condemnatory.

But it was silly to waste her time pondering such possibilities. Elizabeth was not going to tell anyone else her secret.

Ever.

Chapter 37

Elizabeth had gone off to have lunch with two former colleagues. Petra had met both Emma and Tristan at a holiday party given by the principal of the school a few years before. She had liked them both—actually, she had found everyone at the gathering pretty nice—and hoped that her mother was enjoying herself and not succumbing to nostalgia for the old days at Eliot's Corner Primary.

"Did I ever meet the friends Mom's seeing?" Cam asked. She had come north once again, on her own. For a person spending so much of her time on the highway, she looked remarkably calm and collected. Petra hated highway driving, especially in the summer.

"I don't think so," Petra replied, handing her sister a glass of ginger iced tea. "I only met them once, at a Christmas party."

"I guess there's an awful lot about Mom's life her daughters will never know, small things as well as large. Wow, this tea is gingery!"

"That's kind of the point." Petra, recalling how Cam had so abruptly ended the last Zoom call, decided that now was as good a time as any to repeat the question Cam had not answered.

"So," Petra went on, "what did Ralph have to say about Mom's secret? I bet he was pretty shocked. It's not the sort of thing you expect to hear about your mother-in-law, is it? Though I don't know why anyone should be shocked by anyone else having secrets. We all have them, no matter how hard we might pretend not to."

Cam smiled briefly and awkwardly. "I haven't actually told him yet. It's not that I don't want him to know," she went on hurriedly. "I'd like to have someone to help me come to terms with the news. Of course, I have you and Mom and even Jess in one of her better moods but—"

"But Ralph is your husband," Petra said. "So why aren't you talking to him? Is it because of Lily?"

Her sister sighed. "Yes. I'm still not sure of what's going on between Ralph and Lily, and the last thing I want is to open up to someone, to make myself vulnerable to someone whose attention is so focused elsewhere."

Petra nodded. "I think I understand. But you can't go on keeping something so important from him. I mean, he's bound to find out from one of us at some point. Maybe you should think of telling Ralph about Mom and Chris as a sort of test. His response to our family crisis—if you can call it that—might tell you a lot about his feelings for you."

Cam frowned. "And telling him about Mom's extra-marital affair is meant to what, prompt him to admit he's having one of his own?"

"If he's having an affair it might, I suppose, compel him to come clean. If he's not actually having an affair, but he's feeling guilty about his obvious crush . . ." Petra shook her head. "Oh, I don't know. I've never been married, or even been in a long-term relationship. I don't really know what I'm talking about."

"That's okay," Cam assured her. "It helps me to share this craziness with you. I don't expect you to have a solution. I just appreciate that you listen."

Suddenly, the back door opened, and Jess came striding into the kitchen. Because it was the weekend Jess was dressed down; for her, this meant an oversized white shirt worn with dark skinny jeans. Though every hair was in place, Petra thought her sister looked stressed. The sudden collapse of her planned business venture clearly was taking a very large toll on her.

"We were about to go out back," Cam said. "Join us?"

"What's there to drink?" Jess said in response. She went over to the counter and sniffed the pitcher of ginger iced tea. "This will do," she said. "Okay, let's go."

When the sisters were settled in adjacent Adirondack chairs, cold drinks in hand, Cam turned to Jess.

"Any news on the business front?" she asked.

"I don't want to talk about it," Jess said shortly.

Petra shared a look of concern with her oldest sister. At the moment, there were two obvious topics that seemed to be off-limits. Jess's business venture, and Jess's boyfriend. How long, Petra wondered, would it be before someone brought up the third topic of contention . . .

Suddenly, Jess slapped the arms of her chair. "I'm so freakin' annoyed about this whole Mom and Chris thing. I can't stop thinking about it, night and day. It's obsessing me. I so don't want to have to rethink the subject of my parents. In fact, I resent having this situation dumped on me. I'd made my peace with Mom and Dad—"

"You mean," Cam said, "with your version of them."

"All right, if you want to put it that way, but so what? That's all any of us can do, come to terms with a person as we know them. And I did just that. But now that Petra's torn the veil off the past—"

"Not Petra," Cam corrected. "Mom."

"—and revealed all sorts of secrets and deceptions and compromises, I feel like I never knew my parents at all, that the people I'd made them out to be never really existed."

"No child ever really knows a parent," Petra said quietly. "No one ever really knows anyone other than herself. If even that's possible."

Jess rolled her eyes. "Yes, I know, but that's dragging what I'm trying to say into the territory of existential philosophy or something. I'm talking about something much more . . . much more powerful. I'm talking about feelings. I'd felt somehow . . . secure in my idea of Mom and Dad. Now, that sense of security or surety is gone. If I can't know my own parents, how can I ever know myself?"

My question exactly, Petra thought.

"It doesn't have to be so dire, Jess," Cam argued. "Mom and Dad are still who you thought them to be, but they're also other people. You must understand that, don't you?"

"Okay, of course I do. I'm not stupid! Look, Cam, you're acting all calm and rational, like nothing at all has happened. Isn't this freaking you out to some degree?"

"No, it's not freaking me out," Cam said after a moment. "It has given me a lot to think about, to sort through, that's for sure. But I'm not doubting my own identity. I'm an adult. I've made a life for myself. Mom and Dad have no real influence on me at this point in my life."

Petra doubted that a parent ever ceased to have at least some degree of influence on a child's life, no matter how old the child, but she said nothing. Maybe Cam was just attempting to reassure herself, tell herself aloud that she was fine, hoping she would convince herself it was true.

"Why did Mom marry Dad, I wonder?" Jess said suddenly. "Was she really in love with him? Then again, why does anyone marry anyone? The older I get, the more I ask myself that question, and the more puzzled I become."

"Love?" Cam suggested. "Love is a pretty popular reason."

Jess rolled her eyes. "Please."

"Maybe Dad bullied her into accepting his proposal," Petra suggested gently. "You know how forceful he could be. He could convince you that you wanted something you'd never even thought about wanting. Dad, of course, thought it was charm; he said it was what made him such a successful salesman. But you could also say it was bullying. Maybe Mom just eventually got tired of his asking her to be his wife and gave in."

Cam nodded. "Which might go a long way toward explaining why someone like Chris Ryan held such appeal for her. The total opposite of Dad, at least from what Mom's told us about him and from what I know of his professional reputation. Chris Ryan possesses a lot of tact and diplomatic skill, two qualities Dad was lacking."

"Still, Chris was Dad's friend," Jess said. "It was wrong for Mom to have an affair with him."

"I know," Petra agreed. "But since when does right or wrong come into consideration when passion is at play? That's a rhetorical question, of course." And one she couldn't even attempt to answer from her own limited experience.

"I agree that Dad could be tough," Jess said musingly. "No one can dispute that. If he had discovered the truth about Mom and Chris, I can easily imagine him confronting Chris and beating him up, you know, 'teaching him a lesson,' as Dad would say. In my opinion, a lesson Chris would have deserved."

Petra felt troubled. "I don't think Dad was a violent man. As far as I know he never hit anyone, never even threatened anyone."

"I agree," Cam said. "Dad wasn't violent. Anyway, it's all conjecture. Dad didn't know about the affair, so we can't know how he would have reacted if he had found out."

"And," Petra said with some heat, "I don't believe physical violence ever serves a good purpose. It certainly doesn't teach a lesson. Violence just begets more violence."

Jess shrugged. "You're probably right about that, though there are times Eddie makes me so mad I'm tempted to—"

"To what?" Cam asked with a frown.

Jess waved her hand dismissively. "Nothing. Forget I said

anything. And before you ask, no, Eddie has never lifted a hand toward me. He knows I wouldn't stand for it."

Petra suddenly felt queasy. "Fear can't coexist with love," she said. "Or can it?"

"All things are possible," Cam said quietly. "Love gets distorted, corrupted, and, if a person feels trapped in a relationship, scared, like she has no way out, she has to find a way to rationalize staying put. Sometimes that means convincing herself she's still in love with her abusive partner."

"Anyway," Jess went on, "I stand by what I've said before. Dad would never have hurt Mom."

"Certainly, not in obvious ways," Petra said. "But maybe in ways of which he was unaware. We all hurt the people we love, accidentally, mindlessly, however you want to put it."

Another silence descended on the sisters, this one tinged with a sense of real sadness. At least, it seemed that way to Petra.

Finally, with a sigh, Jess rose. "I'm tired," she said. "I'm going home. See you around."

"Bye," Cam said as Jess left the yard. When they heard the engine of her car roar to life, Cam shook her head. "I worry about her. How did she get such a grim attitude? I mean, she's always considered it a point of pride that she was 'just like Dad,' someone who didn't moan and groan, someone who kept an upbeat attitude and got the job done."

"I doubt that's who Dad was all the time," Petra said musingly. "Everyone performs for the people in his life. Maybe when Dad was alone he was very different from how he was when he was with us or when he was at work, or even when he was with Mom."

Cam rose. "Maybe," she said. "I think I'll go inside. It's getting too hot out here for me. Maybe I'm having a hot flash? God, I hope I'm not perimenopausal already!"

Petra remained where she was after Cam had left the yard. She felt a bit depressed. She wished she could really help her sisters in a concrete way. Positive thoughts and sincere prayers were important, of course, but most often action was necessary to really get something significant accomplished. Petra had never really been good at taking action, not for the good of others and certainly not for her own good.

But maybe that was going to change now that she knew she was the daughter of a man who had devoted his life to the service of others.

That, along with so much else, remained to be seen.

Chapter 38

Elizabeth gave the sink one last wipe with the sponge before admitting to herself that she had had enough of housecleaning for one day. Well, at least for the morning. Two people in the house made more of a footprint than one person, especially when that second person wasn't the neatest.

Petra—as if summoned by her mother's thoughts—came into the kitchen then, carrying a plastic bag she brought to the trash can. "It's funny how quickly you can accumulate stuff to throw out," she said. "And to recycle. We really are a wasteful consumer culture."

"I'm afraid it's probably too late to change that radically," Elizabeth said. "I don't believe in environmental or social miracles."

"What about romantic miracles?" Petra asked with a smile.

Before Elizabeth could find a reply, Petra went on.

"I was thinking again about you going back to graduate school. About what inspired you to make such a big commitment, especially with three small children at home. I don't entirely understand what drove you. I guess I'd like to know because of my own trouble with identifying a goal or a purpose and taking a step toward it."

Elizabeth nodded. "I have to admit that from this perspective, the idea seems kind of crazy. But at the time, going back to school for a degree I'd wanted to pursue years earlier, and hopefully having a career after that, wasn't just a crazy or totally selfish desire. I hoped that if I earned a measure of independence, broadened my world, caused myself to think and to be challenged in new ways, I would be a better person all around, a better role model for my girls, even, maybe, a better partner to my husband."

"It could have gone another way," Petra pointed out. "Going to grad school and then getting a job could have taken you even farther away from Hugh. From Dad."

"I suppose you're right. But I loved Hugh, and I knew he loved me. Things needed to change in our relationship—at least, I needed to change—if we were to survive and be reasonably happy growing old together. And luckily, things did change. I changed. But I always loved Hugh Quirk. Please believe that."

"It's just that you also loved Christopher Ryan," Petra said neutrally, a statement of fact.

"Yes," Elizabeth admitted. "As I told you before, he was, in great part, though it wasn't what he intended, the catalyst that helped shake me out of a deep complacency. He was the person who helped me take charge of my life so I could be more than just Hugh's wife and mother to his children. Well, to my children."

"I guess you have a lot to thank him for. Mom, back when you two were involved, did you ever believe you would have a life together one day? Or did you know from the start that the whole thing was doomed?"

Elizabeth shook her head. "Those are very difficult questions to answer. Honestly, I can hardly remember what I was thinking, and the diary doesn't tell me much either about what I did or didn't hope for the future, not until I knew things had to end. I suppose the moment itself was so all-consuming that everything else just didn't seem to matter. Or, maybe I was hiding the truth from myself, unable to put into writing what I suspected deep in my heart."

Was it true, Elizabeth asked herself now, that she had never imagined a blissful future with Chris? Marriage one day, after Hugh had died, or maybe after he had left her for another woman? It was an unworthy thought. But possibly she had considered such a future—and then conveniently forgotten it?

"I don't know anything about love," Petra said quietly. "The kind that's all-consuming, that makes you, I don't know, feel like you're living in an alternate universe."

"I don't know if I want for you to experience that kind of passion," Elizabeth admitted, "or if I pray that you're spared the experience."

"I suspect no one has much choice in the matter. Falling in love isn't something you can schedule ahead of time, is it?"

"No," Elizabeth agreed, "but some people are more open to passion than others, even if they're not aware that they are until passion is upon them."

Petra smiled. "Maybe I'm one of those people who are unaware of their capability for romance until one day, like magic, there it is, a grand passion, staring me right in the face! Hopefully, I'm not one of those people who go out of their way to avoid love when it appears. Because that seems like a shame. Oh, I don't know what I'm saying. What will happen will happen."

"That's probably a good attitude to have. So, have you contacted Chris yet?" Elizabeth asked.

"No. But I'll do it soon. I guess I'm sort of working up to it."

"I'm still worried that by letting you get in touch with Chris, even if you don't immediately tell him that he's your father, I'm being selfish and perhaps cowardly," Elizabeth admitted. "Please let me approach him first."

"I'm not afraid, Mom," Petra said. "I want to be the one to reach out. He can't hate me. He's my father and I'm his daughter."

"Of course, he won't hate you," Elizabeth said firmly. "I doubt it's in Chris's nature to hate anyone, not even me. It's just that I don't want you to be hurt if he's not receptive. I know nothing about him, Petra. Not anymore. I don't know what exactly he's suffered all these years, or what's brought him happiness. He might simply be too busy or too tired to be a father now. He's not ancient by any means, but he's not a young man."

"Mom, please," Petra begged. "I'm not a child. I don't need a father now the way I needed Dad when I was growing up. I'll be okay, I promise. And if I'm not okay, if Chris rejects me and sends me away, I'll come home, and you can take care of me like you always have."

Elizabeth smiled though tears glistened in her eyes. "And like I always will," she promised.

Chapter 39

Mrs. Shandy had picked up Elizabeth earlier that morning; they were off to a celebratory luncheon for an occasional member of the book group who, long divorced, was getting married again. Petra had caught only a glimpse of the massive and fanciful pink hat perched atop Mrs. Shandy's head. The sight had made her smile.

When she had first arrived in town for the summer, Petra had asked Michael at Re-Turned if he would be willing to cast a professional eye over her mother's wedding dress and, if he thought it salvageable, recommend someone who could restore it to its original state. If the dress wasn't salvageable as a wedding dress, maybe then Michael could recommend someone who could repair and/or redesign the dress so that it could be worn in some other, less formal way. Michael had said he would be happy to help, and so Petra had finally made an appointment for the consultation.

Petra took the wedding dress from her closet where it had hung since she found it. If she had been being really careful, she probably should have laid it out somewhere, but the dress was in such a sorry state as it was, a bit of hanging wasn't going to make it that much worse.

Looking at the dress now, it occurred again to Petra that her mother might very well have treated it so carelessly if she was unhappy in her marriage. But she claimed she hadn't been unhappy in her marriage. Not really, not for a long time. So, when, exactly, had this dress wound up crumpled in a dusty cardboard box, left to the degradations of the attic and its four-legged or winged inhabitants? Petra might never know, and, in the end, it didn't really matter. Did it?

Draping the gown carefully over her right arm and supporting the skirt with her left, she made her way down the stairs, out of the house, and into her mother's car. With the dress in the backseat, a strange and vaguely creepy passenger, Petra drove to the vintage shop.

Michael was just saying good-bye to a customer when Petra arrived—"He spent five hundred dollars!" Michael exclaimed—and he ushered her into the back room of the shop. It was as neat as the proverbial pin, clear plastic containers stacked and labeled, clothing hung neatly on padded hangers, old hat boxes resting on shelves. In the center of the room stood a long folding table, and onto that Petra laid out her mother's wedding dress, circa 1982.

Michael frowned and began his examination. This included his circling the table on which the dress had been displayed several times, looking very closely at various details—sections of lace, seams, the hem—and turning the dress over to expose the back. After what seemed like an ominously long time, Petra cleared her throat.

"So, is it salvageable?" she asked.

Michael looked up from the dress and sighed. "Depends what you mean by that," he said. "Could it be sold in the state it's in? Unlikely, unless some very ambitious fashion student at Maine College of Art and Design wanted it for a thesis project. Can it be repaired? Maybe. Some of it. But this bit of lace is pretty torn up, it's got to go, and that stain is not going to come out, ever. Could the dress be taken apart and the bits incorporated into a new design? Sure. If someone is creative enough. Repairs or a redesign would all cost money though, and if your goal is to sell the dress for a profit, well, that might be quite a challenge. If, on the other hand, you're invested in saving the dress so that one day you or someone else in the family could wear it, that's another story. You could work with a designer to create something specific, something within your budget."

Michael looked at her expectantly, but Petra realized that she couldn't speak. She felt weepy, almost as if the dress were a living thing and her decision about its future was of life-or-death importance. Perhaps sensing her dismay, Michael offered her a seat on one of the two folding chairs in the room.

"Many years ago," he began, "back when I was still at MECA myself, I met a fellow student, a girl named Carly, who had inherited her great-grandmother's wedding dress, along with a cache of jewelry I would have given my eye teeth to own. When I expressed an interest in seeing it all, she invited me to her apartment. I was absolutely blown away by what she showed me. The dress was gorgeous. My friend thought Matilda, her great-grandmother, had been married in 1928 or so, but she wasn't sure. The dress had been perfectly preserved for all those years by a distant aunt or cousin, I don't remember. That person had died, and, somehow, the dress and jewelry had wound up being sent to Carly." Michael sighed. "Big mistake. This girl had no interest in the work of art she had been gifted. I don't know why someone like that was in art school unless she thought it was going to be easier than earning an academic degree. No soul. No sense of style. Anyway, I tried to make her understand what a treasure she had in her possession, but she didn't seem to care. And I was dirt poor at the time so I couldn't afford to buy any of Matilda's things. Last I heard of the affair, Carly had sold it all, every bit of Matilda's stuff, to some shady vintage dealer for next to nothing. The guy probably sold the lot on for a fortune and retired to the Costa del Sol, trust me."

Petra managed a smile. "That's a shame," she said. "When someone shows a lack of respect for the past. For a person who was once as alive as they are."

Michael nodded. "Another case sticks out in my mind," he said. "About ten years ago a woman came into my shop; it was then in a suburb of Boston. You could feel the tension emanating from her, the anger. She dumped a big plastic garbage bag at my feet and said she would take whatever I could give her for the contents. Then she told me she'd only recently learned that her mother, long dead, had repeatedly cheated on her father, and now the daughter, this angry woman, was determined to get rid of every vestige of the sham that was her parents' marriage, and that included an absolutely gorgeous peau de soie gown that had been designed specifically for her mother. Late 1950s style, lovely long sleeves coming to a *V* shape on the back of the hand. So elegant! I found myself trying to convince her not to be so hasty, to reconsider her decision to trash the dress and the other bits and bobs she'd stuffed into the bag, but her mind was made up. I paid her what the dress was worth to me—a considerable amount—and I'm happy to say it found a good home with a lovely young woman wanting to wear vintage for her wedding." Michael smiled kindly. "It's an emotional world in which we've chosen to work, Petra."

"I know. And I honestly don't know what I want to do about this dress," Petra admitted. "I'd still have to ask my mother's permission before I took any step." She thanked Michael sincerely for his efforts—not only in assessing the condition of the dress—and, dress draped over her arm, made her way back to the car.

As she drove back to Lavender Lane, Petra found herself daydreaming about her own wedding, should it ever come to pass. Would Christopher Ryan, her biological father, agree to walk her down the aisle? Would she want him to; would she want any man to, in effect, hand her over like a piece of property, father to husband? Would she have asked Hugh, her dad, to escort her, knowing his rather endearing old-fashioned attitude about such things?

More important, would she come to regret her choice of husband, cheat on him, divorce him? Would he betray her by running off with his personal assistant or the next-door neighbor? Or would they live happily ever after, if such a thing were ever possible, dying within hours of each other, like those elderly couples you sometimes heard about, married sixty or even seventy years, literally unable to breath without each other?

Tears came to Petra's eyes as she pulled into the driveway of her family home. She didn't want to think any more about couples just then, happy or miserable. Sometimes being on one's own was just simpler.

Sometimes, being on one's own was enough.

Chapter 40

Elizabeth never objected to a visit from one of her children but this was not normal behavior for Cam. How was she justifying leaving her family so often? What excuse was she offering to Ralph, and how did he feel about her frequent absences from home?

"I asked Cam again what Ralph had to say about my past," Elizabeth said softly to Petra—Cam was in the house if not with them in the kitchen—"and she told me she hadn't spoken to him yet. When I asked why, she said something vague about his being under a lot of pressure at work and not wanting to put another burden on his shoulders. I understand her concern for her husband. Still, I find it a bit odd. Or maybe I found her manner when telling me odd. That, and the fact that she's been spending so much time here this summer. Something feels wrong."

Petra said, "Oh. Oh?" She turned away and began to fiddle with the apples and bananas in the fruit bowl.

Elizabeth knew when her youngest child was hiding something. Petra wasn't by nature a liar, and, though she could keep a secret well enough (unlike Jess), it was clear that whatever secret she was keeping at the moment was troubling her.

"You know something I don't," Elizabeth said quietly.

Petra nodded. "But I promised Cam I wouldn't say anything."

"Fair enough. But if the knowledge is troubling you, you might consider sharing it with someone who—"

"Cam thinks Ralph's having an affair," Petra blurted, a look of relief on her face. "Or that's he's contemplating having one. Oh, damn. I really didn't mean to say anything!"

Elizabeth was truly surprised. "What makes her think that Ralph would cheat on her? He's so obviously honest!"

Petra explained Cam's concern about Ralph's long-ago girlfriend. "Lily's always been a friend to Cam. Honestly, she's not even sure Lily is aware of Ralph's—infatuation."

"Has Cam spoken to Ralph about this?" Elizabeth asked.

"No. I think she's afraid of what she'll hear."

Elizabeth shook her head. "My timing couldn't have been worse. Dropping the news of my affair on my children when they're going through crises of their own."

"Come on, Mom. There's never a perfect time to share difficult news. Besides, how were you to know Jess's business partner would back out? And I did promise Cam not to tell you about Ralph. I shouldn't have. I'm sorry. Don't say anything to Cam about it, please."

"I won't. And if she tells me of her own accord I'll pretend I knew nothing." Elizabeth sighed. "So many lies and half-truths and secrets."

"What have I missed?"

It was Cam. Her expression was open, not wary. Clearly, she didn't suspect her mother and sister of gossiping about her.

"Nothing much," Elizabeth said brightly. "What's that, my wedding album?"

Cam nodded. "I hope you don't mind. I mean, it was just there on a shelf in the den. I guess I was curious about—about Chris. I mean, my memories of him are so vague; I thought that maybe by looking at the pictures of him in here . . . I'm sorry. I'll take it back to the den."

"No," Elizabeth said quickly. "It's okay, really. Petra, are you okay with this?"

"Yes," she said, taking a seat at the table. "Frankly, I know I've seen the album before, but I can't really remember what Chris looked like. I guess I never had a reason to pay him any attention. Huh. What's even stranger is that since I've known the truth, that Chris is my father, I haven't once thought about searching for his picture."

"Maybe seeing his image now that you know who he is to you is the final step to it all becoming real, irrevocable. Maybe you weren't ready to do that until now." Cam smiled. "Just an idea."

Petra nodded. "And a good one."

"I haven't looked at the album since I was planning our thirtieth anniversary party," Elizabeth admitted. "I had fun choosing photos to display at the party, pictures of Hugh and me as children, then teens, then as young parents, right up to the present."

"But seeing these photos," Cam said, tapping the album, "can't have been much fun. I mean, you were celebrating thirty years with Dad and the other man with whom you'd fallen in love was right there in these pages."

"You would think so, but I was oddly unmoved by Chris's image," Elizabeth explained. "By that time in my life, no doubt partly as a self-protective measure, I had put all thoughts of him out of my daily consciousness. I don't mean that I had forgotten him and our brief time together. It's more as if the memories had moved deep into me, gone from my mind to someplace even more interior and protected. I don't mean that I actively repressed my memories. They just— Retreated to somewhere safe. Does any of that make sense?"

Petra nodded. "I think I understand."

"I'm not sure I do," Cam admitted with a small smile, finally opening the album.

On the first page, there was a classic photo of the wedding

invitation styled with the bride's bouquet. On the next page, there was a photo of the score and lyrics for "The Twelfth of Never," the song to which Hugh and Elizabeth had first danced as husband and wife. Elizabeth couldn't help but smile as she recalled Hugh's comment about the song. "It makes no sense," he had said. "How can there be a twelfth of never? Who comes up with this stuff?" She turned to the third page, and here was a portrait of the bride and groom with the maid of honor and the best man.

"They were so very different," Cam observed quietly. "Dad and Chris. Not just physically. You can tell they were, I don't know, opposites attracting somehow."

Elizabeth nodded. "That's very true," she said.

"Chris looks so serious," Petra observed. "Well, I guess he would. I guess he was sad."

"But happy for me and for Hugh," Elizabeth added firmly. "He was unselfish about the happiness of others. And I was happy that day. I won't deny that. I was young. There I was, the center of everyone's attention, being congratulated, kissed and hugged, and offered best wishes. Who could withstand all that good will? Anyway, I couldn't."

"What ever happened to your maid of honor?" Petra asked. "I don't remember her being around when I was growing up."

Elizabeth sighed. "Nothing stays the same, even the things you think will be stable forever. Harriet had been a good friend since grade school. There was no one else I wanted to be my witness that day. And she promised me that I'd be her maid of honor when the time came."

"So, what happened?" Cam asked.

"Less than a year after my marrying Hugh, Harriet moved to California on a whim—at least, it seemed that way to me—and I lost track of her. We communicated for a while through letters, phone calls, but then, I honestly don't know how or why it happened, our relationship just sort of petered out." Elizabeth shook her head. "It's one of my biggest regrets, not fighting for that friendship."

Petra put her hand on her mother's arm. "Maybe it wasn't worth fighting for," she suggested gently. "Maybe the friendship had simply run its course."

"Maybe you're right," Elizabeth admitted. "Anyway, what's done is done. Let's take a look at the rest of this album."

There were photographs of the bride and groom standing on their own outside the little stone church where they had been married, Elizabeth holding Hugh's arm. There were photographs of the bride's and groom's parents and other family members, taken at the reception hall. There were photographs of the guests dancing and of them sitting around tables decorated with pretty floral centerpieces. In every photograph, people were smiling. Elizabeth wondered now if Chris had been the only person not entirely swept up in the general feeling of goodwill and hopefulness that most weddings conjure. In truth, she had paid scant attention to him that day, even though just the day before they had shared a poignant moment. She had been too wrapped up in her role as bride, the center of attention, her head turned by all the compliments on her appearance, by all the congratulations she received for having found such a strong, handsome husband, someone who would take good care of her.

"What are you thinking, Mom?" Petra asked when they had perused the entire album.

"When Hugh died," Elizabeth said quietly, "I knew I needed to tell Chris, supposing he hadn't already learned of Hugh's illness and death. But I couldn't bring myself to do it, so I asked Mrs. Shandy—she had offered to be of help to me in whatever way necessary—to contact a few people who lived at a distance, people Hugh and I hadn't seen in a long time. Chris was one of those people. Mrs. Shandy sent each one a brief, handwritten note with information on how to make a donation to Hugh's favorite charity, the Disabled Veterans League. Later, I got a note from the charity telling me that Chris had made a very large donation in Hugh's memory. But Chris didn't send a personal note of condolence to me. I never knew what to make of that."

"But he didn't harbor hard feelings toward Dad for having, well, for having won out I guess," Cam said. "He wouldn't have contributed to the DVL if he had."

Elizabeth smiled. "It wasn't Chris's style to hold a grudge. I suspect he still loved his old friend, even though they hadn't been in contact for so long. And that distance had been kept for my sake."

"Did you ever make an attempt to contact Chris after Dad died?" Petra asked. "I mean, after some time had gone by?"

Elizabeth shook her head. "I wanted to but, again, I could never bring myself to act. I recognized that my need to reach out to Chris was entirely selfish. I had to ask myself what it was I wanted from him. Consolation? A declaration of undying love? Forgiveness? All were unfair, so I conquered the need."

"But how could you know for sure that he didn't want to hear from you?" Petra pressed. "Maybe after Dad died Chris really hoped that you would get in touch, in spite of his not sending a note of condolence. Maybe he was just leaving the decision up to you, like he had been doing all along."

Elizabeth simply nodded. She had thought through every possibility so many times.

"Were you afraid of what Chris might say to you?" Cam asked. "Afraid that he might refuse to see you or even to talk with you?"

"Yes," Elizabeth admitted. "And the thought of telling him about Petra terrified me. Because of course, if I was going to contact him, I'd have to tell him about his child."

"Did you and Dad ever go to couple's therapy?" Petra asked suddenly.

"I never asked him to," Elizabeth told her daughters, with

a laugh. "I knew he'd say no, tell me I was nutty for thinking something was wrong between us. Then he would have bought me flowers or jewelry or chocolates, genuinely sure the gift would magically lift my spirits and cure everything that ailed me."

"You assumed all that," Cam noted. To Elizabeth, her tone sounded slightly accusatory.

"Yes," Elizabeth admitted. "Because it had happened before, that pattern of appeasement, and at that point, before the affair, nothing about Hugh had changed. As his wife, I knew that for sure."

Elizabeth was beginning to feel worn out by her daughters' questioning. Still, she felt she owed them what truthful answers she could supply.

"Why didn't you ever ask for a divorce?" Cam went on. "I know divorce is an ugly thing and sometimes the process is so drawn-out, but . . ."

Elizabeth put her hand to her forehead. How to explain something she didn't fully understand herself, even after all these years?

"A divorce isn't really what I wanted," she began, but then shook her head. "Maybe it was. Honestly, I don't know what I wanted, like I told Petra the other day. I was living in the moment as much as it was possible for as long as it was possible."

"Was the affair a way of punishing Dad?" Petra asked. Her tone was not accusatory. "For his not really knowing you?"

"Absolutely not," Elizabeth said firmly. "You can be sure I asked myself that question over and over, and the answer was and still is the same. I might have felt stifled by your father, misunderstood, but I never felt the need to punish him. He did nothing wrong. He was just being Hugh. Maybe the fault was with me, after all, for not being able to appreciate him for the good, straightforward, loving person he was. Another woman, someone unlike me, might in the long run have been a far better match for him."

Cam put her hand over her mother's. "I doubt Dad would say that. He was head over heels in love with you. Everyone could see that."

Elizabeth smiled ruefully. "I know. And knowing that added terribly to the guilt. But I'm not asking for pity. I don't want or deserve it. Like I told you, it was only after Petra was born that I realized if I was unhappy in the marriage and with my own behaviors, it was up to me to make a change. I spoke up for myself, and after a bit of a struggle, Hugh listened." Elizabeth sighed. "I often wondered what would have happened if I'd spoken up long before that, if I had trusted myself and trusted Hugh enough to demand a change in our marriage. If I had spoken up before Chris and I were virtually thrust together, we might never have acted on our love for each other. We might never have betrayed Hugh." Elizabeth reached out to take Petra's hand. "But then I might never have had my third child. And that is unimaginable."

"What-ifs can be dangerous if pursued too far," Petra said quietly.

Cam nodded. "But tell me one person who doesn't indulge in what-ifs."

Elizabeth rose from the table. "How about I open a bottle of wine and put out some cheeses and the baguette I bought earlier at Chez Claudine? We could sit out in the backyard. And maybe leave the past in the past for an hour or two."

"That's a wonderful idea, Mom," Cam said. "I'll grab the glasses."

Petra nodded. "I agree. Most times, the present is the best place to be." In spite, she added silently, of the undeniably compelling allure of the past.

Chapter 41

Petra was alone in the house. Her mother was at the library, where she had been volunteering for as long as Petra could remember. Petra had waited until the house was empty before she sat down to compose a message to the man who, along with her mother, had given her life. It took her some time to write the few simple lines.

> *Dear Mr. Ryan,*
> *I'm the youngest daughter of your old friends Hugh and*
> *Elizabeth Quirk. Though I never met you, I know that you*
> *were important to my family. I wonder if we could talk.*
> *E-mail or Zoom or phone would be fine.*
> *Thank you.*
> *Sincerely,*
> *Petra Quirk*

It was bland and maybe not tantalizing enough to encourage a positive response. But Petra wasn't interested in teasing Chris Ryan by hinting at another, darker reason behind her stated request to speak to an old family friend.

The words would do. She hit *send* and leaned back in her

chair. She had taken the first step—looking at the photos of Chris at her parents' wedding had indeed been a bit of a catalyst—but toward what end, she didn't and couldn't know. All she could do now was wait. Waiting wasn't always easy.

A good, vigorous walk was what Petra needed, so she left the house and headed into town, with no particular destination in mind. For a moment, she considered stopping into Re-Turned to say hello to Michael, but she quickly realized she wasn't in the mood to chat with anyone. Besides, after their last conversation about the fate of old wedding dresses, Petra was a bit wary about accidentally opening up a topic that would make her feel sad again.

Today, with the weather hot and humid, the walk into downtown Eliot's Corner felt long and wearing. But rather than turn back, Petra kept going. By the time she reached Main Street, she felt pretty wilted and decided to stop at Chez Claudine for a bottle of water. On the way to the café Petra found herself walking not far behind a middle-aged man and woman. They didn't look like a couple—it wasn't hard to tell that sort of thing; they might, instead, be colleagues on their lunch break—and suddenly, it seemed to Petra from the way their heads were tilted toward each other, and the way the woman seemed to be nodding in a meaningful way, that they were gossiping about someone. A colleague, a neighbor, a mutual friend, it could be anyone.

Petra hurried around the pair. Busybodies. She hadn't heard that term used in a while; clearly it had been lurking in her mind. She wondered if anyone in Eliot's Corner had suspected her mother of having an affair. But if anyone had, how likely was it that he or she wouldn't have spoken? People with suspicious minds needed to share their suspicions about the behavior of others for reasons they would claim were altruistic but that were really mean-spirited and self-righteous. And good, old-fashioned gossips came in all shapes and sizes; it was silly not to admit that men as well as women could be gossips, the young as well as the old.

In having sent a message to Christopher Ryan, her mother's erstwhile lover, Petra realized she had taken a terrible risk. True, she hadn't revealed anything of importance in her e-mail, but surely a hacker invading the private correspondence of Christopher Ryan could possibly make a vital connection between Petra Quirk, Elizabeth Quirk, and the famous man. No means of communication was entirely safe or private. Suddenly, Petra realized that she had told a lie by claiming to be the youngest child of Elizabeth and Hugh Quirk. Well, it wasn't entirely a lie, but Petra hated to lie.

Another disturbing thought clouded Petra's mind as she approached the café. It could be argued that her mother had been supremely selfish, wanting both Hugh and Christopher in her life, wanting what each could give her without thought as to what it cost the men. Petra felt a surge of anger toward her mother. She thought she had conquered that unhappy emotion. She knew that her mother felt genuine guilt for her duplicitous behavior. A guilty conscience was punishment enough.

Petra opened the door to Chez Claudine, enormously grateful for whoever had invented air conditioning. She bought a bottle of cold water and gulped it greedily. The vigorous walk she had hoped might distract her had failed; the intense heat and heavy humidity had probably even contributed to her suspicious and paranoid mood.

Somewhat refreshed, Petra left the café and headed back to Lavender Lane. A nap in her childhood bed seemed like a very good idea. She would put her phone in silent mode. She couldn't allow herself to become obsessed with checking for a message from Christopher Ryan, a message that might never come.

A message for which Petra might regret ever having asked.

Chapter 42

Elizabeth and her friend Mrs. Shandy had been doing volunteer work at the Eliot's Corner public library for the past fifteen years or so. Once upon a time their services would have been paid, their work performed by high school kids in need of pocket money. But kids didn't seem to want to take an afterschool job at the library for a tiny salary when they could make a heck of a lot more money working at one of the clam shacks out by the water or at the midsized retail stores a few towns inland.

At the moment, the two women were filling wheeled carts with books to be re-stacked, grouping volumes by subject and call number.

"Do you remember learning the Dewey decimal system when you were young?" Elizabeth asked, as she placed a general history of the English Civil War next to a study of the Plantagenet dynasty.

"Most certainly. I thought it was a brilliant. I suspect I was the only child in my class who did."

"I learned it on the job," Elizabeth said. "I worked for a summer in high school at my local library. It was a dream come true.

Being surrounded by all those books! The temptation to slip behind a stack and read was strong, but I managed all right. At least, I wasn't fired."

"Elizabeth. Mrs. Shandy. I knew we could rely on you to help out."

Before Elizabeth could respond with a word or a nod, Jane Stodden, the head librarian, sighed grandly and went on. "It's the women with husbands you can't rely on. Husbands always demand precedence, especially when it comes to activities that don't directly benefit them in some way. If Mr. So-and-So finds it inconvenient that Mrs. So-and-So spend two or three hours volunteering at the library—after all, who will make his lunch?—then Mrs. So-and-So stays at home." Jane shook her head, and as she turned to walk away, she added, wearily, "It's the way it's always been."

Elizabeth looked to her friend. "Um," she said, "what are we to make of that?"

Mrs. Shandy smiled. "Besides the fact that Jane has never been married and therefore doesn't entirely understand the give-and-take of a domestic relationship?"

"But she is right to some extent. I mean, there are still plenty of husbands—mostly over a certain age—who find it difficult to accept that their own needs aren't always primary."

Mrs. Shandy looked closely at Elizabeth. "We've known each other a long time, haven't we?" she said. "First as colleagues and then as friends."

Elizabeth nodded. "Yes. We have. Forgive me if I don't count up the years."

In a lower voice, Mrs. Shandy went on. "I'm sure you've wondered why I refer to myself as Mrs. Shandy when, clearly, there's no Mr. Shandy at hand, and I've never made any mention of such a person, not once in all the years you've known me."

"I have wondered," Elizabeth admitted, more than a little

surprised that her friend had introduced the topic. "But I figured you would tell me about Mr. Shandy at some point if you wanted to."

"Like if he ever existed? Come now, I'm sure you've considered that I might have invented a husband along the way for my own interesting reasons."

Elizabeth nodded. "I've entertained the possibility, yes. For one, the title 'Mrs.' still carries some weight socially; right or wrong, it gives a woman a bit of standing. And when no husband is at hand it suggests widowhood, which always has an air of dignity, or seriousness. Of course, it could also suggest divorce but somehow . . . No. I've never thought that you were divorced. Don't ask me why. Just a feeling."

"Well, you're right there," Mrs. Shandy said. "I'm not divorced. I'm a widow."

Elizabeth was truly surprised, though the possibility had occurred to her often enough. "I'm sorry," she said.

"Thank you," Mrs. Shandy replied brusquely. "The sad truth is that my husband died on our honeymoon. There was a boating accident. We'd dated for only three months before running off to marry, an act that infuriated my parents and wound up alienating them forever. I was all of seventeen at the time—Ross all of nineteen—a bit of a hippy, and totally on my own. Of course, I contacted my parents after Ross died. I suppose I thought they'd feel bad for me and tell me I could come home, not that going home would have been such a smart idea. Well, they responded promptly and made it clear that I'd let them down, betrayed my faith—rather, that I'd betrayed their faith—and that I was on my own."

"So much for Christian charity," Elizabeth said with a frown, "assuming they were Christians. Or for familial bonds. I'm sorry."

Mrs. Shandy nodded. "I'm sorry, too, or, I was. A lot of time has passed. You see, my family were members of a small and very strict religious sect that had adopted some aspects of Catholicism and some aspects of the more extreme forms of evangelism. I was only about eight or nine when I realized it was all hooey—at least, for my purposes. But it wasn't until I met Ross that I found the courage to get out. Not that I used him as a way to escape; I truly loved him, and he loved me."

"I believe you. What a sad story. Oh," Elizabeth exclaimed. "Something just occurred to me. Your first name. You never told me how you came to be called Foundation, but now I think I have a notion. . . ."

Mrs. Shandy laughed. "You've hit upon the truth. The sect my parents belonged to favored giving babies odd and ponderous names, sure to cause bullying by outsiders. My father chose to name me Foundation as a reference to Jesus's naming Peter as the rock upon which he would build a church. Why they couldn't call me Petra or even Peter—I could have dealt with that—I'll never know except that they were, as you will have gathered, strange people."

The irony—was that the right word?—wasn't lost on Elizabeth, who had chosen Petra as a silent nod to Chris's confirmation name: Peter. The apostle upon whom Jesus declared he would build the church.

"You could have left your first name behind," Elizabeth noted.

"It turned out that I couldn't. It had stuck. So much of what I'd been taught, so much of my childhood didn't stick, thankfully, but my name did. And Shandy was really Ross's last name; I kept that and happily."

Elizabeth put her hand on her friend's arm. "Thank you for telling me all this."

"I don't know why exactly I did!" Mrs. Shandy declared. "After all these years. I hope I'm not getting batty in my old age."

Elizabeth laughed. "You're not old nor are you in the least bit batty. And by the way, there's no need to ask for my silence. You have my word I'll say nothing to anyone."

"Thank you. I suppose in some ways it wouldn't matter if

people knew, but I have grown very fond of my mystique, if you like. I often wonder what fantastical stories the good people of Eliot's Corner have told themselves about me."

"I honestly haven't heard a one. Though as I said, I've always wondered about Mr. Shandy's whereabouts. It's natural to be curious about one's friends and neighbors."

"Curious or obsessed. Well, I'm off to tidy up the children's room now. The staff is supposed to be teaching the children how to bring the books to the librarian when they're done with them, not just leave them lying around on the floor and who knows where. But the lesson doesn't seem to have taken."

Left on her own, Elizabeth continued to load her cart with books—literature here; social science there—though what she was really thinking about was her own massive secret and the impossibility of her ever revealing it to anyone in Eliot's Corner, even Mrs. Shandy. Like her friend, Elizabeth wondered if she was going batty, telling her children something about her past that was so potentially damaging.

But it was too late for regrets or retractions. And honestly, her family hadn't fallen apart or exploded upon the revelation of her affair.

At least, they hadn't yet.

Chapter 43

Petra was propped against the pillows on her bed, having a FaceTime chat with Cam. She didn't particularly like video calls or whatever they were called now; in spite of her youth she had never fully absorbed the dynamics of the current media/tech culture. Sometimes she was teased for her lack of interest and proficiency, called a Luddite, even irresponsible. Not that she cared.

"Where's Ralph?" she asked now. Cam was at her kitchen table, wearing a plain blue T-shirt, her hair tied back.

"At his mom's, with the kids. What's going on in Eliot's Corner?"

"The same," Petra replied. She continued to keep her silence regarding the fact that she had reached out to Christopher Ryan. If he failed to respond, or, if his response was dismissive, she might never let her sisters know what she had attempted.

Cam frowned. "Have you seen Jess? I left her a voice mail the other day and sent her two texts, but once again, she's radio silent. I hate when she gets like this."

"I'm sure she's okay," Petra said automatically, but was she sure? "I'll call her again this afternoon. Or maybe I'll drop by her apartment this evening."

Cam laughed. "I wouldn't risk a pop-in. Not with Jess."

"You're right. I might not make it out alive. Look, I've been thinking about the Ralph and Lily situation."

"Sorry," Cam said. "I mean, I don't want my problems to engulf you."

"They're not engulfing me," Petra assured her. "But . . . You said before that you suspect Ralph is in love with Lily but that you believe he still loves you. I've been wondering. Don't you think it might be better in the long run to have someone love you and not be crazy mad about you? I'm beginning to think that crazy mad passion never holds up in the end. It certainly doesn't in all the great stories. Look at *Wuthering Heights*. Passion leads to misery and madness. Or death. Or separation, like it did with Mom and Chris."

"I think anyone in a serious, committed relationship," Cam responded, "will tell you that a bit of both mad passion and loving concern is what she—or he or they—wants."

"Of course," Petra said quickly. "I didn't mean . . . Honestly, I don't know what I meant. I have so little personal experience with relationships."

"You might be lucky in that." Cam sighed. "I don't know. It worries me that Ralph might look at Lily and see life with her as an escape from the life he's got with me, a what-might-have-been if he hadn't married and had three kids. I mean, Lily's life is so carefree compared to ours. She's got a glamorous career, no dependents of any sort, a gorgeous condo kept in perfect shape by an army of house cleaners." Cam poked at her midsection. "And no mommy body."

Petra felt her blood begin to boil. "Well, if that's the case," she said, "Ralph's not really in love with Lily, he's in love with his idea of her, which is insulting to both you and Lily, really. He's acting like the sort of man who objectifies women rather than accepting each woman as an individual with her own unique qualities. Because there's no way Lily's life is carefree. No one's life is, no matter how cushy it seems from the outside."

Cam seemed to reflect on that for a moment. "I've never thought of Ralph as a misogynist," she said finally, "or as a guy who objectifies women, though maybe that's the same thing. But maybe there's a trace of that—I don't even know what to call it; prejudice?—in every man, no matter how intelligent and sensitive he is."

"I don't know the answer to that, either," Petra admitted. "Look, Cam, I just wish you would talk to Ralph!"

"I know I should, but he could easily lie, deny he has feelings for Lily. Or, maybe worse, he might tell me a very ugly truth. He might say that he's fallen back in love with her, or that he never actually stopped being in love with her, even when he married me. What am I supposed to do with that sort of information? Ignore it? Not possible."

Petra sighed; she was beginning to feel as if they were going in a very silly circle. "I get what you're saying, Cam, I really do. You're afraid. Believe me, I know all about being afraid! But is it really better not to know the truth? To wait until he comes clean to you, which could take months? You're already worn down by the situation. Just talk to him!"

Her sister suddenly looked guilty, or maybe it was ashamed. "I haven't told you this yet," she said, "but Ralph's mother shares my suspicions. I mean, she is a bit nutty, but she's not stupid or blind. And she knows her son."

"She said something to you?" Petra asked. She had met Mrs. Perry a few times over the years and found her formidable, not at all above butting in on her son's personal life. As for nutty, well, Petra had thought she was kind of fun, a true individual.

"No," Cam admitted. "But she's given me enough meaningful, thoughtful looks when we're all together to make me certain she knows something's going on." Cam paused. "Like at the party we gave back in April for Beth's birthday. We both saw Ralph practically drooling over Lily. It was embarrassing. I'm sure we weren't the only ones who noticed. I dread being questioned by one of my friends or neighbors, you know, the so-called well-meaning ones, who are really hoping to hear some story of marital misery so they can feel better about their own not-so-great domestic situation."

"I'm sorry you feel so exposed," Petra said. "Truly, I am. But Ralph acting goofy when Lily is around isn't necessarily proof of an affair." Petra considered before going on. "It sounds to me like just silly flirting, stupid behavior at worst, that's all. If something really were going on, wouldn't Ralph and Lily want to keep things super quiet? Why would they be so blatant?"

Cam squirmed in her seat. "I don't know the answer to that question, but there's something else I haven't told you. Only yesterday Ralph mentioned in an overly casual, offhand way that Lily spent last Saturday afternoon with him and the kids at the children's museum in Boston."

Petra felt slightly sick to her stomach. "Whose idea was that? I mean, did Ralph invite her to meet them or did she instigate the outing, suggest Ralph and the kids come down to Boston for the day?"

"I'm not sure. I didn't have the heart or the nerve to ask." Cam laughed unhappily. "What really hurt was that Beth never told me they had gone to the museum. She always tells me everything. Why keep that a secret? I know she adores Lily; she always babbles on about how cool she is. So why the silence? Did Ralph tell her not to tell me?"

"I'm sorry, Cam," Petra said, aware she was speaking a bit too loudly, "but this is getting ridiculous. You have to have it out with Ralph. If your children are being dragged into a subterfuge, then now is the time to act. I know you don't want to cause them harm."

"Of course, I don't," Cam said. "And I will act. I promise. But in the meantime, I'm bringing Beth with me to Eliot's Corner this weekend. To keep her away from Lily. Not that Ralph will have time to fool around. His sister and her husband and their baby are visiting. They should keep him safely occupied."

Fool around? Safely occupied? Petra realized that she almost felt more distressed by the situation in her sister's marriage than she had upon learning that the man she thought was her father was not in biological fact her father.

"Do I have a right to ask Ralph not to see Lily without my being there?" Cam said suddenly.

"Absolutely!" Petra declared. "Look, do you still think Lily can't tell that Ralph is into her?"

"I don't know. I mean, I can't see how she could miss his schoolboy devotion. Unless she's so used to men falling at her feet it doesn't really register! But if she is aware that Ralph has feelings for her, she should be adult enough to stay away from us for a while, give Ralph's obsession time to die out. She would know that his behavior is hurting me."

"I agree that it would be nice if Lily backed away for a while," Petra admitted, "give you and Ralph some time to breathe. But it's not her marriage at stake, so it's not her responsibility to fix things."

Cam sighed. "I know. Honestly, before Ralph's infatuation I enjoyed spending time with Lily. We've always got on pretty well, and like I said, Beth adores her. She's the glamorous aunt figure, the one who wears prettier clothes than Mommy and always shows up with a gift, usually something Mommy said no to, like a ridiculously expensive pack of glittery barrettes."

"There's nothing wrong with having that sort of person in your life when you're a kid," Petra noted. "In a way, Chris played that role for you and Jess, didn't he? Different from Dad. Traveling all over the world and bringing back interesting or exotic souvenirs for you."

"I hadn't thought about it that way, but you're right." Suddenly, a look of horror came to Cam's face. "Oh, Lord, and Chris had an affair with Mom!"

Petra put her hands to her head. "I'm such an idiot!" she cried. "I didn't mean to make that comparison at all! I'm so sorry, Cam. Whatever's going on, I bet that in the end it will all be much ado about nothing."

"I certainly hope so. In spite of what I told Jess, learning that Mom and Dad's supposedly rock-solid marriage wasn't always so rock-solid has made me feel a bit dispirited all around."

Petra didn't know what else to say; she was afraid anything but a generic farewell might cause her sister more upset. When Cam had signed off, Petra put her laptop aside and scrunched down on the bed. She felt worn out. This latest conversation with Cam, coming as it had so soon after her sending an e-mail to Christopher Ryan, had really taken a toll on her spirit.

Suddenly, Petra rolled over and reached for her copy of *The Wild Swans*, that cherished childhood book.

Within moments, she was in another world.

Chapter 44

Elizabeth had finally gotten her wish of a visit from her grand-daughter and namesake, but at the moment, Beth had little time for her family. There was a gentle tide in which to wade, shells and stones to be collected, and other kids to make friends with, all more appealing than sitting with the grown-ups and listening to their boring talk.

"Getting her a neon-colored bathing suit was a smart idea," Elizabeth commented. "She's impossible to miss, even among the other children."

Cam smiled. "Beth was actually the one who wanted a neon yellow suit. She has such a love of bright colors. But yes, it makes it easy to keep an eye on her."

The women were seated on folding chairs. A beach blanket that had been in use since Elizabeth's children were small was spread out at their feet. A cooler loaded with bottled water, sliced fruit, and sandwiches—ham and cheese with lettuce and tomato for the adults; peanut butter and grape jelly for Beth—sat nearby.

Petra had heard of a new flea market a few towns away and had taken Elizabeth's car—with her blessing, of course. She had said she was annoyed with herself for neglecting the search for vintage goods to sell on Past Perfect's website. Elizabeth felt certain that Petra's neglect of her online business was at least partly due to her preoccupation with Christopher Ryan. That was natural enough.

"Have you spoken with Jess lately?" Cam asked, squeezing more sunblock onto her thighs.

"She's still being elusive," Elizabeth said with a sigh. "I don't know what she's up to. But I do know it's futile to press her to talk. It would only send her farther away."

"You're right there. She's as stubborn as Dad was. If he didn't want to do something, he simply wasn't going to do it." Cam paused before going on. "You know, Chris Ryan brought me a little wooden wishing well from one of his European trips. He had a gift for Jess, too, but I can't remember what it was. I was enchanted with my wishing well. I've kept it all these years. Now, it belongs to Beth. She thinks it's magic, that a fairy lives inside."

Elizabeth nodded. She thought of the lavender agate pendant Chris had given her after that same trip, but she chose not to mention it to Cam. Elizabeth wasn't sure why, but she felt the need to keep the origin—the existence—of that pendant a secret between herself and Petra. Another secret. When would all the subterfuge end?

"Was Petra's conception really an accident?"

Elizabeth drew in her breath sharply. "My, that was abrupt."

"Sorry," Cam said hastily. "Forget I asked."

"No, it's all right. But I can't honestly answer that question. I couldn't back then, and I still can't now. Was I careless somehow? Maybe. But I didn't ever consciously want Chris's child, at least, not unless we were legitimately together. I honestly didn't set out to get pregnant. That would have been madness. And then when it happened . . . Well, I told you. I panicked. The joy didn't come until later."

"Kids change everything. In fact . . ." Cam sighed. "Ralph has developed a major crush on his old girlfriend Lily. Or maybe he's fallen in love with her again. I don't know. All I do know is that it's not right, and the situation is driving me crazy."

Elizabeth kept her expression neutral. She was glad her daughter had finally opened up to her. She had wondered if Cam had been hesitant to talk about Ralph's behavior because of its surface similarity to her mother's situation. A spouse's failure—or possible failure—to keep the marriage vow.

"I'm surprised," Elizabeth said carefully. "Ralph has always struck me as a pretty upstanding man. And I've met Lily on several occasions, at your wedding for one. She seems like a solid person. She might have a so-called glamorous career and appear to some as being a free-spirit—something most single people are accused of being, no matter the reality—but I don't see her as what used to be called a homewrecker."

"Neither did I," Cam admitted. "Until now. The thing is, Mom, Ralph really wasn't sold on the idea of having more kids after Beth. I pretty much forced the issue. Now I can't help but wonder if Ralph's infatuation—pray that's all it is!—with Lily is a result of my having insisted on our having another baby. Which turned out to be two babies."

Elizabeth felt a tiny shiver of fear pass through her. She had thought often enough of how an unwanted child—or children— could become the focus of larger feelings of resentment. She would be lying to herself if she claimed she hadn't considered what might have happened to Petra if Hugh, in spite of being a good person, had found out she was the child of another man.

"There's no tactful way to put this," she began, "so I'm just going to say it. Has Ralph ever been neglectful of the boys? Has he ever hurt them?"

"Not at all," Cam cried. "No way. Ralph is a doting father. I trust him completely with their care. If I didn't I wouldn't be spending so much time with you and Petra and Jess this summer. I feel guilty about that, of course. Being away from my family. But . . ."

"In order to take proper care of others you have to first take proper care of yourself," Elizabeth said firmly. "Not an easy lesson to learn. But I have to wonder if being apart from Ralph at this time when you're worried that his relationship with Lily is or is becoming inappropriate is the wisest thing for you—or for your marriage."

Cam didn't reply for a long moment. "You mean," she said finally, in a subdued way, "am I pushing them together by being away?"

Elizabeth recalled how Hugh had seemed to be doing just that in the long-ago summer of 1991. "It's just a suggestion," she said mildly.

Cam sighed deeply. "Oh, I don't know. I never dreamed I would find myself in this sort of situation. I feel totally ill-equipped to handle it. Do I keep ignoring it, go back home and stay there, say nothing, keep smiling? Confront Ralph or Lily?"

"Not Lily," Elizabeth said firmly. "Ultimately, this is between you and your husband."

"You believe me when I say there's something going on? You don't think I'm imagining things or overreacting?"

Elizabeth shook her head. "Not you. You're not the sort to create drama where there is none. That said, I really don't think Ralph is having an affair. He might be contemplating the idea or he might be unhappy about something other than the marriage, maybe something going on at work, and for some reason he's finding it easier to escape from his unhappiness with Lily than with you. Neither scenario is ideal, of course."

"I know," Cam said wearily. "And before you ask, I've been scrupulous about keeping my suspicions and my . . . well, my annoyance and anger with Lily to myself when I'm home. Beth adores her. I don't want to damage or put an end to that relationship unless I absolutely have to at some point. Of course, it really bothers me that Beth never mentioned that Lily joined them at the children's museum in Boston one Saturday when I was in Eliot's Corner. I had to hear about that from Ralph, who mentioned it in a very awkward, overly casual way."

"That would bother me, too," Elizabeth admitted. "Children are sensitive to everything in their environment. And little girls can be uncanny in their ability to pick up on other people's feelings, even if they don't understand those feelings. If Beth is spending a lot of time with Ralph and Lily, she's undoubtedly made note—in a six-year-old sort of way—of her father's behavior with Lily and compared it to his behavior when he's with you. I'm afraid that's certain, though it needn't become a problem as long as you take action soon."

Cam was silent for a long moment. When she spoke, it was to change the subject. "Enough about me and my woes," she said. "How are you feeling, Mom? What are you thinking? Everything has changed now in a way, hasn't it?"

"I don't know if everything has changed," Elizabeth replied. "What happened between Chris and me, happened. All that's different is that now you and Jess and Petra know about it. Okay, and that knowledge has put into doubt what you thought you knew or believed about your father and me." Elizabeth sighed. "I guess you're right after all. Everything *has* changed."

"No. I was wrong. Our love for you and Dad hasn't altered," Cam said firmly. "That's a fact."

"You can speak for Jess?"

"No. But, I believe she still loves you. She's just not the most . . . receptive person in the world. It's like she's a mass of sharp edges and flat surfaces. It takes time for things to find a way inside and through to her heart." Cam laughed. "A poet I'll never be!"

Elizabeth smiled gratefully. "I know what you mean, though."

Beth suddenly broke away from the group of children she had been playing with at the water's edge and came running toward them across the sand.

"Grandma!" she cried excitedly when she reached her family. "Look what I found!"

Elizabeth leaned forward to examine the object her granddaughter held in her hand. "Oh, wow. That's a beautiful shell."

"And there's no chips, look. It's perfect!" Beth turned to her mother. "Here, Mommy. It's a gift for you."

Cam accepted the shell and kissed her daughter on the forehead. "Thank you," she said, with a hint of tears in her voice. "It's a very special gift, and I'll treasure it always."

"I'll go find one for you, Grandma, okay?"

Before Elizabeth could reply, Beth was dashing back toward the water's edge. Elizabeth reached for her daughter's hand; Cam readily accepted her mother's touch.

Chapter 45

Petra was stretched out on her bed, staring at the ceiling upon which ages ago her father—Hugh—had helped her to paste a sprinkling of glow-in-the-dark stars. The stars no longer glowed and had taken on a dingy look, but they were still stars.

All things changed, if only a little. Nothing stayed entirely the same. Things darkened or brightened. They began to glow or they failed to glow. Like her mother's wedding dress, they remained intact but in tatters, whole but torn.

Much like Petra was feeling right then. In fact, it seemed that feeling disoriented, whole but torn, had become her basic state lately. Take the day before, for example. With a certain level of excitement, she had borrowed her mother's car and set out for a highly regarded flea market. But the moment she stepped from the car in the dusty lot filled with pickups and vans of all sizes and in all sorts of conditions, she had felt intensely dispirited. The sensation was unprecedented. Still, she had made herself walk up and down the aisles of tables and booths displaying everything from rusty old farm tools to vintage Austrian crystal jewelry, from colored prints torn from books to tableware dating from the 1940s, but absolutely nothing had called out to her, not even the sorts of items that usually caught her keen attention, like caftan-style dresses, and fringed suede handbags from the seventies, and bold silver or genuine Bakelite jewelry.

Petra wasn't about to give up on flea markets entirely, but she was bothered by her apathetic response to the stimuli that she usually found so enjoyable, even fascinating. Did her uncharacteristic reaction and general sense of things being "off" have anything to do with the fact of her just having learned that the man who raised her was not her biological father? Of course, it did. No question about it.

Tired of staring at the faded stars on her ceiling, Petra got off the bed, went across the room to her small desk, and opened her e-mail account. And there it was, a message from Christopher Ryan. Petra felt her heart begin to beat faster and realized she felt afraid. Maybe she didn't want to read the e-mail. There was nothing to stop her from deleting it and convincing herself—maybe—that the message had never been delivered to her mailbox. Or she could simply put off opening the e-mail until she felt calmer. She was in control. Nobody was forcing her to act.

And then she opened the e-mail.

Dear Petra, it began, *How good to hear from you. I think often of your parents with great fondness. Time and circumstance often draw people apart, but they can be brought back together in memory. I am happy to talk with you. In fact, I can easily come to Maine. There's a bed-and-breakfast I have stayed at frequently, not far from Eliot's Corner, in Lark's Circle. Would two or three days from now work for you?*

I'll await your word.

Sincerely, Chris.

Not Mr. Ryan, as Petra had addressed her own message. Chris. Her father. One of them.

This was it; what she had wanted was happening—if she still wanted it. Petra's heart continued to pound uncomfortably. She hadn't considered the possibility that he would respond so quickly, and even so eagerly. It had to mean something positive. That was good. But . . .

She would reply now. The message had been sent only two hours ago. Christopher Ryan might be awaiting her response to his e-mail as tensely as she had been awaiting his response to hers.

What to say? Best, she thought, to keep it simple.

Dear Mr. Ryan. She still didn't feel comfortable addressing him by his Christian name. *Thank you for replying. If you let me know a time and location where we can meet, perhaps at a café near your bed-and-breakfast, I'll be there. Thank you. Petra*

She closed the laptop and wondered for a moment why she hadn't written "Love, Petra," or "Sincerely, Petra." Well, what was done was done.

Petra wanted to let her mother know immediately, and found her in in the garage stowing a few gardening tools in a cabinet Hugh had built for that purpose.

"I heard back from Chris," she said without preamble. "He said he'd be glad to talk with me. In fact, he offered to come to Maine to meet me in person."

Elizabeth startled and took a step backwards. "He did? Oh. Good. I mean, I knew he wouldn't turn you away."

Petra looked closely at her mother and saw on her face a mix of emotions. Fear. Anxiety. Relief. "He's coming to meet me even though he doesn't know I'm his daughter. Does that strike you as, I don't know, strange?"

"He might well suspect the truth," Elizabeth said after a moment. "If Cam or Jess had contacted him out of the blue he might simply assume they had been remembering the days when he was a visitor to this house. But you, who's never met him . . ."

Petra nodded. "Maybe it's good he suspects that I'm his child or, at least, that I know about the two of you. It will come as less of a shock when I confirm the fact."

"Yes. That's true."

Petra suddenly felt dizzy, almost sick. Chris's positive response to her e-mail hadn't come as a total surprise; Elizabeth had said several times she felt sure Chris wouldn't turn Petra away, and Petra herself had felt fairly certain of the same. Still, Petra thought, it was fact now. Christopher Ryan, her biological father, was going to meet with her. There was no going back. Sure, Petra could change her mind, decide not to engage with her biological father, but she and her mother would forever know that contact had been made, that Chris had been amenable—and that something good might have been lost by not responding in kind.

"I'm not going to tell Cam and Jess right away," she told her mother. "If things don't go well with Chris, maybe I'll never tell them."

Elizabeth smiled wanly. "Be careful of creating more secrets."

"Secrets are inevitable, though, aren't they?" Petra asked. "We all need to have secrets. And sometimes they're necessary to protect a person."

"Still, secret keeping is messy."

Petra went over to her mother and put her arm around her shoulders.

"It will be okay, Mom, won't it?" she asked. It was not what she had meant to say. She had meant to say: "It will be okay, Mom. Don't worry."

"Yes," her mother whispered. "I promise it will be okay."

Chapter 46

Elizabeth closed the book on her lap. It was no use. The ability to concentrate had flown before she had read to the bottom of page one of what was touted by all of the reviews she had read to be an excellent novel.

She couldn't concentrate because she was unhappy. And she was unhappy because her children were unhappy.

There were Cam and Ralph, locked in an absurd dynamic that was only going to get worse before it was—hopefully—going to get better.

There were Petra and Christopher Ryan, in an unprecedented situation fraught with a potentially wide range of emotional issues.

And there were Jess and Eddie, a strange match from the start and becoming stranger all the time as Jess continued to keep her partner from her family and to verbally dismiss him as useless and irrelevant. Add to that, Jess's sudden loss of a business partner, which seemed to have sent her into an unprecedented mood of despair and self-doubt.

It was difficult for Elizabeth not to think that she had failed her children. It was a fact that relationships could go off the rails for all sorts of reasons and in what appeared to be the steadiest unions. That two of her daughters were experiencing relationship woes didn't mean that Elizabeth was to blame. As for Petra's familial challenge, well, that *was* down to her mother's actions. There was no escaping that truth.

With a sigh, Elizabeth reached for her laptop, which was sitting next to her on the couch.

She had been putting off starting an informal job search, nothing too serious, but now might be the time to make a foray. She would spend some time on Monster.com—that had been Jess's suggestion—looking for local part-time positions that might suit her. But no sooner had she logged on to the website than she began to feel disheartened. Nothing would replace the satisfaction she got from teaching a group of children, from watching them grow over the course of the school year, from guiding them through failures and successes, sending them off into the summer months with a sense of a job well done. Of course, there had been the occasional child who had failed to learn or to engage with the subject, his fellow students, or his teacher—but at least Elizabeth knew for sure that she had tried her best to meet that student's needs.

She supposed she could consider becoming a private tutor. That would be satisfying to some extent, certainly, but a private home would lack the energy of a school environment that had so inspired Elizabeth.

She shut her laptop with a sigh of frustration. She didn't have to work; she was financially secure and used to living within a budget. She didn't need to be considering work as a hostess in a restaurant or as a salesperson in a nice clothing shop, or even a job as a private tutor. Still, at some point she would need to find a new focus for the future.

Could that focus be Christopher Ryan?

Elizabeth shuddered. No. Absolutely not. She could not allow herself to rely on someone else to give her a new life. She had done that very thing when she married Hugh, and she had come too far since then, learned and achieved too much independence to revert to the role of helpless female, looking to a man to mold a life for her.

But there was love . . . And love was often worth a major sacrifice of self. At the age of sixty-two, she could honestly say that she had accomplished a good amount, achieved many things for which she felt proud. Would it be so horrible at this point in her life to put all of her energy into love for another human being, for Christopher Ryan? Would that really be a sacrifice of self at this point in her life, as it most definitely had been when she married Hugh right out of college?

Assuming, of course, that the other human being didn't loathe and despise her for having kept him in the dark about the existence of his child, flesh of his flesh, blood of his blood.

Elizabeth got up, left the den, and headed for the kitchen. What would emerge from Petra and Chris meeting each other? Elizabeth realized that she was facing a very large unknown, and the more she dwelled upon that unknown, the more crowded it became with dark scenarios. Petra turning her back on her mother, devoting herself to her father alone, maybe even rejecting her sisters. More accurately, her half-sisters.

Oddly, maybe even perversely, Elizabeth realized that she missed Hugh. For all the years of their marriage he had been a steadying presence, so commonsensical and practical, never an alarmist. He had helped her to navigate tough times and had been unfailingly unflappable, even during his cancer scare in the summer of ninety-one, and years later, when he did indeed have cancer. Maybe she had failed to fully appreciate the strength he had supplied for her, the lessons he had unknowingly taught her about simply getting through and moving on.

At that moment, Elizabeth's cell phone alerted her to a call from Mrs. Shandy.

"My car broke down two days ago," she told Elizabeth, her annoyance obvious, "and is still in the shop though I was promised it would be ready this morning. You can't rely on anyone these days. Anyway, I need to ask a favor of you. Would you be able to drive me to the dentist this afternoon? My appointment is at two."

"Of course," Elizabeth said readily, relieved to be given a task that would get her out of the house and distract her from her unsettled thoughts. "I'd be more than happy to, and I'll drive you home after."

They arranged a time for Elizabeth to pick up her friend and ended the call. And as she went upstairs to change, it came home to Elizabeth that she need not feel lonely, or of no use in the world, or even particularly anxious when she had a good friend just moments away.

She hoped that Mrs. Shandy felt the same.

Chapter 47

The last time Petra had visited a flea market she had had such a strange and negative experience and still didn't know why, and yet here she was, heading for another one, ostensibly in search of items for Past Perfect. Ostensibly, because it was becoming clear to Petra that what she was really in search of was something intangible. Maybe it was something her father would help her find. Maybe that was wishful thinking.

This flea market was held every other Saturday morning in a small town called Southwerk. Parking was free, but there was an entrance fee of ten dollars, which, for Petra, was pretty steep. The field of tables spread for what seemed like miles, but of course that couldn't be true. Petra, not usually a fan of precise methods, nevertheless had a habit—not really a system—of walking down the right side and back up the left side of every aisle, generally assessing what was on display, before repeating the process, stopping when an item caught her eye. On her second journey through the first aisle she paused at a table with, among other antique and vintage items, several boxes of old photographs, each box labeled to indicate its contents. *Portraits. Death Portraits. Children. Families. Friends at Leisure. Couples/Weddings. Landscapes. Foreign Cities. Ameri-*

can Cities. Seaside/Vacation. Petra was impressed by the precise categorization of subject matter, though she guessed that cross-referencing wasn't a task that the seller had attempted.

As for the seller, the woman standing behind the table was about Petra's mother's age. She was strikingly beautiful, one of those people who have that ever-envied thing, "good bone structure." Her dark hair was drawn away from her face and fixed into a bun at the nape of her neck, accentuating eyes so beautifully brown that Petra felt momentarily mesmerized by them.

"Feel free to browse," the woman said with a smile. "And to ask questions. I do know a fair bit about some of the people shown in my collection, though of course not all. And I have a nice selection of vintage purses down there, at the end, as you can see."

Petra smiled back. "I think I've spent my vintage purse budget already this summer," she said. "But thanks, I'll look through these photographs."

The seller nodded and turned her attention to another potential customer, leaving Petra alone with the boxes of treasures.

She began to flip through the photos in the box labeled *Portraits.* There were images printed on heavy cardboard announcing the name of the photography studio responsible for the unsmiling, stiff portraits of men in narrow suits and women in dresses with a nipped waist and full skirts. Other images, from the box labeled *Friends at Leisure,* dated from a time when more people had access to their own cameras, the kind that didn't require the sitter to remain absolutely still for minutes on end; these photos revealed locations other than inside the home or a photographic studio. Friends were gathered on beaches or in parks; couples were seated alone together in rowboats; families were enjoying picnics in cemeteries.

Next, Petra moved on to the box labeled *Couples/Weddings.* She was almost ready to move on again—oddly, none of these photographs caught her interest—when she was struck by three photos, one after the other. The same couple featured in all three images, one a formal studio portrait, another showing the pair sitting under a leafy tree, and the third depicting the couple, arm in arm, standing in front of what might have been a courthouse or some other municipal building. On the back of the first photo, written in a thin, spidery hand, were the names Philip and Margaret, and the date 1891.

Given the long exposure times necessary to photography in the nineteenth century, smiling people were not necessarily to be expected, but this man and woman, Philip and Margaret, had managed, in each of the three photos, to project, through their eyes and their very stance, a sense of great happiness and even excitement. Had they perhaps been secret lovers?

"I see you're drawn to this couple."

Petra looked up to find that the seller had returned.

"So am I," the woman continued. "To me, these photographs suggest a tragic love story, two passionate lovers somehow torn apart. I wish I were a writer. Then I could try to tell the story of these two, at least what I imagine it might have been. I could give the lovers a happy ending. I could heighten the tragedy, whatever it might have been, but bring them together in the end, in spite of all odds."

"Maybe they wouldn't want to be characters in someone's story," Petra suggested, "even one based on their own."

"Not that they could prevent someone from crafting a story," the woman pointed out. "Philip and Margaret are dead, but these photographs survive. They weren't destroyed, though it's possible Margaret thought Philip had disposed of them and Philip thought Margaret had burned them or tossed them into the ocean—assuming a bad ending to their affair. Anyway, the photos suggest possibilities, and humans need a sense of possibility. People live on in what they leave behind, even if they live on in new ways for everyone who encounters those artifacts."

"I agree with you," Petra told her, "but not everyone would.

I mean, not everyone can believe that something of a person's spirit lives on in a tangible object. Spiritualism of that sort isn't everyone's cup of tea. Why are you selling these three photographs, anyway?" she asked. "They seem to mean a lot to you."

The woman laughed. "I'm an addicted collector," she said. "If I don't periodically pass on some of my stash, I'll have no room for new items. Still, I try to sell to people like me, people who will appreciate the treasured—or even the neglected or the discarded—possessions of people long gone."

The woman turned then to another browser, this one ready to purchase a nineteenth-century color print of the city of Edinburgh.

Petra studied the three photos again and finally decided not to buy them. She didn't think the seller wanted to part with the three photos, not really, in spite of what she had said about getting rid of existing items to make room for new ones. Maybe one day the seller would write the story of Philip and Margaret, as she imagined it might have been.

Petra wandered on, all the while thinking. Would Elizabeth and Christopher have a happy ending at some point in the future? Who could tell their story, given the fact that Elizabeth didn't want anyone else to know it? Who could tell their story if it died with the Quirk family? Or, maybe the love story of Elizabeth and Christopher had already had its ending, an unhappy one, back when the lovers had turned away from each other out of guilt and a sense of duty. Was that a suitable ending for any love story? For a sad and tragic one maybe, for a love story more common than generally admitted, a love story forbidden by custom if not by law.

Petra drove back to Eliot's Corner, ten dollars poorer, but, this time, not displeased with her experience. She wasn't sure what made her choose to travel through the town itself on the way to Lavender Lane; there was a shorter route along a road that ran along a farm that included a large stable of horses. It was always nice to see the horses grazing in the field. But travel through the town itself she did, and there, striding along Main Street in her usual determined manner, was Jess. Petra, who never used a car's horn if she could help it, opened her window and called out "Hello." Jess turned abruptly with a frown—as if expecting to find a harasser?—and when she realized it was her sister who had called out, her frown lessened. Marginally.

"Hey," she said, when Petra had pulled against the curb.

"Want a ride anywhere?" Petra asked.

"I'm fine. Where've you been?"

Petra hesitated. If she told Jess she had been hanging out at a flea market with a self-proclaimed addicted collector of vintage and antique items, Jess would probably roll her eyes. But if she phrased it another way and tweaked the truth just a bit, maybe she could lift her sister's spirits.

"I was meeting with someone who's been in the antique business for a long time," Petra said. "I told her about your suggestions for expanding my business, and she thought they were really excellent. I was wondering if you have any more ideas for me? I could really use your help."

Jess laughed harshly. "Why are you asking me? Clearly, I know nothing about business or I'd have figured out what to do with my own. Wait. I don't have a business of my own!"

"I just thought—"

"Well, don't."

Jess strode off, and Petra sat there, watching her go. She remembered how just the other day Cam had admitted she had done Jess a disservice by assuming she was indestructible, that she could easily overcome any obstacle in her way. "She's vulnerable like the rest of us," Cam had said. "She has Dad's bluster, but we know what his bluster served to mask."

Smarting from Jess's words, aware that she had blundered badly, and that she had lied—Petra had lost the paper on which Jess had written her business recommendations and contacts for her sister, and had never even read what was written on it—Petra started the car again and headed for Lavender Lane.

Maybe she was about to blunder badly with Christopher Ryan, as well. Suddenly, Petra felt overcome with anxiety, with fear. There was nothing preventing her from sending Chris another e-mail asking to reschedule their meeting for some time in the future. For that matter, there was nothing to prevent her from getting the next bus back to Portsmouth and forever putting off a reunion with her biological father. Such a decision might disappoint her mother, or it might instead ease her mind—Petra didn't know.

But as she pulled into the driveway of her family's home, the cloud of fear and anxiety lifted, as quickly and as unexpectedly as it had descended. She would go through with the plan she had made with Christopher Ryan. After that, she would be under no actual obligation to take their relationship any further, assuming her father wanted to know her better. She had to take care of herself, an idea fairly new to Petra and one that made her feel uncomfortable because it implied, of necessity, that one knew oneself well enough to know what taking care of that self really meant. And for Petra, self-knowledge, a unique personhood, had always been elusive.

Chapter 48

For the past fifteen minutes, Elizabeth had been going through her closet and the drawers of the old bureau to see if there was any bit of clothing she might pass on to the local charity shop. Nothing was old or interesting enough to entice Petra or her friend at Re-Turned, but there was a pair of jeans Elizabeth had worn only twice before deciding they were too uncomfortable for her, and a lightweight blazer that was a bit too short and boxy for her taste. Why had she bought it in the first place? Well, she had loved the color and still did, a bright apple green. Hopefully, some other woman would be able to make the blazer work as Elizabeth had not been able to.

Elizabeth brought the small bag of clothing to be donated to the door of her room before going to the safe at the back of the closet and retrieving the diary she had kept in the summer of 1991.

Seated comfortably in the old armchair, Elizabeth recalled that there had been moments, during the few years in which Petra had lived alone with her mother in the house on Lavender Lane before moving on to Portsmouth, when Elizabeth had considered telling Petra the truth about her father. But she had never spoken; she had never felt ready to accept the consequences she could foresee as well as—particularly—those she could not foresee.

Elizabeth opened the small red leather book. She had noted earlier that her handwriting had changed over the years; that was inevitable, she supposed. Now, compared to the handwriting of the young woman she had been back in 1991, her handwriting was less robust, the letters not quite fully formed, hurried. Why her handwriting should be hurried, Elizabeth wasn't sure. Was she really so aware that time was flying by, that she was getting old?

Better, she thought, not to analyze the matter. Instead, she turned the pages of the diary until she reached a passage written shortly before she and Chris had first kissed.

Chris is so very different from Hugh. The truth is I think I've always been in love with Chris, ever since the first time I met him. Still, it wasn't until the day before the wedding that I knew—or suspected—that what I felt was love. And by then, it was too late. I was marrying Hugh Quirk. It was inconceivable that I could walk away less than twenty-four hours before the ceremony that would bind us as husband and wife, through sickness and in health, until death did us part.

Inconceivable. Maybe it wouldn't have been inconceivable for another, stronger woman, Elizabeth thought.

She moved on to a passage written just after that fateful night at the ballet when she and Chris had first kissed.

I hardly know what to think. I feel exalted. Guilt-ridden. Terrified. So very happy. But it can't happen again, that moment of bliss, of completion. It just absolutely can't.

An empty protest in the end. Had she meant it, though, at that moment?

After a moment, Elizabeth went on. The next passage she

chose to read had been written a few weeks after that first kiss, after, indeed, she and Chris had finally made love.

I'm scared about keeping this record of my life but I'm in desperate need of someone to talk to. Even if I had a sibling or a very close and trustworthy friend, how could I expect to find true sympathy with my situation? What I'm doing is wrong. I don't need anyone else to tell me that. What I need is understanding and not judgment. But do I deserve understanding?

Elizabeth sighed. In the passages recorded immediately before the affair with Chris had begun, she had spent a lot of ink praising Hugh for his various good qualities, almost, she wondered now, as if she had been hoping to persuade herself to abandon all romantic thoughts of Christopher Ryan. And then, as the fateful moment drew near, that evening she had spent with Chris at the ballet in Boston, suddenly Hugh disappeared from the pages of the diary. No praise, no accusations. Just absence. A heavy absence.

Elizabeth now flipped back to the entry made on her wedding anniversary in June, not long before she and Chris had finally acted on their love.

Our anniversary today. Having dinner at Dominic's. H. gave me a silver bracelet.

Even after all these years, Elizabeth remembered how she had felt a bit horrified by the fact that she hadn't wanted to celebrate the anniversary, that she had wished it would just pass by unremarked. But that was impossible, of course. Cam and Jess had made a card for their parents, using lots of glitter and glue, and had presented it with childish pride. Hugh's parents had sent a card espousing the usual romantic sentiments written out in flowery script. Elizabeth remembered feeling oddly thankful that her own parents were gone. What would they think if they knew how unhappy their daughter was in her marriage? There was nothing wrong with Hugh, they would argue. He was a fine, upstanding man. He had given her two lovely children. How could any woman possibly be unhappy married to such a man?

Not that Elizabeth would have told her parents that she was unhappy. They had adored Hugh, practically forced their daughter into the marriage. To share with them her frustrations would have been unthinkable.

And how, exactly, had she grown so unhappy in the relationship that the prospect of dinner out with her husband was so objectionable? What did that signify for the future with Hugh? Nothing good. At the time, Elizabeth had truly felt—she had truly believed—that nothing would or could change. At the time, she had truly felt—she had truly believed—that she didn't want anything to change for the better. She had had enough of being Mrs. Hugh Quirk. Not that being Mrs. Christopher Ryan was an option. But better to be on her own . . . than what? To be the cherished wife of a decent man, living in a lovely house, raising two beautiful daughters?

Besides, divorce was out of the question. It always had been. Mrs. Quirk she would remain.

She had felt so very distant from Hugh the night of their anniversary in 1991. It had annoyed her when, before leaving the house for the restaurant, Hugh had made it a point of telling her over and over that she was the most beautiful woman he had ever seen, that he was so proud to be her husband, that she was sure to turn heads wearing that gorgeous blue dress. He had asked her if he looked okay, if he should change his shirt or tie. He wanted to look like he deserved to be with her, though of course, how could a man like him ever deserve a woman like her?

Elizabeth had gone through the motions of toasting with a glass of champagne, of smilingly agreeing that the food was wonderful though she was paying virtually no attention to the meal at what was then Eliot's Corner's one and only significant restaurant. The Quirks knew every other person in Dominic's that evening. They had received so many good wishes from friends and neighbors stopping by the table. It had all been rather exhausting.

After dessert and coffee, Hugh had insisted they move to the bar. He had bought drinks for several people and gotten a bit drunk. He had been so very happy that night, Elizabeth was sure of it. Hugh couldn't lie; it simply wasn't in him to tell even a white lie. It was an admirable quality, one his wife did not also possess.

She had driven them home shortly after midnight, Hugh dozing in the passenger seat. They had not had sex that night; Hugh had fallen deeply asleep the moment his head hit the pillow. Elizabeth was glad, relieved. She hadn't felt sexually attracted to Hugh for some time.

Slowly, Elizabeth closed the old diary and wondered, yet again, what should be done with it. She couldn't just tuck it away and forget it as she had forgotten it for so long, because things were different now. The girls knew of the diary's existence and were curious. She trusted them not to sneak into her room when she was out of the house and hunt it out. Or did she? In this case, curiosity could easily lead to a bending of the rules of good behavior. That was why the diary was residing in the safe Hugh had insisted they install at the back of her walk-in closet for her good jewelry and their important papers. None of the girls had the safe's security code.

But why not just get rid of it now, take responsibility and delete the damning evidence. Well, that was being dramatic. The diary didn't actually prove anything. It could be taken as a work of autobiographical fiction. The only real evidence of the affair the girls had in their possession was their mother's word. Even Petra had at this point no concrete proof that Chris Ryan was her biological father. And if neither agreed to a DNA test, any relationship they might develop would be based on faith in Elizabeth's word.

For the moment, Elizabeth decided simply to return the diary to the safe at the back of her closet, glancing as she did at the black leather ring box in which her engagement and wedding rings, now too small for her fingers, were stored.

Though she wasn't in the habit of drinking before evening, she very much wanted a glass of wine, and headed downstairs to the kitchen. She so wished the meeting between Petra and Christopher was over, a thing of the past. The one who waits often suffers just as greatly if not more so than the one engaging in battle or confrontation. And Petra's first meeting with her biological father could be seen in some way as a confrontation.

Elizabeth sighed and took a bottle of *vinho verde* from the fridge. Just one glass.

Chapter 49

Summer 1991

Elizabeth tightened her grip on the steering wheel. She was meeting Chris in an old diner halfway between his cottage and Eliot's Corner. Chris didn't have much time to spend with her. He was due in Boston that afternoon, and business required him to stay on there for the next week. Elizabeth wished more than anything that they could meet at his cottage where they could be alone, hold hands, kiss, and make love, but you didn't always get what you wanted in life. Sometimes, you got the exact opposite of what you wanted.

She had felt sick to her stomach since the day before when Hugh had received the call from his doctor. As a very young child Hugh had suffered two serious bouts of pneumonia; the trauma had left one of his lungs permanently weakened. In spite of that he had grown into a strong, strapping boy and then a powerful, well-built man, but as a precaution he was in the habit of getting a chest X-ray every two or three years. This latest X-ray had shown a suspicious spot on that weakened lung, a spot that required further exploration.

They had agreed there was no need to say anything to the

girls, not at this point. There was no need to frighten them unnecessarily. And if all went well, the children would never even have to know there had been a scare.

But Chris needed to know. Rather, Elizabeth needed to tell him, though in a way she couldn't describe with words she feared the outcome of that revelation—as much as, if not more than, she feared the medical diagnosis still to come. Interestingly, Hugh hadn't said anything about letting Chris know what was going on; maybe he just hadn't gotten around to considering the idea or maybe, and this seemed more likely, Hugh didn't see a need to share news that might not turn out to be news in the end. He was nothing if not a phlegmatic man.

There was the diner, three letters of its old, once lighted sign missing. Aside from Chris's car, only one other car occupied the small dirt lot, and that vehicle, crusted in rust, had definitely seen better times. Elizabeth parked and went inside.

Chris was seated at a booth near the back of the diner, and she greeted him circumspectly, as they always greeted each other when in public. The waiter—possibly also the owner and cook; the place had a lonely, deserted feel—took their order of coffee, came back with the cups, and then disappeared.

"I'm sorry we had to meet here," Chris said with a smile. "I promise it's clean in spite of being a bit worse for wear."

Elizabeth attempted a smile. "I have something to tell you," she began. "It's about Hugh. It's not something he asked me to share with you, so you'll need to keep it to yourself for now."

Chris nodded gravely. "All right," he said.

Elizabeth stared down at the table for a moment. Since the affair had begun earlier in the summer, Chris hadn't visited the Quirk family as it had been his habit to do once every few weeks or so, and he had turned down Hugh's invitations to dinner on at least two occasions. If Hugh found his friend's absence that summer troubling, he wasn't saying. More likely, due to that famously phlegmatic nature, he simply assumed that Chris was busy elsewhere.

Elizabeth and Chris had never discussed the matter of Chris's relationship with the Quirk family, and they certainly hadn't thought ahead as to how a friendship might be managed in the future. They had simply, carelessly, taken each day as it came, as lovers did and always had done and probably always would do until the end of time.

But now, with the possibility of Hugh's being seriously ill, Elizabeth realized that things had changed. Fantasy time was over; the time for responsibility was near to hand. She swallowed hard before looking up and telling Chris that Hugh, his oldest and dearest friend, might have lung cancer.

Chris reached across the table and grasped Elizabeth's hand briefly but firmly. "I'll be there in whatever capacity you need me to be, for both you and Hugh," he said. "You know you can count on me."

Elizabeth blinked away tears. Of course, she could count on Chris. But how could she allow him back into their daily lives, into their home? How could she allow Chris to be of help to Hugh? His very presence would be an insult to a sick man, a man he professed to love, and yet, a man he was betraying!

More than that, should Hugh prove to be ill, she would have to end her relationship with Chris right away. Elizabeth knew that for sure. To be honest, even before this health scare she had already begun to sense that an end was near, that an end was necessary and inevitable, but until now, that sense had been relatively easy to dismiss, to ignore.

Until now.

"There's no need to make any decisions yet," she said, with more confidence in her voice than she felt in her heart. "We don't know for sure that Hugh is sick, and if he is sick, we don't know how serious it is, and we have no idea what the doctors will propose we do about it."

Chris nodded. "All right. That makes sense. But you know you can rely on me, whatever happens. Hugh is my friend, my dearest friend. And—"

"Yes," she said. "I know."

Elizabeth had never felt the wrongness, the hopelessness of what she and Chris were doing as intensely as she felt it in that moment, as they sat across from each other in the diner booth, untouched cups of coffee on the table, her paper napkin twisted into a ball in her left hand. The look on Chris's face was one of deep sadness; his ordinarily light blue eyes were dark with emotion.

"I should get going," he said quietly then. "I'm due at my publisher at three."

"All right. I . . . I think I'll sit here for a bit. I feel a bit too shaky to drive just yet."

"Do you want me to stay with you?"

Elizabeth smiled and shook her head. "No, thanks. I'll be fine."

Chris rose from the booth, and before he headed toward the door he stopped to lay his hand on her shoulder. "Good-bye, Elizabeth," he said softly. "Call me when . . ."

She nodded and he was gone, on his way back to his life in the larger world, the world outside the boundary of two people in love. Elizabeth sat there alone, cold cup of coffee before her, feeling for the first time in her life true desolation. She knew the end of her relationship with Chris was near, no matter the outcome of Hugh's medical tests.

Chris, she felt sure, must know it, too. She had felt the knowledge in his touch.

Chapter 50

Summer 2022

Petra found herself in a quandary. She had no idea what she should she wear to meet Christopher Ryan, her father, the following day.

Not that she had much choice. She had brought very little with her from her apartment in Portsmouth, and it was all old and comfortable and not what people might consider "adult." But that was silly. What was wrong with her clothing? Nothing. She liked what social media and the established fashion magazines called the bohemian look. She felt comfortable in her flowing dresses, loose linen pants, and strands of stone beads around her neck and wrists. If Chris made a snap judgment about her based on her clothing, well then so be it. Besides, how negative could that judgment be? He might assume she was a contemporary hippie, and in that he would be sort of right.

Petra sighed and wondered why she was dwelling on something as silly as clothing. It wasn't as if she was going on a job interview or an audition. Or was she? Was she in some way auditioning for the role of daughter to this man who had once loved her mother enough to betray his own best friend?

Anyway, Petra was smart enough to know that her focus on creating a suitable outfit was a convenient way to avoid dwelling on the emotional content of the meeting with her newly discovered father. Distraction was a powerful thing.

What to say? Should she start with small talk? Nice weather we're having. How was your drive from Boston? It would only postpone the important conversation she needed them to have, but maybe that was okay, to just sort of ease into it, get a bit comfortable with each other.

She wondered if she should bring a few pictures of herself to show to Chris, a few of her as a baby and then as a child, maybe a graduation picture. But maybe she would save that for the next time they met, if there was a next time. Better not to make too many—or any—assumptions about Chris's interest in his daughter.

One thing was certain, she wouldn't call Chris Dad; she couldn't, and she doubted that he would expect or want her to, not now. Hugh would always be Dad.

And if she felt in the least bit frightened or threatened, she would leave the café immediately. But why would Christopher Ryan frighten or threaten her, no matter who she was? The idea was ridiculous. She had to expect some degree of tension or unease, and she had to be strong and stay put, not run off like a child. In all probability, the meeting would not be particularly pleasant. That was okay.

Suddenly, spontaneously, Petra reached for her phone and sent a text to her housemate Sara, saying hello and asking how her summer was progressing. In all her life she had never, ever before felt the need to reach out to someone like this. Was the impulse due to nerves, or was she truly feeling a need for connection? For a brief moment, she toyed with the idea of telling Sara now, via text, that the man she had presumed her father was not in fact her biological parent. But she only toyed with the idea.

Good to hear from you. All fine here. Lena's got a new guy. Hot!

Petra smiled. *Ok for a cooking lesson when I get back?*
About time! A woman can't live on take-out alone.

The brief exchange had made Petra feel better, more relaxed. Early in the day she had suggested that she and her mother go to the book club meeting that night as a sort of distraction— there was that word again! There was no good reason for them to miss the meeting, and anything would be better than sitting at home counting the hours until morning when Petra would head off to Lark's Circle to meet with Christopher Ryan.

Besides, there would be cookies and brownies after the discussion. Cookies and brownies could put a smile on just about anyone's face.

Even someone as nervous as Petra.

Chapter 51

Elizabeth had agreed to Petra's suggestion that they attend the book club meeting that evening, though she wasn't in the mood to socialize, and no matter that the Arden Forest Book Club considered the book primary reason to meet, gatherings were at bottom a social event.

But once they were in the shop, seated with their friends and neighbors, Elizabeth realized she was glad they had come. Conversation was more stimulating than usual. It was rare there was a serious difference of opinion among the members, but this novel had provoked strong feelings at opposing ends of the love-hate spectrum. Martha Benbow, scion of her family's construction company, had declared it one of the most disappointing tales she had ever read—"Nobody turned out happy!"—while Jeanie Shardlake, the artist, had argued that the whole point of the story was that nobody is guaranteed happiness, in real life or in a novel. The other members took up the argument, with a few deciding that a downer of an ending was balanced by the high quality of the writing, and another few protesting that the writing wasn't all that great, either.

When all talk about the book had wound down to silence, and before the group broke up to indulge in the snacks, Arden announced the next title. "This," she said, holding up a hefty volume, "was suggested by Lydia. As you can see it's called *The Third Room*, and it was written by a young man who grew up in rural Virginia. This is his first published novel though he's had stories published in several respected anthologies and magazines. I'll have books in the shop by the end of tomorrow for those who want to purchase their own copy, and I know the library has two copies on hand."

A warning bell went off in Elizabeth's head as she stared at the book Arden held in her hand, though faintly. Something she had heard about the book? Something she had read about the story, maybe via the LitHub daily e-mail she subscribed to, or the *New York Times Book Review*? What was it?

"Aren't bastards in some cultures seen as special?" Tess Mogan, Tammy's mother, asked, seemingly out of the blue.

Elizabeth startled. She avoided looking at Petra, who sat by her side.

"What brought that up?" Laura, Arden's daughter, asked.

"Our next novel," Tess explained. "I've read about it. There's a subplot about a bastard son who can't forgive his father for having abandoned his mother when he learned she was pregnant. It's not an unusual storyline, but the telling is supposed to be super."

"Well, I certainly can't say," Arden admitted. "I mean, about bastard children being considered special in some way."

"I don't know, either," Jeanie admitted. "I think some cultures accord a place of honor to gay or transsexual people."

Young Tammy frowned. "I don't understand. Why are you equating bastard children with gay and transsexual people?"

Jeanie blushed. "I just meant that some cultures appreciate people who aren't what they consider the norm, rather than punish them. Oh, rats, that didn't come out right, either. I'd better shut up now."

"Did you know," Mrs. Shandy intoned, "that Queen Victoria banned royal bastards from court? She referred to them as 'ghosts best forgotten.' Supposedly there were an awful lot of royal 'by-blows.' Randy bunch, those royals."

"Good old liberal-minded Queen Victoria!" Laura said with a laugh. "And isn't the word itself, 'bastard,' mostly used now as an insult having nothing to do with a person's parentage? You call someone a bastard when they've behaved badly, been dishonest or cruel."

With each comment—good-natured though they were—Elizabeth's stomach tightened until there was a genuine ache in her gut. Though she still couldn't turn her head to look at Petra, she could feel the tension emanating from her as well.

"I don't think there's a stigma against a bastard child in this day and age," Tess said. "I mean, what's so bad about having kids and not being married to the mother or father? It's almost the norm now, isn't it?"

"Maybe," her daughter agreed, "but it's still not cool to have a baby by someone other than your current husband or boyfriend, though. I mean, it's not honest."

"Of course not," her mother said firmly.

"In the bad old days," Mrs. Shandy said, "legitimacy was all about inheritance. A man didn't want to leave his money, his lands, or his title to another man's son. For a wife, trying to pass off a child as your husband's, when he wasn't, was risky business, but often, necessary for her survival, and the survival of the child."

Petra leaned into Elizabeth and whispered, very faintly: "We have to get out of here."

"But how?" Elizabeth murmured.

Marla Swenson, Arden's elderly neighbor, spoke up now. "I remember my grandmother using the expression 'the milkman's child' to describe a girl or boy who stood out from a family of siblings, either physically or in some less obvious way. You know, a dark-haired boy in a family of blonds, that sort of thing, or a bookish kid in a family of athletes. The implication being that the milkman fathered the child."

"The word 'cuckold' must be related to the cuckoo bird lay-
ing her eggs in another bird's nest," Martha said. "Why didn't I
put that together before now?"

Mrs. Shandy nodded. "The Germans say *kuckuckskind.* It
means cuckoo's child."

"Maybe we should save further discussion for our next meeting," Arden said firmly, looking at her watch. "Those chocolate
chip cookies aren't going to eat themselves."

Elizabeth was never so grateful for Arden's leadership skills
as she was at that moment. "Let's skip the socializing," she
murmured to her daughter. Petra nodded. Together, the Quirk
women hurried off to where Elizabeth had parked her car and
got safely inside before either spoke.

"Well, that was awkward," Elizabeth said, turning the key in
the ignition.

"Maybe we should skip the next meeting," Petra suggested
as her mother pulled away from the curb. "Come down with a
twenty-four-hour bug or something."

"I think that's an excellent idea. And we'll pass on reading
the book, too."

"Oh, yes." After a moment, Petra said: "Well, I guess my
idea of using the book group as a distraction before I see Chris
tomorrow backfired."

"The best laid plans of mice and men . . ." Elizabeth murmured. "I think that we both need a glass of wine."

Chapter 52

The drive to Lark's Circle where Petra was to meet her biological father was easily the most nerve-racking one of her life. Still, she managed to arrive at her destination without incident and fifteen minutes before she was due to meet Christopher Ryan at a café he had suggested, ample time to park the car, take several deep breaths—none of which succeeded in calming her—and make her way to Orlando's.

Several of the tables on the café's patio were occupied, but only one by a man on his own. He was a tall, thin man, good-looking in an ascetic, serious sort of way, like Leslie Howard in *Gone with the Wind*, or Daniel Day-Lewis in just about anything. There was a book opened before him, and he seemed intent upon reading it. His legs were crossed, gracefully, one over the other, which emphasized their length. She thought now of Fred Astaire, dapper, elegant, and wondered if Chris was a good dancer. Had he danced with her mother at Elizabeth and Hugh's wedding? An image of the bride and best man in each other's arms came to Petra's mind, and she tried to blink it away.

This man, who she assumed was her father, was wearing a blue oxford shirt under a lightweight blazer, pressed chinos, and a pair of obviously ancient Keds sneakers. Large tortoiseshell sunglasses sat on the bridge of his nose. Petra watched as he turned a page of the book. His fingers were long and fine, yet his hands looked strong. Petra knew that Christopher Ryan's hair had once been blond; this man's hair was a pale gray mixed with white, a non-color, similar to what her mother's hair would be like if she weren't in the habit of coloring it once a month.

Petra also saw . . . herself. A version of herself. It was weird. It was uncomfortable. It was also a bit thrilling. Romantic. The stuff of which daydreams were made.

Would he know at first glance that she was more than Elizabeth's daughter, that she was his daughter, too? Suddenly, again, Petra wasn't sure she was prepared for such a possibility. But bravely, she approached the table where the man sat.

"Mr. Ryan?" she said, not surprised to hear that she had spoken very softly.

The man closed the book he had been reading—Petra saw that it was a novel by Iris Murdoch—removed his sunglasses, and quickly replaced them with a similar pair of glasses with clear lenses. "Chris, please," he said with an abbreviated smile. "You must be Petra." He seemed to look more closely at her then, even searching her face as if for an answer. "You look so much like your mother," he said then. "Please, sit."

And so much like you, Petra thought as she took the seat across from her father. Should she have put out her hand for him to shake? Probably. Why hadn't she? She felt she was beginning to tremble and pressed her hands onto her thighs to steady herself.

"Do you want a coffee or—"

"No," she said quickly, "thanks. I'm fine for now. What are you reading?"

Chris almost seemed startled by the question. "Oh, *The Green Knight.* It's my third or fourth time. I love Iris Murdoch's work."

"I'm rereading *The Glass Bead Game.* I'm sure you know it."

"Yes. It's another favorite."

"For some reason, back when I was in college the absence of women in the story didn't bother me. Now, it kind of does, though I still appreciate the book."

There followed a moment of silence, pregnant with anxiety. At least, it felt that way to Petra.

"What made you contact me?" Christopher asked then; his tone was only mildly curious, not in the least aggressive. "I haven't been in touch with your family in a very long time."

"Before I answer that," Petra said, "I'd like to know what made you agree to see me. I really wasn't sure that you would."

Chris shrugged slightly. "Oh, several reasons. Curiosity. Nostalgia for my friendship with your parents. Besides, I didn't have a good reason to say no to your request."

Petra considered his reply. Chris had to know there was a possibility of Petra's having learned of the affair, and yet he didn't seem at all afraid. He was so calm. Not happy though. Or cheerful. Sort of sober. Careful.

"I heard about your father, of course," Chris said after a moment. "I'm sorry."

"It was a long time ago. Nine years. But thanks. He was a good man."

"He was." Chris cleared his throat. "How is your mother?" he asked then. "And your sisters?"

Petra saw a look of wariness in his eyes. He knew he was approaching, step by careful step, a dangerous place.

"Everyone's fine," she said. "Cam's got three kids. Jess, well, she's trying to start her own business. It hasn't been easy, but she's tough. Like Dad."

"I remember one time when I was at the house, Jess was very young, maybe two or three, and absolutely determined to open a jar of peanut butter on her own. Her little hands just weren't up to the task, but she tried so very hard, and she was so angry with herself when she failed."

Petra smiled. "That's Jess."

"And your mother?" Chris asked again after another moment of silence.

Petra realized she didn't know how exactly to reply to his question. How was Elizabeth Quirk at this moment in time? "She's fine," she began. "Healthy. She was teaching up until this May. Her school is being shut down and absorbed into a larger one a few towns away. There's no place for her on the faculty it seems."

"I'm sorry. Unless she's ready to stop teaching?"

"Oh, no," Petra said quickly. "She loves teaching. She's not ready to retire. She's—She doesn't really know what to do with her life now. The future, I mean. I think she's at a crisis point." It was more than she had meant to say, more than she had meant to share with this stranger of sorts. Too late to un-speak the words.

Chris smiled briefly. "They keep coming, crisis points. They have no respect for age."

"She told me," Petra blurted, unable to hold her tongue a moment longer. "She told us all, me and Cam and Jess. About your relationship. She said that after all the years of silence she finally needed to speak. She said she had no choice, that keeping silent had become impossible."

Petra waited, looking patiently and yet anxiously at the man sitting across from her.

Finally, he spoke. "I see. I have to admit I was half expecting that's what you wanted to tell me when you contacted me, that you knew about your mother and me."

Petra thought that he sounded resigned. Relieved, as well? "Yes," she said. "I thought you might have guessed. Mom thought so, too. She supported my wanting to get in touch with you. She knows I'm here with you today."

"What about Cam and Jess? What do they think?"

"They don't know I'm here," Petra admitted. "I think they're still in shock. But it's different for me. I had to see you."

Christopher's eyes were moist with tears. "Why?" he whispered.

"Because you're my father."

Chris said nothing, did nothing, just continued to look directly at her with the tears standing in his eyes.

"Mom offered to approach you first," Petra went on, a bit desperately, "sort of pave the way for me. But I think she was relieved when I insisted I be the one to tell you who I am. I think . . . I think she's afraid that . . ."

Chris reached for her hand. "Petra," he said finally. "My daughter. Forgive me if I . . ." Chris put his other hand over his eyes and took a deep, slow breath.

"It's okay," Petra said. His hand felt strong, as she had guessed. And it felt like the hand of a gentle man.

"Are you mad at Mom for keeping it a secret? Are you angry with me for getting in touch with you?" she asked when he had taken his hand from his eyes.

"No!" His voice was firm. "I know your mother must have had good reasons for keeping silent. As for you, well, I'm . . . I'm very happy, in fact. Surprised and not surprised. And you've only known this a short while?"

"Yes," Petra admitted. "See, I found a diary Mom had kept around the time you were involved with each other. I didn't know about your relationship at the time, and I didn't look inside the diary, of course. I just gave it to her. I guess her reading the diary acted as a catalyst, helped her to make the decision to tell my sisters and me about you. And so, here I am."

"Here we are," Chris said, with a subtle but distinct emphasis on the word "we."

"Yes. So . . ." Gently, Petra took her hand from his. Suddenly, she felt frozen. What next? Where did they go from here? These were legitimate questions, but somehow, she couldn't bring herself to ask them.

Chris leaned forward a little. "Would you like us to get to know each other?" he asked quietly.

"Yes," Petra said promptly, grateful that Chris—her father—had spoken.

"Good. I would like that, too."

"I think I need a glass of water, please," Petra blurted. "And something to eat. I feel a bit wobbly."

Chris rose promptly. "I'll get you something. Wait right here."

Petra watched as her father hurried into the café. She had done it. She felt relieved. Proud. Exhausted. Elated.

She hoped Chris would bring her a big fat sandwich. And maybe a brownie, too, or a macaron. Unlike Jess, she wasn't fussy.

"So, Past Perfect is in its second year and doing okay. Not great, but that's because I don't work hard enough at making it a success."

"Depends on how you define success," Chris said. "But I love the fact that we share a passion for history."

Petra smiled. She had eaten the sandwich Chris had brought her—and the brownie—in record time and was now enjoying a tall glass of iced tea. They had been sitting together for over an hour and not once after their initial awkwardness had there been a break in the conversation.

"I'd love to know more about your work," she said. "If you had to summarize the purpose of bioethics, how would you do it?"

Chris nodded. "Simply put, it's all about searching for and hopefully finding answers to some of the big questions in life, the ones we all ask ourselves, or should. Like, for example: What are my responsibilities toward others? What does it mean to be a good mother or teacher or construction worker or lawyer? How should I act in the world? What do I owe the world?"

"I think I've been asking myself those questions since childhood," Petra told him. "Sometimes, I feel plagued by them, though I'm not sure I'd want to be the kind of person who doesn't think about social responsibility and what it means to be good at something."

"I agree. It's better to think than to not think. Even when it's exhausting."

"So, can you tell me about a specific area of concern, maybe one that's really close to your heart?"

"One set of questions in particular," Chris went on, "has always been of great interest to me, those concerning the rights of minors to make their own health care decisions. For example, who has the right or is in the best position to decide between a minor's opinion about their medical treatment and the opinion of the parents or guardians if that opinion differs?"

Petra nodded. "Like if a child says they don't want chemotherapy and the parents insist upon it, is a doctor, who has sworn to do no harm, the one who is best positioned to decide?"

"Pretty much. Of course, medical professionals—well, all of us, really—have another question to ponder. Are we, as humans, required only not to harm other people, or are we also required to behave in ways that make other people's lives better?"

"I know what I think," Petra said, "but I'm sure others disagree with me. All ethical questions have the ability to provoke spirited debate and, as you know, in particular situations, real anger."

"You're right. Witness animal rights' protestors of the more violent sort, or, for example, anti-abortionists who resort to acts of terror. The challenge in my job is to really think and analyze, and listen to opposing ideas, not to react on the strength of emotion only, or prejudice or common so-called wisdom."

Petra sighed. "It sounds wonderful, so much more important than what I do."

"Than what you're doing now," Chris amended. "If you want to do something you consider more important than selling vintage clothes, there's nothing stopping you."

Except me, Petra said silently.

"Is there anyone special in your life?" Chris asked, suddenly. "A boyfriend or girlfriend?"

"No." Petra half smiled. "There kind of never has been. I've always bolted pretty early on in my romantic relationships, if you could even call them that. And, to be honest, I've never been good at making friends, close friends. People have tried to befriend me but . . . It's funny but I've never talked to anyone about this before, not even to Mom. I guess you could say I've got a classic fear of intimacy."

Chris nodded. "A fear of intimacy often stems from a person's lack of self-solidity, from her being aware of the fact that she's still unformed and worried that her defenseless self is going be swallowed or eradicated by being too close to another person." He smiled a bit ruefully. "I know whereof I speak. But for that brief moment with your mother, I've never known true emotional intimacy."

"When did you fall in love with my mother?" Petra asked.

"At the risk of sounding corny, the first time I met her. I used to think that love at first sight was a joke or a lie, just a way of disguising overwhelming sexual attraction. But then, it happened to me. The love came first. I saw Elizabeth as an entire human being, and I was done for."

"I've never had that happen to me," Petra said. "As I just told you. But what specifically about Mom was it that drew you to her?"

Christopher shrugged. "Something indefinable. I really can't say why I fell in love with Elizabeth in the way I did. I don't think anyone has ever really been able to say how or why love happens. Poets and philosophers try their best but when it does happen to you, it's entirely unique, and often surprising, unasked for. I certainly never wanted to fall in love with my best friend's girlfriend, but I did, and it went against every idea I held about myself being an upright and moral person, even a person immune to romantic affection." Chris paused. "But I was wrong about myself, naïve. I knew nothing at all about life until I met Elizabeth."

Petra thought about that for a moment. Could one person really have so much of an awakening effect on another person?

Could one relationship, no matter how fleeting, revolutionize a person's life? Well, why not?

"When I told you that I'm your daughter," she said then, "were you worried I'd act out, abuse you in some way?"

Chris shook his head. "No. But maybe I deserve your anger. Yes, I probably do."

"I'm not comfortable with anger," Petra told him, "in any form or degree, whether it be my own or someone else's. I know that anger is normal. I know it can be healthy and justified. Still, I don't like to feel angry. I felt angry with Mom for a bit after she told me about the two of you. But it didn't last, and I'm glad. And if I was angry with you for a bit, I'm not any longer. Anger doesn't seem to get a person very far."

"No. But some people will argue that righteous anger can help get important goals accomplished, like the end of brutal political regimes, racism, misogyny. But that's getting off the subject."

"Mom still has the agate pendant you gave her," Petra said. "Do you remember? It's lavender, her favorite color. It's kind of a cute coincidence that we live on Lavender Lane. Anyway, she wore it when she told us about you. For courage, as a sort of talisman. She said that Dad used to tease her about being superstitious, about believing in a world of spirit and coincidence and miracles."

Chris smiled. "I do remember the pendant, and yes, Hugh was the most earthbound person I'd ever met."

"Tell me about the two of you, Dad and you, I mean."

Christopher seemed glad to oblige. "Hugh and I never had very much in common," he began, "and less so as the years passed. I think what was keeping us together was partly habit, the comfort of familiarity, and an old sense of obligation, at least on my part. I met Hugh when we were in second grade. I was being routinely bullied by a few of the kids, and one day Hugh came upon them in fine form. They had me backed into a corner of the school playground, and two of them were taking turns shoving me back against the fence. They stopped pretty quickly when Hugh—he was always big for his age—made an appearance and warned that if they ever harassed his 'good friend Chris' again they'd have to answer to him."

"Did they leave you alone after that?" Petra asked.

Chris laughed. "Oh, yes. What people didn't know was that Hugh's bark was much worse than his bite. I don't think he ever had to follow through on a threat, and I think he was glad about that." Chris smiled. "Hugh Quirk always had a sense of fair play. He was a natural caregiver—even if he had to convince someone they needed to be taken care of."

"Like he did with Mom?" Petra asked. "Dad needed attention. Being a savior got him plenty of it."

"Yes. But don't be hard on him. He always meant well, even if he tended to blunder or to make the other person feel less than in some way."

"What do you mean?" Petra asked.

"I say this without rancor or disrespect," Chris assured her. "But I think Hugh enjoyed feeling somehow more adult than me, more capable somehow. He had the wife and the family. Oh, he knew I had the brains, and he respected my work, but it pleased Hugh—and I wasn't angry about this—to be the one who could offer a home-cooked meal to his bachelor friend, to play the lord of the manor if you will, dispensing hospitality to someone who didn't have home comforts of his own. Sometimes I think he imagined me eating cold beans out of a can for dinner and sleeping on a ratty old sofa, when in reality I'm a pretty good cook and sleep in a very good bed under clean, high-thread-count cotton sheets."

"But you must have meant more to him than, than what? Than someone he pitied?" Petra asked.

"I think so," Chris agreed. "Hugh was a very loyal man. Once he declared you his friend—wife, child, whatever—you were his friend for life. No matter what. It wasn't in him to walk away. It also wasn't in him to—" Chris shook his head. "Never mind. I've said more than I probably should have."

"It wasn't in Hugh Quirk to grow and change?" Petra guessed. "To acknowledge growth and change in others?"

"I always thought so," Chris admitted. "Though from what I was able to gather over the years, Hugh did eventually acknowledge your mother's need to forge a career, and his acceptance of that was indication of his own growth. You've got to admire him for that."

"Yes," Petra said. "I do. Still, I can't help but wonder if he agreed to Mom's going to graduate school because he sensed he'd lose her if he didn't."

Chris shrugged. "And what if that was the case? Hugh knew that Elizabeth was the most important aspect of his life, that without her he would be badly diminished. He did what he had to do to keep her. It was a good decision that benefited them both."

Petra had to agree. Like Hugh Quirk, Chris Ryan had a sense of fair play, willing to accord praise where it was due.

It was only after another hour had passed that Petra realized she should probably head back to Eliot's Corner. She knew her mother would be eager to hear about her meeting with Chris. And she figured that Chris might be worn out from having met his previously unknown thirty-year-old daughter!

Before they parted in the parking lot of the café, having arranged a time and a place to meet again, Petra dared to hug her father. He returned the hug with no awkwardness and waved until her car was out of sight.

Petra, driving along the road with a smile on her face, was happily aware that her life, however improbably, had suddenly started anew.

Imagine that!

Chapter 53

The anxiety brought on by waiting helplessly for Petra to return from her meeting with Christopher Ryan was threatening to make Elizabeth physically ill.

Just think, coming face-to-face with a parent or a child for the first time as an adult! Well, Elizabeth reflected, that was what Laura Huntington, Arden Bell's daughter had done. And, in some way, the meeting had been a first for Arden, too, who had only been allowed a glimpse of her infant daughter before she had been taken away. How many parents and children experienced such an emotionally overwhelming situation? Maybe more than Elizabeth had ever imagined.

Elizabeth sighed and tossed the New England lifestyle magazine she had been flipping through onto the couch next to her. Not long after Petra had left the house late that morning, Elizabeth had been rehearsing one of the last conversations she had shared with Hugh before his death. In the last months of his life, he had spoken several times of his sorrow and regret that his friendship with Chris had melted away. Friends made in childhood inhabited a special place in a person's heart, maybe even their soul; no one could argue that.

One morning, when Hugh was feeling relatively calm after

a particularly rough night of pain, he had asked if Elizabeth would sit with him while he got something off his chest. She had perched on the bed alongside him, holding his hand, smiling encouragingly.

"As you know, I've been thinking a lot about Chris lately," Hugh began.

For a moment, Elizabeth felt sure that her husband was going to tell her that he had had suspicions about her and Chris once upon a time. "Yes?" she said quietly, hoping her face didn't reveal her guilty fear.

"I've been thinking about how we lost track of each other, of how he faded out of our lives. I hope it wasn't something I did or said that sent him away. You know how ham-fisted I can be. Always barging or bumbling into situations and conversations. Blustering. Laughing too loud." Hugh had smiled ruefully. "Who knows what damage I've done in my life by always having to be the center of everyone's attention."

She had tried to comfort him, assure him that he had done nothing wrong or hurtful to Chris. "Sometimes people just— things happen and people drift apart," she had said. "No one's to blame."

"I know," Hugh replied, "but still, I miss him. I always thought that Chris and I would be, you know, a team until the end. An unlikely duo, but buddies. Friends. But I guess I was wrong. When I'm gone . . . When I'm gone, will you find him again? Let him know I, tell him I . . . Tell him that I loved him."

She had promised that she would find Chris and give him Hugh's message. She had been deeply touched by her husband's accurate and honest assessment of himself. It was one of the few times he had ever displayed a sense of self-knowledge.

But Elizabeth had not kept that promise. Nine long years had gone by. She often felt remiss, guilty, but still, she had never acted. Why? Fear? Cowardice? Yes. Because she was haunted by the fact that she was the one responsible for the melting away of the friendship between the two men.

Could it possibly have been otherwise, Elizabeth wondered now, again? Could she and Chris have continued the family friendship for Hugh's sake? Why hadn't they? It would have taken a great deal of sacrifice, and they would have had to live with the dangerous possibility of it becoming clear over time that Petra was Chris's child. It might have become difficult to ignore the physical similarities as well as other resemblances, like those of personality, that would have emerged as Petra matured.

Too late now. The men's relationship had been broken.

Elizabeth got up from the couch in the den and went to the backyard. The air was wet with humidity, unpleasant really, but she didn't return to the house. Instead, she remembered how, just after discovering she was pregnant with Chris's child, she had tried to imagine what sort of day-to-day family life the three of them would have if they were free to be together. Chris's career was steadily building, and it necessitated a great deal of international travel, which meant long periods of time away from home. She had feared that she and their child would be left largely on their own. Would she become less of a wife and more of a hanger-on? Would she be lonely? She had thought that she might. She didn't want a lonely life. She enjoyed—even relied upon—her busy, small-town world, taking the kids to and from school, hosting birthday parties, shopping at the local farm stands, volunteering at the public library. Would she fit in with Chris's colleagues and friends? The last thing she wanted was to cause him misery if they took that step, make him regret his decision to marry her.

And they would have had to be married in the Catholic Church. She would have had to raise their child in the Catholic faith, which meant that she herself would have to convert, an idea to which she wasn't exactly opposed, but could she honestly say she wanted to become a Catholic? How could she, when she didn't even know what that entailed? She didn't even know if a person who had been divorced before she converted to Catholicism was allowed to marry in the Church! She had grown up in a fairly secular home. If the Ten Commandments were obeyed, and Jesus was acknowledged as a good man who didn't discriminate against the poor and social outcasts, that was about the extent of her so-called religious training. Chris's faith meant so much to him, and it was not a simple faith. Several times during the course of his career he had met with criticism of his ideas on certain matters, ideas that didn't strictly follow the Church's doctrinal line. You had to be brave to profess a faith and, at the same time, to think for yourself.

All in all, there had been a sense of relief in convincing herself that a married life with Chris was out of the question, child or no child. If that made Elizabeth—yet again—a coward, well, so be it. There was no use in denying the truth. She had gone on to pretend that the child was Hugh's, to stay married to him, to be a good wife.

At least, she had truly tried.

Elizabeth sighed. She didn't remember ever feeling as impatient as she did right then on this muggy summer afternoon. To make the situation even worse, she realized that in some small way she felt jealous of Petra meeting with Chris when Elizabeth herself had been denied his presence for so many years. It was appalling to be jealous of her daughter; still, she couldn't deny that she was.

"Oh, please, Petra," Elizabeth whispered into the unhappy, sticky air. "Come home!"

Chapter 54

Petra arrived back at the house on Lavender Lane at seven that evening.

"I've held dinner," Elizabeth announced as soon as Petra had come through the door. Her mother's expression looked strained, weary.

"Good. I had a huge lunch, but I'm starved."

"You were gone for a long time. I was worried. But you look— happy. Relieved."

Petra nodded. "I am. It went better than I could ever have hoped it would."

Her mother put a hand to her heart. "I'm so glad," she said. "I was . . . I worked myself up into a state, wondering, worrying that it was going to be too much for you, that you would regret seeking out your father in the first place."

"I probably would have done the same in your shoes." Petra smiled and reached for her mother's hands. "Mom, I look so much like him! Anyone seeing us together would know immediately that we were father and daughter."

"Does he seem well, healthy?" Elizabeth asked.

"I think so. He's a handsome man, more so than he looks in photographs. He was reading a book when I got to the café."

Elizabeth finally smiled. "Of course, he was. He was always reading. Come, let's eat."

Mother and daughter took their places at the kitchen table. Elizabeth had prepared a cold pasta salad with smoked salmon.

"What was it that he was reading?" Elizabeth asked after a moment.

"A novel by Iris Murdoch. I'm afraid I've never read her books."

"He always loved her work. I remember reading a few of her novels after we ended the relationship because I knew Chris was a fan. It . . . It brought him closer."

"Did you enjoy the books?" Petra asked. Though maybe it hadn't mattered if her mother had enjoyed them, not if they connected her with Chris.

"Oh, yes. Very much. So . . . Do you think he . . . No, forget it."

"Does he forgive you for keeping me a secret?" Petra guessed. Her mother nodded.

"I'm not sure he believes you need to be forgiven. He seems very understanding, very calm about things." Or resigned, Petra thought. Maybe that was a good thing.

"He was never a rash or excitable person," Elizabeth said. "I think people tended to see him as cold or removed, but he wasn't either, just perhaps reserved."

"Still, it was so easy to talk to him, even to reveal something as huge as the fact that I'm his child. Maybe because of his demeanor. Wait, that's not the right word. He . . . Gosh, Mom, he's so different from Dad. I mean, I guess I expected that, given what you told me about him, but still. I can . . . I can see why you would be drawn to him. His sensitivity. His intelligence."

"Will you see each other again?" Elizabeth asked.

"Yes. He's going to stay on in Maine for a few days."

"I'm pleased. So, what did you talk about?"

Petra laughed. "What *didn't* we talk about? My work, his work, our shared love of history. We talked about Dad, too, their friendship, and about you, how Chris fell in love with you at first sight, how you taught him about the world, about love."

Suddenly, Elizabeth bowed her head and put her hands over her eyes. "I don't know why I'm crying," she said weakly.

Petra leapt from her chair and went over to her mother. "Because you're happy," she said, putting her arms around Elizabeth's shoulders. "So am I. And so is Chris. My father."

Chapter 55

Elizabeth sat at the kitchen table, her old diary unopened before her.

Only that morning she had remembered an incident long forgotten. A few months after Hugh's death, a former colleague of his who had been widowed the year before had called her and asked her out to dinner. She had last seen Gerry Lane at Hugh's funeral, where they had barely spoken beyond the required exchange of sympathy and thanks. In fact, since she had first met Gerry, about fifteen years before, they had met only a handful of times and had never shared a one-on-one conversation. Elizabeth had liked his wife well enough, though she had found Cheri a bit silly.

Gerry's offer had puzzled her. It was so unexpected. Had he been attracted to his colleague's wife all along? If so he had admirably kept his feelings to himself. Gerry seemed pleasant and Hugh had spoken highly of him, but still, Elizabeth had politely refused the date. She had no interest in getting involved with another man. There had only ever been two men in her life, Hugh Quirk and his friend Christopher Ryan.

She wondered what had happened to Gerry Lane, if he had remarried, if his kids had accepted his new wife. Vaguely, she considered looking him up but dismissed the idea. They had never been friends, and there was no reason to pursue a friendship now.

Elizabeth drained her cup of the last bit of coffee. It was cold. Blah. She wished she could talk to someone about the crazy situation she had created, about what she was feeling, but there was only Petra, poor Petra, the person right at the heart of the mess. Petra had been burdened enough; she didn't need to hear more intimate knowledge from or share more soul-searching with her mother.

The old diary beckoned, and Elizabeth opened it at random. The entry dated from about a week before the end of her affair with Chris.

It has happened as I knew it would. I've gone from a state of extreme joy to one of extreme sadness. I know now in my heart, in my gut, that our relationship isn't going to last, that it can't, that one of us has to end it before we cause any more damage. But I don't think I can break away. This is the most alive and yet the most miserable I've ever felt. Oh, what am I going to do? The longer it goes on, the harder it will be to leave, but not even for Chris's sake can I act . . . What sort of person does that make me? I'm afraid to find out.

With a shiver, Elizabeth closed the diary again.

Petra's approaching Chris, and Chris's willingness to respond, had opened a door into the family's future. It was inevitable now, or at least highly probable, that she and Chris would come face-to-face again. She was undeniably excited about the prospect while, at the same time, the idea terrified her. Maybe Chris had lied to Petra about having forgiven her mother for keeping his child a secret. Maybe he had been protecting Petra, reserving his anger for when he and Elizabeth were alone.

Oh, what she wouldn't have given to be the proverbial fly on the wall at that first meeting between father and daughter, watching Chris and Petra talk, listening to their words!

Suddenly, Elizabeth got up from her chair and dashed up to her bedroom to put the diary back in the safe and to grab her handbag. It wasn't her day to volunteer at the library but she decided that she would just show up. There was always work to be done, and she was going mad being on her own, rereading the emotionally charged words she had written all those years ago, wondering, hoping, dreaming.

As Hugh had been fond of saying, "work cures most ills." He was right.

He was often right.

Chapter 56

Petra had returned to Orlando's Café in Lark Circle to meet her father. This time, almost immediately she noticed small things that had escaped her attention before: a pale, scraggly scar on the back of his left hand; the way his hair curled slightly at the base of his neck; the fine line on either side of his mouth.

She noticed, too, that there was a vague scent of something clean and fresh about him, maybe the result of his soap or shampoo. She remembered giving her dad, Hugh, a bottle of cologne one Christmas, a typical kid's present for a father, cologne and ties. Had Hugh ever worn the cologne? Had her mother helped her select the scent? These things, Petra couldn't recall.

Today, Chris was wearing a slightly different version of what he had worn the other day. Petra made the assumption that it was his uniform, his trademark, much as her wild prints and flowing fabrics had been hers since college.

"Sometimes," she went on, after a lull in the conversation when they had taken the opportunity to eat their pastries, "I wonder why I don't feel angrier with Mom for having kept my real parentage from me. My sister, Jess, asked me the same question. She said if she were in my situation she'd be furious, and I believe her. But I don't see the point in faking anger so . . ." Petra shrugged.

"Do you ever get genuinely angry?" Chris asked. "You told me the first time we met that anger upsets you."

"Sure, I get genuinely angry. I just don't like it. Does that make me weird?"

Chris laughed. "If it does, then I'm weird, too. I've been told on more than one occasion that I'm a minimizer and an avoider—I agree with that assessment by the way—but sometimes I wonder if those accusations were in fact made because no one has ever witnessed my anger."

Petra thought about that for a moment. Was she, too, a minimizer and an avoider? It bore further exploration.

"Why do you think my mother married Hugh Quirk?" she asked then. It was a question she had been wanting to ask from the start.

Chris didn't answer right away. Only after a few long minutes did he say: "I can only tell you what she told me many years ago. Your mother married Hugh because she loved him— that's the truth—and because she thought he could give her a life. Well, that's what he—and her parents—convinced her to believe. The reality was that he took away what was already there of her life. Granted, it was in seedling form, but it was there. By marrying Hugh, she gave up the opportunity to nurture those seedlings. At least, for a long time she believed that she had."

"How does anyone get it right?" Petra said with a sigh. "How does anyone know for sure that the person he or she decides to marry is really the person who's best for them at that particular time in their life?"

"You can't know anyone else—to the extent it's possible to really know anyone—without having a fairly good idea of your own place in the world," Chris said. "What do you believe? What do you need? What do you reject? If you haven't answered those questions for yourself—or if you haven't begun the process of figuring out the answers—you can too easily be convinced to grasp on to someone else's answers, latch on to their life, find yourself along for someone else's ride."

Petra nodded. "It makes sense. Like you said, I think that's what Mom did, unconsciously, when she married Dad. Hugh. She went along for his ride." And, she thought again, maybe it was why she, Petra, kept her distance from other people, because she knew she might, through close contact, very well lose what tiny bit of herself she possessed.

"I have so many questions," she went on. "I don't mean to be obnoxious or to pry, but I feel I have to at least ask about things. I know you have a right not to answer my questions."

"I'll answer every question I can as honestly as I can," Chris promised.

"Did you intend to ask my mother to leave Hugh?"

"I truly wasn't sure I had a right to ask such a thing of her," Chris admitted. "Even if Elizabeth had offered to leave Hugh, if she had taken the lead, I think I would have been forever bowed down by guilt, which would have seriously damaged any legitimate relationship Elizabeth and I might have built." Chris sighed. "It was all so terribly complicated. It—the affair itself— never should have happened, but it did in spite of our best efforts. I don't regret one moment I spent with your mother. She was the one and only love of my life. Even after all these years, sometimes I still wonder . . . What if I'd had the courage to ask her to marry me before she married Hugh? But I didn't have the courage, and nothing can change that."

"Were you so sure she would have accepted your proposal?" Petra asked with a smile.

"No. But maybe that shouldn't have stopped me from asking. Faint heart never won fair lady."

"But you weren't faint of heart when you and Mom . . . You must have known that you were hurting Hugh. Dad. He was a good man. He didn't deserve to be betrayed by his wife and best friend."

Chris nodded briskly. "No, he didn't deserve that at all. I betrayed him terribly."

Was it inevitable, Petra thought, that everyone would at some point in her life betray someone and be betrayed, with or without intention? Possibly. Probably.

"So," she said after a moment, "at some point not long after the affair was over you must have found out that Mom was pregnant. That sort of thing doesn't stay quiet for long. Didn't it occur to you that you might be the father? Didn't you want to know the truth?"

"Yes," Chris said quietly. "And no. I admit that a part of me was relieved I wasn't being asked to be a father, assuming I was one. I know that sounds awful."

Petra tried but failed to smile. "It does sound awful."

"Let me try to explain what I mean," Chris went on. "I never felt equipped to be a parent; even as a young man, the thought terrified me. I wasn't like Hugh. There was never any question that he would grow up to marry and have children. It was what he wanted and expected of himself from the start. He told me so often enough. He used to tease me about my aversion—that was his word—to what he called the messier side of life, the down and dirty of marriage and family. He used to ask why I didn't just enter the priesthood and 'get it all over with.'"

"Why didn't you?" Petra asked. "Enter the priesthood, I mean, not 'get it all over with'? Gosh, Dad had a way with words!"

"I thought about it," Chris admitted. "But I had no calling. I don't regret my decision to remain a layperson."

"I know I'm repeating myself," Petra said then, "but I still don't understand. Why, if you had any suspicion whatsoever that I might be your daughter, didn't you confront my mother?"

"I don't know if I can explain," Chris admitted. "I could simply say that I don't really remember what I was thinking back then and that would be truthful, if not the whole story. I know that I never wanted to put pressure on Elizabeth. She put enough pressure on herself. I suspect that I believed she would always act in the best interests of the child, no matter the father. And, well, let's say I had asked Elizabeth if I was the father and she had told me that yes, I was, what could we have done? I would have been compelled to accept your mother's need for silence and secrecy. I would have had to come to terms with the fact that my child could never be a part of my life." Chris shook his head. "Maybe I was too much of a coward to bear that burden."

"You wouldn't have fought for access to me?" Petra pressed. "You wouldn't have demanded that I be a part of your life?"

Chris held her eye and spoke firmly. "It would have been terribly selfish of me to demand a share in your life. It would only have harmed the woman I loved above all other people, certainly above myself."

"Okay," Petra said after a long moment, feeling very slightly ashamed. "You're right."

And then she thought about how much her father, Christopher, had suffered for the sake of Elizabeth, and how much Hugh, as well, had suffered, and for a moment Petra once again felt angry with her mother for having engineered a situation in which no one really benefited—no one but Elizabeth that is. By keeping silent, she had been able to keep herself safe and unpunished. Well, safe and unpunished by everyone but her conscience, and Petra knew for a fact that her mother's conscience had never let her rest easy. The moment of anger passed.

"So," she went on, "when I was born in May 1992 you—"

"I sent a congratulatory card and continued to keep the promise I'd made to your mother to fade away from the family, and more specifically, not to be in touch with her. Maybe I was wrong to keep the promise."

"Do you think she would have told you the truth if you'd broken your word, gotten in touch with her and demanded she tell you if you were my father?" Petra asked.

"I don't know." Chris sighed. "She might have thought that

if I knew I was the father I'd confront Hugh, tell him that his wife and I were in love. But I would never have done that, not unless Elizabeth asked me to. In fact, no, I'm sure she never really feared my doing something rash."

"But if she *had* asked you to confront my father, tell him you were in love, would you have done it?" Petra asked. "Would you have had the nerve," was what she really wanted to ask.

"I honestly don't know," Chris said after a moment. "Your mother saved me from having to do anything, from having to make a courageous decision. She was the brave one. I'm afraid I've always been somewhat of a coward."

Petra wondered. She had always seen herself as somewhat of a coward. Maybe this was another way in which she and her biological father were alike. "She named me after you," she said.

Chris smiled. "Of course. How could I not have made the connection? Peter is the name I took when I made my confirmation. I must have told her about it once. I'm honored, but not surprised, that she remembered."

"So, years passed . . . And still, you kept away."

Chris nodded. "Yes. I conquered the occasional impulse to make contact and sincerely hoped Hugh and Elizabeth had found peace together. When their thirtieth wedding anniversary was announced in the local paper—I knew the anniversary was approaching so I checked the Eliot's Corner paper for any mention of a celebration—I felt my heart contract. I was pleased for them—thirty years of marriage is a great achievement—but I was overwhelmed yet again by thoughts of what might have been."

"If you and my mother had married before she married Hugh?" Petra suggested. "When it could have been simple and uncomplicated, no ex-husbands and stepchildren, no secret love child."

"Yes," Chris admitted. "But pondering what might have happened is rarely a productive way of spending one's time. I brought myself around. I wanted to send an anniversary card, debated with myself about the wisdom or folly of such an act . . . Would Hugh see it as a gesture of renewed friendship? Would he reach out to me, invite me into his home again? That could only cause Elizabeth distress. In the end, I did nothing. I let the occasion go unremarked by the old bachelor friend, hoping that out of sight did truly mean out of mind."

Petra took a last sip of her iced coffee. She realized she felt worn out by this conversation with her biological father. Still, she needed to know more.

"I know you're Catholic," she said, "and that the Church doesn't allow divorce, but Mom wasn't Catholic. Didn't it occur to either of you that she could get a divorce?"

"Of course." Chris paused. "But your mother was afraid of your father in some ways. He was a formidable man. She was worried he'd manage to get you children."

"Mom indicated as much, but I never thought of Dad as vindictive," Petra said. "I can't believe that he was."

"Maybe not," Chris admitted. "I'm just telling you what your mother feared. After all, Hugh could be self-righteous. He felt himself a paragon of virtue and morality. That belief might have compelled him to try to take you children away from their cheating mother."

"But he was a good person, wasn't he?" Petra said. "You said so before."

"Yes," Chris said. "His problem was that he couldn't see or admit to his flaws. That blindness resulted in his exalting himself over mere mortals." Chris shook his head. "I'm sorry. That was nasty. I suppose even after all this time it makes me angry to think that he would have condemned your mother for her relationship with me without even trying to understand why or how it came about."

Petra realized that she felt slightly sick. "You assumed that Dad would have acted badly. You and Mom both made that assumption. Maybe you underestimated him. Maybe he would have surprised you both. Maybe he would have understood."

Chris shook his head. "I don't think so. People don't radically change. Not usually. But yes, Elizabeth and I assumed that Hugh would act and react as he always did, as he always had."

"But after he died, weren't you ever tempted to contact my mother? It has been a long time now, almost ten years. Surely, there could be nothing wrong with making a phone call or writing a letter?"

"I was tempted," Chris admitted. "But you see, I found out about Hugh's death via one of your mother's friends. I got a formal note from this woman, I can't recall her name offhand, an announcement of Hugh's passing, with no personal message, just information about Hugh's favorite charity to which I could offer a donation in lieu of sending flowers to the funeral home. I took it as a sign that Elizabeth didn't want me to contact her. Yes, I assumed. Was I acting the coward again? Very possibly. I left it to her to contact me if she wanted to. And she never did."

Always the gentleman, Petra thought. Never the hero? But that was unfair. "Were you upset when you heard that Dad died?" she asked.

"Of course," Chris said promptly. "My vibrant friend was gone too soon. He'd left a wife and family bereft. All the old guilt and sadness I'd felt about the affair came rushing back to life. I was pretty depressed for a long time. Eventually, the psychological and emotional pain eased. It usually does, though I'm not sure it really dies; it just goes to sleep, as it were."

Petra realized that it was time to put an end to this second meeting with Christopher Ryan. She needed to get away, to process all that she had heard, to consider what Chris had said about cowardice, emotional pain, sacrifice, and so much more.

They parted with a handshake. Petra thought that Chris might have expected another hug, but she didn't feel capable of making the gesture. But they also parted with a promise to continue their conversation at another time. Christopher's eyes had looked sad.

The drive back to Eliot's Corner was a bit of a challenge

for Petra. Her nerves were jangling and her mind racing; both made it difficult to focus on the road.

Earlier, she had told Chris that she understood why he hadn't fought for access to his child. He had explained that he was only acting in Elizabeth's best interests. But wasn't his withdrawal from any relationship with the Quirk family an act of convenient passivity, even of cowardice?

You could say one thing about Hugh Quirk, Petra thought. He was never a coward. He had a forceful nature, and it caused him to take action, maybe even at times to rush in where he possibly shouldn't have. But there was something admirable about that. The reckless hero, careless of his own safety.

As for Christopher Ryan . . . When was passivity, when was doing nothing, or taking the path of least resistance, the right thing? When was it cowardly? The answer to that question depended on the circumstances of the situation, as well as on the moral, emotional, mental, and physical fitness of the person who was in the position to act, or to not act.

Petra sighed. She felt bothered by this second meeting with her father in ways she hadn't by the first. But that shouldn't be a surprise. They had spoken with so much honesty about so many things, many of them disturbing.

This was reality, Petra realized, as she was finally within blocks of Lavender Lane, not the stuff of fiction or of childish daydreams. Christopher Ryan was a flesh and blood man, not a glamorous romantic hero from a film, not a puppet prince from a fairy tale. He had loved and lost; he had erred and tried to make amends. He was just like every other man who had gone before him, and every other who was to come.

Merely human.

Chapter 57

Elizabeth had suggested a get-together with her middle daughter. She had no other motive beyond having a hopefully pleasant—or, at least neutral—exchange with Jess. And if she waited for Jess to initiate a date, she would be waiting until the crack of doom or just about.

Jess was almost ten minutes late arriving at Chez Claudine, which was unlike her. Like Hugh, she believed that punctuality was a virtue. She offered no explanation or apology and sat with a large sigh that could signify annoyance or exhaustion.

"How's your day been so far?" Elizabeth asked.

Jess shrugged. "Okay. Wait, I need a coffee."

She got up again and went to the counter to place her order. Elizabeth took a sip of her cooling cappuccino and waited for Jess to return.

"What's up with Petra?" Jess asked, sitting again with a cup of steaming espresso. "Not that I've seen much of her these past two weeks but she seems distracted, more spacy than usual. Has she met someone? When was the last time she had a boyfriend? Do you think she's ever going to get married?"

Yes, Elizabeth thought. Petra had in fact met someone. Her father.

"To be honest, I can't remember the last time she was involved with a man, and of course I have no idea if she'll ever marry," Elizabeth said. "But Petra's love life, or lack thereof, isn't really our business."

"Isn't it?" Jess laughed. "She's always asking me about Eddie. Sometimes I think she can't wait to hear that we've broken up."

Elizabeth frowned. "That's not true. Petra is genuinely interested in you and in Cam. She wants you both to be happy."

"Fine. Then she should stop asking me about Eddie."

"It's perfectly normal for her to do so," Elizabeth argued. "It's perfectly normal for me to ask, as well. We're your family."

"Speaking of family," Jess said, sitting back and folding her arms across her chest, "I wonder how Petra's finding out that Dad wasn't really her father is going to affect her love life, if she ever has one. I mean, she might totally distrust relationships now, assuming she ever trusted them. She might even come to hate men. Though that might not be such a bad thing. The older I get, the less use I have for them, I swear. Except for Dad. He was one of the good guys, in spite of whatever problems you might have had with him."

Elizabeth felt as if she had been kicked in the stomach. Jess had a right to be angry, but she didn't have to remind her mother that she had possibly—probably—damaged Petra by revealing the truth of her parentage. That was cruel, and gratuitous. And there was really no need for Jess to comment on the nature of her parents' relationship with each other. Elizabeth felt a strong urge to fight back but managed, like a mature adult, to conquer that urge. It wasn't easy.

"Have you spoken to Raven?" she asked. It was an obvious tactic, a change of subject.

Jess frowned. "Why would I?"

"Because you said she had a family crisis that was preventing her from going ahead with the new business. Don't you want to see if she's okay, if she needs some support?"

"We weren't friends," Jess pointed out. "It was all just business. Never mix business and friendships, that's my motto."

Elizabeth realized that she had chosen another potentially dangerous topic of conversation. But on she went. "Your father mixed business and friendships," she said, "all the time."

"But he was a salesman. It was his job to be nice and make friends. Ugh. I could never."

Then it was a good thing after all, Elizabeth thought, that Jess's business venture never made it off the ground. If she found being nice and making friends so unappealing, good luck finding and keeping clients.

"I don't mean with his customers," Elizabeth said. "I mean with his colleagues at the company. It was a pretty tight-knit group at one point, and right up to the time he got sick your father was spending time with some of the guys after office hours. Friendship and business aren't necessarily incompatible."

Jess frowned doubtfully. "Aren't they?"

"I was on good terms with the majority of my colleagues at the school. And Mrs. Shandy and I became genuine friends."

"Well, we're different people. You're all . . . I'm more discriminating than you are."

Was she? Elizabeth wondered. Then how did Jess explain having chosen Eddie as her partner, a nice enough guy but, if Jess was to be believed, someone whose taste in companions ran toward the willfully unemployed and the boastingly uneducated? Presumably, if only on occasion, Jess spent time with these people. Did she enjoy their company? Or did she sit with her arms folded across her chest, frowning and judging?

Again, Elizabeth struggled to hold her temper. "What about the people at your office?" she pressed. "I've met a few of your colleagues. They seem like decent people. You really don't ever socialize with any of them?"

"No. I mean, not really. A few times this woman Paula has asked me to go for a drink after work with some other people, but I haven't gone. Don't get me wrong," Jess added hurriedly.

"I'm perfectly pleasant at work; I just don't feel the need to be best friends with the people I spend eight to ten hours a day with. Anyway, why are we even talking about this?"

"I asked about Raven."

Jess sighed. "Look, if it means so much to you I'll call her tomorrow."

"It's up to you," Elizabeth pointed out. "It shouldn't matter what I think."

"I know that. God, sometimes . . ." Jess shook her head. "Look, I'm out of here."

Elizabeth didn't try to stop Jess from leaving the café. In some ways, she worried about Jess more than she worried about Cam and Petra. If Hugh were alive he might be able to help his favorite daughter negotiate what was clearly a stressful time in her life. Was Elizabeth misremembering, or had Jess been a happier, or at least a more amiable person, when Hugh was alive? Oddly, Elizabeth found it difficult to answer that question. What she did remember clearly was that Jess had moved out of the house immediately upon graduating from college and had never come back. Elizabeth remembered, too, that before Eddie there had been two other long-term boyfriends, neither of whom Jess had brought around much at all. For all of her adulthood thus far she had kept her personal life far apart from her family life. Elizabeth realized she wasn't even sure that Jess had ever had a close friend after college, male or female. Certainly, no one came readily to mind.

Three women came into the café in a flurry of chat and laughter. Each one was carrying several shopping bags, suggesting they had been on a bit of a spree at the boutiques and craft shops around town. Elizabeth got up, brought her cup and Jess's to the bussing station, and left the café. The women seemed perfectly pleasant, but Elizabeth didn't feel in the mood for witnessing the sort of easy friendship her middle child might never have known, and, if she kept on the way she was going, might never even know in the future.

Chapter 58

Petra was aware she had been somewhat ignoring her sisters since Chris had come into her life, but it was easier to keep the burgeoning relationship a secret if she spent less time with them. If things between her and her father continued to be positive—and after their last meeting, she wasn't really sure that they would—she would tell Cam and Jess before long.

For a third time, now with some trepidation, Petra had driven to Lark's Circle to meet her father. The idea of meeting closer to home hadn't been mentioned, and she was glad about that. Word that Petra had been seen in the company of a stranger, an older man, didn't need to be passed around Eliot's Corner. Who knew what some people might make of it?

Today father and daughter met at a little park on the outskirts of town. The grass hadn't been mowed in some time; Petra liked the slightly wild, natural look of the place.

"I like to come here early in the morning," Chris told her, "before the sun is quite up."

Petra smiled. "I'm afraid I haven't seen a sunrise in a very long time! I go to bed kind of late."

"Is that a new habit?" he asked.

"Nope. Ever since I was a kid I'd stay up past bedtime whenever I could get away with it."

"Doing what?"

"Reading, mostly. You know, a flashlight under the covers sort of thing, though maybe most kids my age were using the flashlight on their cell phones. Not me. I had this old, bright yellow thing I'd found at a yard sale for a dollar!"

Chris laughed. "I did the same thing way back when. But I probably didn't need to be secret about staying up late and reading. Both of my parents were bookish types. In fact, I'm sure they knew what I was up to and approved."

They had just begun their second turn around the little park when Petra finally worked up the nerve to ask if Christopher was in a committed relationship with a woman. If the answer was yes, that meant that someone had legitimate emotional claims on him, perhaps claims more legitimate than Petra and her mother had.

"No," Chris replied promptly. "No relationship."

Petra felt a palpable sense of relief. "Okay. Has there ever been anyone else important since Mom? I'm sorry," she added hurriedly. "I probably have no right to ask that."

"It's perfectly fine for you to ask," Chris assured her. "And the answer is no. Many years ago, I got to know someone through my work. I liked her, and she made it clear she would be open to a relationship, but I knew that there was no future for us. I'm afraid I'm one of those very odd, very old-fashioned people for whom there is only one love. One soul mate."

"That didn't have to stop you from dating, though," Petra pointed out. "I mean, you know. People have . . ." She stopped, embarrassed. "People need companionship."

Christopher laughed. "I've always had plenty of companionship, often more than I'm comfortable with. There have been so many times in my life when I would have done anything for a moment alone. But I was never interested in dating, as you put it."

"Sorry. I suppose you want to know about Mom and other men. I mean, since Dad died."

"Only if she wants to tell me," Chris said pointedly. "She owes me nothing."

"She thinks she owes you a lot," Petra said. "But there hasn't been anyone since Dad died. Just so you know."

"Okay," Chris said after a moment. "But she has friends, I hope."

"A few," Petra told him. "Now that she won't be going back to work in September though, I don't know. She might find herself feeling lonely. I hope not, but I didn't plan on staying in Eliot's Corner forever. Not that I have all that much to go back to in Portsmouth. I mean, I like the city and the people I know there, my roommates and all, are great but, well, the truth is that I've been losing interest in working in the vintage business, not entirely but . . ."

"There's a saying of Montaigne's that's always stuck in my head," Chris said. "'The soul which has no fixed purpose in life is lost; to be everywhere, is to be nowhere.' It's given me pause for thought more than once in my life when I've found myself doubting the meaning or direction of my work, wondering if I'm really focusing on what's most important for me."

Petra nodded. "I read a bit of Montaigne in college though I'm afraid I don't remember much. But what he said, to be everywhere is to be nowhere, well, I finally know that's true."

"If you had to choose one field of study to pursue," Chris said, as they began their third round of the little park, "one topic or area you felt most deeply about or that interested you above and beyond all others—but not to the absolute exclusion of every other concern in life; being well-rounded isn't the same as having no fixed purpose—what would that be?"

"I guess I would have to say literature and philosophy." Then, Petra smiled. "And history. I'm not sure how I would choose. I've continued to read in all three areas since college though not in a very disciplined way. And it's hard to really come to understand concepts and even the workings of a piece of writing without dialogue with other people, without having access to a teacher or a mentor. Self-education works really well for some people, and I guess it works for me, but it doesn't feel like enough."

"So? What's holding you back from entering into dialogues with others, from turning to a teacher or a mentor for guidance?" Chris asked. "What's stopping you from going back to school?"

"I worry that it's mostly laziness," Petra admitted. "Graduate school would be a big commitment, and it would mean setting a course of action for my life after I had earned a degree. I mean, I believe in learning for learning's sake, but I want to make a positive difference in the lives of other people. I want what I learn to be of use somehow. At least, one day."

"Are you sure what's holding you back isn't fear of success?" Chris asked.

Petra smiled. "You mean, do I suffer from imposter syndrome? Maybe. I don't know. I've never really done any work in which I could achieve a level of success I'd feel I didn't deserve, that I'd achieved accidentally or through sheer luck. Does that make sense?"

Chris laughed. "Yes, I think so."

Suddenly, on that August morning, walking alongside her newly discovered father, Petra had what she thought was a genuine epiphany, and she remembered what she had been wondering about only weeks before, about revelations and how they came about. She began to talk, looking somewhere in the middle distance, as if watching a screen on which the story of her life was playing out.

"My father, Hugh," she said, "always made fun of me, not really mocking me but kind of gently laughing at my tendency to 'space out' as he called it. He used to tell me I thought too much and that too much thinking would only get me into trouble, that if I went on the way I was going I'd never be able to support myself and that people would take advantage of me.

Somewhere along the line," she went on, "I think I stopped being me. Mostly, I mean. I came to believe that being me was silly and wasteful. But I didn't really have anything to replace me. I mean, here I am, thirty years old, barely scraping by, doing something I enjoy but not something big enough to really satisfy me, not something that really benefits people in any deep and important way."

Petra looked at Chris now, and he nodded, his expression rapt with attention.

"Dad died not long after I graduated from college," Petra went on. "He'd thought the idea of my going on to grad school for a degree other than business was impractical, not to mention ridiculous. Mom tried to encourage me, she really did, but Dad was a force of nature, and I never seemed to find the strength to stand up to him. I always just folded. I know Mom thinks I'm not using my full potential. She told me that . . . Well, she said that my being your child means that I have it in me to do if not great things then at least something more important than what I'm doing now. I've told her that I'm fairly happy and satisfied, but I'm neither. I've been lying to everyone for so long."

Chris reached for Petra's hand, and she grasped his tightly. It felt right.

Petra shook her head. "I just thought of something else. What if one of the reasons Dad kind of put me down all the time about my 'thinking too much' was because I reminded him of you, the friend he had lost to a world that to him was so foreign, the life of the mind as he saw it? I'm not saying he suspected I wasn't his biological daughter, but that maybe . . . Maybe on some subconscious level he was punishing you for what he saw as you leaving him behind by trying to discourage me from going in the same direction? Is that crazy?"

"No, it's not crazy," Chris assured her. "Unfortunately, we'll never know what Hugh was thinking or feeling, but whatever that was, it can't be allowed to stand in the way of your living your life in the way you want to live it."

"I know," Petra admitted. "It's just—I'm scared."

"Maybe being scared can morph into being excited."

"Maybe you can help me with that."

"I'll do my best," Chris promised. "And a bit of fear can be a good thing. It gets the adrenaline going, at the very least."

"Still, I don't like feeling scared."

Chris laughed. "Then you're a very normal person. How about we get something to eat? All this walking in circles has made me hungry."

"Yes, please." Petra smiled. "You should probably know that I'm always hungry."

"Then you are most definitely my daughter."

Chapter 59

Elizabeth was feeling good about the relationship that was developing between Petra and her father. After her second meeting with Chris, Petra had admitted to feeling unhappy and unsettled, but after the third afternoon she had spent with him, the negative feelings had been dispatched, and Petra believed she had experienced a sort of personal breakthrough. She felt that she was beginning to see a way into her future, beginning to define a purpose.

That was indeed good news, but Elizabeth had refrained from asking Petra for details. She was worried that she had been a pest since father and daughter had met. Still, Petra hadn't once complained about her mother's inquisitiveness. And if she was holding certain things back, that was her right.

Perhaps the most important bit of information Petra had shared was that there had been no other woman in Chris's life since Elizabeth. "I believed him," Petra told her mother. "I mean, why would he lie? Anyway, he doesn't seem like a liar. Neither do you. You never have. It must have been really difficult to keep your relationship a secret, totally against your natures."

Elizabeth had been so grateful for Petra's kind words and

the depth of understanding behind them. And she had felt an undeniable thrill knowing now for sure that no other woman had replaced her in Chris's heart. If that thrill was tempered by concern that Chris had lived a lonely life in the past thirty years, well . . .

Now, Elizabeth opened her laptop and logged into her e-mail account. The only message of any interest was from a travel company for single women she had discovered a few months back, before she had told her children about her affair. The fact was that she was financially secure enough to travel in some style, and for the first time in many years she had no major commitments to keep her in Eliot's Corner day after day. Tour groups were an obvious option, but so was travel on her own. There was something very tempting about being in a position to determine the direction of one's own wanderings. No partner—or fellow tour group members—with whom to negotiate a destination or the sort of accommodation they would occupy or the type of food they would have for their dinner. Tropical island or large metropolis. Airbnb or high-end hotel. Haute cuisine or street food. On her own, she could seek out unusual exhibits in local museums. On her own she could wander crooked cobblestoned streets and charming little alleys for hours on end. On her own she could eat whenever, wherever, and whatever she wanted to.

This current message from Women on the Road featured several photos of destinations to which the company was offering tours in the fall and spring: Provence, Tuscany, Lisbon. The photos were enticing, as were the testimonials given by women who had traveled with the company, yet Elizabeth still couldn't muster the enthusiasm to make a commitment to a journey of adventure.

The thought had flitted across her mind again the night before as she was getting ready for bed that she might be holding back on making plans because of Chris. After all the years since the end of their affair, could she possibly be counting on him to come back into her life and sweep her off her feet? After all the years of residing under—and often resenting and resisting—Hugh's old-fashioned male dominance, was it possible that she was falling back into the trap of waiting for, of hoping for a man to rescue her, to give her a life she was too timid to create for herself?

If that was the truth, then she was in trouble.

But was it the truth? Why was it so hard to be honest with herself? Did she really want to see Chris? Was she truly ready for a reunion, no matter the result? Did she have the courage to call him, send him an e-mail or a letter? And if the answer to these questions was yes, what was the genuine motive behind that yes? How much of her intention was about Chris and what might be best for him, and how much was about her, about what she wanted? How much could be put down to altruism and how much to selfishness?

Petra, Elizabeth knew, would approve if she did reach out to Christopher; Petra had made that very clear. She might not cherish hopes that her parents would reunite after thirty years apart, but she would very much like them to be on good terms.

Elizabeth shut her computer and grimaced. To be tormented in this almost adolescent way at her age was an embarrassment, even if she was the only one to know what was going through her heart and mind. Did people ever truly grow up and leave the desire for romance behind? Or was everyone potential prey to desire, to the need for intimate recognition, until the very end of their lives?

At the moment, Elizabeth thought, she would rather not know the answer to those questions. Instead, she went into her favorite search engine and typed the words: *essential sights for a weekend in Paris.*

A little research couldn't hurt.

Chapter 60

Summer 1991

"We can't go on doing this," Elizabeth said.

"I know."

"I've never been more miserable in my life. And yet, just weeks ago I was never happier."

"I know. I feel the same way."

Elizabeth sat hunched in one corner of the couch in the living area of Chris's little cottage. Her eyes were red and swollen from crying. Her head ached. Chris sat at the other end of the couch, but she couldn't bring herself to look at him.

She should, she supposed, be happy. Hugh had been declared cancer-free. The scare had been just that, a scare, though one that had deeply rattled Hugh, Elizabeth, and Chris. Of course, Hugh had no idea that Chris knew of his health scare. If Hugh had known, he might very well have wondered why his wife had spoken, even to his dearest friend, when they had agreed to "keep things quiet."

"I'm so sorry," Elizabeth whispered. "How did this happen to us? How could something so beautiful and wonderful and real have become . . ."

"Our love is still all of those things." Chris's voice was rough with emotion. "Don't think otherwise."

Elizabeth laughed bitterly. "Poor timing? An ill-fated romance? Oh, God, what a nightmare. What a clichéd nightmare."

She turned to Chris and saw him flinch. Her words had hurt him. She hadn't meant them to hurt.

"I'm sorry," she said. "None of this is your fault. You've been nothing but—"

"What have I been?" Chris interrupted. "Good? Honest? Heroic? I've been none of those things! A coward? Yes. I'm the one at fault, Elizabeth. I'm the one who should feel guilty, and I do feel guilty, terribly so."

Elizabeth pushed herself up from the couch. "Oh, this is ridiculous! We're both to blame! We should have ended this weeks ago, we should never have allowed this to happen in the first place, we should . . ."

"We should part now before we come to hate each other."

Elizabeth felt the words as a slap. "That's not possible," she cried. "I could never hate you! And you . . ."

Chris now rose. "I'm sorry. I could never hate you, either. Of course, I couldn't. But you're right; we have to end this relationship. What we're doing to Hugh is . . ."

"You know I can't leave him. I'm scared to leave him."

"Yes. I know. So . . ."

Elizabeth sighed and put a hand to her aching head.

"Hugh wants the three of us to go out to dinner. But you'll have to tell him you can't, that you'll be out of town or something."

"Yes."

"And I think it's best . . . I think you should . . ."

"I'll absent myself from the friendship. Slowly, kindly, but I'll stay away from your family."

Elizabeth felt her knees begin to wobble. "I think it's the only way I can go on," she said hoarsely. "And we, you and I . . ."

"We won't speak again, unless you want to. I promise."

"It's not about what I want. It's about what has to be."

Suddenly, they were in each other's arms, holding on more tightly than they ever had, for one last moment. And then, that last moment came to an end, and Elizabeth, still trembling, ran from Christopher Ryan's cottage.

She didn't look back. She knew what looking back would cost her.

She managed to drive on a mile or two before she had to pull off the road, too distraught to continue. She leaned her forehead against the steering wheel and moaned. Would she really never feel Chris's lips on hers, or the touch of his hand on the small of her back? Would she really never be allowed to gaze into his eyes as they lay together in his bed? So much loss! How would she ever bear so much loss?

Maybe, she wouldn't have to. She could turn the car around, drive back to the cottage, tell Chris she had been wrong, tell him that she would leave Hugh, let Hugh have the children if he demanded them, walk away and . . .

No.

Just a dream.

Eventually, Elizabeth raised her head. She wondered if she had been seen by anyone passing, a woman in distress, alone in her car, sobbing. What did it matter now if she had been seen? What did it matter if someone went to Hugh, told him he had seen his wife on the side of a lonely road out in the middle of nowhere, her head on the steering wheel of her car?

It *didn't* matter, because in some very important way, her life was over. Oh, she would go on, day to day, week to week, year after year, God willing. For the sake of her children, if not for her own sake. But going on wasn't living.

Not really.

Elizabeth wiped her eyes one last time, started the car again, and headed back to her very nice house and to her loving family on Lavender Lane.

Chapter 61

Summer 2022

Cam had brought a foldable chair from the house. Jess and Petra preferred to sit on the beach blanket that had been in use in the Quirk family since Petra's childhood. The blanket was almost threadbare, but Petra couldn't imagine anyone in her family wanting to throw it in the garbage and replace it with something pristine.

The cooler, though, was fairly new, bought since Hugh Quirk's passing. At the moment, it was stocked with reusable bottles of water; chunks of watermelon and green grapes in plastic containers; and a bag of sea salt and vinegar flavored potato chips. In Petra's opinion, no outing to the beach was complete without a bag of chips.

"Did I forget the napkins?" Cam wondered, rummaging in her voluminous striped canvas bag. "Nope, here they are."

"Remember how when we were kids we wiped our dirty, sticky hands on the blanket and Mom would scold us?" Jess smiled. "Good ole blanket. It's no worse for wear in spite of sticky fingers."

"Are you really oblivious to the stains and holes?" Cam asked with a smile. "Or do you find the flaws charming?"

Petra only half listened to her sisters' good-natured banter. Her plan was to tell them about her new relationship with Chris. She was a bit nervous about the reception her news would receive but not concerned about her ability to handle any possible criticism. Petra felt bolstered by her growing relationship with Christopher Ryan. She felt as if she had found a genuine ally.

"I've met with Chris Ryan," she announced. "My father. Actually, I've seen him three times in the past weeks."

"And you're only telling us now?" Cam asked, turning to look at her sister, her eyes wide. Petra thought she sounded hurt.

"I'm sorry. I wanted to see how things went before I let you know. If Chris had been dismissive or angry, I might never have told you. But he hasn't been either of those things. He's been nothing but kind and receptive."

"Yeah, but is he being honest?" Jess snapped. "He's lied before."

Cam sighed. "Jess, be quiet. Just let Petra talk."

This was exactly what Petra had expected, Jess's negative attitude.

"Sorry," Jess said, her face still marred by a frown. "So, it must have been pretty weird meeting him that first time."

Petra laughed. "Uh, you could say that. But at the same time, it felt totally natural."

"Weird and natural? Yeah, that sounds healthy."

"Wait, when you first met did he know you were his daughter?" Cam asked.

"No. I had reached out to him," Petra explained, "saying I was Elizabeth's youngest child and asking if we could talk, maybe meet. He responded pretty quickly and said yes to both."

"No questions, like why are you contacting me and why now?" Jess asked.

"Nope. But it turns out he had guessed it had something to do with my knowing about the affair. He came up to Maine— it was his suggestion—and we met at a café in Lark's Circle where he stays when he visits the area. I told him then that we all knew about his relationship with Mom, and that I was his daughter."

"Just like that?" Jess said. "I have to hand it to you, Petra. That took courage. So, how did he react? Was it a big dramatic scene? Tears and wailing and breast-beating?"

Petra rolled her eyes. "Not quite. That's not Chris's style. Like I said, he knew that some sort of revelation was coming."

"So, how will this change things for you?" Cam asked. Her genuine concern was clear. "I mean, will you go on seeing him once he goes back to Boston—if that's where he still lives—and his . . . I was going to say when he goes back to his life. But you are his life now, a big part of it."

Petra nodded. "Oh yes, we fully intend to keep the relationship alive. Honestly, I know it hasn't been long since we found each other, Chris and I, but our relationship feels essential to me. In a way, I'm already relying on him, not for day-to-day things, but for—I can't put it into words."

"Just be careful," Cam said gently. "None of us wants to see you get hurt. He might not feel as strongly about your relationship as you do. At least, not yet."

"What does Mom think about all this? I mean, is she going to start seeing him again? Does he want her back in his life, too?" Jess frowned. "A little, ready-made family of his own after all those years of bachelorhood?"

"Jess, don't," Cam said angrily.

Jess shrugged but didn't apologize.

Petra felt sorry for Jess; it couldn't be easy facing the world with such a suspicious, cramped attitude. "I don't know what will happen between Mom and Chris, if anything. I'm trying to stay away from that issue. I mean, it's up to them if they want to resume their friendship—"

"Or something more," Jess put in.

"Or something more. And I have absolutely no need for my birth parents to reunite, though of course I'd like it if they were on good terms. I'm an adult. I had a good father in Hugh. I'd be content to enjoy my own relationship with Chris, in whatever form that takes, aside from any relationship he and Mom might decide on."

"No awkward family dinners at the holidays? Good. I'm still not sure I want to know this guy."

"That's your call, Jess," Petra said calmly, though her sister's attitude had worn on her nerves. Petra had never been Eddie's biggest fan, but at times she felt sorry for the guy, living with her prickly, judgmental sister. How did he do it? Did he simply ignore her? That couldn't be easy.

Suddenly, Cam rose from her chair. "Gosh, it's hot. I'm going in for a swim. Anyone want to join me?"

"I will." Jess leapt to her feet and began to stride down to the surf.

Cam smiled down at Petra. "You okay?"

Petra nodded. "Yeah. Thanks."

"Thank you for telling us."

Petra watched her sisters at the water's edge, wading in up to their knees, then further. She loved them both deeply if not in every way equally. And she would very much like it if one day she could share them with Chris. But only time would tell. Both women had a lot on their minds right now, their own crises to resolve.

Cam turned to look back at Petra and waved. Petra smiled and waved back, just as both Cam and Jess dived into the surf.

Chapter 62

Elizabeth was downtown for the sole purpose of visiting Motifs, a shop that sold locally made, all-natural lotions and creams for dry and troubled skin. She had met the women who produced the stuff, a married couple in their forties, back when they started their business, selling their products at a weekly farmers' market. Since then the business had grown remarkably, and now the products were sold in several stores in and around Eliot's Corner. Though not inexpensive, the Misty Morning line was worth every penny as far as Elizabeth was concerned.

She was just leaving Motifs, having successfully made her purchases, when she spotted Arden Bell across the street, looking particularly glowing and youthful in a rosy pink blouse over pistachio-green linen pants. Lately, Arden's wardrobe had become more colorful and playful; Elizabeth thought that the look suited her.

Elizabeth waved, and in response, Arden dashed over to join her.

"I'm on my way to Chez Claudine for an iced coffee," Elizabeth said. "Care to join me? Iced coffee is an American thing, isn't it?"

Arden smiled. "Yes, I'll join you, and I don't know. All I know is that iced coffee is very refreshing on a day like this, more so than iced tea in my opinion."

The women entered the café, placed their orders for two large iced coffees, and took the drinks to a table. The café was otherwise empty; it was after lunchtime but not quite time for a midafternoon, sugar-rush snack.

"I'm sort of busting with some big news," Arden said after she had taken a sip of her drink. "May I share it with you?"

Elizabeth nodded. "Of course."

"Gordon and I have decided to move in together. If all goes well, and I feel sure it will, we'd like to get married next year."

"That's wonderful, Arden," Elizabeth said warmly. "I'm so happy for you, truly. He's a lovely guy—well, you know that—and you seem so suited to each other. So, are you buying a place together or . . . ?"

"For now," Arden explained, "I'm moving into Gordon's place and making a few major changes, to all of which he's agreed. His taste in home furnishings is, well, it's awful! Laura will move into my place. She's enjoyed being housemates with Deborah, but she feels it's time to be on her own again."

Elizabeth nodded. "That all sounds reasonable."

"Honestly," Arden went on, "I never thought I'd fall in love again after losing Rob in the way I did. I certainly never imagined that I'd be thinking of marrying one day. I'm still sort of in shock about it, but I know it's the right thing for me."

Elizabeth couldn't help but admire Arden's courage in welcoming love and romance after the brief and tragic experience of her youth. And, Arden's happy news gave her yet more to consider about the possibilities inherent in her own situation with Chris Ryan. That is, if he didn't refuse to have anything to do with his former love. Assuming she ever found the courage to reach out without the selfish intention of using him as a crutch to prop up her post-career life.

"How does Laura feel about this development?" Elizabeth

asked. "About you and Gordon making such a big commitment."

"She's happy for me," Arden said. "I won't deny that the idea of my marrying is a bit startling for her. I mean, she's come to idolize her father in a way, and I think that's probably very normal given the circumstances. An innocent young man, killed and tossed away without concern. I asked Laura outright if she felt I was in some way betraying Rob by moving in with Gordon. To be honest, I've asked myself the same question often enough. But Laura denied feeling that I was sullying Rob's memory by moving on after all these years. Still, we're both aware that this is a big step, one that will change our dynamic, mother and daughter, to some degree."

"Are you worried the change will be for the worse? I'm sorry," Elizabeth added hurriedly. "It's just that you and Laura only found each other a short time ago. It would be a shame to damage or to lose such a precious gift."

"It would," Arden admitted. "But Laura and I have come so far in that short period of time. It's like we've been making up for all those years apart. We're very close, closer than I could have ever hoped for. So, yes, my moving in with and marrying Gordon will change things, but not for the worse. I have to believe that." Arden glanced at her watch. "Guess I should get back to the shop now. I don't like to leave the interns on their own for too long. It seems unfair given the pittance I pay them."

The women left the café, Arden turning toward the bookstore and Elizabeth in the direction of her car. Arden was a brave woman, Elizabeth thought yet again. And so was Laura, to be so generous about her mother's happiness. So many adult children couldn't offer that level of generosity to their parents. Adult children like Jess?

Elizabeth started her car and began the short trip back to Lavender Lane. She remembered that just the other day, as Petra was about to leave the house to meet her father, Elizabeth had almost said "Give Chris my love" but had caught herself.

What did it mean to send her love? What was her love worth to Chris? And was she really in possession of love to send?

Yes, she thought now as she drove along. She was. Love came in different degrees and shapes. Her love for each man, for Hugh and for Chris, had been and continued to be valid. She believed that. But to send one's love meant little; in most cases, it was just a standard greeting, even a meaningless one.

And Elizabeth's love wasn't meaningless. She had felt such a strong surge of happiness, of hope and possibility, upon learning from Petra that Chris was single. For while Elizabeth had always hoped that Chris had found someone with whom to share his life, at the same time, she had dreaded discovering that he had fallen in love with another woman. The possibility of learning that Chris had moved on was definitely one of the major reasons she never reached out to him after Hugh's death. She knew that she would feel wounded by the news that Chris had married, maybe even had children. The fact of that marriage— if it existed and assuming it was a good marriage—would have, of necessity, reduced her importance to Chris, even in his memory. This was right and to be expected.

But it was not what Elizabeth, selfish as she was, wanted to acknowledge

Elizabeth parked her car in the drive, picked up the little shopping bag of Misty Morning products, and went into the house. In spite of the large coffee she had drunk at the café with Arden, she felt tired. A nap in the sanctuary of her bedroom seemed a very good idea.

Chapter 63

"Did you see this article about the wildfires out west?" Petra asked her mother.

"I did. It's horrifying. I can't help but feel that the planet is angry—rightfully so—and in the process of kicking us out. Climate change is real, no matter what some people insist on believing."

Before she could reply, Petra became aware of Jess approaching the kitchen; it was impossible not to become aware. She stomped rather than walked and always had. When she was angry or frustrated, the stomping got louder. Today's stomping seemed to indicate a pleasant, or at least a neutral, state of mind.

"Look what I found," Jess announced, joining them in the kitchen. "Dad's senior yearbook. It was hiding in plain sight, on the top shelf of the bookcase in the den, along with a few yellowed issues of *Sports Illustrated*, and a file folder containing a few handwritten recipes. Here's one for Irish soda bread, one for tuna casserole, and oh, yum, one for red velvet cake."

"Those recipes belonged to my mother," Elizabeth explained. "I wondered where they'd gone."

"I love red velvet cake," Jess went on. "One of my roommates in college used to get these amazing care packages from home and sometimes there was an entire red velvet cake inside. She was always on some ridiculous starvation diet, so the other girls and I were the real beneficiaries."

"Then I'll make you one for your next birthday," Elizabeth promised. "Let's take a look at this yearbook."

"Did Chris go to Dad's high school?" Petra asked as they sat at the table. "Maybe I knew once but if so, I forgot."

"No," her mother told them. "He went to a private Catholic school, but the boys remained good friends."

Jess opened the book at random. "Oh, my God, the hairstyles!" she exclaimed. "How much hair spray do you think this girl went through in the course of a year?"

"I can't imagine spending that much time on my hair," Petra admitted. The girl's helmet-like hair stood a good six inches above her scalp. "What a nightmare."

Elizabeth smiled. "Hair was definitely easier to negotiate by the time I got to high school. Teasing and back-combing wasn't as big a thing, but then came the eighties . . ."

"I kind of love the short skirts," Jess said, "but what a pain in the butt it must have been to keep those bouffant hairdos so . . . puffy. I mean, how is someone supposed to sleep on that? Wouldn't it all fall apart by the morning, or morph into weird shapes? And have you ever accidentally sprayed hair product in your eye? It's not good, let me tell you."

Elizabeth smiled ruefully. "Being a woman has always been a hazardous job."

Petra pointed to another photo. "This girl went for the hippie look. That's more my style. Long, straight hair. Strands of beads. Fringe suede jacket. I'd totally wear that."

"That's because you're the vintage queen," Jess said, not unkindly, as she turned to a two-page spread. The heading on the left page read: *Home Economics Department.*

"You know," Jess went on, "a mandatory home economics class is a very good idea. It costs money to live like a civilized adult, and learning how to make a budget and stick to it is a valuable—Wait a minute. Listen to this. Here's a description of one of the classes on offer. 'Personal Management, where a girl can learn how to make herself more attractive.' WTF?"

Petra laughed though there wasn't anything remotely funny about the idea of teaching a young woman how to make herself more attractive to men, because of course that's what must have been taught in the class. Flirting, dieting, and conversational skills.

"It's outrageous!" Jess cried.

"It was 1968," Elizabeth pointed out. "Lots has changed for the better since then. Not enough, but we've made some headway."

"Our culture is still fixated on women looking a certain way though," Petra pointed out. "If not always on grooming them for marriage and kids and housekeeping. Even the body positivity movement has its downside, or so I've read. And look at female Olympic athletes, still required to wear bikini bottoms to play certain sports. It's insane."

Jess grunted and flipped a few pages forward. "Oh, man," she cried again. "It just gets worse! Listen to this: 'Being chosen a member of the Hostess Committee is one of the highest honors a girl at Allendale High can achieve.' Really? Serving tea and showing visitors around the school building? I think I'm going to be sick! How about academic achievement? Athletic success—without resorting to bikinis? And I don't see any classes teaching boys how to be more attractive to girls, like learning how to keep it in their pants when it's not wanted and—"

"Maybe we had better put the book back where it came from," Elizabeth cut in. "Some things are better left in the past."

"No," Petra said. "Let's go on. I want to see some pictures of Dad."

Jess nodded. "I promise to control my temper. At least, I promise to try."

"Find the senior portraits," Petra suggested.

Jess did. And there was an eighteen-year-old Hugh Quirk, undeniably handsome in an all-American sort of way, straight-backed and smiling confidently, even cockily, into the camera.

"I remember that look," Petra said fondly. "Super confident, like he could meet any challenge that came his way. He didn't change all that much as he got older, did he?"

Her mother smiled. "No. Not all that much. But maybe most people don't."

"Let's check out the football team," Jess said, and Petra thought she heard a catch in her sister's voice. Jess had worshipped Hugh; even after all the years since his death she must still miss him deeply, maybe more than Petra or Cam did.

Jess flipped ahead to the section that covered the high school's various sports teams. She leaned closer to the page and frowned. "Wait a minute. It says here that some guy named Hank Mathis was voted Player of the Year." Jess frowned and looked to Elizabeth. "I thought Dad said *he* held that title in his senior year. He was always so proud of how good he had been at football. He told me that his coaches wanted him to consider going pro, but that he got bored with the game and decided not to continue playing in college."

Elizabeth didn't answer at once. When she did, Petra noticed that her mother's face looked strained. "Your father did have a tendency to brag," she said, "and to, well, to elaborate on the truth when it came to his past achievements."

"What you really mean is that he had a tendency to lie about himself," Jess said flatly. "Great. Another golden myth blown to pieces. Dad was a cheat."

Petra winced. "Jess, that's not fair."

"No," Elizabeth said firmly. "He was not a cheat. Yes, for whatever reason—a deep-seated insecurity, probably—he felt the need to augment his own achievements in the telling. To self-mythologize. It's not entirely uncommon in men of his sort. Otherwise, he was totally honest, sometimes scrupulously so."

Petra nodded. "He was. I remember one time we went shopping for hiking socks at Renys, and when we got out of the store he suddenly stopped and pulled out his wallet. It seemed the cashier had given him an extra dollar in change, so he went right back inside and gave the dollar back. A lot of people would have just kept the dollar and called it luck."

Jess sighed and flipped to another section of the yearbook. They were looking at pictures taken at the homecoming dance.

"Oh, come on!" Jess cried. "I distinctly remember Dad telling me that his date was the homecoming queen. But that's not Dad standing on the stage next to the Stepford wife with the ridiculous sash and crown. Did he lie about everything?"

"He embroidered the truth," Petra said, carefully. "That's not the same as lying." In fact, she wasn't entirely sure she believed that.

"And you're splitting hairs," Jess snapped. "Why are you defending him? He's not even your—"

"I'm not defending him," Petra said a bit desperately. "I'm just—describing him."

"Well, I've had enough." Jess closed the yearbook and pushed it roughly across the table. "Mom's right. Some things are better left in the past."

Petra saw her mother frown, but neither woman said anything. The silence went on for some moments, Jess staring down at the table, her expression glum; Petra trying to think of something to say that would brighten her sister's mood. Change the subject radically, Petra thought. Bring the conversation into the present and make it not about family. And ignore the fact that Jess had been on the point of unnecessarily reminding them that Hugh Quirk was not Petra's "real" father.

"What do you think about the remake of *Jane Eyre* that's in the works?" she said suddenly, brightly. "There's been a lot of hype about it. It's definitely on my list to see."

Jess looked up briefly, and her frown deepened. "Haven't they made that thing often enough? I mean, what else can be done with it? Hero is a macho jerk. Heroine loves him anyway, don't ask me why. In the end, heroine gets maimed hero. Big deal."

Petra shot a glance at her mother; it said, "Help me."

"I'm looking forward to it," Elizabeth said. "I like the actress they got to play Jane, gosh, what's her name? Anyway, I saw her in a series on PBS last year and was really impressed."

This raised no comment from Jess, and Petra, feeling a bit desperate now, found herself bringing up a topic not at all mood-brightening. The moment the words were out of her mouth she regretted them as ill-timed and insensitive.

"Have you been rethinking your original business plan?" she began. "Maybe you can start a business on your own after all if you come at the problem from a different angle. Think out of the box. Think laterally. Though I have no idea what that means."

Jess sighed and looked directly, wearily, at her sister. Petra tensed for an attack, but what came was something quite different.

"Do you think I haven't considered about a million ideas since Raven walked away from the project?" she asked rhetorically. "I have. It's just that I can't seem to focus. I've never had this problem before. I've always just—done things. It's driving me mad. It's like I don't even recognize myself. I used to be this, I don't know, go-getter, and now I'm—flailing. And Eddie's no help. Not that I expected him to be."

Elizabeth sat quietly, hands folded on the table, seemingly content to let her daughters continue the conversation on their own.

Petra sighed. She felt very bad for her sister; she had never seen Jess in such a depressed state. "Jess," she said gently, "why the heck are you still in a relationship with Eddie if he's such a disappointment to you?"

Petra half expected her sister to tell her to mind her own business but again, she was surprised by Jess's response.

"I don't really know anymore," Jess admitted. Her voice was a bit unsteady. "Maybe Eddie's not the problem. Maybe I'm the problem, and I don't want to face that possibility. Maybe I'm too demanding. Always dissatisfied. Always complaining. I mean, Eddie hasn't really changed since I first met him. He's still the same sort of happy-go-lucky person, not terribly intelligent but not stupid, either. Likable. Charming at times." Jess shook her head. "And sexy. Good-looking. Gorgeous, frankly. Not that I feel attracted to him these days. But in the beginning and for a long time after . . . Was it all about sex? That's so . . . pathetic."

Elizabeth reached across the table and laid her hand on that of her middle child. "You might be doing Eddie a disservice staying with him if you don't love him. And I think that's what you're saying. Am I right?"

Petra watched the expression on her sister's face change from one of knee-jerk resistance to one of acceptance or realization. Finally, Jess nodded.

"You know what I think?" Elizabeth said briskly. "I think you need that red velvet cake sooner than your birthday. It won't solve your problems, but it might make you feel happier for a bit."

"Sugar rush?" Jess managed a smile. "Thanks, Mom. That would be really nice."

Petra got up from her seat. "I'll see what ingredients we need from the store. I'm pretty sure we don't have any buttermilk or cream cheese, and you can't have red velvet cake without the cream cheese frosting!"

"And a lot of it," Jess added. "Heaps."

Chapter 64

"Gardening is an instrument of grace."

May Sarton had said—or written—that. For a long time, Elizabeth hadn't understood what Sarton had meant by those words, but as each year came and went, her understanding grew. Right then, in that moment, kneeling by the hosta plants, she felt deeply content, almost serene. It was amazing what time spent digging in the earth—planting seeds, tending new growth, maintaining the health of mature plants—could do for one's mood, one's attitude, no doubt for one's soul. Yes, she believed in a soul. It was one of those beliefs, one of those communal myths, that Elizabeth had never been able to do without.

She had been working for close to half an hour when she became aware of a car pulling alongside the curb. Only mildly curious, Elizabeth glanced up; she didn't recognize the vehicle and looked back to her work, only to look up again when she sensed someone standing a few yards away.

The sun was in her eyes but . . .

"I hope I didn't startle you," the man said. "I see you're busy."

The voice . . .

"Does Petra know you're here?"

The question came out more harshly than Elizabeth intended. She wasn't angry. She was just in shock. She had imagined a reunion countless times over the years, even longed for it. So many different scenarios had played out in her mind. A rainy night in a foreign city, probably Paris, maybe Venice. A windswept northern coastline at dusk. A pink sunrise over white sands. Each scenario had been based on an accidental meeting, a meeting fated to happen, a scene of high romance having nothing to do with grass-stained knees and an aching back.

Christopher Ryan stepped forward. "I'm sorry," he said earnestly. "I should have called first, asked if it was a good time for me to come by, but to be honest, I wasn't sure you would agree to see me. So, I took the risk. And no, Petra has no idea I'm here."

Elizabeth took a deep breath. She wanted to speak, but words wouldn't seem to come.

"Maybe you're not ready for this," Chris went on, stepping back again. "I'll go if you'd like me to."

"No. No, it's all right." Elizabeth climbed to her feet with less grace than she might have wanted to display. "It's just . . . Let's go inside."

Silently, he followed her across the lawn, through the back door, and into the house.

It took a moment for Elizabeth's eyes to adjust to the dimmer light of the interior. Only then did she really see the man who stood before her. There were lines around his eyes and at the corners of his mouth. His shoulders were ever so slightly stooped. His hair had faded. Otherwise, he was still Chris. Her Christopher Ryan. A memory, a fragment of a memory, flashed through her mind, her hands against his chest, his hands grasping her shoulders, their lips meeting.

"I'm frightened," she said simply when the image had receded. "I know you have every right to be angry with me, to want nothing to do with me. . . . Why did you come here?"

Chris's expression, so nakedly open, so vulnerable, threatened to break Elizabeth's heart. "Because I wanted to. Because I had to, for my own sake."

"Not for my sake?" Elizabeth asked, though she wasn't sure she wanted to know the answer to that question.

"That remains to be seen," Chris replied. "I can't predict what you'll feel when I walk back to my car and drive off. Relief that I've gone. Happiness that I showed up at all. Anger at my presumption in doing so. I just don't know. I do hope that you won't still be frightened."

But Elizabeth knew what she would feel. It was what she was already feeling right then, standing only feet from Christopher. Love. She had never fallen out of love with this person. She would not—did not—want him to leave. Ever.

"Let's sit and talk," she said, her voice a whisper. "We owe that much to each other."

And so much more, she thought. So very much more.

"Petra told me you still have the lavender agate pendant I gave you when I came back from one of my trips abroad."

Elizabeth and Christopher sat across from each other at the kitchen table. She had made them tea and put out a plate of shortbread cookies, though the food and the drink had barely been touched. Elizabeth was highly aware of his closeness; every nerve in her body felt alive to his presence. She had never expected to feel this way again at her age. But she had never expected to be reunited with Christopher Ryan. Hoped, yes. Feared, also yes. But expected?

"I wore the pendant the day I told the girls about you and me," she said with a brief smile. "I needed all the strength I could muster, and I felt the pendant would be of some help. I know, it's superstition. But sometimes, it's necessary."

Chris smiled. "I agree. You know, I remember worrying that the pendant was too personal a gift to bring back for you. I remember wondering if it was acceptable for a man to give a woman who wasn't his wife or his girlfriend or his mother or his sister a piece of jewelry. But I took a chance."

"And I remember you saying you chose the stone because

you knew that lavender was my favorite color. And then Hugh said—"

"'No, it isn't. Blue is her favorite color.' And then you pointed out that blue was Hugh's favorite color. And Hugh laughed and said something about not being able to remember things like that."

Elizabeth nodded silently. The kinds of things that Hugh didn't make the effort to remember were exactly the kinds of things that Christopher did.

A silence, more of a hush, not uncomfortable, settled over the two old friends. To Elizabeth it felt almost sacred, a gift of rest. Only after some time was the silence broken.

"The day before your wedding to Hugh," Chris said quietly, "when I found you sitting on that bench at the edge of the village green. I . . . I remember hating myself for asking if you were excited about the wedding. But I couldn't stop the words from being said. And then I was so confused, unsure of what you were telling me about your feelings or even if you were telling me anything at all. If Hugh hadn't come along when he did . . . I don't know. What else might I have said? Or done. I watched the two of you walk off toward the church, hoping, praying you would turn around for one last look at me, dreading that you would. And you didn't."

"I wanted to," Elizabeth told him earnestly. "I wanted to turn back, but . . . I was confused as well. Afraid almost of what I was feeling, not even entirely sure that what I was feeling was love for you. In a moment, I convinced myself that it was madness, all pre-wedding lunacy, jitters. So, I walked on with Hugh."

"I know we've talked about this before, back in ninety-one, but if only one of us had had the courage to speak that day. Think of what might have been."

"But would the other have had the courage to respond honestly?" Elizabeth shook her head. "I'm not sure I would have."

A brief smile flitted across Chris's lips. "I suppose we need to accept the fact that it wasn't our time."

Elizabeth considered the unspoken question. Was this their time then?

"At one point during our affair," she said, "I believed I could have left Hugh for you, but you didn't ask me to, and I didn't have the nerve to suggest the idea. I remember coming across my college copy of the letters Abelard and Heloise wrote to each other, and as I was leafing through the book one evening I came upon the story of Heloise's refusal to marry Abelard. Her reason, she said, was twofold. First, she feared her uncle's angry reprisal, and she was right to be afraid of the man. Second, she felt that to marry Abelard, such a famous scholar and teacher, would bring disgrace to him. A man meant for the world, she believed, should not be taken away from his rightful duty in order to live a private domestic life with one woman. I took it as a sign, the book showing up when it did. A sign that I wasn't to marry you."

Chris shook his head. "'Who finally, intent on sacred or philosophic meditations, can bear the screams of children?' That was Abelard, years after both he and Heloise had entered the religious life. I'd like to be able to say that I would have endured any consequence if I could have been a husband to you and a father to Petra. But then, how could I have put you both through the publicity that inevitably gathers around the adultery of someone in the spotlight? And, for better or worse, my name is a public one, if not on the same plane as J. Lo."

Elizabeth raised an eyebrow. "You know about Jennifer Lopez?"

"Everyone knows about Jennifer Lopez, even if they've never heard her music or seen her movies. Neither of which I've done."

Elizabeth laughed. "Me too. I mean, me neither. Pop culture and I parted ways back in the eighties I'm afraid. Honestly, I'm not sorry."

"Elizabeth, we have a child together."

Chris spoke those words not in the tone of an announcement, but with a sense of wonder.

"I'm so sorry I never told you. I'm so sorry I kept your daughter from you."

"I'm sorry, too, but I understand why you did what you did."

"Do you forgive me, though?" Elizabeth didn't know how she would go on if Christopher said that no, he didn't, couldn't, wouldn't forgive her.

"Yes," he said. "I do."

Elizabeth felt her body relax; she hadn't realized how tensed it had been. "Thank you," she said. "Thank you." And then, she went on: "Strangely, our relationship acted as a catalyst, allowing me to make changes to my relationship with Hugh, to reshape it into more of an equal partnership. I know that was hardly your intent or mine when we came together. We had no ulterior motive, did we? No impetus other than allowing ourselves to recognize and to acknowledge our love for each other."

Chris nodded. His eyes were slightly misted with tears.

"What tangible benefit did you get from our relationship?" Elizabeth asked, hoping that Chris could tell her something that would ease the guilt she felt about her behavior toward him. "What good did you gain in the end?"

"The experience of love," he said promptly. "That was more than enough."

Elizabeth wasn't sure that she believed him, or, that he really believed himself. There had to have been times when he felt that he had been deprived, even used, abandoned, left without anyone or anything. No lover. No best friend. What could only the memory of love have provided Chris during all the years of their separation?

But she didn't protest or question his reply. He had given the answer he had for a reason. However unlikely, it was the truth.

Boldly, utterly surprising herself, Elizabeth reached across the table and grasped Chris's hand in hers. "Don't go away again," she whispered urgently. "Please don't ever go away."

Chapter 65

When Petra had left the house on Lavender Lane to walk into town, her mother had been about to start some work on the flower beds in the front of the house. Petra wondered if one day she, too, would come around to gardening. Though she loved flowers as much as the next person, the idea of nurturing them held almost no appeal. She was beginning to wonder why.

That was a question she hadn't asked her father, Christopher: if he enjoyed gardening or if, like his daughter, he preferred simply to observe the beauty and variety of flowers and plants. She would ask him the next time they spoke. Chris had returned to Boston to attend to a bit of business; he hadn't been entirely clear on when he would return to Maine. His lack of specificity had caused Petra a twinge of anxiety. Would he never return? Would she receive a note of apology, an explanation, of why he couldn't or wouldn't continue their nascent relationship?

She didn't really believe that Chris could abandon her, but the situation, so unexpected and certainly unprecedented in her experience, was fraught with anxiety. She had even found herself wondering, however fleetingly, if Chris was primarily spending time with her as a way to access her mother. How genuine, how deep was his interest in Petra Quirk, as an individual, not just as a person who might bring him together once again with his one true love?

So many questions!

Petra had reached the heart of Eliot's Corner almost without realizing it, so absorbed in her thoughts had she been. A guy about her own age passed her, eyes fixed on his phone. To Petra he looked vaguely familiar, but she couldn't place him. So many people came into one's life and then passed on, leaving barely a trace. It was sad though inevitable; no one could retain the memory of every person she ever met.

But if you did remember someone . . . Memory was like possession, wasn't it?

At this very moment, someone might be remembering a little girl or a young woman called Petra. A former classmate; the teacher who had taught her math back in fourth grade; the receptionist at the local dentist's office; someone she had worked alongside once upon a time at the crystal shop in Portsmouth; a guy she had dated briefly in college. She existed in the memories of other people. How odd. And other people, people whose names she couldn't recall, whose faces were a blur, nevertheless, had a sort of life in her mind, even if they were no longer physically alive.

There was always so much to think about! Was this what Chris experienced, too, a mind always wondering and asking questions and positing solutions and pondering possibilities? One thing Petra knew for sure. She rarely if ever bored herself!

And she certainly felt that she was learning a lot about herself since Christopher Ryan had come into her life. He was a fatherly figure of a different sort than Hugh had been. Hugh had been an advisor but not a director; he had encouraged but hadn't pushed; no doubt he had developed some of his particular communication skills over the years of his career as a salesperson.

Hugh had taught her how to ride a bike, a two-wheeler like big kids rode. Would Chris have done that? Did he even know how to ride a bike? Would he have been home most weekends or on the road or holed up in his study, researching and writing papers, articles, books? Would he not have wanted to be disturbed while he worked, annoyed if his child came bursting into the room to share her latest crayon drawing or to sing him a song she had learned in school?

No one would deny that Hugh Quirk had been the sort of father with seemingly endless patience. He had happily opened bottles of bright purple and sickly green nail polish for Petra, and spent hours playing catch on the lawn with Jess. On Saturday mornings, he made pancakes from scratch for the family. When Cam had a sprained ankle in seventh grade, Hugh had driven her to and from school every day for the two weeks she was on crutches so she wouldn't have to deal with climbing onto and off the school bus. He had helped Petra make a prize-winning poster in second grade. He had cheered the loudest at his children's graduations.

Would Chris have brought his daughter with him on some of his trips to foreign cities? Would Petra have had a passport by the age of nine and already have been able to speak bits of other languages, enough to get by without being rude? By the age of twelve, would she have met fabulously interesting people, great intellects in the fields of science, medicine, theology?

There was no way to know for sure.

There was an expression Petra had heard on a British television show once. "Those two are chalk and cheese." It meant that the characters were totally different people, like Hugh Quirk and Christopher Ryan. And yet, in life, Hugh and Chris had been friends. Opposites attracting? Or had their friendship been purely a relationship of circumstance? Had it really mattered in the end?

Probably not.

Suddenly, Petra decided that as long as she was in town she would pay a visit to Re-Turned. She liked Michael and felt a sharp need of retail—or in this case, resale—therapy. In the past few days, and after years of wearing only loose skirts, dresses, and harem pants, she had found herself suddenly interested in wearing jeans again. Maybe jeans with a flare leg; maybe jeans with some patchwork. Something with a seventies vibe. Where had that interest come from? Well, it didn't matter. Maybe it would lead to another new interest. One thing always led to another, good or bad.

Change. It was inevitable.

Chapter 66

"You're wearing the pendant."

"There's no reason for me to keep it in hiding now, is there?"

Elizabeth had driven to Lark's Circle, the town in which Chris had made an occasional home in the years since Hugh's death.

"Did you choose Lark's Circle because you hoped to run into me one day?" Elizabeth asked, with a smile. They were sitting at the café where Petra had first met her father. An umbrella shaded them from the direct sun, and iced coffees helped keep them cool.

"I didn't think it likely," Chris admitted. "What would bring you to visit little, out of the way Lark's Circle? But after Hugh died, I needed to be closer to you than I had been after selling the cottage when we broke up and living solely in Boston. Lark's Circle seemed a decent compromise, even if you never knew I was here."

Elizabeth gazed at the man for whom she had once risked so much. She wasn't entirely sure she believed that they were sitting so close to each other after having spent so many years apart, so many years in self-imposed separation. She felt that she would be satisfied if her life ended in that moment, and yet, she strongly hoped that she and Chris would spend many, many more years together.

"I hated that Hugh called you 'sweetie,'" Chris blurted. "It seemed so demeaning."

Elizabeth laughed. "I hated it, too. At one point, I can't remember when exactly, I started asking Hugh not to call me 'sweetie' or 'honey' or any other clichéd term of endearment, but he went on as always, laughingly apologizing when I next protested. I suspected he didn't really try to change his behavior, and after a while I just accepted that he wasn't going to change. Then, years later, it was during our relationship, I finally lost my temper with Hugh one evening. I remember shouting at him, telling him I was sick and tired of not being heard, that if he called me 'sweetie' one more time I'd do something drastic. Thankfully, I didn't specify what, exactly, I would do! Poor Hugh was badly shocked. It was the first time I'd ever raised my voice with him. I apologized, of course, and from that day on Hugh complied with my request. I was never again 'sweetie.'" Elizabeth paused. "I think I learned a lesson from that incident. That if I spoke up loudly enough, Hugh would hear me."

Chris looked uncomfortable. "Why should a person be forced to scream in order to be heard?"

"They shouldn't. But . . ."

"I'm sorry," he said quickly. "I don't mean to criticize Hugh. Really."

"I know. Chris," Elizabeth asked, "I've often wondered if you went to confession after we broke things off. We were both so burdened by guilt."

Chris shook his head. "No. I never sought official absolution. Instead, I asked God for forgiveness on my own, without intercession. It's not the Catholic way, but it's the decision I made."

"Do you regret that decision?" Elizabeth asked.

"No," he said. "I don't regret it, though at times I've wondered why I didn't seek formal absolution."

"A ritual of forgiveness is something I've never had access

to, not having been raised a Catholic. Well, it's more than just a ritual. Confession is a sacrament, isn't it?"

"Yes. And a sacrament means nothing if you don't have faith. No," Chris added hurriedly, "that's not true. You can be full of doubt, not sure of what you believe if anything, and still draw comfort from the faith of others, as well as from ritual or participation in a sacramental act."

"I see what you mean. Was there ever any real interest in Catholicism in Hugh's family?" Elizabeth asked. "Or was it just one of those things the family did by rote, go to church Sunday morning, say this prayer at meal times, that prayer when you went to bed, all with no real thought or interest?"

Chris shook his head. "I can't really say I knew what went on with Hugh's parents. They seemed sincere enough, but Hugh and his brothers never took to their religion, if you can put it that way. And interestingly, Hugh wasn't close to his brothers. You met them. They were a lot like Hugh, blustery, forceful. Maybe he saw them as competition, whereas with me, there was never any chance of our being in competition for anything—not even for you. We were playing two very different games, each of us in possession of two very different sets of skills."

"I know. By the time Jess was born," Elizabeth said, "Hugh had already lost touch with his brothers. I felt bad about that. I'd only met them a handful of times, and had seen them last at the wedding, but they were Hugh's flesh and blood. I sent Richard and George and their families Christmas cards every year for my entire marriage, signing both my name and Hugh's. Their wives would do the same. But the brothers never bothered with one another."

"Were they at the funeral?" Chris asked.

"No," Elizabeth said. "By the time Hugh passed, Richard had been dead for almost two years. As far as I know George is still alive, but maybe not. The last holiday card I got from his wife was the year after Hugh's death. Then, nothing."

"It's strange how families fall apart. It makes you wonder if they were ever really strong and coherent in the first place, or just pretending to be so."

"Hugh's mother would have very much liked her sons to be close," Elizabeth said. "She told me so more than once. But there really wasn't much she could do about it once the boys were no longer living under her roof."

"Your daughters," Chris said. "They're close to one another?"

"Overall, yes. Maybe not always the best of friends, but there's never been any major conflict among them, not even when they were growing up."

"And now? Since they've learned of my part in your life?"

"There might be a degree of conflict now," Elizabeth admitted. "But it's not as if Jess has renounced her family in reaction to my relationship with you. I'd like to think—to believe—that all will be well again between us."

There followed a long moment of silence. Elizabeth found herself staring at Chris's hands, one around his iced drink, the other in a relaxed fist on the table. She remembered as if it were yesterday the first moment his hands had touched her in an intimate way. Could it really have been thirty years before?

"I've missed Hugh over the years," Chris said quietly, "particularly at specific times of my life, when the pressures of work or the news of the world got to feel like too much. Growing up, whenever I got too melancholic he would jostle me out of my dark mood and sometimes even make me laugh at my habit of 'too much thinking.' One or two times I resented what I saw as an intrusion rather than as an act of friendship, but in the end I was always glad he had cared enough to speak."

"I don't remember Hugh ever being really down," Elizabeth said, "and if something was bothering him at a given time, it certainly didn't bother him for long. He was almost ridiculously resilient. I envied him that ability to rebound." Elizabeth smiled a bit. "When it didn't drive me crazy, and make me wonder if he had ever felt anything deeply at all."

"I think he felt very deeply," Chris said, his voice breaking.

"I failed Hugh in more ways than one. I'll never forgive myself for not being a better friend."

Elizabeth swallowed hard. She felt a bit sick to her stomach and wondered if she would ever be truly done with the lying that brought on guilt. "I have another admission to make," she said quietly. "Just before Hugh died he asked me to let you know that he loved you. He was worried he had said or done something to put you off. I tried to reassure him that he was in no way to blame, that people drifted away from each other for all sorts of reasons. I'm not sure I succeeded."

"And you didn't seek me out to pass on Hugh's message." It was a statement, not a question.

"No," Elizabeth said softly. "I'm sorry for that. I owed it to Hugh to fulfill the promise I made when he was near the end. It was the usual story. I was afraid, afraid of so many things. I knew that I would be compelled by what's right to tell you more than just what Hugh had asked me to say. That you had a daughter. It seemed too much for me to handle. I'm sorry."

Chris nodded. "It's all right. You're telling me now."

"Better late than never? I'm not sure that's always true." Elizabeth leaned forward. "Chris, should we have tried to keep going on as we had before the affair, the three of us, family friends, pretending for Hugh's sake that nothing had gone on between you and me?"

"I don't know," Chris admitted. "It's an unanswerable question now, so maybe it doesn't really matter. But it does matter, doesn't it?"

Yes, Elizabeth thought. It did still matter, what they had decided thirty years ago. And it made her wonder if they should continue to be punished for their mistake, their crime of passion. Should they keep punishing themselves and each other by choosing to stay apart? Or could they acknowledge the harm they had done, accept the blame, agree that they had tried to atone for the harm ever since it had been committed, and move on to find happiness and contentment together? All the while aware of having been chastened, tempered. All the while grateful for Hugh in their lives. Not only had he brought them together—however unwittingly—but he had been a good friend and a good husband in spite of his ham-handedness in emotional matters.

"I'm going to let Petra know that we've been meeting," Elizabeth said now. "I'm not comfortable keeping it a secret from her."

Chris nodded. "All right. There's no reason she should be kept in the dark. For once, we're not doing anything wrong by being together."

Elizabeth reached for his hand. She so hoped that he was right.

Chapter 67

"Look at these tomatoes! They're gorgeous!" Petra exclaimed. "Caprese salad tonight for sure."

"We'll need to pick up some mozzarella on the way home," her mother noted. "Corn. We need corn."

Elizabeth headed to the mountain of bright green corn on the cob while Petra lingered over the array of freshly picked herbs for sale. She was happy to be back in Maine, though her excursion to Massachusetts the day before had been a real pleasure. She and her father had met at the Peabody Essex Museum in Salem to explore a few of the ongoing exhibits, like *Japanomania! Japanese Art Goes Global*, and the galleries that housed the works of American Art. Petra had been pleased to discover that her father shared her habit—her need—of silence while regarding art. She hated going to an exhibit with a person who couldn't stop chatting or who wouldn't stop commenting.

Chris hadn't had time to linger afterward; he was finishing an article that needed to be submitted to the journal's editor first thing the following morning, so Petra had headed back to Eliot's Corner, glad she had learned even more about the man who had helped give her life.

"I love this kind of day," her mother observed a few minutes later, as they pulled back onto the road loaded down with ten ears of corn, a large bag of tomatoes, another bag of zucchini, and a fistful of fragrant basil from the farm stand. "Meandering through the countryside."

"Even if we're not on foot," Petra noted. "Is it really meandering if you're in a car?"

"I don't know," Elizabeth admitted. "But I kind of think it is. Look, I've been wanting to tell you something. I've seen Chris. Actually, we've gotten together twice now."

Petra's eyes widened. She felt stunned and the tiniest bit betrayed. Why hadn't her father said anything yesterday? Should he have? Could she possibly be jealous of her mother, now, too, spending time with Chris? "You have?" she said finally, pushing the strange thoughts and feelings away. "I thought you didn't . . . I thought you . . . Wow."

"Yes," her mother said, her eyes on the road. "Wow. I'm sorry I didn't tell you sooner. It's all been a bit . . . A bit surreal, if that's the right word."

"So, how did this come about?" Petra asked. "Did you call him? Did he call you?"

"No. Chris just showed up one day, not long after you'd left to walk into town. I don't know if he knew you wouldn't be home, or if it mattered either way to him. Of course, I recognized him immediately. He hasn't changed all that much, but to say it was a shock seeing him standing there in our front yard is putting it mildly. I never expected him to just appear like that, with no warning, without asking."

"I'm really surprised he took that risk," Petra admitted after a moment, remembering all of the times when she had considered many of her father's actions cowardly. "That was pretty brave of him. You could have closed the door in his face. In a nice way, I mean. But I wonder why he didn't tell me he planned to contact you."

"Maybe he wanted to spare you from knowing that I had

refused to talk to him," Elizabeth suggested. "Assuming I had refused—and Chris had to know that was a possibility, in spite of everything that's happened this summer."

Petra shifted so that she could look more directly at her mother. "What did you feel in that first moment, Mom, face-to-face with Chris, with my father?"

Elizabeth shook her head, her eyes still firmly on the road. "It's hard to put into words, really. Shock, like I said. Self-consciousness. I wished I'd looked better, had put on some makeup that morning! Maybe a twinge of anger or annoyance, directed at who or what I can't say. But after a few minutes, it was all okay. He was my Christopher Ryan. I was happy he was there with me."

"You must find him changed in some ways though," Petra pressed. "No one stays exactly the same over time."

"Yes. I do find him changed," her mother admitted. "He seems more mature, but maybe that's just a consequence of ageing with your eyes open, of coming to understand and accept more and more of what you witness and experience in life. Oh, I don't know. But Chris is definitely a stronger man now than he was all those years ago. I can feel it."

"What do you think he found changed about you?" Petra asked.

Her mother laughed. "Aside from the wrinkles around my eyes and my expanded waistline?"

"Mom! Like he cares about those things! Has he said anything about his feelings for you now? Tell me everything!" Petra felt tears come to her eyes. "I'm very happy for you, Mom," she went on, "and for Chris. For all three of us, really. I mean, who knows what will happen in the future, but to finally know and acknowledge that this family exists and has existed for thirty years, well, that's huge."

"It is huge," her mother agreed. "Again, I'm sorry I didn't tell you right away that Chris had come by. In some moments,

I still feel that our relationship needs to be kept secret, that it's shameful. It might take some time to get past that, to remember that things are different now."

"Well, please do get past it," Petra urged. "Because if you feel shame about your relationship with my father, then what am I supposed to feel? I mean, nothing good can come from a shameful or sinful situation, right? So, what does that make me? A mistake? A monster?"

"My gosh, Petra," her mother exclaimed. "You're certainly not a mistake or a monster! There's nothing at all for which you should feel ashamed or embarrassed or guilty. But I do understand your need for me to stop beating myself up about having fallen in love with a man not my husband. It's a waste of time, for one, and time is just too precious to waste."

"Is enjoying a beautiful summer afternoon with your mother a waste of time?" Petra asked with a smile.

"Not at all."

Petra nodded. "Good. Because spending time with you is one of my favorite things ever."

Chapter 68

Elizabeth was in a remarkably good mood.

She hadn't expected understanding and forgiveness from the man—one of them—she had hurt, but those were the very gifts Chris was offering. Just how well had she known Christopher Ryan? How well did she know him now? Because how, knowing him, could she have feared his condemnation or his rejection?

Being on her own for many years had caused Elizabeth's mind to create all sorts of enemies and hobgoblins; she had begun to focus only or mostly on negative outcomes to a reunion of the two lovers and had failed to imagine happiness. But in reality, in the here and now, Chris was neither an enemy nor a hobgoblin; he was the person she had loved so well, the person for whose love she had risked so much. He might even still be the friend he had been long before they had come together as lovers. In Chris's friendship, she might have found a remedy—one based on equality—for the isolation she had feared in her post-career life.

She had asked him not to go away again. He had promised that he wouldn't.

And so, now it was time to come clean to Cam and Jess about this renewed friendship.

Conveniently, Cam had announced her plans to visit Eliot's Corner again. Getting Jess to stop by during her sister's stay wasn't difficult though Jess did grumble about having "a lot to do" and "being very busy." Well, she was always grumbling about something.

Petra hadn't said where exactly she was going, but she had been firm about not wanting to be present when Elizabeth spoke to her sisters.

"Cam will be okay about it," Petra had said. "But Jess will be Jess, and I'm not sure I need to hear any more of her bitchiness at the moment. But if you want me to be there, sort of as an ally or support, I will be, no problem."

Elizabeth had thanked Petra for her offer but told her to do what she needed to do for her well-being. Now, though, sitting across from Cam and Jess in the backyard, Elizabeth half wished she had accepted Petra's offer of support. After her first big revelation earlier in the summer, this one was pretty tame and even to be expected. Still . . .

"Where's Petra?" Jess asked. "Off hunting through someone's discarded stuff again? Hoping to find a hidden treasure in a trash heap?"

Cam sighed. "Jess, will you never stop—"

"Stop what?" Jess said, turning to her sister. "Being myself?"

Cam just frowned.

"Seriously, Mom," Jess went on, "where is Petra?"

"Honestly, I have no idea. She took the car and headed off. Though I'm pretty sure a trash heap is not her destination," Elizabeth added dryly.

Jess shrugged. "Sorry."

"Chris and I have seen each other," Elizabeth announced, before Jess could spout more nonsense.

Jess frowned. "I should have known this was coming. So, what's the deal? You guys are dating or something?"

Cam sighed. "Good 'ole Jess, always getting straight to the point."

"No, we're not dating," Elizabeth responded calmly. "We're talking."

"Whose idea was it to get together? Did Petra put you up to it?"

"Nobody put me or Chris up to it," Elizabeth replied harshly. "Really, Jess, sometimes you make it very difficult to have a civil conversation."

Jess had the grace to look slightly ashamed. "Sorry," she mumbled.

"Well, I'm glad you two are communicating," Cam said. "You must have an awful lot to talk about."

Elizabeth nodded. "We do. And not just the standard 'what have you been doing with your life all these years' sort of topics. In the two times that we've met over the past week or so, we've covered so much emotional territory. Even at the time of our relationship thirty years ago we were able to talk about everything under the sun, with never an awkward silence. This time, after a very brief moment of discomfort, our friendship easily reawakened."

"Has he apologized for what he did?" Jess demanded. "For betraying my father, his best friend?"

Elizabeth flinched. "There's no need for him to apologize to me. We both—"

"You don't have to explain things, Mom," Cam said quickly.

"Wait," Jess went on, sitting forward. "I have another question. It's no secret I'm not exactly a huge fan of this Christopher Ryan, and I'm not letting him off the hook for the damage he did to our family, but on some level, he has a serious right to be pissed off. I mean, you've effectively been lying to him, Mom, every single day for the past thirty years. You can't tell me there was only a 'brief moment of discomfort.' He must have been furious when he found out he had a kid."

Elizabeth lowered her head. How to make Jess understand that Chris's capacity for understanding and forgiveness was as genuine as it was all-encompassing? Finally, she looked up again. She thought—she hoped—that Jess's expression was not quite as dark as it had been a moment ago.

"I can't make you believe me," she said carefully, "but I'm telling the truth when I say that Chris isn't angry with me, that our love and friendship for each other is stronger than it ever was."

Jess frowned but sat back in her seat.

"So," Cam said quickly, "how does he look? What I mean is, has he changed much? Okay, that's a silly question. Thirty years have gone by since you last saw him. Of course, he's changed."

"Honestly, he hasn't changed all that much physically," Elizabeth said. "But what's important is that I recognize him as the man with whom I was very much in love. He's not a stranger to me. And I'm not a stranger to him."

"True love never dies." Interestingly, Jess's tone was unclear. Cynical? Wistful? Elizabeth just wasn't sure. "Anyway," Jess went on, "I still need time before I can play happy new family. Not that I'll ever consider him my stepfather, just so you know."

"I wouldn't expect you to," Elizabeth assured her.

"If you do decide you'd like us all to meet, I'm game," Cam told her mother. "But that's your call."

"I gotta go," Jess said suddenly, rising quickly and reaching for her bag.

"An appointment?" Elizabeth asked.

Jess didn't reply, just waved and stalked off to her car.

"Don't worry about her, Mom," Cam said soothingly. "She'll be okay. She won't do anything stupid. And in spite of her feeling down about the business, she hasn't lost her common sense."

"What do you mean?" Elizabeth asked. At that moment, common sense and rationality weren't qualities she associated with her middle child.

"I told her about the situation with Ralph and Lily. I'm not really sure why I did, other than that I felt uncomfortable with there being yet another secret floating about among us."

"What did she advise you do?" Elizabeth asked, all too aware that her secret had been and remained the most troublesome of all for her family.

Cam looked down at her hands in her lap. "Same thing both you and Petra advised. Confront Ralph."

"Good advice. But have you acted on it?"

"No." The word was spoken softly.

"Cam, please—"

"Look," Cam said, raising her eyes, "I'm doing what I can. And after the conversation I had with Jess the other day, at least I had the courage to finally tell Ralph about you and Chris."

Elizabeth nodded. "And what did he say?"

Cam sighed. "He said he was sorry things hadn't worked out between you and Chris. I'd always suspected that Ralph was kind of intimidated by Dad, and his response clinched the idea for me. He also said he hopes that Petra gets to know her real father."

"Ralph's always been a generous man," Elizabeth said. "But what did he say when you told him you'd known about my past for some weeks? Assuming you admitted to holding on to the news."

"He wasn't happy that I'd kept the story to myself for as long as I had," Cam admitted. "He was upset and asked why I felt as if I couldn't trust him."

Ralph's response, it seemed to Elizabeth, wasn't the sort that came from a man guilty of cheating on his wife. "That would have been a perfect moment to tell him how uncomfortable you feel about his dealings with Lily," she pointed out. "Cam, he gave you an opening. Why didn't you take it?"

"I don't know. I don't. What's wrong with us this summer? With me and Jess, I mean? Neither of us is behaving as we normally do. It's like we've both suddenly lost our nerve. And no, Mom, this is not about you and Christopher Ryan. This is about my sister and me needing a mental and emotional reset." Cam managed a smile. "Talk about bad timing."

Elizabeth's heart ached for her children, but she had to keep reminding herself that they were adults and that her attempting to fix the problems of other adults could only result in disaster.

"You'll be all right," she promised, gently pressing her daughter's hand between her own. "I really believe that both you and Jess will be okay."

"If you say so, Mom. Mothers know best, right?"

If only, Elizabeth thought. If only they did.

Chapter 69

Petra, Elizabeth, and Christopher had arranged to meet together at the little park in Lark's Circle.

"I'm glad you did the driving," Petra said as her mother parked the car at the entry to the park. "I'm so wound up I just know I would have gotten us into an accident."

Her mother smiled briefly. "Now that we're here in one piece I have to admit there were moments I thought I was going to run us off the road, my hands felt so shaky."

"There he is." Petra stepped out of the car. Her father, Christopher Ryan, was walking toward them, all long legs and preppy chic, which is how Petra had come to describe his style.

"I hope we're not late," Elizabeth said when Chris was close.

He smiled and shook his head. "It wouldn't have mattered if you were."

Chris kissed her mother's cheek, and the act caused Petra to cringe just a bit. The only man she had ever seen touching her mother in that intimate sort of way was Hugh. Her dad. In her life, Dad and Father had become two different individuals. That was okay. It probably wasn't even all that uncommon.

Chris turned to Petra then, and they hugged.

"Let's walk to the far end of the park," Chris suggested. "There's a bench in the shade of a giant old oak."

The three began to walk, side by side, Petra between her parents. She wondered if her mother was feeling as she was, both awkward and excited. All those years ago, Elizabeth had been the primary architect of the separation of father and mother, of father and child. But this summer, she had been the primary architect of the family's reunion. That was something about which to be proud.

When they reached the wooden bench, they sat, with Petra remaining between her parents.

"This is pretty wild," she said, taking her mother's hand and then her father's. "We're a family. We always were and we always will be, even if we never live together under the same roof. It's kind of amazing."

Elizabeth smiled. "Blood ties. Blood is thicker than water. It's universal, isn't it, the reverence in which human beings hold the idea of family, even when a particular reality can be pretty horrible."

"'Happiness is having a large, loving, caring, close-knit family in another city.' That's George Burns speaking," Chris added hastily. "Not me."

Petra laughed. "What was your family like, Chris?" *My family, too,* Petra thought. *Wow.*

"Well, for one," he said, "it wasn't large. I was an only child, as you know, as were both of my parents. So, no hordes of aunts and uncles and cousins around the Sunday dinner table."

"What were your parents' names? My grandparents."

"Eileen and Thomas, or Tommy as he was called by his friends."

"Were you a lonely child?" Petra asked. "Not that only children are necessarily lonely."

"No, I wasn't lonely," Christopher told them. "But I was fairly solitary, by choice, which is probably why I was a target for bullies. I didn't really know how to be comfortable socially with my peers. Honestly, my best friend—before I met Hugh—was my maternal grandfather. Your great-grandfather, Petra. He was a lovely man. He didn't have much formal education, but that didn't stop him from reading everything he could get his hands on. We would talk for hours about all sorts of topics, from history to the natural world to what was going on in professional baseball. He was a big fan of the game. Early summer mornings we would take long walks or go fishing on the river at the edge of our town."

"That sounds pretty perfect," Petra said. "Idyllic even."

"His name was William, yes?" Elizabeth asked. "I remember you telling me about him."

Chris nodded. "Hugh knew him. I remember the three of us going ice skating on a local pond a few times. In summer, Grandpa would take us for ice cream at the old-fashioned ice cream parlor in our town, the kind with paper placemats with scalloped edges and printed with puzzles and word games, and twenty or thirty flavors of ice cream on offer."

Petra reflected. Her fathers had shared so much of their lives together. It made the idea of their both falling in love with the same woman more understandable, as well as more poignant. "How old were you when your grandfather died?" she asked after a moment.

"Nineteen," Chris told her. "It was a devastating blow, the first real loss I'd experienced. My parents held a wake and funeral of course; my grandfather was Catholic; his faith was simple but strong. Hugh came, which was good of him. Grandpa died in the middle of term, and Hugh, who was away at college like I was, drove two hours to be there. We didn't have much time to speak, but I remember Hugh patting me on the shoulder and looking genuinely sorrowful."

"He never did know what to say when we kids were sad or upset," Petra noted. "But he did know how to be there and what to do."

Hugh Quirk, Dad, the man who had helped nurture and

care for Petra from the day she was born until the day he died. There and then Petra decided that she wouldn't ask her mother again about selling the dress Elizabeth had worn at her wedding to Hugh. The dress shouldn't be sold, not now, not after all that had been revealed. If one day her mother allowed Petra to have it—to wear or simply to treasure—that would be just fine. In fact, it would be wonderful.

"Chris and I have been talking about the possibility of me going to grad school," Petra announced. "That's what I meant, Mom, when I said I thought I might finally have a vision, at least a glimpse, of my future."

Elizabeth smiled. "I'm so happy to hear that. I'm sorry I didn't press the idea more when you were a senior in college," she said. "I guess I've always believed that to push someone in a particular direction, even one she's expressed an interest in taking, is a bad idea. But maybe I should have been more obviously supportive. I'm sorry."

"Don't blame yourself, Mom," Petra said firmly. "I'm responsible for my life. I really wasn't ready to take that step back then. Enrolling in a master's program would probably only have resulted in my dropping out. A waste of time and money."

Suddenly, taking Petra completely by surprise, tears began to stream down her face.

"Are you okay, Petra?" her mother asked worriedly. Chris put his arm around Petra's shoulder.

It took a moment or two before Petra was able to reply. "Yes," she said, wiping away the last of her tears with a tissue her father had given her. "I'm okay. But I'm not going to lie and say that on some level, in some moments, I don't feel the shock all over again. I won't lie and say that I don't suddenly feel disoriented, feel that my life has been deeply disrupted. The feeling doesn't last, but I suspect it will keep popping up for a while, at least until the truth of my parentage becomes commonplace. And I believe that it will become commonplace at some point." Petra smiled. "Human beings are incredibly resilient and adaptable."

"Still, I'm sorry," Elizabeth said, shaking her head in regret. "I'm sorry I put you through this."

"The fault is mostly mine," Chris added. "I apologize, too, Petra."

"You shouldn't be sorry, either of you. It's right that I know the truth of my origins—everyone should—and I'm glad that I finally do. How can you know where you're going if you don't know where you've been?" Petra smiled again. "Or something like that."

"Anybody in the mood for a coffee?" Chris asked. "I suddenly feel the need for refreshment."

"Can we make that a glass of wine?" Elizabeth suggested. "Maybe Prosecco? I feel this is a moment that should be celebrated. I feel like we should mark this occasion, our first family outing, with bubbles."

"There's a restaurant not far from where I'm staying that has a very nice bar, old and quaint," Chris suggested. "It's usually pretty quiet until six or so. We can go there if you like."

Petra smiled. "I think it's a great idea. And we'll toast to our future. Whatever it brings, it will be ours."

Chapter 70

Elizabeth was doing a few gardening chores in the backyard. The day was overcast and humid but there was a bit of a breeze that made working conditions bearable. Still, she was looking forward to autumn weather, to being able to pull out her tweeds and her wool sweaters, to traipsing through a carpet of red, yellow, and orange leaves, to needing no excuse for drinking hot chocolate.

"Mom?"

Elizabeth turned to see Jess standing a few yards off. She looked subdued, slightly troubled.

"Do you have time to talk?" Jess asked.

"Sure," Elizabeth said as she got to her feet. "Do you want to go inside?"

"No. Let's stay here. The weather sort of fits my mood."

Dark and melancholic, Elizabeth thought, as they made their way to the chairs on the patio.

"It's about me and Eddie," Jess said after a moment. "The thing is, I finally came to my senses about our relationship. I mean, I've known for a long time that it wasn't a good one, but I just couldn't seem to find the strength or the courage I guess to end things. I kept asking myself why, why couldn't I take a stand the way I did in other areas of my life? Why was I clinging to something so unsatisfactory? And if I was so unhappy, how could Eddie be happy, even though he never complained? Not much, anyway. I'm thirty-six-years old. Why was I in a relationship that was so obviously wrong for me? You don't have to answer that question; I already have, at least partly."

"So, what did you conclude?" Elizabeth asked gently. She hadn't heard Jess speak so openly and honestly about her feelings since once or twice in high school when hormones had been just too much for Jess to handle on her own. Introspection wasn't Jess's strong suit; neither was sharing her emotional struggles with others. In those ways, she was so much like Hugh.

Jess offered a wobbly smile. "I'm not sure I came to an actual conclusion about much, but I do think I've made a start in understanding stuff. I think I actually came to rely on Eddie's being kind of lazy. I think I needed him to be dependent so that I could feel better about myself, like I was the strong one, the smart one, the person in control. I think I might have developed a bit of a martyr complex, you know, like don't worry, I'll take care of everything, and secretly—or not so secretly—feeling smug about it all." Jess sighed. "Anyway, last night I broke it off with Eddie. He's moving out today; he'll text me when he's gone."

Elizabeth took her daughter's hand; Jess didn't pull away. "I'm proud of you, Jess. It can't have been easy. What did Eddie say? How did he take it?" Though Elizabeth wouldn't voice her concern aloud, she was afraid that Eddie might not have behaved himself as he should have. As far as she knew he didn't have a history of violence, but nobody liked being dumped, and Jess could be pretty harsh when she opened her mouth. Not that it would be Jess's fault if Eddie couldn't control his temper!

"That's the thing," Jess said, with a bit of a wondering laugh. "He was fine. Totally fine. He said he'd been wanting to end things for a while, too, but that he was afraid of hurting me. Can you believe it? We were so many miles apart in our ideas about each other! It would be laughable if it weren't so sad. Then he told me he knew he needed to make some big changes in his life and that staying on with me was making him even more dependent and less pro-active than could be explained by his usual tendency toward laziness. In the end, we both actually laughed. And I cried a bit, which I absolutely hate doing, but I couldn't help it. Then Eddie packed a bag and went to his friend Danny's for the night. It was all so civilized. We even hugged right before he left."

"Wow," Elizabeth said. "It does sound very civilized." But would her daughter remain friends with Eddie? Elizabeth thought it was doubtful, and probably not advisable, for either of them.

"Was what I felt for Eddie early on in our relationship love?" Jess went on. "Or was it just lust dressed up as something more legitimate? Do you know, Mom, that in the five years we were together, neither of us ever mentioned the idea of getting married? And we never once talked about the future, about our future. I mean, okay, we were living together for four of those years, but so what? Without a formal, even a private commitment, without having once promised the other to be faithful and all that, what did it matter? In effect, we were just roommates."

"And that's something it turns out neither of you wanted," Elizabeth noted.

"Yes. You know, I haven't thanked you yet for your words of wisdom that last time we talked about Eddie and me, the day we were looking through Dad's yearbook. You said that maybe I was doing Eddie a disservice by staying with him. You were right."

A tiny flicker of uneasiness suddenly raced through Elizabeth. Assuming Eddie now knew about her affair with Chris Ryan—and back in early July he hadn't seemed to know—could he be relied upon to keep the secret, especially now that Jess had broken up with him? "Um," she began, "did you tell Eddie about my—"

"No," Jess said quickly. "There was no reason he needed to know. I guess deep down I knew we wouldn't be together much longer so there was no point in sharing something so important."

Elizabeth was relieved. If that was selfish, so be it.

"You know," Jess went on, "I've been thinking about the lies Dad told us about his high school days, and about how he could be a braggart, always going on about being the best salesman in the office, better at golf than all his friends, in better shape than most men his age. And I've come to the conclusion that I'm even more like Dad than I thought, and I'm not so sure that's a good thing."

Elizabeth sighed. "Jess, none of us are perfect, far from it. Try not to focus on what you feel are your flaws, whether or not they have anything to do with your father. And remember that you take after him in many positive ways. You get your natural athleticism from him, as well as your incredible energy and ability to get things done."

Jess looked close to crying, but the tears held off. "Thanks, Mom," she said, her voice husky with emotion. "You know, it dawned on me the other day that in a way you and I are in a similar situation career-wise. I mean, we're each facing a big challenge. Your career was yanked out from under you, and mine was, too, in a way. But Raven's backing away forced me to stop in my tracks and reconsider a lot of things."

"Not the worst thing to have happened," Elizabeth said. "An enforced reset."

"Maybe." Jess paused before going on. "I think I'm going to step back from the idea of starting my own company, at least for a while. I mean, why do I need the additional stress? Anyway, I like my current job, my boss appreciates me, like you said the other day, my colleagues are nice enough, and the pay is good, so why am I rushing to walk away? To prove to myself that I can make life even harder than it already is without my interfering with it? I feel like I've spent so many years of my life all wound-up and for what? I feel like I need to . . . like I need to breathe."

Elizabeth felt very proud of her middle child at that moment.

Self-knowledge was never easy to achieve, and she knew that for someone like Jess it could be a monumental task. "I'm glad you've come to the decision to stay on at ATD," Elizabeth said. "It seems to me a very wise one."

"I'm sorry I've been so harsh this summer," Jess went on, suddenly looking pretty sheepish. "Well, more than harsh. I've been a pain in the butt. I guess I've been feeling afraid of pretty much everything, doubting everything I thought I knew for sure, even apart from learning about you and Dad and Chris. It's kind of amazing I made it this far in my life before having an existential crisis!"

"I hear some people get through life without any form of existential crisis," Elizabeth noted with a smile. "But I don't believe it."

"Dad might have been one of those people," Jess replied. "I can almost believe he never allowed himself to follow dark thoughts and big questions to the point of crisis. I can almost believe he simply turned his back on them. That said, I do believe that by the end of his life he'd finally realized that you were competent in ways he'd always denied. I guess he needed to feel important, to believe you weren't as capable as he was in what he would call the 'serious things,' that without him you wouldn't get by. Dad badly needed to feel needed."

"He did. Until he got sick he'd never let me pay the bills or talk to repair men or replace batteries in smoke detectors. God knows what he thought would happen if I tried! Now, I have to admit I didn't enjoy taking over those tasks—I still don't find any real satisfaction in doing them well—but they have to be done so . . ."

"He was too young to die," Jess said. "Poor Dad."

"Yes, he was," Elizabeth agreed. "And I was too young to lose my husband. Fifty-three. I remember feeling so . . . crushed by the thought of living on alone for another ten, twenty, thirty years. Without your father, the person with whom I'd made a life, raised a family. The idea of marrying again never ever crossed my mind as a possibility. That's the truth. All I saw for a very long time was a sort of slow descent into old age and, eventually, oblivion."

"Grim." Jess shook her head. "I'm sorry, Mom. I guess I didn't ever pay much attention to your being, well, being a woman on her own, not just my mother. You know, Mom, perfectly okay with being a widow forever, with hanging her life on a hook and taking to her rocking chair. Gosh, I was so selfish, so naïve. I totally failed to see things from your perspective, not 'Mom's,' but Elizabeth's."

"It's all right," Elizabeth assured her daughter. "It's certainly not uncommon for even an adult child to have trouble acknowledging a parent as something other than or in addition to a mother or a father. I know that I never thought of my mother as anyone other than Mom. Frankly, I'm not sure she would have wanted me to."

"Depressing, isn't it? In some ways, we never grow up, no matter how hard we try to be mature! Anyway, now that Chris is back in your life, well, things have changed, haven't they? You don't have to consign yourself to a rocking chair!"

"Yes," Elizabeth admitted with a smile. "I'm not sure how, exactly, things have changed, what form they're going to take, but time will tell."

Jess sighed. "I wish I could be as philosophical as you are. Or as patient. I know change and growth take time, and that there are lots of things we can't control in this world, but it drives me nuts!"

Both women laughed.

"Have you told your sisters about you and Eddie?" Elizabeth asked after a moment.

"Not yet. I wanted to talk to you first. I'm sure neither Cam nor Petra will be surprised that Eddie and I have broken up."

"They just want you to be happy," Elizabeth said.

Jess smiled wanly. "Being happy isn't so easy. But I'm going to try. I promise, Mom, that I'm going to try."

Chapter 71

Petra observed her sister as she went about the kitchen, putting things to right. Jess had seemed a bit subdued but not unhappy since she had ended things with Eddie. Petra didn't blame Eddie for her sister's recent woes, but having him out of her life, along with Jess's having come to the decision not to leave a job she enjoyed, could only mean something positive for Jess. Cam, who had showed up again at their mother's house the evening before, agreed with Petra.

"Does Mom have any more paper towels?" Jess asked, waving an empty cardboard cylinder.

"If there are any," Petra replied, "they're in the pantry."

Her sister went off to rummage, while Petra took the broom from the narrow closet next to the fridge. The family had gotten a surprise that morning around eleven thirty when a large, olive-green vehicle had pulled into the driveway and parked behind Elizabeth's car.

"Isn't that Ralph's SUV?" Petra had asked, peering through the window.

"Let me see. Yup. What's he doing here, I wonder." Jess had walked to the foot of the stairs leading to the second floor and bellowed to Cam to come down and greet her husband and kids.

Why, indeed, had he come, Petra had thought? Had Cam asked him to join her? Petra didn't know the answer to those questions for sure, but if she had to guess, she would say that Ralph's visit had come as a complete surprise to his wife. The look of confusion and even, briefly, fear on Cam's face as she came racing down the stairs, and the speed with which she dashed outside, had convinced Petra that Cam hadn't been expecting the arrival of her family and was probably beside herself with anxiety as to what had prompted the visit.

When the family had trooped into the house, Petra had tried to catch Cam's eye but in vain. She, Jess, and her mother had greeted Ralph and the kids and helped to get everyone settled. It was clear from the number of travel bags that Cam's family would be spending at least one night in Eliot's Corner, and Petra foresaw being on occasional diaper duty. In truth, Petra had never changed a child's diaper. How hard could it be?

Everyone knew that Ralph was one of those transparent people who, try as they might, couldn't hide their true emotions. (Which was the major reason it had been so easy for Cam to see that when he was in the presence of his ex-girlfriend he became gaga.) Now, while he smiled at and hugged his in-laws and asked after everyone's health, it was clear to Petra—and most probably to the others—that he was a bundle of nerves. Well, he had reason to be, Petra supposed. Whatever was actually going on in Ralph's head wasn't making anyone around him happy. It probably wasn't making him happy, either.

It had been quickly agreed that lunch was in order, and it was, predictably, a chaotic affair, what with the boys being very excited to see their grandmother and Beth being Beth. Ralph had of course brought food for the twins and Beth's favorite juice drink and the cup in which she insisted it be poured. On the one hand, Petra kind of admired her niece's fierce preference for a particular drinking vessel. On the other, she found her sister and brother-in-law's catering to this preference a bit much. She had been witness to a tantrum on an occasion when the cup was unavailable. Beth's wailing and crying had seriously upset Petra, though Beth's parents had seemed to take it in stride.

After lunch, the twins were put to bed to nap; they had been more than ready. Beth set off for an impromptu playdate with the little girl who lived across the street; the Bauers had a golden retriever puppy, a big enticement for Beth, who was obsessed with animals and was constantly begging for a dog of her own. Cam and Ralph discreetly disappeared into the den and closed the door behind them.

Elizabeth went off to the bathroom, leaving Petra and Jess alone in the kitchen, clearing away the remains of the messy meal.

"I am so never having kids," Jess said firmly, dropping several dirty paper napkins into the trash can. "Who wants to be cleaning up after them all the time?"

"I think there's more to having kids than cleaning up," Petra replied. Then she recalled her niece's high-spirited antics at the table. "But I think I feel pretty much the same," she added. "I'm content being an aunt, at least for now."

"By the way," Jess said softly, "Cam told me her suspicions about Ralph and his old girlfriend. I urged her to 'woman up' and confront him, but I'm thinking she hasn't acted yet."

"We've all been telling her to confront him," Petra admitted. "And I think you're right. I suspect she hasn't spoken to him yet."

Jess tossed the dish towel she had been using onto the counter by the sink. "Well, maybe now is the moment she's been waiting for. Let's find out."

"What do you mean?" Petra asked.

"I mean that we should listen in to whatever it is Cam and Ralph are saying in the den. Look, I tried to get her aside just before lunch, and she literally turned away from me. The only way we're going to find out what's going on is by eavesdropping."

"Are you crazy! We can't spy on them!" Petra whispered fiercely.

Jess rolled her eyes. "We can't just wait around until it's over and Cam's ready to talk. The suspense would kill me."

"Why can't we just be patient?" Petra countered. "I thought we were civilized human beings!"

"Fine. Then you go away and I'll listen, but I'm not going to tell you anything."

"Jess! Ugh! Mom would kill us if she knew."

"Knew what?"

Petra startled. She hadn't heard her mother come back into the room.

"Cam and Ralph just went into the den and closed the door behind them," Jess explained in a whisper. "Ralph's got the look of a guilty man if ever I saw one. I mean, just showing up the way he did? I want to hear what's going on. Petra's being all ethical about it."

Elizabeth frowned. "We'll have to be quiet," she said softly. "Cam can't know that we invaded her privacy."

"We'd better listen from outside the window," Jess pointed out. "It's less likely we'll be caught."

"We can't!" Petra cried. But she followed her mother and sister as they tiptoed out the kitchen door and around to the other side of the house. As expected, the windows of the den were wide open to the summer warmth; the three women crouched under the center window. Petra hoped that no neighbor or passerby took notice of them. She was sure they looked ridiculous, if not actually criminal.

"Enough small talk. You didn't tell me you were coming."

That was Cam. Petra was surprised—and embarrassed—to find that she was now very interested in what was happening in the den.

"I know," Ralph said. "I guess I thought if I told you my intentions maybe you'd tell me not to come."

"Why would I do that?"

It was difficult to make out the next bit of the exchange. Maybe, Petra thought, her sister and brother-in-law had moved away from the window. But then, she could hear Ralph as plain as day.

"I don't know if you've noticed, well, of course you have, that in the last few months I've been, well, a bit . . . I mean, lately I've . . . See, the thing is . . . Boy, this is hard. Okay, it's like this. I got it into my head that—that I was still in love with Lily. I know, it was crazy of me," he raced on, "and wrong; I absolutely am not in love with Lily. Sure, she's a friend, our friend, a friend of the family, but nothing more."

Jess grimaced and ran a finger across her throat. Elizabeth frowned at her. Petra bit her lip. Cam was silent.

Then, Ralph spoke again. His voice was shaky. "When you told me about your mother and her friend, Christopher Ryan, that you'd known for weeks about their affair but hadn't told me, it was a wake-up call. I realized just how far I'd checked out of our marriage this summer. It shocked me. It scared me, badly."

Petra thought she could hear Cam sigh. "Why did it happen?" Cam asked then. "Why did you turn to Lily of all people?"

"I've been giving it a lot of thought," Ralph said after a moment, "and I finally admitted to myself that after the twins came along, well, really about the time they turned one, I began to wonder what if things had been different. What if—oh God— what if you and I hadn't gotten married. What if I . . . what if I'd married Lily, not that she would have had me, I mean, she dumped me, not the other way around. It's just that I started feeling overwhelmed by all the responsibility of having three kids, and I began to think, what if I lose my job, what will happen to the children then, and when I finally retire am I going to be too worn out to do anything other than sit in a chair and watch television. Or maybe I won't be able to retire, not with having to send three kids to college. And then there was you. I thought, Cam is still young and attractive and vibrant and what if she gets tired of me and leaves. Who would possibly want me? I know I'm not exactly the most exciting guy out there and . . ." Here, Ralph stopped talking and laughed nervously. "I think I was having an early midlife crisis."

Silence followed Ralph's fraught speech. Petra felt her stomach clench with tension. She thought her mother looked gray. Not surprisingly, Jess looked angry.

"Cam," Ralph pleaded. "Say something."

It was another moment before she did.

"Don't you think I get overwhelmed by the children, and the house, and my own job?" she said, her voice remarkably calm. "Do you think I don't worry about money and growing old and getting sick and all the other things middle-aged people worry about? Do you think I don't sometimes feel exhausted, being the one having to deal with our extended families, my mother and sisters, your parents and siblings and their kids?"

Jess's frown deepened. Elizabeth closed her eyes. Petra held her breath. Ralph must have responded in some way to Cam's words, though she hadn't heard him speak.

Then, Cam went on. "But I never once fantasized about our not being married." Cam laughed. Was there a trace of bitterness or regret in the laugh? Petra couldn't tell. "Maybe if there was an eligible man around I could fantasize about I might have, but there isn't. Besides, I don't want to fantasize. I don't need to. I'm happy with who and what I have, you and the children. If things aren't perfect, so what? I never expected them to be. I don't need them to be."

"This is the moment of truth," Jess whispered. "He'd better not blow it."

Petra half wanted to cover her ears, to block out the critical moment. Instead, she listened more keenly.

"I'm so sorry, Cam," Ralph said. His voice was rough with emotion. "I really am. But what I need you to believe is that I never, ever said anything to Lily to suggest . . . To make her think . . . Because I never really wanted to be with her, not deep down. It wasn't even Lily that I thought I wanted. It was . . . It was a life that was relatively carefree. But I've come to my senses. No life is carefree, is it? Everyone has responsibilities and burdens and troubles. There is no fantasy life or fantasy partner. And that's okay. It really is okay."

Cam was silent. Petra tried and failed to imagine what her sister might be feeling at that moment. And then, Ralph was speaking again.

"Honestly, this is not a blame thing, but you being away so much this summer didn't help matters. I got to thinking that maybe you were tired of me, and I wouldn't blame you if you were. Like I said, I know I'm not the most exciting guy around. I never was. Anyway, finally, I came to realize, to remember, how much I love you and our life together. How much I need you, respect you, rely on you. Look at the children we created! They're pretty great, aren't they?"

Petra strained to catch her sister's response; she thought she heard a murmur of laughter.

"One more thing," Ralph said hurriedly. "I really think we should adopt a dog because Beth has been going on about wanting one, and I think it would be good for the boys, as well, and I promise to be the one to walk him in rain and snow. Really. I swear."

There was a long moment of silence. Petra felt the proverbial butterflies take wing in her midsection. She felt almost as invested in a happy outcome for her sister as if in that moment, she herself was Cam.

"We've both been so foolish. I'm sorry."

That was Cam speaking, her voice muffled.

"I'm sorry, too."

And then there was silence again, a silence that, to Petra, spoke of a private reunion between two people who loved each other and always would.

Jess, who had been crouching, suddenly fell back onto her

butt. Elizabeth smiled and wiped a tear from the corner of her eye. And Petra, who truly did believe that she and her mother and sister had done something wrong, still felt the urge to laugh merrily as the butterflies in her stomach flew away.

"Grandma, what are you guys doing?"

Petra gulped. It was Beth, back from her romp with the Bauers' puppy and staring wonderingly at the grown-ups tumbled together on the grass beneath an open window.

"We thought we saw a frog," Elizabeth said, at the exact moment Jess said, "I lost an earring," which was also the moment Petra said, "We were pulling weeds."

Beth frowned. "I'm hungry. Can somebody make me a snack?" she said.

"You just finished lunch!" Jess exclaimed.

Petra scrambled to her feet and took her niece's hand. "Let's go inside and I'll make you a snack. Growing up takes a lot of energy."

"Are you grown-up?" Beth demanded.

Petra looked seriously at the little girl. "I'm really not sure," she said.

Chapter 72

Shawcross Farm was in fact a nature preserve managed by a private trust. It featured beautiful walks along groomed trails, some of which were meant for those with hiking skills, but the majority were for the average walker. A central building housed a small natural history museum, a very nice gift shop, and a room for lectures, performances, and art exhibits.

Chris had gone back to the car to fetch his sunglasses—he claimed he was getting more forgetful by the day—and Elizabeth, standing outside the central building, was waiting patiently for him to return.

The night before, she had decided that no matter what happened between Chris and herself going forward, she would keep the old diary from the summer of 1991, honor it as a testament to a significant moment in her life, a moment when she had committed herself to an act that had resulted in, among other things, the bringing forth of a new life. What did it matter if one or all of the girls decided to read it when their mother had passed on? Every word in the diary was heartfelt, and no word was vicious or mean-spirited.

Chris came back in sight, and, as Elizabeth watched him walking toward her, she thought back to the day before her wedding to Hugh, when she had watched Chris coming toward her across the village green. Now, almost forty years later, she wasn't scared to see him approach, and didn't feel the urge to run away. Now, there was no need to be afraid or to run.

And yet, in a way, she still had trouble believing that Chris was real, there with her in the present, and not just a dream or a figment of her desperate imagination. She reached for his hand when he joined her; it fit so well, so easily with hers. Her hand had gotten crushed in Hugh's loving grip. But that was the past.

"So, start with the A trail?" Chris suggested, pointing to the visitors' map he held. "It's considered the least difficult."

Elizabeth agreed and they set out, a pair of binoculars hanging around Chris's neck—he had had them since childhood, he explained—and Elizabeth wearing a backpack containing two water bottles, a handful of snack bars, and the usual odds and ends a woman tended always to have with her.

"How are the girls?" Chris asked as they walked; then, he winced. "I suppose I shouldn't call them girls, not anymore."

"Don't worry," Elizabeth replied. "They'll always be my girls, no matter how old they get! To be honest, earlier in the summer I wasn't sure things would be okay any time soon. But Cam's marital woes have been brought out in the open, and I foresee a fresh start for her and Ralph if they can keep talking. Jess's career crisis led to real self-discovery, even concerning that odd relationship she was stuck in with Eddie. Now, maybe both Jess and Eddie can move on and be with someone who really loves them."

"And Petra?" Chris asked.

Elizabeth smiled. "Since you saw her just a few days ago? Seriously though, it makes me very happy to know that Petra enjoys your company as much as she does." Elizabeth paused. "I hope," she went on, "that you enjoy her company, as well, that you're not spending time with her primarily—"

"Out of a sense of duty?" Chris's tone revealed that he had been hurt by Elizabeth's remark.

"I'm sorry," she said hurriedly, pulling him to a stop so they could look directly at each other. "Really. I don't know what made me say that, what made me think such a thing. I should know you better. I do know you better. Please forgive me."

Chris smiled and squeezed her hand gently. "It's okay. This is difficult for all of us in some ways. We're bound to say things we don't really mean or wish we hadn't. Personally, this is something I never expected to happen, being together with you again. And knowing that Petra is my daughter, well, that's wonderful, but it's still a shock. I wake up some mornings in that sort of blank state, and in a split-second I suddenly remember that I have a child and I wonder if I'm still dreaming or if I've gone crazy overnight."

Elizabeth felt reassured, and they continued to walk along through a wooded area dense with green ferns and thick, velvety moss.

"You know," Elizabeth said musingly, "it is all strange, isn't it? Just a little while ago, when I watched you walk across the field to where I was waiting, I remembered you crossing that village green forty years ago, and for a moment, there was no difference at all in time. It's as if we've always been together and always will be, as if there's no real past or future, only a perpetual present." Elizabeth shook her head and laughed. "Well, you know what I mean."

"I think I do," Chris said. "But I'm not sure I have the skills to even attempt to describe the feeling!"

When they had reached what was marked on the map as the halfway point of the trail, just out of the wooded area, Chris suggested they stop and take in the view. There were three beautiful benches crafted from logs for just that purpose. From their seat, they looked out on an expansive field of grass thick with wild flowers. A bird of prey, possibly a hawk, was circling far above; a chipmunk darted in and out of cover not far from their feet. The air was still and quiet.

"I've been thinking," Chris said after a few minutes. "Now

that you've retired, however unwillingly, and are free to, well, free to pretty much do what you please—"

"Short of rampaging through Eliot's Corner in my birthday suit and shouting fire in a crowded movie theater."

Chris raised an eyebrow and laughed. "Yes, short of that. Anyway, would you consider our going away for a while? It needn't be far; it could be out West. Or we could go to Europe, maybe settle for a month or two in a city or province, live like locals as much as is possible, then move on. Or come home. Whatever you'd want. As long as we can be together, have time alone at last."

Elizabeth felt a tingle of sheer joy flow through her. Things were moving swiftly between them, but that was okay. It felt comfortable and right. Neither of them was a child. Both knew all too well that a long future wasn't guaranteed. Carpe diem.

"Yes," she said. "I'd consider our going away together. Rather, yes, I want us to go away together. Wherever it is. You could show me places that have been important to you in the past. We could find new places that will mean something to the both of us. Yes. I think we should do it. I've always wanted to travel."

Chris beamed. "Wonderful," he said. "There are a few loose ends I need to tie up, but it shouldn't take long. And you'll need to get a passport if you don't already have one and make arrangements here, I imagine, like finding someone to check in on the house and such. We might be able to leave by mid-October if we're lucky."

"As long as we can agree on where to go first," Elizabeth pointed out. "You might be sick of it, but I've never been to Paris, so that's a must at some point. And I've always wanted to visit the Black Forest. And St. Petersburg. Maybe we could fly to Mexico to see the Incan ruins. And—"

Chris laughed. "I'm a seasoned traveler, but I am in my seventies," he said. "One country at a time, please."

"Okay, then. Maybe we could rent a cottage on the West Coast of Ireland. We could visit the Aran Islands and the Cliffs of Moher. And some days we could just stay put and spend the mornings taking long walks over the ruggedly beautiful landscape, and the afternoons drinking tea and reading in our cozy little cottage, and our evenings in the local pub listening to live traditional music."

"It sounds perfect," Chris said. "Ireland is magical. There's a good chance you won't ever want to leave."

Elizabeth smiled and leaned in to kiss him. And upon their return to the States, what then, she wondered. Maybe they would buy a home together. Maybe they would marry. She believed—she knew—that they would never part again.

"How do you think the girls will feel about our going away?" Chris asked then.

"They'll be all right," Elizabeth assured him. "Well, Jess might grumble a bit, but that's what she does. She might have freed herself from a dead-end relationship and decided to stay the course with her job, but she's still my grumbling, critical-minded middle child."

"Are you happy?" Chris asked, reaching for her hand. "Or is that a silly question?"

"Silly or not, the answer is yes. I am happy. And you?"

"Yes. I'm happier than I ever hoped to be."

Elizabeth got to her feet, pulling Chris along with her. "Good," she said. "Then let's keep walking. There's a lot still ahead of us."

Chapter 73

Petra had asked Chris to meet her at Chez Claudine in Eliot's Corner. He was after all a legitimate friend of the Quirk family, and, in that role, there was no reason for them not to meet for coffee and a pastry in full view of the neighbors.

"I like this place," Chris said when they were seated with coffee and croissants. "It's very authentic. It makes me miss Paris."

"I'd like to travel one day," Petra told him, dusting flaky croissant crumbs from her fingers, "really try to understand different peoples in different countries."

"It will happen. There's no substitute for experience, though armchair traveling through books and film is certainly better than nothing. Speaking of books, I want you to know that I'm prepared to cover your expenses during graduate school. It's something I truly want to do. I can't make up for the important times I missed with you, birthdays, school plays, graduations, but, well, I hope you'll accept this gift now."

"Thank you," Petra said earnestly. "I will accept your gift. I mean, assuming I go ahead with—"

"Here." Chris interrupted by handing her a folded piece of paper. "I did some investigating and came across a few respected graduate programs that will allow you to craft your own program of study to combine your interests in philosophy, literature, and history. It won't be easy to create such a program, to find a meaningful focus, but you'd have the help of a seasoned advisor. I hope you don't mind or think that I'm interfering. Of course, you're free to ignore this list and conduct your own research."

"No, I don't mind," Petra assured him, opening the paper and glancing at the information Chris had written down. It was the first time she was seeing his handwriting. From now on, her life would be full of firsts with her father. "Thank you, again. It all feels so overwhelming and I'm grateful for your help. It's just that . . ."

"That what?"

Petra sighed. "It's been a long time since I've been in school, since I've lived a disciplined life. Maybe I've permanently lost the ability to work in a really concentrated way. Maybe I won't be able to turn away from all the distractions I've allowed to clutter up my life and really devote myself to my studies. Do you know how much time I spend on Instagram? Watching cat videos on Facebook? Maybe I'm just not intelligent enough to go on for another degree."

"You are."

"But—"

"Don't contradict your father." Chris smiled. "I've been wanting to say that since we met. Or another of those typical dad-like statements."

Petra laughed. "Just don't start wearing dad jeans, please."

"That's a promise I can keep easily," Chris assured her. "I've never been into wearing jeans, even when I was a young man. Hugh used to tease me about my sartorial stuffiness."

"Again," Petra said, indicating the piece of paper Chris had given her, "I do really appreciate your doing this initial research for me. I wouldn't have known where to start. But going forward, I'd . . . Please don't take offense at this, but I'd like to keep our connection a secret. At least until I'm accepted in some program or other. If people know I'm your daughter they might assume you used your influence to get me into a good school or . . . I'm sorry."

Chris smiled. "Don't be sorry. I think that's a wise decision. But I'm not planning on keeping our relationship a secret in other quarters. I'm not ashamed in the least that you're my child, and I'm happy to let people know that I'm your father. But a revelation can wait until you're ready. And until your mother is ready."

Petra was deeply moved. "You're not worried about it affecting your career, the news that you had an affair with a married woman?" she asked.

"In this insane culture where nobody in the public eye seems able to keep their clothes on for more than five minutes at a time?" Chris laughed. "What I did hardly merits a mention, not compared with what so many people get up to. Don't worry, my career will be just fine. The work I've done stands for itself. Besides, I'm pretty much retired from working now. I do what I feel capable of doing, which these days is mostly advising, but my years of hectic world travel and all the turbulence that goes with globe-trotting are over. I'm glad of that. Frankly, I'm tired."

"You're okay though?" Petra asked. "I mean, you're in good health?"

Chris smiled. "A few minor aches and pains but nothing major. I've been lucky so far. And longevity tends to run in my family, so maybe my luck will hold out."

"Your family is my family, too," Petra reminded him.

"Of course. And like I said before, it's a small group. There might be a stray third or fourth cousin somewhere; if there is, I don't know about them. But yes, your family, too."

Suddenly, a thought occurred to Petra. "I suppose I should know about more than longevity, like if there's a history of cancer or, I don't know, Alzheimer's in the family."

"I'll tell you everything I know," Chris promised. "But there's time for that later on. I was wondering if you'd be interested in taking a drive to the Coastal Maine Botanical Gardens some afternoon. I haven't been there since it first opened in 2007. I hear it's grown enormously."

"That sounds great. For some crazy reason, I've never been there, and that needs to change. Oh," Petra said, "by the way, what's your favorite flower? Or is that too difficult a question?"

"Not at all. Peonies, hands down."

"Mine, too! Imagine that." It was a minor thing. Lots of people loved peonies, and those people had nothing to do with Petra Quirk and she had nothing to do with them. A love of a particular flower wasn't, as far as Petra knew, an inherited preference. But the fact that she and her father shared that preference felt nice. It felt more than nice.

"Sadly, peony season is over," Chris went on, "but we can plan to attend a peony festival or two next June, maybe the one at the Maine Audubon nature preserve in Falmouth."

Next June. Her father was looking ahead, making plans for them to spend more time together. "That sounds great," Petra said. "I can't wait."

Chapter 74

"So, as soon as I've got a passport," Elizabeth explained, "and made some arrangements here, and as soon as Chris has taken care of loose ends regarding his current projects, we'll be off. We've decided to go to Ireland, with an open-ended ticket. Next year, who knows?"

Elizabeth hadn't expected a universal cheer to erupt at her announcement, but she had hoped for a more energetic response than the silence that met her. Petra, to Elizabeth's right, looked down at her lap. Cam, who was sitting across the little outdoor table from her mother, wore a slightly strained smile. Jess, sitting to Elizabeth's left, was frowning.

"When, exactly, are you planning to leave?" Cam asked after a moment.

"Like I said," Elizabeth replied, "as soon as we've got our ducks in a row, probably by mid-October."

"This running off together concerns me, Mom," Jess said in that crisp tone of voice she hadn't given up in spite of her avowed desire to change and become less wound up. "I mean, how well do you really know Chris? Until this summer, you hadn't seen or even spoken to him in thirty years. He could be a cad for all we know! I mean—"

Petra finally looked up. "Jess, that's enough," she said, calmly and firmly. "Be reasonable. You're forgetting that I've spent hours with Chris this summer, and I'm a pretty good judge of character. Chris Ryan is a good man, and he's my father. He loves Mom and Mom loves him. And they're not 'running off' together. There's nothing secret or clandestine about it. I'm sure they'll give us an itinerary if we ask for one, and we can all keep in touch via FaceTime or whatever."

"Petra is right," Elizabeth said. "It's not as if I'm going into the abyss. And there's nothing to say that one or all of you can't pop over to visit us. We could plan a week together somewhere, maybe London or Edinburgh."

Cam took a drink from her glass of iced tea before saying: "I'll admit this news comes as a bit of a surprise, not that it should, not after everything that's happened this summer. But I think we owe it to Mom to trust in her intelligence and good sense. And I, for one, might just take you up on that idea of meeting you and Chris for a wee vacation. Ralph and I could use a romantic getaway."

Jess sighed, and a sheepish smile came to her face. "I suppose. But if Chris runs off with your passport and money, Mom, leaving you stranded in some boggy Irish landscape, he's going to hear from me."

Elizabeth nodded. "Fair enough! Look, I'm very glad you all support my decision to travel with Chris. Not that your disapproval would have stopped me," Elizabeth admitted. "At one time it might have, but not now."

"Good." Petra nodded. "Life is short. And precious. When happiness beckons—"

"Without the complication of a prior personal commitment," Jess added slyly.

Petra nodded. "Without the complication of a prior personal commitment, follow it."

"I'd like to meet with Chris soon, Mom," Cam said now, "if you think he's ready. Maybe Petra could be with me."

"And not me?" Elizabeth asked. "Why? So that you two can tell Chris that I'm addicted to Apple Jacks or that I've been wearing the same slippers for the past ten years?"

"I am so not mentioning the slippers!" Cam said with a laugh.

"It's not like I don't wash them once a month," Elizabeth protested.

"And I like Apple Jacks," Petra added. "What's wrong with Apple Jacks?"

"Jess?" Elizabeth asked.

Jess shook her head. "Sorry, Mom, but I'm not ready to meet Chris just yet. If Cam says he's okay, that's enough for me for the moment. Not that I don't trust your opinion, or Petra's but . . . Cam is more of a disinterested party. In a way."

"I'll miss you, Mom," Petra said suddenly, and her eyes were wet with tears. "And I'll miss Chris, when you go away."

"And I'll miss you all, truly. Thank you for being honest," Elizabeth said feelingly. "Thank you for everything."

Elizabeth replaced the receiver of the landline in its cradle.

The call had taken her completely by surprise. Rather, it was the caller's news that had surprised her. Marie Keogh, principal of MidCoast Primary, had explained that the woman who had been promoted to the position of full-time instructor in English grammar and literature at the school, the woman who, justly or unjustly, had been chosen over Elizabeth to fill the position, had just announced that she had taken another teaching position out of state. The woman was sorry for the last-minute announcement. She hoped she hadn't caused too much trouble, but the offer was just too good to refuse.

"We thought of you immediately," Ms. Keogh had told Elizabeth. "I know this must come as a bit of a shock but, well, we would be thrilled if you were to accept the position at Mid-Coast. Classes start in just a few days so I know you might be inconvenienced; maybe you have travel plans. But please, I hope that you consider our offer."

Elizabeth put the receiver back to her ear. "I'm sorry," she said. "Could you repeat what you just said? There was some trouble on the line."

The woman complied with Elizabeth's request, and after what seemed an interminable amount of time, during which Elizabeth heard only vaguely something about salary, benefits, and other, unofficial perks of the job, like a brand-new teachers' lounge and bathroom, Ms. Keogh said: "So, can we have your answer by the weekend?"

"All right," Elizabeth said. Her reply was automatic, more of a way to end the call than an agreement. "Thank you. Goodbye."

Now, here she was, faced with a dilemma she had never anticipated. And there were only three days in which to decide. Accept the teaching position, return to a career she loved—and see Chris only on weekends and holidays through the coming academic year. Or, turn down the offer and go away with Chris as planned.

Chris would understand if she chose to work for another year, or maybe even two years. He knew she had loved her career as much as he loved his. But . . .

To return to teaching, a life she had truly enjoyed. Or, to seize life with the man she had loved in silence for so many years. The man who was the father of her youngest child.

Elizabeth realized that she felt angry. She hadn't asked for this offer of a teaching position. Finally, finally, the way was clear for her to be with Chris, for him to be with her, and the path forward was being muddied by opportunity. Strange. Be careful what you wish for.

One thing was certain. She would not tell her daughters about the job offer. This was a decision she had to make on her own, not a problem for her children to solve or to worry about. Especially not after having learned just that morning that their mother was planning on going abroad with her lover.

And whatever Elizabeth decided—to go away with Chris now or to ask him to postpone their life together yet again—and whatever that decision led to, at least Petra had come to know her father this summer. That was, Elizabeth truly believed, the most wonderfully important thing in the end.

Chapter 75

Cam was driving, and Petra was glad. Her sister was an excellent driver and that was something about which Cam could be proud, but like most people who excel at a particular activity, she tended to be critical of others less skilled. Normally, Petra was relaxed and confident behind the wheel of a car (unless there was a lot of traffic), but when Cam was sitting beside her, commenting on her driving performance, Petra found herself making mistakes and poor decisions.

"So," Petra said when they were close to the lobster pound where they were to meet Chris Ryan for lunch, "what have you and Ralph decided to do about Lily? Are you just going to pretend that nothing odd happened this summer? I can't see how that would be possible. Lily is smart. She had to have seen Ralph falling into crush mode, even, if for some weird reason, she chose to pretend everything was normal."

"I'm not sure what to do," Cam admitted, eyes fixed to the road. "Part of me wants to ask Lily out to lunch and have a heart-to-heart. Tell her I was aware of Ralph's behavior, let her know we're working on making the marriage whole again, and maybe, if I have the nerve, ask her what role she really played

in it all. I mean, I found out that she was the one who orches-
trated that day at the children's museum in Boston with Ralph
and the kids. Why? She'd never done anything like that before.
What was she thinking, co-opting my family like that?"

Petra thought for a moment before saying: "I think it's
Ralph's responsibility to sit Lily down and confess his temporary insanity. I think he's the one who should make it clear to
her that you're the one he loves and apologize for anything else
he might have suggested. I mean, you're the victim here. Why
should you have to clean up the mess Ralph made?"

Cam pulled into the parking lot of the lobster pound and
turned off the engine of the car before replying. "We both
made a mess of things," she said quietly. "But Ralph and I will
figure it out together. Don't worry about it."

Petra was happy enough to back away from a problem that
wasn't hers to solve. The sisters got out of the car and made
their way toward the deck on the far side of the restaurant
where they had agreed to meet Chris.

"That's him," Petra said when they had reached the hostess
station. "In the far right-hand corner. The man reading."

"My gosh, you look so much like him," Cam whispered as
they were led Chris's table.

Petra's heart began to race, and she realized that she felt
proud to be introducing her half-sister to her biological father.
If anyone had told her back at the start of her summer in Eliot's
Corner that such an event would be taking place in the very
near future, she would have dismissed the idea as preposterous,
worthy of a novel or a movie, not likely to happen in real life.
And yet, here they were.

"Chris?" she said.

He looked up from his book and smiled. "Petra. And Cam."

The women took seats, one on either side of Chris, and
before they had said another word, a waitress appeared with
menus and asked for their drink order.

"What are you reading?" Cam asked when the waitress had gone. Petra thought she sounded nervous, which was not like Cam. But this was a strange and unprecedented situation.

Chris slid the book over to Cam. "It's a new novel, out a few months I think. It's the writer's first published work of fiction."

"I've never even heard of it, let alone read it," Cam admitted.

"Me, neither," Petra said, peering at the cover of the trade paperback. "The title is okay. *The Darkest Forest.*"

"I wouldn't bother getting yourselves a copy," Chris said. "The title is the only decent bit of it. The book itself is pretty bad. Awful, really. The only reason I gave it a go was because a colleague recommended it, and usually, he has good taste in literature. But this . . . I'm not sure what I'm going to say when he asks my opinion."

Cam laughed; Chris's honesty seemed to have relaxed her. "People take their taste in reading material very seriously. Your friend will probably feel personally insulted if you tell him you found the book bad."

"True. I'll probably just say that it wasn't to my taste and leave it at that."

Petra nodded. "Good idea. I lost a friend because we disagreed about an author she loved and I didn't. It was back in college. I couldn't make her realize that just because I didn't really like Shelley's poems didn't mean that I didn't like her."

"Her loss," Chris said with a fond smile.

"The funny thing is," Petra added, "I came to love Shelley's work after college. I wonder if my old friend would find me redeemed."

The waitress reappeared with their drinks, took their food order, and hurried off again. When she had gone, silence descended on the three. Petra felt it was her responsibility to keep a conversation going, but just as she opened her mouth to ask Chris if his latest work venture had been successful, Cam looked to him.

"I still have one of the gifts you brought me when I was very young," she said. "It's a little wooden wishing well. Do you re-member it?"

Chris smiled. "I do. I remember the fun I had choosing pres-ents to bring back for you and Jess."

"Well, now it lives in my daughter's bedroom. She's in love with it. She's convinced a fairy lives at the bottom of the well and that one day the fairy will come popping up for a visit. She's only six, after all."

"I hope she still believes in fairies when she's sixty!" Petra said.

"Do you have photos of your family?" Chris asked.

Cam reached for her phone and, after a moment of scrolling, handed the phone to Chris.

"That was taken just last week at a birthday party," she told him. "Here's my daughter, Beth. She's named after Mom, obvi-ously. And here are the twins, Jake and Joe. The big guy is my husband, of course. Ralph."

"You have a lovely family," Chris said sincerely, handing the phone back to Cam. "You look very happy together."

Cam nodded. "We are. We really are. I try not to take that for granted, though sometimes I fail."

Their waitress appeared carrying an enormous tray on her shoulder. Petra had never worked as a server in the food indus-try. She just knew she would be fired before the end of her first shift. The number of glasses and dishes she broke in her own home was astounding.

"I'm sorry that Jess isn't here today," Cam said, as they began their meal. "She's still, well . . ."

"It's fine," Chris said. "I'm fine. No one owes me any expla-nations."

"She'll come around," Petra promised. "She's just sort of prickly. And she's going through a lot of challenges right now. I told you, she broke up with the guy she was living with, and then there's the stuff about her career."

"She doesn't need an excuse for not meeting me," Chris said.

"Of course, for your mother's sake, I hope she comes to accept me as a part of—well, I was going to say 'the family,' but that might be hoping for too much. If Jess and I could be on pleasant terms, I'd be satisfied."

Cam laughed. "I'm not sure anyone is ever really on 'pleasant terms' with Jess! She tends to do extremes, which means that if she likes you, she's your friend forever. And if she doesn't like you . . ."

"Like her father," Chris said quietly. "Hugh was one of the most loyal—and most black-and-white—people I've ever known."

"But there should be a limit to loyalty," Petra said. "I mean, there can be a time when it's silly to stay loyal to someone or even to a thing. Remember how Dad refused to throw out that old flannel jacket he'd had since college? It was literally falling apart. Every time it came out of the wash it was more and more in shreds. It drove Mom crazy that he wouldn't get rid of it, but he was determined to hang on to it until the bitter end."

Cam rolled her eyes. "How could I forget the Battle of the Flannel Jacket? It only ended when a sleeve finally fell off!"

For a while the three concentrated on eating their lobster rolls, French fries, and coleslaw, and conversation was light and general. When they had finished lunch, Cam turned again to Chris.

"So, tell us about your plans for your trip to Ireland. Mom's beyond excited."

"I've rented a cottage in Galway on the West Coast of Ireland for two weeks," Chris explained. "It's one of my favorite spots, and I think Elizabeth will love it, too. Hopefully, from there we'll travel on to London and Edinburgh, maybe get to Wales. The itinerary will be loose and depend on what takes Elizabeth's fancy." Chris smiled. "And on my old bones."

"You're not old," Petra said firmly.

"Well, I'm not young!"

"With three small children," Cam said, "sometimes I can't

remember ever being young. My life just feels like one long moment of exhaustion. But you, Petra, at thirty, you've truly got your life ahead of you."

Only weeks ago, Petra would have found that statement—that opinion?—worrisome or challenging. But now, she realized that she felt stronger than she had upon first returning to Eliot's Corner, more rooted, and that was largely thanks to her mother's bringing her together with her biological father. Petra just might be ready after all to accept the challenge of living her life to the fullest and for a purpose.

"You look like the cat that swallowed the cream," Chris noted.

"You do. What are you smiling about?" Cam asked, with a smile of her own.

"Everything," Petra told her father and her sister. "I'm smiling about everything."

Chapter 76

Ordinarily, Elizabeth was not one to just drop by a person's house unannounced—unlike her middle child. To be honest, she wasn't entirely sure what had prompted her to do just that today. A compulsion, a need to seize the moment, to not waste another minute. Whatever had caused her unannounced appearance, Elizabeth hoped that her friend would forgive her rudeness.

Elizabeth pressed the doorbell and, while she waited for Mrs. Shandy to come to the door (her car was in the driveway; she was home), Elizabeth glanced at the houses on either side of her friend's home. They were similar but not identical, built at some point in the 1950s, compact and generally unremarkable, but well-kept, as were all of the houses in this part of Eliot's Corner.

Before Elizabeth could remark anything more, the door opened.

"Fancy you just turning up," Mrs. Shandy said. "Come in, come in."

Elizabeth followed her friend into the house. It was as neat as the proverbial pin, with a place for everything and everything in its place. Elizabeth had been to the house many times before but never failed to be struck by its almost extreme tidiness. And yet, the house felt like a home, lived in and loved, and this in spite of the absence of photographs of friends or family. Now, knowing about Mrs. Shandy's husband, a young man who tragically died on his honeymoon, Elizabeth wondered if her friend kept a photo of Ross in her bedroom, a place that was off-limits to visitors. It seemed likely, but it wasn't a question she would ever ask.

"I'm sorry I just showed up like I did," Elizabeth said as they walked through to the kitchen at the back of the house.

"No worries. I wasn't doing much of anything other than trying to decide what book to start reading next. Simon Schama's *Landscape and Memory* or Zadie Smith's most recent novel. Your presence is a relief, to be honest. Such choices!"

The women settled at the kitchen table with glasses of very cold, very tart lemonade and a plate of thin, sugary lemon cookies.

"But I am curious as to what brought you here today," Mrs. Shandy said then. "We've known each other a long time and you've never come by without a call first."

"I'm sorry, really," Elizabeth began. "It's just that I want to tell you something. I feel I owe you the truth after you were generous enough to share your story with me, I mean, to tell me about your parents and your husband."

Mrs. Shandy shook her head. "There's no tit for tat in friendships, Elizabeth. You don't owe me anything in return for my sharing a tragedy from my past. But if you truly want to tell me something, then I'm quite prepared to listen."

So, Elizabeth told her friend about the history of her relationship with Christopher Ryan, her husband's dearest friend. As she spoke, she felt another layer of strain peel away. The expression on her friend's face remained steady, an expression of calm interest and focus. Not until Elizabeth had finished her story did Mrs. Shandy nod, smile, and speak.

"That is quite a tale indeed, Elizabeth. Thank you for telling me. I imagine this is to be kept between the two of us, and, of course, your daughters."

"Yes," Elizabeth said, "please. For a long time, I was afraid of the truth getting around town, and I'm certainly not going to advertise my less than honest past, but now I'm not so afraid of being exposed. I'd prefer that nobody but you know about my long-ago relationship with Chris Ryan, but if word did somehow get around, I won't allow myself to be destroyed by the opinions of my neighbors."

"Good for you. I must say, your romantic tragedy might just trump mine! Well. I understand why it's not something you want made general knowledge. Too many people enjoy other people's heartache." Mrs. Shandy smiled. "But now, it seems that something has supplanted your heartache."

"Yes. The possibility of a genuine, legitimate future with Chris. Something I'd long ago given up hoping for."

"Something for which you'd long ago given up hope. Sorry. I've been pretty good lately about controlling the impulse to correct but not perfect."

Elizabeth smiled. "I'm glad I told you."

"Long-lost diaries." Mrs. Shandy shook her head. "All they cause is trouble. There's a lesson there, but no matter."

"Well, my long-lost diary didn't cause trouble as much as it provoked a major change. It was the catalyst I didn't know I needed. The spur to be honest with my family. That and Petra's uncovering my wedding dress in the attic, more than a bit worse for wear. And hearing an old song on the radio! You know how music can send you hurtling into a specific time in the past."

"You were receptive to the signs."

"I suppose. There's another twist to this story, if you can bear it." Elizabeth went on to tell Mrs. Shandy about the teaching offer she had unexpectedly been offered.

"It never rains but it pours," Mrs. Shandy noted.

"Yes. Now the question is, should I take the job and stay in

Eliot's Corner for another year or two? My being around might be a help to Jess. She's newly single and facing a pretty major personal rethink. And there's Cam's family. If I go off traveling the world I might not see my grandchildren for some time. And then there's Petra. She might be terribly disappointed if I *didn't* go away with Chris, though she's told me she'll miss us both."

"You can't let your children's thoughts and feelings override your own, not now." Mrs. Shandy's tone was firm.

"My head tells me the same," Elizabeth admitted. "But how does a parent ignore the thoughts and feelings of her children, even a parent of an adult child?"

Mrs. Shandy sighed. "I can't say, not having had children of my own. But I can remind you that you're making assumptions about your daughters' needs and attitudes. And that sounds to me like cowardice, like making lame excuses not to go off with the man you love because maybe you're afraid that things won't work out or that he'll grow tired of you, or who knows what. Ask Jess if she wants your advice about her love life or her work. Ask Cam if she really thinks you'll do irreparable damage to the grandchildren if you only see them on Zoom once a week for the duration of your journey. As for Petra, you have no worries there. She's the smartest of the lot, and the most understanding. She'll be okay with whatever you decide."

Elizabeth smiled awkwardly. "Cowardice. It's not the first time I've been accused of that though it is the first time the accusation—a just one, by the way—has come from anyone other than myself."

Mrs. Shandy reached across the table and patted Elizabeth's hand. "I didn't mean to be insulting. Just honest. You asked for my advice, rather, for my take on the situation. But honestly, I'm not sure I'm qualified to give advice in matters of the heart. Look how abbreviated my own experience turned out to be."

"But it was genuine," Elizabeth said firmly. "You and Ross were in love."

"Yes. We were."

"Well, then you possess the greatest wisdom there is, Mrs. Shandy."

"You might make me cry one of these days, Mrs. Quirk."

"Anyway, you're right about the girls," Elizabeth went on. "The grown women, I should say. Everything will be okay. And to be honest, before the unexpected job offer I felt firm in my decision to go away with Chris. I guess I might have had some lingering doubts I wasn't acknowledging."

"So, now the question remains: What will Chris think about your accepting another teaching position? And why aren't you hashing things out with him, rather than coming to me?"

Elizabeth sighed. "My cowardice is showing again. It's just that, well, I let Chris down so badly in the past. Can I really do that to him again? He's flesh and blood, after all. He has deep feelings as well as lofty thoughts; he's vulnerable as well as worldly-wise."

"You have to try to put yourself first, even before Chris," Mrs. Shandy insisted. "He's an intelligent adult. He knows all about disappointment and the dangers of assuming the reality of anything other than what you are holding in your hand at any given moment. He wouldn't have shown up on your doorstep not understanding there was no guarantee of future happiness with the mother of his child."

Elizabeth nodded. "You're right, of course. I have to learn how to be in a genuine, honest relationship with Chris. And that means respecting him, not selling him short. And it means talking to him. Anyway, whatever I decide about the teaching position, I'd like for you to meet Chris. I've told him about our friendship and how much it means to me. Would that be okay?"

"Don't be silly! Of course, it would be okay. I'd be honored to meet the under-the-radar famous Christopher Ryan. And I'd be honored to meet the man you've loved for so long in silence. It must have taken an enormous degree of inner strength to tell your children about what happened in the past. And an enormous amount of courage to embrace having Chris back in your life, even if you're both still learning the ropes, as it were. You're a downright romantic heroine! Someone should put you in a novel."

"Me? Hardly! But thank you for the support."

Elizabeth left soon after. On the drive back to Lavender Lane, she found herself thinking about Hugh, about how he had loved her, about how his devotion to her had never wavered, even when she had puzzled and maybe even frightened him by growing in ways he had never anticipated. She thought, too, about what a good father he had been from the moment each girl had been born until the last time he had been well enough to speak with each of them in turn. She wondered if she had deserved a life with such a genuinely good man.

But that was a moot question, especially now. *Hugh*, she said to her husband as she neared home, *please understand what I'm about to do and know that I have always loved you and that I always will love you.*

And she felt in her heart that he had heard her words and accepted them.

Chapter 77

The Sea Breeze Diner in Cousins Corner had caught fire and been virtually destroyed at the start of the previous winter, and now, late summer, it was finally reopening. The owners were hosting a week-long celebration. Those owners, who also ran the diner on a daily basis, were a husband and wife, named Herb and Janet LaFond. They had two small children, whose grandparents helped care for them during the hours the diner was open. Herb's cousin, Rene LaFond, worked as a second cook, making the Sea Breeze Diner a truly family affair.

"I'm so glad the LaFonds were able to rebuild after the fire," Petra said. "Did they ever find out what caused it?"

Jess nodded. "Faulty wiring. The original building was pretty old. Herb and Janet were planning a big overhaul in January and February, when they usually shut down for the season. In a weird way, the fire came at just the right moment."

All three sisters had ordered scoops of homemade, hand-churned blueberry ice cream and were enjoying the treat at a picnic bench outside of the diner.

"Blueberry ice cream might be my new favorite thing," Jess announced. "Ice cream isn't exactly on my healthy eating plan, but I think I'm going to make frequent exceptions for this stuff. Besides, blueberries are chock-full of antioxidants."

"I love the color," Petra said, examining the bowl before her. "Bluish purple. Periwinkle but deeper. Kind of celestial. Whenever I get my own place, I mean, a place that's truly mine, a place I own, I'm going to incorporate this color, maybe paint a wall with it, maybe the bedroom ceiling."

Cam laughed. "Beth would be in heaven. She's color addicted, as you know. She's been clamoring to have her room painted hot pink with lime green accents, but neither Ralph nor I have the stomach to face those colors in our home. Bathing suits and hair ties are one thing, but walls and furnishings?"

"Beth will win out, you know," Jess said, licking the last ice cream from her spoon. "She's like me. Forceful."

"Well, hopefully she won't win out for some time. So, what are Mom and Chris up to today? Gosh, that still takes getting used to. Mom and Chris."

Petra shrugged. "They're together, but that's all I know. She said she'd be home in time for dinner. So, I've got some news to share."

Jess groaned. "Oh, my God, more news. Can't anything just stay the way it is for, like, five whole minutes?"

"Don't worry, it's nothing bad, though it is big for me. Well, next to Mom's big news this summer it's not so big but—"

"Just tell us, Petra," Jess said with another groan.

"I've decided to apply to a few graduate programs. I'm hoping to create a course of studies that will combine in a meaningful, but especially in a practical way, my love of philosophy, literature, and history. "

"Is that all?" Jess's eyebrows were sky-high. "Better woman than I am."

Cam nodded. "I'm glad to hear it. Back when you graduated from college I wondered why you weren't going on to grad school like you'd talked about, but I was so focused on building my career and on my relationship with Ralph I never got around to asking you what was going on."

"I never even knew that you wanted to continue in school," Jess admitted. "Sorry. Talk about being self-centered."

"Don't worry about it," Petra told her. "Really." The fact that Jess had admitted to a degree of self-centeredness was in itself a wonder.

"So, why now?" Cam asked. "What prompted you to act?"

"The simple answer is meeting Chris, spending time talking with him, listening to what he has to say about . . . oh, things like finding a purpose in life and learning one's identity. He's the one who really gave me the courage to make the decision to apply. And he helped me choose a few schools that might suit me. Of course," Petra went on, "I'm applying as Petra Quirk, so no one will know I'm the daughter of the celebrated biomedical ethics professional. I don't want anyone to think I'm trying to catch a free ride on the strength of his reputation. And, honestly, I don't need anyone comparing me unfavorably—and it would be unfavorably!—with my celebrated father. I'm nervous enough as it is. I want to prove my worth on my own."

"You'll do just fine," Cam assured her. "What will you do with your online shop when you're back in school?"

"Keep it, at least for a while," Petra said. "If I get too busy with my studies, I'll sell my stock to someone else in the business of vintage. Maybe Michael at Re-Turned would be interested. Past Perfect is a pretty small enterprise, as you know, but I'd like to think the content of the collection is special."

Jess nodded. "I know it is. You have a good eye for style and design. Certainly, a better eye than I have."

"You have a perfectly fine style of your own," Petra said. "I'd even go so far as to call it a brand."

Cam nodded. "Definitely."

"It's dull," Jess said flatly. "I'm dull. But I'm going to do something about that. This summer, with everything that's happened, it's shaken me up. I wasn't happy about it at first—

as you guys know!—but now, well, okay, I'm still not happy about being forced to reevaluate stuff and make changes, but I've stopped fighting the necessity for change. And that's half the battle. Isn't it? Please tell me it is!"

"What about meeting Chris?" Cam asked, a bit mischievously. "Are you reevaluating your thoughts about that?"

"Yeah," Jess admitted. "But I figured I'd wait until he and Mom get back from their jaunt before I meet him face-to-face. By then, Mom will be 100 percent sure she wants to be with him, or she'll have dumped him."

Petra shook her head. "Jess, come on. I've told you before. Mom's already 100 percent sure about the relationship. But as for meeting Chris and getting to know him, I'm glad you're finally at least open to the idea. Thank you. It means a lot to me."

"Whatever," Jess said with a shrug. "I mean, if Dad liked him in the first place, how bad can he be? And Cam, you said he was okay, right?"

Cam nodded. "I was on high alert for any signs of his being a lunatic or a criminal, and there was nothing. Hey," she went on, "did Mom say anything about selling the house? Somehow, I can't see Chris moving in and their staying on in Eliot's Corner. For one, Chris still takes on a project here and there. I'd think they might want to live closer to an airport or even a major railway line for the convenience. And let's face it, they'd be a sort of celebrity couple in Eliot's Corner, and that's not something I think either of them wants. The gossips would be watching their every move even without knowing the real story of their relationship, or knowing that Petra is Chris's child. Local widow marries dead husband's best friend. It would keep people talking for months."

"She didn't say anything to me about her plans," Jess admitted. "Now I wish I had asked her."

"I did ask her about what she foresees for the future," Petra told her sisters. "She said she was making no decisions about the house or anything else until she and Chris got back from Europe."

"I suppose it's possible Mom will sell the house and move to his place in Boston, or maybe they'll buy a new place of their own, a condo on the waterfront maybe." Jess sighed. "Boy, I'll miss our house if that's the case. I mean, we grew up there. So many memories."

"Maybe that's a reason Mom and Chris should start fresh in a home of their own," Cam suggested. "Being surrounded by reminders of another life, and of, well, of Dad, might not be so healthy."

Petra sighed. "It would be odd not celebrating Christmas and Thanksgiving on Lavender Lane. Gosh, none of us has missed one holiday gathering there since we were born, have we?"

"Not one," Jess confirmed. "But come on, we're jumping the gun. We have no idea what Mom's going to do in the future, and neither does she, so let's not dwell on the possibilities, good or bad."

"Besides," Cam put in, "there's this holiday season to plan for. Why can't the three of us celebrate in the house, even if Mom is still in Europe? Someone's going to have to be looking after the old place while she's gone."

Petra smiled. "I think that's a fantastic idea! As long as Mom leaves us her recipe for chestnut stuffing. Christmas isn't Christmas without her chestnut stuffing!"

"And Brandy Alexanders," Jess added. "Dad was a whiz with Brandy Alexanders. I haven't had one since he died. I wonder if I'd even like them now. I'll make a pitcher anyway!"

"And we'll decorate the tree with all the old ornaments, like we've done every year," Cam said. "We'll even use the old chains we made as kids, the ones made of Scotch tape covered with silver and gold glitter. Maybe we can teach Beth and the boys how to make new chains."

"Would it be too goofy to say that we'll make this the best Christmas ever?" Petra asked, only half-jokingly.

Jess rolled her eyes. Cam groaned. And Petra laughed.

Chapter 78

The cemetery where Hugh Quirk was buried was not the oldest cemetery in the area by far, having been established in the mid-nineteenth century, but for Elizabeth, it shared with all long-established New England cemeteries the same sense of peace, calm, and security. And, it even held a certain warmth and charm.

There was an ever so slight hint of fall in the air that day. There wouldn't be many more days of sun and heat before the light changed to gold and the air took on an invigorating crispness, to be replaced all too soon by the piercing chill of winter. And, Elizabeth thought, she and Chris might not be there, in Eliot's Corner, to welcome those chilly days and nights of winter. They might still be far away across the Atlantic, celebrating Christmas and ringing in the New Year all on their own in a foreign land.

Together, Elizabeth and Chris walked along the cemetery's central path, holding hands. If her fingers weren't as slim and graceful as they had been, if her nails were a bit ridged, if Chris's knuckles were larger, if his skin was rougher, well, none of that mattered. The years had passed. Their love had not.

"I've been keeping another secret from you," Elizabeth said

suddenly. "I'm sorry, but I needed to make an important decision without anyone's influence. Well, I did make an exception for my friend Mrs. Shandy, but by the time I talked with her, my mind was pretty much made up."

Chris nodded. "I understand. No need to apologize. Unless, of course, what you have to tell me is—"

"Nothing bad," she said hurriedly. She told him about having received the surprise offer of a teaching position at MidCoast Primary, and that she had decided to turn down the offer. "It would have meant delaying our trip a year or more, and honestly, I don't want that."

Chris turned to look at her closely. "Are you sure it's the right thing to do? Petra told me how upset you were to be leaving teaching. You've told me so yourself. I can wait." He gently squeezed Elizabeth's hand. "I'm very good at waiting."

"I was upset to be forced out of my career," Elizabeth admitted. "But this is different. A lot is different, not only the fact that this time I was given a choice. It's amazing how having a choice in determining the direction of your life, even just the next step in it, is so important."

"True. Well, I can't deny I'm glad you'll be able to run off with me, as selfish as that is. So, you didn't tell Petra and the others about the job offer?"

"No," Elizabeth admitted. "Like I said before, I didn't want a lot of outside opinions. In the end, it wasn't my children's decision to make. Of course, it's possible, even probable, they'll find out that I was offered the position at MidCoast Primary; I can't imagine it was a deep dark secret, and now the school will be openly scrambling to find someone qualified for the job. But I'm not worried about that."

"You shouldn't be worried about anything. This is our time now, at long last. But I do hope that going forward we can get in the habit of facing the big decisions together, right from the start."

"I do, too," Elizabeth assured him. "No more unilateral decisions when it comes to anything more important than what sort of pie to buy at the farm stand."

"I'm partial to cherry."

Elizabeth laughed. "I remember."

"As long as we're talking about unilateral decisions we've made lately, I want you to know that I've changed my will. I've named Petra as my sole heir. Now, I hope my life will go on for some time, but when I do die, Petra will be pretty secure."

Elizabeth leaned her head against Chris's shoulder for a moment. "Thank you," she said softly. "That's very kind."

"It's not kind as much as the right thing to do. I wasn't around to help my daughter when she was a child. The very least I can do is to offer what help I can now that she's an adult."

They walked on for another moment or two before Elizabeth pointed to the left. "It's down this aisle a little way."

A few moments later, they stopped before a classic gray granite headstone, standard size, inscribed with Hugh's name, the date of his birth, and that of his death. Above that information was engraved a cross.

Chris held a handkerchief to his eyes for a moment. "I didn't expect there to be a cross on his headstone," he said finally, his voice husky with emotion. "When I knew Hugh, he was so adamantly opposed to the religion in which he had been raised."

"He never officially returned to Catholicism," Elizabeth explained, "and I'm not sure he ever regained his faith, assuming he'd had any faith early on. But a year or two before he died he told me he wanted to make a few changes to the document he'd prepared citing his wishes for a funeral and burial. One of those changes was what he wanted depicted on his headstone. I was a bit surprised but didn't question him about his decision." Elizabeth smiled. "You know how he was. Not a great talker when it came to his feelings."

"Yes. And many people turn back to the religious traditions

of their childhood when they know their life is ending. The traditions can be of great comfort. Maybe Hugh was one of those people. Was there a funeral mass?"

"Yes, though before he died he didn't ask for a priest to administer last rites. I half expected him to. I guess he asked his God directly to forgive his sins, as small as they might have been."

Elizabeth watched as Chris made the sign of the cross. She wished she possessed real faith; she never had possessed it and had come to think it unlikely that she ever would. But all sorts of things might happen now, moving into a future with Chris.

"I believe that Hugh has given us his blessing," Elizabeth said, sliding her arm through Chris's. "In fact, I'm sure of it."

Chris pressed her hand. "I am, too," he said. "I truly am."

Epilogue

One Year Later

"I'm glad we're all here," Petra said with a smile. "Well, here together in cyberspace."

"It's as close as Jess and I are going to get to you for a while, so we'll take it."

Cam looked happy, Petra thought, observing her sister in her square-framed Zoom box. Certainly, happier and more relaxed than Cam had looked—and had been—last summer, during that awful craziness with Ralph and his ex-girlfriend. The result of that early midlife crisis or whatever it had been was that Cam and Ralph had decided that for the health of their marriage and family, they would banish Lily from their lives—and not a moment too soon. At the very end of the summer Cam had indeed sat down with Lily, in a typically Cam non-confrontational way, to ask about her involvement—if any—in Ralph's massive crush; much to Cam's surprise—and horror—Lily had admitted that she had developed feelings for her old flame, and, seeing Ralph's growing interest, had nudged his feelings along.

Well, that had been the end of that friendship. According to Cam, neither she nor Ralph regretted having jettisoned the troublemaking Lily from their lives. For about a month, Beth, who had been enamored of "Aunt Lily," continued to wonder why she wasn't coming around anymore, but then, Beth stopped asking and didn't seem to care. Now, with Beth gearing up for second grade and the twins well into their terrible twos, the family was busier than ever—which hadn't, however, prevented Cam and Ralph from joining Elizabeth and her beau in London that spring for a much-needed romantic holiday. In an unprecedented act of generosity, Jess had moved into the Perry house in South Portland to care for the kids while their parents were away. The experience had served to confirm her resolution never to have children of her own.

"So, how's it going in Chicago? The City of the Big Shoulders, right? Who said that?"

"Carl Sandburg, in his poem 'Chicago,'" Petra told Jess. "Everything's going really well. I'm working harder than I ever have on anything in my life and learning so much. I still kind of doubt my abilities, but the more I go on, the more confident I become." Petra laughed. "The more marginally confident, anyway!"

As he had promised he would, Christopher Ryan had been a huge help in steering Petra toward a university that would allow her to craft a graduate degree program that would incorporate her passion for history, literature, and philosophy toward a socially useful end. And, though he and Elizabeth had spent the last year largely out of the country, Chris had made himself as available as possible for consultations about how to negotiate the application process, and later, how to choose courses that would best serve her purpose, and perhaps most importantly, where to find the best deep-dish pizza in the city. Chris Ryan, Petra was happy to have discovered, made an excellent father.

Still, she missed her mother and was looking forward to her return. Petra knew that her sisters missed Elizabeth as well.

"When was the last time anyone spoke with Mom?" Cam asked. "She told me they might be out of range while in certain really remote areas of the Black Forest, but I'm getting a bit worried."

"Don't," Jess commanded. "Mom's with a seasoned traveler, and it's not like they're backpacking and sleeping under the open skies. They're staying at a top-rated hotel. I'm sure we'll hear from them as soon as it's possible."

Jess, too, had faced changes and challenges since the summer before, and, in Petra's opinion, seemed much better off for them. After ending her five-year relationship with Eddie, Jess had decided to concentrate on herself for a time, and not to dash into another monogamous but otherwise unsatisfying union. More difficult for Jess to negotiate had been the letting go of her desire to start her own business, a desire she had come to realize was not in her best interests, at least, not at this point in time. At the start of the summer she had received a promotion to vice-president of new business at ATD Marketing and seemed genuinely content. Well, as content as Jessica Quirk was ever going to be. She was still the prickly sister but less judgmental than she had been. At least, these days, if she was still making harsh judgments, she was keeping most of them to herself.

"So," Petra said, "I'm definitely coming back to Maine at Thanksgiving. I can only spare a few days, but since Mom and Chris have promised to be in Eliot's Corner for the holiday I don't want to miss my opportunity to spend time with them."

"It will be the last Thanksgiving in the family home," Cam noted. "We'd be crazy not to be there together."

Jess nodded. "Agreed. I'm dying to see the new condo in Boston, though. Mom sent me a few photos, but without Mom's and Chris's stuff in it yet, well, it doesn't tell me much. Excellent views, though!"

"I hope the new owners of Lavender Lane will cherish the old place as much as we did," Petra said earnestly. "As we still do. Homes, houses, have feelings. I really believe that. They're alive."

Jess laughed and rolled her eyes. "Same old Petra! It's a good thing we love you so much."

"I love you guys, too," Petra said.

"Meet at the same time next week?" Cam asked. "No matter what?"

It was a deal.

Please turn the page for a very special Q&A
with Holly Chamberlin!

Q. You've been writing novels for many years now. Do you ever worry that you'll run out of stories to tell? Does it get more difficult over time to come up with fresh ideas?

A. There are endless stories to invent and to tell. Ideas—no insult to them—are a dime a dozen! I've never had a problem "making stuff up." In fact, I entertain my husband whenever we go out by telling stories about the people passing by or sitting at the next table. He's half amused and half freaked out that I can spin complex tales so easily. (Can I add and subtract? Not so much.) And I must give credit where credit is due. My editor, John Scognamiglio, is the master of story ideas. He throws me a tantalizing line, and I'm off. We make a good team.

Q. In previous books, you've explored family dynamics that might be termed dysfunctional, but in *A Summer Love Affair*, for the first time, you write about a young woman who discovers that the man she thought her biological father is not. Any particular reason why you chose this topic?

A. Well, sadly, Elizabeth's story is probably way more common than not in real life. The idea of being "in trouble" and of feeling compelled to keep a child's true father a secret from the world is, however painful for the character, pretty interesting for the reader. There are so many moral nuances involved, so many opportunities for an observer to blame or to feel compassion (sometimes both at once), so many reasons to choose forgiveness or to withhold it. Historically, women have been forced to think on their feet in such situations, to take extreme risks, to make painful choices for the sake of expediency—and then, to live all alone with the consequences. I find that heartbreaking and terribly compelling.

Q. Do you have a favorite character in this book? Do you always, or often, find one particular character most interesting or sympathetic?

A. Over the course of writing a novel, a writer develops a relationship with each of her characters, a relationship that changes as the story unfolds. In this case, my relationship with Jess and with Cam was, as to be expected, less strong than it was with the point of view characters, Elizabeth and Petra. Of those two, I felt most drawn to Petra and her search for identity and purpose. I may be almost sixty years old, but in my experience, that search never ends! And in Petra's character I found myself depositing bits of my younger self: the daydreamer, the one with her head in the clouds, lacking ambition, et cetera. (Well, I still lack ambition though I am fairly grounded.) I suspect it's common for a writer to have a favorite character, and not necessarily because she relates to that character, like I did with Petra. Loathsome characters can be pretty compelling! Pretty much everybody finds Satan way more interesting than the good guys in *Paradise Lost*. Maybe Milton did, too.

Q. In *A Summer Love Affair* as well as in *Barefoot in the Sand*, a reading group is featured. Are you a member of a reading group?

A. I have to admit that I'm not and, except for a very brief time many years ago, I have never belonged to a book group. I think they're fantastic but as I've never been good about committing to associations of any sort (I didn't make it very far in Girl Scouts), a book group is not for me. My friend Carmen belongs to a book group that has been intact for thirty-two years! She herself has been a member for over twenty years. I find that really amazing.

A SUMMER LOVE AFFAIR

ABOUT THIS GUIDE

The suggested questions are included to enhance your group's reading of Holly Chamberlin's *A Summer Love Affair*!

DISCUSSION QUESTIONS

1. Chris and Petra spend a good deal of time talking about the search for identity, purpose, and emotional intimacy. He says: "You can't know anyone else—to the extent it's possible to really know anyone—without having a fairly good idea of your own place in the world." Discuss this idea in relation to the main characters, in particular, to Petra and her journey toward a state of self-knowledge.

2. "Feel the fear but do it anyway" is a handy but perhaps deeply unrealistic bit of advice. Fear, cowardice, and courage are important themes in this book. Talk about Cam's reluctance to confront Ralph about his feelings for his ex-girlfriend, Lily. A usually strong person, Cam admits to being afraid of what Ralph might tell her and of what actions that information might force her to undertake.

   Chris admits to having been a coward in the aftermath of his affair with Elizabeth. He acknowledges that Elizabeth, by taking action, allowed him to avoid accepting the responsibility of fatherhood.

   Mrs. Shandy tells Elizabeth that making assumptions about, in this case, her daughters' needs, is a form of cowardice. Elsewhere in the story, the characters talk about how assuming the reactions of another person can be a convenient way to avoid taking responsible action.

   Elizabeth reflects about her life: "so much (about her life) had come about because of fear." She also admits that for a long time she was afraid of Hugh and his forceful personality. At one point with her sisters, Petra, in relation to her mother's admission that she feared Hugh, wonders aloud if fear can coexist with love, to which Cam replies, "All things are possible. Love gets distorted, corrupted . . ."

Even Jess admits to being afraid when she tells her mother that for a long time she lacked the courage to leave Eddie. She wonders if she was ever in love with Eddie. Earlier, Jess pronounces that "People in love are careless. They don't think about the consequences of their words or actions on other people. They're selfish." Petra counters: "Some might say that people in love are courageous." Are both characters right in their assessment?

3. Petra wonders if she lacks the courage to do something truly productive with her life. She tells us that Hugh Quirk could never have been called a coward, but perhaps she is failing to acknowledge that fear causes every human being at some point in his life to act against his best interests and the interests of those he loves. For example, Hugh regularly embroidered the truth about himself. Is that a habit of cowardice?

4. The POV characters look to those around them as examples of courageous behavior. Elizabeth considers Mrs. Shandy a courageous woman for having married in defiance of her parents and for having built a worthy life on her own after the untimely death of her husband. Elizabeth views Arden as brave for taking a chance on love with Gordon. Petra sees Laura Huntington as strong for having returned to her studies after a messy and expensive divorce, and the shocking discovery of her birth parents. Which character do you feel shows the most courage in this story?

5. At one point in the story, Cam says: "Honesty is . . . complicated." At another point, Elizabeth reflects: "Secrets had a mind of their own." Discuss how the habit of secrecy has affected the lives of the main characters in this story.

6. The sisters try to understand why their mother made the choices she made regarding Hugh and Chris. Petra seems to suggest that a definitive answer might not be possible. "Do you understand everything you do?" she asks Jess. "Why must a person's motives always be explored, brought to light? Maybe not every word or action can be understood. Maybe mystery or confusion is simply part of the human condition." Jess argues that: ". . . people don't just do stuff. There has to be a reason why they do what they do, say what they say. Otherwise it's all just chaos." Talk about this interesting and perplexing topic.

7. Early in the story, Petra thinks fondly of her father—Hugh Quirk—and reflects that: "It was funny the things you remembered. Not always the big moments, the official turning points, demarcations like graduations from high school or college, but the small moments, the feel of your father's jacket against your cheek as you dozed against his chest, the smell of the pine-scented candles your mother brought out in the winter months." What are some of the small but significant moments you recall from your childhood?

8. Elizabeth is reluctant to retire from her job as a teacher. She reflects on the definition of retiring: "To withdraw. To fall back. To take out of circulation. To go to bed." What does retirement mean to you, personally? Do you regard it as an exciting, welcome prospect, or as a threshold opening into a frightening unknown? Or maybe, as a bit of both?

9. If you could create a sequel to *A Summer Love Affair*, what would happen to the characters? Do you foresee a happy future for Elizabeth and Christopher? For Petra going forward with her studies? For Cam and Ralph mending their marriage? For Jess finding peace of mind?

Visit us online at
KensingtonBooks.com
to read more from your favorite authors,
see books by series, view reading
group guides, and more!

BOOK **CLUB**

BETWEEN THE **CHAPTERS**

Visit us online for sneak peeks, exclusive
giveaways, special discounts, author content,
and engaging discussions with your fellow readers.

Betweenthechapters.net

Sign up for our newsletters and be the first
to get exciting news and announcements about
your favorite authors!
Kensingtonbooks.com/newsletter